SOMETHING IN
THE DARKNESS

THE UNOFFICIAL
AND UNAUTHORISED
GUIDE TO
TORCHWOOD SERIES TWO

SOMETHING IN THE DARKNESS

THE UNOFFICIAL AND UNAUTHORISED GUIDE TO *TORCHWOOD* SERIES TWO

Stephen James Walker

First published in England in 2008 by

Telos Publishing Ltd
61 Elgar Avenue, Tolworth, Surbiton, Surrey KT5 9JP, UK
www.telos.co.uk

Telos Publishing Ltd values feedback. Please e-mail us with any comments you may have about
this book to: feedback@telos.co.uk

ISBN: 978-1-84583-024-3 (paperback)
ISBN: 978-1-84583-025-0 (hardback)

Something in the Darkness: The Unofficial and Unauthorised Guide to Torchwood *Series Two* ©
2008 Stephen James Walker

The moral right of the author has been asserted.

Internal design, typesetting and layout by Arnold T Blumberg
www.atbpublishing.com

Printed in the UK

1 2 3 4 5 6 7 8 9 10 11 12 13 14 15

British Library Cataloguing in Publication Data.
A catalogue record for this book is available from the British Library.

CONTENTS

Introduction 7

Part One: Series One – The Aftermath 9
Chapter One: Bouquets and Brickbats 10
Chapter Two: *Torchwood* Goes Global 15

Part Two: Gearing Up for Series Two 33
Chapter Three: Back in the TARDIS 34
Chapter Four: Retooling the Format 37
Chapter Five: Into Production 41

Part Three: The Series Airs 45
Chapter Six: Toward Transmission 46
Chapter Seven: Into Transmission 51
Chapter Eight: The Series In Progress 56
Chapter Nine: Series Two Hits America 61
Chapter Ten: The Second Series Ends … And a Third is Confirmed 66

Part Four: The Fiction 71
Chapter Eleven: *Torchwood* Timeline 72
Chapter Twelve: Main Character Biographies 86

Part Five: The Fact 93
Chapter Thirteen: Main Cast Biographies 94
Chapter Fourteen: Principal Creative Team Biographies 99

Part Six: Episode Guide 107
Series credits... 108
2.01: Kiss Kiss, Bang Bang.. 112
2.02: Sleeper 124
2.03: To the Last Man.. 135
2.04: Meat 144
2.05: Adam 153
2.06: Reset... 161
2.07: Dead Man Walking 171
2.08: A Day in the Death 181
2.09: Something Borrowed... 190
2.10: From Out of the Rain 199
2.11: Adrift.. 208
2.12: Fragments.. 216

2.13: Exit Wounds..227
Series Overview 241

Appendix A: Tie-In Merchandise...245
Appendix B: Original Novels, Audios and Comic Strips 249
Appendix C: Torchwood Declassified 260
Appendix D: Ratings and Rankings..269
Appendix E: Webwatch..275

About the Author 280

INTRODUCTION

Readers of my earlier book *Inside the Hub* (Telos Publishing, 2007) will already have a pretty good idea what to expect from this follow-up volume as, given that the format was thankfully well-received last time, I've basically taken the same approach again, with just a few variations in certain of the sections to try to keep things fresh and avoid repetition.

For the benefit of any newcomers, I ought to explain where I'm coming from here. The fact is, *Torchwood* is one of my favourite TV dramas of all time. It is simply my kind of show: dark and urban, rain-soaked and blood-drenched, sexy and thrilling. It is not without its flaws, of course; but then, what is? It's the sort of show that gets under your skin, worms its way into your head and keeps you thinking about it long after each new episode has come and gone. So, in short, I have approached the writing of this book very much as a fan, and any readers hoping for a damning indictment should look elsewhere. *Something in the Darkness*, while not shying away from criticism where it is due, is essentially a celebration of Series Two of *Torchwood*, giving all the facts and figures, all the dates and details, but also, and more importantly, examining its appeal in depth, discussing the strengths – and weaknesses – of the 13 individual episodes and highlighting exactly what it is that makes the show so special.

The basic contents are as follows. Part One recalls the mixed reactions to Series One and details its scheduling and reception in those international markets where it has been screened. Part Two then looks at how the *Torchwood* production team prepared and paved the way for Series Two. In Part Three, I move on to describe events that occurred during the eight month period from mid-November 2007 to mid-June 2008, covering the build-up to, transmission and aftermath of Series Two. Part Four then explores the show's mythology, with a fully annotated timeline of events in the *Torchwood* universe and fictional biographies of all the regular characters, based on information gleaned from the televised episodes and officially-licensed tie-ins. Part Five presents capsule biographies of the show's main cast and production team members. This then leads on to the most substantial section of the book, Part Six, which consists of a detailed guide to and analysis of the 13 episodes. Lastly there are five appendices, covering more peripheral matters: tie-in merchandise; original *Torchwood* novels, audios and comic strip stories published during the period covered by this book; the *Torchwood Declassified* mini-documentaries; the series' ratings and fan rankings; and a brief overview of *Torchwood*-related websites.

In summary, I have aimed to make this a fitting companion volume to *Inside the Hub*, giving a comprehensive overview of everything that has happened in the world of *Torchwood* since that first book was published, right up to the BBC's announcement that a third series – albeit in a rather different format – had been commissioned to go into production in August 2008 for transmission in the first half of the following year: an announcement that has already got the show's many fans buzzing with anticipation and excitement, coupled perhaps with a little apprehension about the apparently significant changes that lie in store.

Roll on 2009!

Stephen James Walker
17 June 2008

PART ONE: SERIES ONE – THE AFTERMATH

CHAPTER ONE: BOUQUETS AND BRICKBATS

As the first-ever series-length spin-off from the phenomenally popular *Doctor Who*, *Torchwood* was bound to attract a lot of attention from the very start. If nothing else, people would be intrigued to see what it was like; and interest was heightened by the fact that it was being aimed not at *Doctor Who*'s traditional family demographic but at an adult audience, with the episodes debuting in a post-watershed slot on BBC Three.[1] Even allowing for this, though, Series One proved a bigger hit than anyone could have reasonably anticipated. Two-and-a-half million viewers tuned in to its opening double bill, 'Everything Changes'/'Day One', on Sunday 22 October 2006, making it the most-watched non-sport programme ever on a UK digital channel to that date. A further three million viewers caught the BBC Two repeat the following Wednesday; a figure exceeded by only two other BBC Two programmes that week. Factoring in the ratings from other repeats within the same week, the two episodes won a total audience of around six-and-a-half million viewers – a quite phenomenal achievement. Although, as is generally the case with any new series, the ratings then dropped for subsequent episodes, *Torchwood* still ended up taking nine of the top 15 places in the chart of the highest individual audiences for programmes broadcast on BBC Three during 2006[2], making it by far the most successful show ever to be screened on the channel. On BBC Two as well, the repeats continued to pull in large numbers of viewers, being usually amongst the channel's highest-rated programmes each Wednesday and within its top 30 for the week of transmission.

Leaving aside the higher figures for the first three episodes – which benefited not only from the show's novelty value but also from some heavy advance publicity – the total audience remained remarkably constant over the course of the run, with just a small mid-series dip. Taking into account the figures from same-week repeats as well as debut transmissions, Series One ended up averaging 4.62 million viewers in total per episode – which would be a very respectable tally for a (single-screening) BBC One drama, let alone a BBC Three one. *Torchwood* was never going to rival *Doctor Who* in terms of viewing numbers, being aimed at a smaller, exclusively adult audience, made with a considerably lower budget and first transmitted in a late-evening slot on a digital channel; but, judged on its own terms, the spin-off had arguably proved just as remarkable a ratings triumph as the parent show.

What's more, the BBC's Appreciation Index (AI) figures indicated that not only were people tuning in to *Torchwood* in impressive numbers, but they were also greatly enjoying it. The average AI figure for a drama programme broadcast by BBC One or ITV1 is 77, but every single episode of Series One, both on BBC Three and on BBC Two, scored higher than that. The average figure on BBC Three was 84, with a still-very-good low of 82 for the season opener 'Everything Changes' and an excellent high of 86 for the closing double-bill of 'Captain Jack

---

1 9.00 pm is regarded in British broadcasting as a 'watershed', after which the transmission of programmes with adult content is acceptable, on the assumption that most children will have gone to bed by then.

2 Had 'Captain Jack Harkness' and 'End of Days' been transmitted a day earlier, rather than on 1 January 2007, they would have made it into this chart as well, giving *Torchwood* ten of the top 15 places (with 'Random Shoes' knocked down to number 16).

Harkness'/'End of Days'; the average on BBC Two was 81, with a low of 78 for both 'Ghost Machine' and 'Random Shoes' and a high of 84 for the closing double-bill. So not only were the figures all higher than the average for drama but, again, they were also remarkably consistent, the difference between the lowest and highest being only four points on BBC Three and six points on BBC Two.

In short, the British viewing public had clearly fallen for *Torchwood*'s charms, quickly and in a big way! It was thus no surprise to find that the show was soon in the running for some prestigious TV awards, as noted by reporter Karen Price in a 3 April 2007 story headed 'Doctor and Captain Jack Go Head to Head' in the leading Welsh newspaper *Western Mail*:

> *Doctor Who* and its spin-off series *Torchwood* go head-to-head at this year's BAFTA Cymru awards.
>
> The BBC Wales dramas, both written by Swansea writer Russell T Davies, have a total of 21 nominations between them – 13 for *Doctor Who* and eight for *Torchwood*.
>
> The two series are in direct competition to win best drama series along with another BBC Wales programme, *Belonging*.
>
> And *Doctor Who*'s David Tennant will be up against John Barrowman, *Torchwood*'s Captain Jack, for the best actor gong, while former *Doctor Who* star Billie Piper and *Torchwood*'s Eve Myles are both in the running for the best actress award.
>
> *Belonging*'s Charles Dale is also nominated for best actor and *Con Passionate*'s Beth Robert for best actress.

As if to prove that there was no more than a friendly rivalry between *Torchwood* and its fellow award nominee *Belonging* – an English-language drama shown only in Wales on terrestrial TV but viewable elsewhere in the UK via satellite and cable services – 4 April 2007 saw the debut screening on BBC One Wales of an amusing trailer for the latter show, shot on the set of the former. This opens with a *Torchwood* clapperboard snapping shut and a crew member announcing 'Scene 10, Take 1', followed by a shot of John Barrowman, in familiar Captain Jack costume, bracing himself to pull shut by hand the Hub's cog-like circular entrance door. After a few seconds, the actor asks, 'Anyone gonna call "Action"?', but receives no reply. He notices that the crew are gathered around a TV monitor. Crossing to join them, he asks 'What are you guys watching?' When one of them replies '*Belonging*', he eagerly takes a seat beside them, enthusing, 'Oh, I love that! Hey, are Ceri and Robbie still together?' Then, as a voiceover announces '*Belonging*, the new series, coming soon to BBC One Wales', he sees a shot of Eve Myles on the screen, appearing in her regular *Belonging* role of Ceri Lewis, and wonders 'How do I know her?' This trailer was shown numerous times in BBC One Wales programme breaks over the days that followed.

While *Doctor Who* proved to be – for the second year running – the winner of the highest number of awards at the BAFTA Cymru ceremony, held in the Cardiff International Arena on Saturday 28 April, *Torchwood* pulled off a notable coup by beating its parent show in the Best Drama Series category, while Eve Myles was preferred to Billie Piper for the Best Actress gong. Rounding off a highly successful evening for the spin-off, it also won the awards for Best

Director of Photography: Drama (Mark Waters) and Best Design (Edward Thomas), taking its tally to four in all. BBC Wales Controller Menna Richards was quoted in news reports as saying: 'I'm very proud indeed of the success of all those who've made such wonderful programmes for BBC Wales. It's great to see BAFTA Cymru recognising the talents of all those who make programmes of the highest possible standards.' Looking back on the occasion in a *Western Mail* interview published on 9 February 2008, Myles said that she had been 'shocked' to be named Best Actress, adding: 'I had been nominated three times before but it never worked out.[3] A year on and it remains one of the best nights of my life, and the trophy has pride of place in my living room.'

These were not the only accolades that *Torchwood* would receive in 2007: in a ceremony on 3 September at the Dorchester Hotel in London, it was announced that it been voted Best New Drama by readers of *TV Quick* and *TV Choice* magazines in their joint annual TV polls. John Barrowman, producer Richard Stokes and co-producer Chris Chibnall were on hand to collect the award.

For those who had missed Series One the first time around, or who simply wanted a chance to enjoy it all over again, BBC Three began another complete run of weekly repeats at 9.00 pm on 14 September, each episode being followed by the appropriate *Torchwood Declassified* mini-documentary.

Torchwood's status as a *Doctor Who* spin-off had in many ways been a blessing, guaranteeing it a high profile from the outset and giving it a rich fictional universe to draw on in terms of characters, concepts and overall ethos. In other ways, however, it had arguably been a curse. Many genre TV fans, and *Doctor Who* fans in particular, had their own pre-conceived, and sometimes deeply-entrenched, expectations as to what a *Doctor Who* spin-off should be like – expectations that an entirely original show would not have had to face. When, as was inevitable, not all those expectations were met, some – albeit a minority, even within *Doctor Who* fandom[4] – were quick to express their dissatisfaction. Fans, by their nature, tend to feel very strongly about such things, and the criticisms expressed were often scathing. A number of TV journalists – some of them admitted *Doctor Who* devotees themselves – picked up on these criticisms and reflected them in their own reviews and commentaries. One of the most prominent and persistent detractors was Charlie Brooker of the *Guardian*. In the 28 October 2006 edition, for instance, he wrote:

> *Scooby-Doo* (more than, say, *The X-Files* or *Buffy*) is probably the show most analogous to *Torchwood*, in that both … revolve around a fresh-faced team of meddling kids tackling an ever-shifting carnival of monsters in a world of childlike simplicity. The Torchwood gang even have their own version of the Mystery Machine, although theirs is a spectacularly ugly SUV with two daft strips of throbbing LED lights either side of the windscreen whose sole purpose is to make the entire vehicle look outrageously

---

3 These earlier nominations had been for her role in *Belonging*.

4 Online polls conducted in the forum of the Outpost Gallifrey *Doctor Who* website, for instance, indicated a strongly and consistently positive reaction to *Torchwood* overall.

silly ... The inside's not much better – LCD screens embedded in every available flat surface, each urgently displaying a wibbly-wobbly screensaver ... It must be like driving around in a flagship branch of PC World.

The show came in for further stick in Brooker's overview of the year's TV, published on 16 December 2006:

> The award for the Year's Most Jarring Show goes to the *Doctor Who* spin-off *Torchwood*, which somehow managed to feel like both a multi-coloured children's show and a heaving sex-and-gore bodice-ripper at the same time. The constant clash of mutually-incongruous tones meant watching it felt like stumbling across a hitherto secret episode of *Postman Pat* in which Pat runs down 15 villagers while masturbating at the wheel of his van. Interesting, but possibly aimed at madmen.

High-profile brickbats such as these arguably led to the growth of a more general assumption in the media that public dissatisfaction with the show was rife – an assumption that was demonstrably false, as evidenced by its excellent ratings and AI figures and awards successes.

BBC Two's satirical comedy show *Dead Ringers* got in on the act the following year, presenting a number of sketches poking fun at *Torchwood*, with impressionist John Culshaw taking the Captain Jack role. The first two of these sketches, both in the episode transmitted on 8 March 2007, lampooned amongst other things the show's alleged preoccupation with sex, its Cardiff-centred settings and its supposedly one-dimensional characters, characterising these as 'Annoying' (Owen), 'Dull and Annoying' (Ianto), 'Camp and Annoying' (Jack) and simply 'Welsh' (Gwen).

Interviewed by Caleb Woodbridge for an edition of the Cardiff University students' magazine *Quench*, Russell T Davies was asked what he made of all this negativity, and responded: 'Um, we don't pay much attention to it really. Equally, when *Doctor Who* is praised to the skies, we don't pay any attention to that. Praise is just as unhelpful as criticism. We watch the show, we work on it, we know what's working and what isn't – which is not necessarily what you think is working and what isn't, and never will be – and we'll work on that.

'And that Charlie Brooker column is hilarious, brilliantly written; the man's a fantastic polemic writer. But if you turned round to Charlie Brooker and said, "So does that mean you think television dramatists should listen to the word of TV columnists?", he'd run away in horror!

'It's the same sort of argument that happened about whether we should have a focus group of two thousand people telling us what to do. Absolutely not – it's just not the way to work.

'So some things worked, some things didn't, [and] we'll work on it. There [are] new things [planned and] we'll see if they work as well. But industry-wise, it's a record-breaking programme, a huge success ... It is seen as a programme in need of a lot of work, and that's what we do, keep it working.'

Given his assertion that he and his team were unswayed by the criticisms that had been made, Davies's acknowledgment that *Torchwood* was 'seen as a programme in need of a lot of work', seems somewhat contradictory, not to say strange in light of the general viewing public's overwhelmingly positive reaction to the show. But whether he had indeed been influenced by the negativity within certain sections of fandom and the media, or whether he – or possibly even his BBC superiors – had quite independently reached the conclusion that some retooling of the format was required, one thing seemed certain: there would be some changes in store for *Torchwood* in Series Two …

CHAPTER TWO: TORCHWOOD GOES GLOBAL

While *Torchwood*'s second series was in production in the UK, viewers in other countries around the world were getting their first opportunity to see the debut series.

ISRAEL

Quickest off the mark was Israel, where the show premiered on 14 May 2007 on Yes Stars 2 – a satellite channel devoted to American and British programming. It drew a positive response from viewers and critics alike. In a preview in the 3 May edition of the *Jerusalem Post*, Aryeh Dean Cohen wrote:

> Beware the deadly spin-off, my son, the jokes that bomb, the plots that die. Yes, generally speaking, shows that spring from other shows don't fare too well in TV land. See under: *Joey*.
>
> So it was all the more pleasant to catch a spin-off that not only works, but is a wonder unto itself, Yes Stars 2's new *Torchwood*, debuting locally at 22.30 starting a week from Monday.
>
> We didn't even really know about this series' noble heritage until we checked it out on the web after being dazzled by the sci-fi/detective show hybrid. For *Torchwood*, dear Watson, is an anagram of *Doctor Who*.
>
> What? Okay, if you're not a Brit or a dedicated sci-fi nerd, you may not have heard of the legendary series, which ran from 1963-89 originally … The series was relaunched in 2005 by Russell T Davies, the creator of controversial series about homosexual life, *Queer as Folk*.
>
> Davies built *Torchwood* around a character from the new *Doctor Who* series, one Captain Jack Harkness, a bisexual Mulder type assigned to track the misdoings of aliens in beautiful Cardiff, which just happens to be the place where 'there's a rift through space and time' allowing 'creatures, time shifts, space junk, and debris' to reach its shores.
>
> …
>
> The writing, acting and effects are excellent, with all the little bits just right … Comic touches … plus the cool technology, the smooth acting, fine music and a fast-moving plot make *Torchwood* a hot addition to Yes Stars' line-up, proving that not all that is spin-off is necessarily dreck.

AUSTRALIA

After the ABC (Australian Broadcasting Corporation), the traditional home of *Doctor Who* in Australia, and SBS (Special Broadcasting Service) both declined the opportunity, a reported bidding war between Seven Network and Network Ten, otherwise known as Channel Ten, resulted in the latter picking up the broadcast rights to *Torchwood* down under. This news was announced in a BBC Worldwide press release dated Wednesday 28 February 2007:

BBC Worldwide Australasia has licensed dazzling adult drama *Torchwood* (13 x 50') to Network Ten, it announced today.

The series follows the adventures of an international team of investigators, led by Captain Jack Harkness (John Barrowman), the enigmatic American air force renegade who first appeared in *Doctor Who* in 2005.

Set in the UK in 2006 [sic], the team use scavenged alien technology to solve crime; both extraterrestrial and human.

Torchwood is separate from the government; outside the police; beyond the United Nations. Everyone who works for Torchwood is young – under 35. Some say that's because it's a new science. Others say it's because they die young …

Transmitting first on BBC Three in the UK, the first episode of *Torchwood* was the most watched (non-sport) programme ever to air on a UK digital channel.

Ten has also committed to a second series, which is currently in production.

'*Torchwood* is a thriller sci-fi cop show with a very human heart,' said Amber Knight, Senior Sales Manager for BBC Worldwide Australasia. 'It's sexy, clever, wild and perfect for Ten's audience.'

'*Torchwood* brings a sexy new twist to the traditional cop show genre that we at Ten are thrilled to have as part of our 2007 slate,' added Beverly McGarvey, head of programming at Network Ten.

Following this new sale, nine countries have now acquired the series, including Spain, New Zealand and Sweden.

The series is written by Russell T Davies, the extraordinary talent behind *Doctor Who*, *Casanova* and *Queer as Folk*, who described it as a meeting of *The X-Files* and *This Life*. He named the series after the anagram that was used to protect the secrecy of early *Doctor Who* rushes and preview tapes.

Torchwood is a BBC production in association with CBC.

As Amber Knight had observed, *Torchwood* seemed a good fit for Network Ten's audience: the channel had a good track-record of appealing to young adult viewers, and had previously screened a number of other – primarily American – science fiction-themed shows, including *The X-Files*, *Battlestar Galactica*, *Veronica Mars*, *Supernatural* and *Smallville*. Some fans, however, were apprehensive about the treatment that *Torchwood* would receive from the channel, noting that a number of these other series had been consigned to late-night slots, suffered erratic scheduling changes or had interrupted runs – *Veronica Mars*, for instance, had been taken off mid-season, and then suddenly brought back without any advance publicity. This was in stark contrast to the favourable scheduling given to crime dramas such as *Law and Order*, and to the channel's own home-grown reality show programming, to which it appeared to accord a higher priority. In addition, the channel often had banner adverts scrolling across the bottom of the screen, particularly during what it considered to be 'non-mainstream' programmes, making for a less-than-ideal viewing experience.

These concerns initially seemed unwarranted as Network Ten mounted a strong promotional campaign for its new acquisition – albeit one that, surprisingly, gave little hint of the show's science-fiction content and, perhaps less surprisingly, made no mention of the fact that it was a spin-off from ABC's *Doctor Who*. This included placing newspaper and radio adverts and running a competition with a weekly prize of $2,000 in Australian currency. From 20 May 2007, the channel started screening a number of 30-second trailers for the show. Giving away a rather important plot point regarding Jack, these opened with the line: 'The man who can never die!' In mid-June, a new series of promos began appearing; these consisted of specially-shot material, with the regular cast members wearing Series One-style costumes and delivering lines such as 'I believe in Captain Jack Harkness' (Eve Myles), 'I believe in science' (Burn Gorman), 'I believe there's no better place to be' (John Barrowman), 'I believe the 21st Century is when it all changes, so be prepared' (John Barrowman) – 'I believe' being a catchphrase used by Network Ten in all its programme publicity – and '*Torchwood* is coming soon, exclusively to this channel' (Gareth David-Lloyd).[5] Channel Ten also launched its own *Torchwood* website – at http://ten. com.au/ten/tv_torchwood.html – featuring an introduction to the show by Russell T Davies; cast and character information; a photo gallery; and text interviews with Eve Myles and Naoko Mori. Asked how she thought an Australian audience would respond to *Torchwood*, Mori said: 'Well I think you guys have a really acute sense of humour, and I think that's one of the big things that you would really like. We have a character called Owen who's played by Burn Gorman, he's incredibly funny, a lot of little quips, so I think that's one of the main things … The great thing about *Torchwood* is that it's a real mix, for want of a better word. It's sci-fi but it's more modern, it's urban and there's something for everyone, there's action and there [are] good storylines, plus there is humour.'

On 14 June, the Melbourne newspaper the *Age* ran a preview article incorporating quotes from Russell T Davies and Burn Gorman. Responding to the suggestion that he takes risks with his TV projects, Davies commented: 'I don't take risks deliberately, it's the way my mind works, I can't help it. But I do watch a lot of television science fiction, and it is a particularly sexless world. With a lot of the material from America, I think gay, lesbian and bisexual characters are massively underrepresented, especially in science fiction, and I'm just not prepared to put up with that. It's a very macho, testosterone-driven genre on the whole, very much written by straight men. I think *Torchwood* possibly has television's first bisexual male hero, with a very fluid sexuality for the rest of the cast as well. We're a beacon in the darkness.' Gorman meanwhile noted: '*Torchwood* is unlike any other sci-fi show. It's quintessentially British, because it's pushing boundaries. It's not bland; viewers either absolutely hate it or absolutely love it. It has awkward situations that aren't particularly resolved in a good way and that's what I like … When we started off episodes one and two, they were still writing the other episodes, so they've written to our strengths and weaknesses. It really was a work in progress, and very satisfying to get a story that shows different sides of your character … It's a dream job for an actor: you get to shoot guns in the morning, have sex before lunchtime, and drive a brilliant car

---

5 A behind-the-scenes video of the recording of these Australian promos was subsequently placed on the BBC's official *Torchwood* website. This showed *Torchwood* brand executive Matt Nicholls and associate producer Sophie Fante supervising the shoot as the cast members delivered their lines in front of a white backdrop – with John Barrowman and Eve Myles also indulging in a little clowning around.

in the afternoon.'

The opening episode, 'Everything Changes', eventually went out in a 9.40 pm Monday slot on 18 June, with no cuts apart from the insertion of commercial breaks, but – as the fans had feared – with banner adverts for other shows scrolling across the bottom of the screen at certain points. Then, the following day, the accompanying *Torchwood Declassified* mini-documentary was added to Network Ten's *Torchwood* website – the first time that *Torchwood Declassified* had been officially made available to view outside the UK – establishing a pattern that would be followed for subsequent episodes. 19 June also saw initial ratings figures become available for the premiere screening. These indicated that it had performed extremely well, averaging 1,003,000 viewers in the five major capitals, beating both Channel 7 (average 964,000 viewers) and Channel 9 (average 963,000 viewers) in its time slot and gaining a 40% audience share in the 18-49 age group. It was the second-highest-rated Network Ten programme of the day, being bested only by the reality show *Big Brother*.

Initial press reaction was largely positive. On 17 June, the TV magazine of the *Sun-Herald* – the Sunday edition of the *Sydney Morning Herald* – featured a *Torchwood* front-cover photograph, an interview with John Barrowman and a four-star review in which Rachel Browne hailed the show as 'highly original and very watchable' and stated that it benefited considerably from 'creator/writer Russell T Davies' ever-present droll sense of humour'. Then, on the debut transmission day itself, the entertainment section of Perth's *West Australian* newspaper ran a photograph of Eve Myles on its cover and an upbeat interview with the actress; the *Sydney Morning Herald* sported a front-page banner with a photograph of Barrowman and the headline 'Dr Who for Adults' and presented both an interview with Davies and a review in which Robin Oliver described the show as 'a stunner'; and Jim Schembri of the *Age* gave the following appreciative assessment:

> It's important to know that the creator of *Torchwood* is a gentleman called Russell T Davies, who 'masterminded' (press release quote) the rebirth of *Doctor Who*. In other words, please ignore the advertisements that have been trying to sell *Torchwood* as a cross between *The X-Files* and *Star Trek: The Next Generation*.
> It's much more fun than that. Think *Men in Black*, but without the budget.
> …
> The appeal of *Torchwood* is not so much that it's gloriously implausible sci-fi pulp, but that it knows it's gloriously implausible sci-fi pulp. There is plenty of talk about perceptual distortions and temporal displacement and that sort of thing to explain some of the odd things that happen, but far more typical of the dialogue is this golden exchange between Gwen and Jack: 'So, you catch aliens?' 'Yep.' 'You catch aliens for a living?' 'Yes, we do.' 'You're an alien catcher.' 'Yes I am.' 'Caught any good aliens?' 'Tons of them.' 'That's a hell of a job.' 'Sure it is.' (Pause.) 'This is so weird.' The adult timeslot for *Torchwood* is a bit of a pity, because it's precisely the kind of fast-paced sci-fi mulch children would love, though the notion that 21st Century kids would be in bed by this time is admittedly a little old-school. Yes, there's blood in the show, but it's of the raspberry-syrup-oozing-through-a-pressure-hose variety.

More critical, albeit in a rather tongue-in-cheek way, was Ruth Richie in the 23 June edition of the *Sydney Morning Herald* – the same newspaper that just a few days earlier had been so complimentary:

> Was it wrong to approach *Torchwood* with suspicion? What is a new Russell T Davies drama doing on Ten, on a Monday night, if it's any good? *Torchwood* is not bad. It's just the slightly club-footed issue of a one-night stand between *Doctor Who* and *The Mod Squad*.
>
> …
>
> For those who can't find Ten on the remote, *Torchwood* is about a team of investigators who use alien technology to solve crime. (Okay, what was I thinking?) The team, in the best *Star Trek* tradition, has a member of nearly every race and colour, except that it is a very small team, so apologies to the Inuits. Of course, a very bright, pretty, round-eyed female copper (they're everywhere this season) with no training and very little skill happens upon the *Torchwood* people as they are reviving corpses and, after a rather convoluted story involving amnesia and leading men with flashing white teeth, she joins the crew.
>
> It's a likeable bit of work, at first glance. Perhaps my suspicions were ill-founded. But then two telltale signs sealed its fate. The ultra-white sexy knight at the head of the group has a funny name and an American accent. (Here's a tip. Run, don't walk, from any drama with a leading man who goes by the name of Captain Jack anything.) Captain Jack Harkness (how made up is that!) plus the American accent – well, it just smells wrong.
>
> Even so, Davies deserves more consideration, so by the magic powers vested in TV critics I watched next week's episode, a completely silly business in which a girl possessed by an alien bonks half of London [sic] and reduces her prey to little piles of dust. But that's not the bad part.
>
> They moved a lamp. The coffee table lamp in the pretty round-eyed cop's flat pops up in the second episode on the desk at the fertility clinic. Definitive proof that UFOs don't exist. I rest my case. Absolute rubbish.

Far more representative were the views of Amanda Horswill of Brisbane's *Courier-Mail*, who wrote in her 17 June piece:

> …*Torchwood* is *Doctor Who* in a dark room and on Viagra.
>
> That's because it's based on Earth and has ordinary humans (or so we think) using extraordinary alien technology to solve crime. Imagine *Law and Order: Alien*.
>
> It has an ensemble cast, so there's all those wonderful, completely human troubles to explore. Like how do you keep what you do for a living secret from the man you love? And what happens when you fall in love with a workmate? And how does a mere mortal resist tampering with all that powerful alien technology? Lust. Love. Greed. Love it.'

Concluding on a cautionary note, however, Horswill echoed the concerns previously expressed by fans:

> Sci-fi fans will add *Torchwood* to their regular viewing schedule. It's on a Monday, a couple of days after the new episodes of *Doctor Who* (which starts next week, on 28 June). But unfortunately, *Torchwood* is also at the same time as *Battlestar Galactica*, on pay-TV's Sci-Fi Channel at 9.00 pm.
>
> Once upon a time that fantastic show was on Channel Ten, until they shifted it later and later and began replacing it with repeats of *Law and Order*, of the non-alien variety.
>
> So, perhaps it's not wise to get too comfortable with Ten's allotted timeslot for *Torchwood*. If it starts to be scheduled later, you will know it's time to get pay-TV.

These pessimistic words proved prophetic as, from 'They Keep Killing Suzie' at the beginning of August 2007, Network Ten shunted *Torchwood* to a midnight slot on Tuesdays, citing as the main reason the strong competition it had faced from other channels. This move had perhaps been on the cards for some time: although the show had been nominally scheduled in a 9.30 pm slot on Mondays, it had often started late due to the preceding coverage of *Big Brother* overrunning. 'Greeks Bearing Gifts' – the episode immediately prior to the scheduling change – had suffered particularly badly, being delayed by as much as 55 minutes after *Big Brother*'s season finale; no doubt partly because of this, it had gained the show's lowest ratings to date, averaging only 563,000 viewers in the five major capitals.

While press comment remained largely positive toward the show – and critical of Network Ten's handling of it – the move to a midnight slot inevitably resulted in a further sharp decline in *Torchwood*'s Australian ratings. 'They Keep Killing Suzie' averaged a mere 98,000 viewers, although the figures for 'Random Shoes' and 'Out of Time' were rather better, at 149,000 and 151,000 respectively, and 'End of Days' did exceptionally well for the slot, with 160,000. There were however other opportunities for viewers down under to catch the show, which also aired on two regional channels affiliated with Network Ten – Southern Cross Ten, serving the southern states, which screened the 13 episodes simultaneously with Network Ten, and Imparja Television, covering the remote areas of eastern and central Australia, which ran them a few weeks later[6] – and subsequently on the new high definition channel Network Ten HD. UKTV, a subscription channel specialising in British imports, also picked up the rights to the show; its screenings launched at 8.30 pm on Tuesday 11 December 2007 and continued into the spring of 2008. In addition, the DVD sets previously available in the UK were released in Australia as well, the first appearing on 31 July 2007, with the complete Series One box set following on 6 February 2008.

---

6 Imparja Television's long-standing Network Ten affiliation ended on 3 February 2008, and it was not expected to show any further episodes of *Torchwood* after that date.

SWEDEN

The digital terrestrial, satellite and cable channel TV4 Plus picked up the rights to screen *Torchwood* in Sweden, where it debuted on 24 June 2007.

MEXICO

In Mexico, XEIMT-TV, otherwise known as Canal 22, began transmitting *Torchwood* on Monday 9 July 2007 in a half-hour twice-weekly slot. Each episode was split into two, often in a completely inappropriate place, with a voice-over at the end of the first part stating (in Spanish) 'This programme will continue next Wednesday' and a superimposed caption reading 'Continuara' ('To be continued'). Principally an arts and educational channel, XEIMT-TV was not a particularly apposite home for *Torchwood*, and although ratings were initially good, they soon fell, not helped by the unsympathetic presentation and the fact that episodes were sometimes bumped back in the schedule in favour of other programming more in keeping with the channel's basic remit.

SPAIN

One of the first overseas countries to acquire *Torchwood* was Spain, where – as reported in a 16 January 2007 story on the website of the industry journal *Variety* – the terrestrial channel Cuatro TV quickly snapped up the rights. All 13 episodes were shown, starting on Sunday 5 August 2007, with no cuts made, although they were dubbed into Spanish and scheduled in a very late night slot, with two episodes shown back-to-back each week – a common practice on Spanish TV. The Spanish DVD box set release of Series One was a disappointment: although the original English soundtrack was offered as an alternative to the Spanish-dubbed one, the picture was in 4:3 ratio rather than the original 16:9 and there were no extras at all.

LATIN AMERICA

In Latin America, *Torchwood* premiered on Tuesday 28 August 2007 on the People+Arts channel, dubbed into Spanish. To the astonishment of fans, all references to same-sex relationships were cut out of the episodes, and 'Greeks Bearing Gifts' and 'Captain Jack Harkness' – both of which revolved around such relationships – were reportedly omitted from the run altogether.

ITALY

The show's Italian debut came on Monday 3 September 2007 on the Jimmy channel. Viewers were given a choice between dubbed Italian and original English soundtracks. The Italian titles of the 13 episodes were as follows (with English equivalents in brackets where these differed from the originals): 'Tutto Cambia', 'Primo Giorno', 'La Machina Dei Fantasmi', 'La Donna Cybernetica', 'La Fate Cattive' ('The Bad Fairies'), 'Il Villaggio Degli Orrori' ('The Village of Horrors'), 'Un Amore Venuto Da Lontano' ('A Love from Far Away'), 'Continuano A Uccidere Suzie', 'L'occhio Alieno' ('The Alien Eye'), 'Fuori Dal Tempo', 'Combattimento', 'Il Capitano Jack Harkness' and 'La Fine Dei Giorni'.

AMERICA

Arguably the most important overseas market for BBC programmes is the USA. Early speculation that *Torchwood* might be picked up for broadcast there by the Sci-Fi Channel, on which the new *Doctor Who* had already been a hit, proved incorrect: a press notice dated 2 April 2007 revealed that it would actually screen on BBC America as one of a range of new acquisitions due to debut later in the year in the course of a 'radical makeover' for the channel.

BBC America has first refusal on the US rights to all BBC programmes, provided it at least matches any other offers from rival bidders, and although it had let *Doctor Who* go to the Sci-Fi Channel in 2006, it was now under new management, who regretted that earlier decision – which they tried to make up for in part by picking up the second-screening rights to the show – and who were not about to make the same mistake with *Torchwood*. On the downside, BBC America has a smaller audience reach than the Sci-Fi Channel, being available only as part of a premium subscription package of digital cable channels in most areas, and not carried at all by some cable providers – although the relatively small proportion of viewers with a satellite service as opposed to cable are generally able to receive it without extra charge.[7] In addition, as programmes on BBC America are interrupted by frequent commercial breaks, each episode of *Torchwood* would need to have about two or three minutes' worth of material cut out of it in order to fit a standard hour-length slot – although probably less than would have been the case had it been acquired by the Sci-Fi Channel, the commercial breaks on which are longer. However, BBC America President Garth Ancier assured fans that the episodes would be edited for timing only, and not for content. Those viewers whose cable providers carried the complementary BBC America On Demand service would also have a chance to see the episodes complete and without commercial breaks, as they would be made available in that form shortly after their BBC America debut screenings. In line with the network's established practice, though, certain swear words such as 'fuck' and 'twat' would be muted out on the soundtrack (although 'shit' would be left in), both for the standard BBC America screenings and for the On Demand service.

The separate rights to screen the show in high definition were meanwhile acquired by the HDNet cable and satellite channel (BBC America having no high definition service itself), which would present it complete and uncut, with even the strongest language left intact and the original 'Next Time' trailer at the end of each episode retained. HD Net's co-founder and president Mark Cuban was quoted as saying: 'We're thrilled to be airing *Torchwood* in HD. This is certainly a Russell T Davies signature show. *Torchwood* explores adult themes and doesn't shy away from anything. Whether it's the diverse storylines or the hero's ambivalence to sexual boundaries, this is not your typical show, and I love it.'

Like Network Ten in Australia, BBC America mounted a strong advance publicity campaign for *Torchwood*. Going well beyond the sort of promotion it would normally afford to a new show, this even extended to placing huge roadside billboard adverts in major cities, including Los Angeles. These depicted the Torchwood team against a dark background featuring a pair of sinister alien eyes, with a caption at the top reading 'Saving the Planet (One Alien at a Time)'

---

7 BBC America is also available in some countries outside the USA, for instance in the Caribbean.

and one at the bottom declaring 'From the creators of *Doctor Who*' (a little artistic licence obviously being employed here, given that *Doctor Who* had actually been created back in 1963). Smaller adverts of a similar design were placed at bus-stops and in other prominent locations. In addition, radio and TV commercials for the show were aired on many local stations, again using the 'From the creators of *Doctor Who*' tagline. Video trailers – some of them of several minutes' duration – were made available via a number of US media websites.

BBC America itself first began running a *Torchwood* trailer on 28 May 2007, in commercial breaks during a '*Doctor Who* marathon', and announced that the show would premiere at 8.00 pm Eastern on Saturday 8 September 2007 as part of its new 'Supernatural Saturday' strand. A few weeks later, however, two new promos appeared, the first consisting of a brief teaser depicting the show's 'T' logo in red and the word 'Torchwood' in white and the second of a full trailer, and the latter of these indicated that the time slot had now been moved back an hour to 9.00 pm Eastern[8].

US media interest in the show was boosted by two sets of personal appearances by cast and production team members: the first in mid-July by star John Barrowman and executive producer Julie Gardner at the Summer Press Tour junket organised by the Television Critics Association at the Beverly Hilton in Los Angeles to give the networks an opportunity to promote their upcoming shows; and the second on 26 July by producer Richard Stokes, co-producer Chris Chibnall, writer Noel Clarke and special effects supervisor Matt O'Toole on a well-attended, two-hour-long panel, moderated by *TV Guide*'s west coast bureau chief Craig Tomashoff, at the latest Comic-Con International event in San Diego, a convention that drew over 125,000 attendees in total. Interviews conducted at these events appeared in a number of online and print journals over the weeks that followed. These included UK genre magazine *Starburst*, which quoted Gardner's response when quizzed on what she thought the US reaction to *Torchwood* would be like:

'I hope it'll be good. Who knows. I'm talking as a British person, but it feels like an American show in terms of its pace and format … Certainly when Russell [T Davies] and I were [planning] *Doctor Who* and then *Torchwood*, we were talking about all the shows we love, and a lot of those shows are [American ones like] *Buffy the Vampire Slayer*, *Angel*, *Smallville* and now *Battlestar Galactica*.[9] We were talking a lot about the pace of storytelling, the way that those shows mix a lot of comedy [with the drama] – certainly the Joss Whedon shows. I think it's more about TV series in Britain and America starting to share attributes, in terms of production, quality and pace.'

---

8 In other time zones, this equated to 8.00 pm Central, 7.00 pm Mountain, 6.00 pm Pacific, 5.00 pm Alaska and 3.00 pm Hawaii.

9 Another American show that may have had an influence on the development of the *Torchwood* format was the short-lived *Special Unit 2*, transmitted on UPN in the USA in 2001 and 2002 and on the Sci-Fi Channel in the UK in 2003. This combined science fiction, horror and comedy and involved a small team of Chicago police force agents operating covertly to protect their city against various mythological threats, often dismissed by the public as hallucinations or optical illusions. The team's secret base was concealed behind the façade of a Chinese laundry, and the agents drove around Chicago in a conspicuous unregistered sports car.

Asked to comment on the differences between British and American shows in terms of production process, Gardner continued: 'We're much slower in our production process than you are in the States. But I think that's a combination of things [including] different union rules [and] the size of our crews. It's kind of much smaller than here. Our equipment is much smaller. It's a very, very different way of a system working. For example, we'll keep a director in the edit for much longer. So a director on something like *Torchwood* would have probably about four weeks' prep. We'll shoot an episode in, say, ten, 11, 12 days, and that director will be on that episode for the next two weeks, and [the executive producers] will come in to the final mix.'

The TV.com website on 4 September published an interview with Chibnall and Clarke, conducted just before they made their panel appearance at the San Diego event. Chibnall summed up *Torchwood* as follows: 'I would say it's a group of mates in Wales, who hunt down aliens and gather alien technology to arm the human race against the future. It's an informal, roguish group led by Captain Jack Harkness, who's an omni-sexual, 51st Century ex-Time Agent. It's the greatest show in the world. And it's enormous fun!' Clarke meanwhile commented: '[On *Torchwood*], you can go with the adult themes that you can't go with on [*Doctor Who*], and not just in violence and sexual stuff, but really sort of delving into the moral stuff ... *Torchwood* is about the dark side of humanity and understanding what it's like to be human in the 21st Century, with all the problems and temptations that are around.'

Much of the other American media coverage consisted of interviews with and features on Barrowman. These typically covered not only his role in *Torchwood* but also his background as a Scot who grew up in the USA and his openness about being gay. The MediaBlvd website, in a piece published on 9 September, quoted him as saying: 'In the series, you will always learn something new about Captain Jack on each episode, but it's not going to be so blatantly in-your-face. It will be delivered in a line of dialogue where you'll go, "Oh, my God! I just missed that." You're really going to have to listen, but you will learn new things about Jack. He is dark, he is charismatic, he has a past. There's two [years] of his past that has disappeared from his memory and we don't why. He is completely passionate about the human race and saving it from anything that might be detrimental to it, which he has learned from the Doctor. You're going on a journey with Jack because, as you learn about him, so does the team of Torchwood.' Asked for his take on how US viewers would react to the series, Barrowman replied: 'I don't know. I think American audiences are smarter than some television shows make them out to be. BBC America has a very intelligent audience that watch their programmes. And I hope it draws in the sci-fi crowd, because I wanna say that they're gonna love it. I hope they love it. We're going to have to wait and see. It will be interesting, because they've never seen a character like this on television before, with his omni-sexuality, as we call it in the sci-fi world. In terms of wording that you need to use in today's day and age, he's bisexual, and I don't know whether they're going to be able to deal with that or not, but I really think they will. I don't think it's going to bug them. It might bug the politicians. It might bug the people who are so far up their own arses that they don't want to let other people live their lives. But, I think the more people who watch it and let people know they like programming like this, the better it will be for us.'

The Out.com gay interest website meanwhile noted: 'On Planet Barrowman, it's normal to be inundated by kids in supermarkets seeking autographs on their Captain Jack action figures. The

Royal Air Force even asked him to do a fly-by and pose for in-character photo ops. While such a request of an openly gay actor is unthinkable in the current climate of the US military, the United Kingdom drafted a new code of conduct in 2000 allowing gay men and women to serve openly in its armed services. "That's why I said I'd do it." Out comes the wicked grin. "I'd like to think my pilot was gay. How many gay boys want to go in the cockpit? I did that!'"

On 23 August, BBC America launched its own slickly-designed *Torchwood* website – at www. bbcamerica.com/content/262/index.jsp – with information about the show and its characters and some publicity photographs. In addition, at around the same time, it started placing adverts for the show in a number of prominent media journals, including *Entertainment Weekly*. In the week beginning 27 August, it added the 'Welcome to *Torchwood*' mini-documentary from the *Torchwood Declassified* team to the On Demand service as an introduction to the show.

The extensive press coverage culminated in the pre-eminent listings magazine *TV Guide* devoting no fewer than three separate articles to *Torchwood* in its 3 to 9 September edition – including a positive review from the notoriously hard-to-please critic Matt Roush, who described Captain Jack's team as 'TV's sexiest alien hunters', and an interview with Barrowman – as well as running another of BBC America's paid adverts for the show.

All this advance publicity paid off handsomely when 'Everything Changes' finally debuted on Saturday 8 September, as reported three days later in a story headed 'Premiere Delivers Biggest Audience for Drama in BBC America History' on the Multichannel News website:

> BBC America said the premiere of *Torchwood* on Saturday night delivered the biggest audience of any drama premiere in the 58-million-subscriber network's history.
>
> The grown-up science fiction series, a spin-off of Russell T Davies's recent edition of *Doctor Who*, attracted 297,000 viewers at 9.00 pm ET and 6.00 pm PT in the target demographic of persons ages 25 to 54, network officials said.
>
> That's slightly ahead of how action drama *Robin Hood* performed when it premiered last year, at about the same rating (0.42). Viewer numbers were higher for *Torchwood* than *Robin Hood* because BBCA is in more homes now.
>
> The relatively heavily promoted *Torchwood* premiere delivered 496,000 total viewers, network officials said.
>
> A second airing, at midnight ET and 9.00 pm PT Saturday, delivered a 0.19 rating (139,000 viewers) in the target demographic, or 241,000 viewers overall, BBCA said.
>
> Figures cited are live viewing and same-day viewing, which adds in a day's worth of digitally recorded watching.

The episode was added to the On Demand service two days after its premiere – a practice that would be followed for the rest of the series, with the three or four most recent episodes being available for viewing at any given time – and later estimates put the total audience for all screenings of 'Everything Changes' at 1.6 million. This was a record-breaking figure for BBC America – not just for drama, but for all programming – recalling *Torchwood*'s original ratings triumph when it had debuted on BBC Three in the UK; and the achievement was soon being trumpeted by the channel in new on-air promos for the show. The figures for subsequent episodes not only maintained this strong start but, contrary to what normally happens with new series, actually improved on it. *Torchwood* was even out-performing BBC America's screenings of Series Two of *Doctor Who* – a fact that Barrowman would note with some satisfaction in subsequent interviews – although this is perhaps not an entirely fair comparison, as *Doctor Who* had already been shown on the Sci-Fi Channel and, unlike *Torchwood*, was already available to buy on DVD in the US.[10]

HDNet meanwhile began its unedited high definition run of *Torchwood* with three screenings of 'Everything Changes', at 7.00 pm and 10.00 pm Eastern on Monday 17 September and 1.00 am Eastern on Tuesday 18 September. Two further screenings followed, at 11.00 pm Eastern on Wednesday 19 September and 2.00 am Eastern on Thursday 20 September. Similar multiple screenings of the subsequent episodes then followed on a weekly basis. Although no official ratings are available for these screenings, it seems that HDNet was well pleased with *Torchwood*'s performance.

Not only had *Torchwood* proved a big hit with BBC America and HDNet viewers but it had also found favour with American critics, who were almost unanimous – not to say, at times, almost rapturous – in their reviews of the show, for which BBC America had made available preview discs of the first four episodes. Robert Lloyd, writing in the 8 September edition of the influential *LA Times*, called it 'indescribably delicious', while Ray Richmond of the well-respected *Hollywood Reporter*, in his piece published two days later, commented:

> I'm not big on the whole aliens/fantasy thing in general, so it takes something particularly enthralling in this genre to grab my attention and keep it. This is the highest praise I can give to *Torchwood*, a new BBC America sci-fi/thriller that's so good and unsettling and creepy that even grumps like me can't help but be in its thrall. The genius of the hour from creator/executive producer/writer Russell T Davies (*Doctor Who* and *Queer as Folk*) is the way it takes the audience's natural scepticism and stands it on its head as we watch all manner of outrageousness unfold through the eyes of a disbelieving cop. It also doesn't hurt that the male lead, the mega-intense John Barrowman, is a near dead-ringer for the young Tom Cruise. He even sounds like Cruise. This in itself is a form of science fiction come to life.
>
> Compelling, convoluted and camp all at once, *Torchwood* tells the tale of a British crime-fighting team that works independently of all law enforcement and government oversight. They operate by their own rules, but not in a Dirty Harry kind of way. It's far more sinister than that. They work for good under the guise of evil, privy as they are to Area 51-style alien info and absurdly advanced technology as they battle the monstrous flotsam and jetsam of both the extraterrestrial and human worlds here on Earth.

Variety's Brian Lowry, whose review appeared in the 3 September edition, was just as impressed:

---

10 In addition, in a rather strange move, BBC America was cropping the *Doctor Who* episodes from their original 16:9 picture ratio to 4:3, which it was not doing with *Torchwood* and indeed had not done with Series One of *Doctor Who*.

The Brits have seldom excelled in science fiction relative to their strides in other genres, but this semi-spin-off of the new *Doctor Who* from its writer, Russell T Davies, yields *X-Files*-ish charms with *Buffy the Vampire Slayer* bite – a smart, occasionally salacious hour wryly populated by cheesy monsters. Built around another one of those crack teams assigned to protect the Earth, the quirky interaction within the group (which loses members here and there) elevates the material, as does John Barrowman's *Who*-originated performance as intrepid and mysterious Yank leader Captain Jack Harkness.

Brian Tellerico of the UnderGroundOnline website wrote of the show:

> It could develop an even more loyal following than the latest version of [*Doctor*] *Who*. The truth be told, it's more instantly accessible. *Torchwood* accomplishes what the Sci-Fi Channel has been valiantly attempting with good-not-great shows like *The Dresden Files* and *The Lost Room* – it perfectly weaves different styles and tones to create one complete package. For sci-fi fans, it will be appointment television and one of their favourite shows of the year.

Newspapers in cities across the States – including San Jose, Seattle, Salt Lake City, Philadelphia, Pittsburgh and Kansas – printed equally glowing reactions to the show; in fact, fans who kept a tally reported that there had been around 70 positive reviews and only two negative ones. The following extract from a 1 September-published piece by Jeanne Jakle of the *San Antonio Express-News* was fairly typical:

> This offering is my favourite [new TV show], as it introduces a uniquely provocative character to weekly sci-fi: the sexually open Captain Jack Harkness (John Barrowman).
>
> The time-travelling adventurer, who's as heroic as he is witty, was introduced in the first season of *Doctor Who* and returns in the latter part of the show's current season.
>
> In his new fast-paced and eccentric drama, he heads a secret organisation in Cardiff, Wales, called Torchwood that's devoted to examining and fighting extraterrestrials who pose a threat to Earthlings.
>
> He's aided by an intriguing group, which includes local policewoman Gwen Cooper (Eve Myles).
>
> The new show features some fascinating aliens, but what really sets it apart is its adult feel. There's also the no-holds-barred sexuality of Captain Jack – who's had relationships not only with women and men, but with all kinds of varying species. The male and female members of his crew are just as experimental and get lusty as heck in several episodes.
>
> Yes, this is not your grandfather's sci-fi show.

Torchwood already had some American devotees even before its BBC America and HDNet screenings, these having generally become acquainted with it through an interest in *Doctor Who* and having either imported the British DVD sets or managed to acquire copies of the episodes through more illicit means such as file-sharing websites. Now, though, they were joined by a whole legion of new fans – and, like many of the American journalists who had written about the show, these were often people who had not come to *Torchwood* via, or even seen, *Doctor Who* and had only a peripheral awareness of its status as a spin-off. This was thus a very different situation from that in the UK, where just about every *Torchwood* viewer must have had at least a basic understanding of its connection to *Doctor Who* and most were doubtless regular followers of the parent show. This may perhaps help to explain why the US reaction to *Torchwood*, from viewers and media commentators alike, was so overwhelmingly positive, with little hint of the kind of cynicism and resistance it had attracted from a proportion of British genre fans and certain sections of the British press. Without their British counterparts' strong and persistent awareness of its *Doctor Who* connections, and all the associated preconceptions and expectations, new US viewers were able to judge *Torchwood* purely on its own merits.

The established fans were meanwhile pleased to note that, as promised by channel President Garth Ancier, the edits that BBC America had made to each episode to bring its running time down to fit a standard hour-length slot had been chosen with obvious care and sensitivity, and were not significantly detrimental to the narrative flow.

Testament to *Torchwood*'s favourable Stateside reception was an upsurge of American interest in online fan communities and the advent of a number of regular blogs and commentaries on US media websites.[11] The After Elton gay lifestyle website even started running a series of roughly ten-minute-long weekly video podcasts in which Michael Hinman, founder of the SyFy Portal website, and Meredith Hogan, a well-known American sci-fi radio personality, could be seen discussing each episode shortly after its debut screening – although, to the disappointment of its regular viewers, this was discontinued part-way into the run for unspecified technical reasons. BBC America meanwhile updated its own *Torchwood* website on a regular basis, and on 15 October 2007 launched a poll giving fans a chance to choose between two different proposed cover images for the US version of the complete Series One DVD box set. This set was eventually released by BBC/Warner on 22 January 2008, sporting the image that had gained the most votes in the poll, and gave those in the US their first opportunity to buy the episodes (other than as imports) as, unlike in the UK and Australia, there had been no previous double-disc releases of three or four episodes at a time.

The US media's love affair with *Torchwood* showed no sign of cooling off as the weeks went by. In November 2007, novelist Lynn Harris, writing on the Nerve.com website, described the show as 'polysexually perverse' and gave the following intriguing assessment of its appeal:

> In reference to [the] preponderance of sex, reviews of *Torchwood* tend to label the show an 'adult *Doctor Who*' and leave it at that. But all the shagging signifies much more than the show's original post-9.00 pm timeslot. The constant thrum of desire is central to *Torchwood*'s theme: the tension between the need for intimacy and the

---

11 See Appendix E for more details.

danger, perceived or otherwise, of getting too close. When police officer Gwen Cooper … joins the crew in episode one, it's made clear that she'll be a humanising influence on the team, who spend so much time underground that they're not sure how to have it any way other than furtive and fleeting. 'How do you switch off from all this stuff? What do you do to relax?' Gwen asks Owen (who, in a major violation of house rules, takes home some sort of alien cologne that causes both men and women to jump his bones). His answer: 'I torture people in happy relationships.'

What's especially interesting is that the show resists the implication that happy relationships are better than casual snogs – or even possible. Two other early episodes demonstrate the palpable danger of getting *too* involved, especially when your girlfriend has become half-cyborg and is threatening, quite plausibly, to destroy the human race. And tellingly, the show suggests that even when humans achieve the ultimate contact – evidence that we are not alone in the universe – they turn their backs.

The *Torchwood* production team were naturally delighted by the show's popularity with US viewers, as Chris Chibnall told *SFX* in an interview first published on the magazine's website on 9 January 2008: 'It's been really thrilling and unexpected and a lovely little bonus that they've taken to it so brilliantly. And what I think is interesting is they're not viewing it through the filter of *Doctor Who*, they're actually seeing it as a standalone show, and I think it's benefited from that to be honest, and I think there's probably been a more even discussion of the merits and demerits of *Torchwood* in the US than there has been [in the UK]. BBC America have really done us proud.'

Such was the public interest in *Torchwood* that it had reportedly prompted many viewer requests to local cable providers to add the channel to their subscription package in areas where previously it had not been available. Understandably keen to build on their success with the show, BBC America managed to gain agreement to screen Series Two just a short while after its UK debut, as they announced in a press release dated 20 November 2007:

JANUARY IS *TORCHWOOD* MONTH WITH THE RETURN OF BBC AMERICA'S HIT SCI-FI SHOW AND DVD RELEASE

BBC America's all-time highest rated show, *Torchwood*, is back with a US premiere second season, beginning January 26, 9.00 pm ET/PT. Created by Russell T Davies, lead writer on the current *Doctor Who* series, *Torchwood* (13 x 50') is a BBC production, distributed by BBC Worldwide.

With guest stars including James Marsters (*Buffy the Vampire Slayer*, *Smallville*), Alan Dale (*Ugly Betty*, *The OC*) and *Doctor Who*'s Freema Agyeman, the show will air close to its UK premiere.

Richard De Croce, VP Programming, BBC America, says: '*Torchwood* has legions of loyal fans in the US and we wanted to bring them the next season as soon as possible.'

And fresh from its critically acclaimed airing on BBC America in September, *Torchwood: The Complete First Season* goes on sale January 22. The seven-disc DVD set includes over six hours of bonus features including outtakes and cast interviews.

Torchwood is an action-packed, adrenalin-fuelled sci-fi series following the adventures of a team of investigators, lead by Captain Jack Harkness (John Barrowman), who use alien technology to solve crime. With fearsome new aliens and compelling storylines, the second season takes the close-knit Torchwood team through daredevil action, temptation, heartache and a life-changing event for one of the team.

Hollywood Reporter called it '… a crackling good, brilliantly conceived sci-fi series that targets actual grown-ups' while the *Philadelphia Inquirer* said it was '… super-slick, raw, bizarre, hilarious, spooky, scary and sublimely sexy.'

BBC America brings audiences a new generation of award-winning television featuring razor-sharp comedies, provocative dramas, life-changing makeovers and news with a uniquely global perspective. BBC America pushes the boundaries to deliver high quality, highly addictive and eminently watchable programming to viewers who demand more. BBC America is distributed by Discovery Networks. It is available on digital cable and satellite TV. For more information about BBC America visit www.bbcamerica.com.

Before long, BBC America had confirmed the exact US premiere date for Series Two: Saturday 26 January 2008.

CANADA

The Canadian Broadcasting Corporation (CBC) had been credited as a co-production partner on Series One of *Torchwood* by virtue of having paid up-front for the Canadian broadcast rights, so it was a foregone conclusion that it would screen the show at some point during 2007. As things transpired, however, the episodes actually had their Canadian debut on the high definition service HDNet Canada, starting with 'Everything Changes' at 7.00 pm Eastern on Monday 17 September. CBC lagged not far behind, though, beginning its run – also in high definition, where available from local cable operators – at 9.00 pm Eastern on Friday 5 October. In both cases, subsequent episodes followed on a weekly basis, although there was a break of a month in the CBC screenings after 'Out of Time', and the last three episodes were then shown over a single weekend, with 'Combat' going out on Friday 4 January and 'Captain Jack Harkness' and 'End of Days' then forming a double-bill on Sunday 6 January. French-speaking Canadians in Quebec had rather longer to wait before they could enjoy the show in their first language: Ztélé began its run of dubbed transmissions – again in high definition – at 10.00 pm on Friday 11 January 2008.

CBC set up only a modest webpage for *Torchwood*, presenting a brief series description and some promotional images, and gave the show far less publicity than BBC America had in the USA, preferring to devote the lion's share of its promotional effort at that time to *The Tudors*. It also edited the episodes far more heavily than BBC America had. Perhaps as a result of these factors, ratings were not particularly good, averaging around the half a million per episode mark

– although CBC claimed that they were happy with this, pointing out that it was better than *Doctor Who* achieved on the channel. There was some positive critical response, too, such as in the following piece, headed '*Torchwood* is Getting Even Better', written by Alex Strachan of the CanWest News Service and published in a number of regional newspapers on 23 November:

Torchwood, the finest Friday night supernatural sci-fi/fantasy hour you're not watching, is winding down the end of its first season. Tonight's episode of the *Doctor Who* spin-off about a secretive government agency that investigates claims of paranormal phenomena – it's not as dull or derivative as it sounds – has already aired in Australia, Israel, Mexico, Sweden, the US and the UK, where *Torchwood* originated

...

Torchwood owes its origins to the newly resurrected, revitalised *Doctor Who*, but it's a far darker, more adult and, in tonight's outing ['They Keep Killing Suzie'], more violent programme than its forebear. *Torchwood* lacks the star sizzle of a David Tennant or Christopher Eccleston, but its stories in recent weeks have packed a heavy emotional punch, from last week's outing about a mysterious pendant that allows the wearer to read other people's thoughts – not as much fun as it sounds, it turned out – to an episode two weeks earlier that mixed elements of a traditional fairy tale with a modern parable about extreme weather patterns.

...

Torchwood has already done something most new series fail to do, and that is improve with age. Each new episode, it seems, has more snap and vigour than the one before, and tonight's sets a new benchmark ...

Torchwood is a much bloodier series than *Doctor Who*, and more sexy – it's decidedly not for the kiddies. It lacks the silliness of *Moonlight* and the weepy sentimentality of *Ghost Whisperer*, Friday's other spook shows, and it has a remarkably eclectic taste in music ('Gorecki' by Lamb, and Funeral for a Friend's 'Red is the New Black' are featured in tonight's episode).

Torchwood will probably never match *Ghost Whisperer* and *Moonlight* in the ratings, even though it airs on the widely available CBC (*Ghost Whisperer* and *Moonlight* air on CTV). *Torchwood* warrants a look, though – especially if you like your murder mysteries with a twist and a dash of the unexpected.

FRANCE

Torchwood began a highly successful run on channel NRJ 12 in France with a triple bill of 'Everything Changes', 'Day One' and 'Cyberwoman' – 'Ghost Machine' being omitted for the time being – at 8.50 pm on Friday 12 October 2007. The episodes were dubbed into French and edited both for timing and for violent content. Other episodes later in the run were also screened out of sequence – 'They Keep Killing Suzie' preceded 'Greeks Bearing Gifts', for instance. The French titles for the Series One episodes were: 'Tout Change', 'Premier Jour', 'Machine Fantome', 'Femme Cybernetique', 'Petits Mondes', 'La Recolte' ('The Harvest'), 'Cadeau Grec' ('Greek Gift'), 'Ils Tuent Encore Suzie', 'Chaussures En Vrac' ('Jumbled Shoes'), 'Hors Du Temps', 'Combat',

'Capitane Jack Harkness' and 'La Fin Des Temps'. NRJ 12 also made the first episode available to view via their website – at www.nrj12.fr/op/torchwood_episode1/index.html.[12]

HONG KONG
ATV World began transmitting *Torchwood* in Hong Kong on Thursday 8 November 2007.

FINLAND
In Finland, the long-established YLE TV2 picked up the rights to *Torchwood*, transmissions beginning on Monday 3 December 2007. Series Two followed straight on from Series One, with 'Kiss Kiss, Bang Bang' debuting on Monday 10 March 2008.

BELGIUM AND THE NETHERLANDS
The Sci-Fi Channel began transmitting *Torchwood* in Belgium and the Netherlands from Tuesday 8 January 2008.

RUSSIA
Most recently, at the time of writing, Series One of *Torchwood* was one of the first shows to be seen on Sci-Fi Channel Russia, which launched on 31 May 2008, with episodes airing daily from that date.

AND ELSEWHERE ...
Other countries where channels acquired the rights to screen Series One included the Ukraine, Japan, New Zealand (where TV2 planned to launch the show in the spring of 2008, its acquisition having been announced by parent company TVNZ – the long-standing New Zealand home of *Doctor Who* – as early as 10 January 2007), South Korea (channel KNN, which also screened *Doctor Who*), Turkey (channel TRT) and Germany (channel RTL2). BBC Worldwide's own BBC Entertainment Singapore and BBC Entertainment Poland were also due to air all 13 episodes in 2008, the latter under the titles 'Wielkie Zmjany', 'Dzień Pierwszy', 'Maszyna Duchów', 'Cyberkobjeta', 'Male Światy', 'Mordercza Wioska' ('Murder Village'), 'Strzez Sie Darów!' ('Gift that Backfires!'), 'Wciaz Morduja Suzie', 'Nie Do Pary' ('Incompatible'), 'Spoza Czasu', 'Walka', 'Kapitan Jack Harkness' and 'Koniec Świata' ('End of the World').

By the spring of 2008, *Torchwood* had firmly established itself as one of BBC Worldwide's hottest overseas sales properties, and a big hit with viewers worldwide.

---

12 For anyone curious to hear *Torchwood* dubbed into French, this link is still live at the time of writing.

PART TWO: GEARING UP
FOR SERIES TWO

CHAPTER THREE: BACK IN THE TARDIS

Torchwood's Series One finale 'End of Days', first transmitted on New Year's Day 2007, concluded with the sound of a TARDIS materialisation echoing through the Hub and Captain Jack disappearing, leaving scattered papers in his wake – a cliff-hanger designed to lead in to the character's long-anticipated return to *Doctor Who*, the show in which he had made his debut back in 2005. That return came in the episode 'Utopia', first transmitted on 16 June 2007, in which it was revealed that the TARDIS had actually materialised not in the Hub – as most fans had assumed – but above it, in Roald Dahl Plass. The reason for this apparent discrepancy was that, at the time when 'End of Days' was recorded, it had still not been decided exactly how 'Utopia' would begin. In fictional terms, however, one can only surmise that the materialisation sound must have carried down from the Plass into the cavernous space below, perhaps through the entrance to the invisible lift sited there (a gust of air through which would also account for the scattered papers) or perhaps via a microphone system set up by Jack in conjunction with his 'early warning device' – which is linked to a jar containing the Doctor's hand, severed from his arm by the Sycorax leader in the 2005 *Doctor Who* Christmas special 'The Christmas Invasion'.[13] Jack goes running out to the TARDIS, presumably exiting the Hub via the stairs leading up to the fake tourist information office at its front entrance (given that the lift leading to that entrance must already be in use by his Torchwood colleagues, who are seen to arrive in the Hub moments later, and that the other, invisible lift is obviously now blocked by the TARDIS). He has on his back a rucksack that is later revealed to hold the jar containing the Doctor's hand, which he must have picked up quickly on his way out; and the haste of his exit may also account for some of the scattered papers. Jack then leaps at the TARDIS and clings on to its police box form as it dematerialises and travels through the time vortex to the planet Malcassairo in the year 100 Trillion, where he is reunited with the Doctor – now in his tenth incarnation as portrayed by David Tennant – and meets the Time Lord's latest companion Martha Jones – played by Freema Agyeman.

During the course of 'Utopia' and the following two episodes, 'The Sound of Drums' and 'Last of the Time Lords', which together made up Russell T Davies's concluding story of Series Three of *Doctor Who*, light was thrown on certain aspects of Jack's recent past that had been puzzling fans for some time, and a number of developments occurred that would prove significant for his future characterisation and portrayal in Series Two of *Torchwood*.

Early on in 'Utopia', Jack reveals that he escaped from the Game Station in the year 200,100, where he was left by the ninth Doctor at the end of *Doctor Who*'s Series One finale 'The Parting of the Ways', by using his Time Agent's vortex manipulator – the device he wears on a leather strap on his wrist – which when operational gives him a rudimentary ability to travel in time. He arrived back on Earth in 1869, but the vortex manipulator burnt out and became 'useless' for further time travel. Jack eventually based himself at the time rift in Cardiff, knowing that the Doctor would return there at some point to refuel the TARDIS – as previously witnessed in

---

13 The Doctor was able to grow another hand, by virtue of the fact that this occurred within a few hours of his regeneration from his ninth incarnation to his tenth.

'Boom Town', when the rift was temporarily opened in 2006. (It may or may not be a coincidence that 1869 is another of the years in which the time rift in Cardiff became active, as seen in 'The Unquiet Dead'.) Jack has had numerous opportunities to contact other incarnations of the Doctor over the period of almost 140 years during which he has been living on Earth – he says that he has been following him 'for a long time' – but has had to wait for a version that 'coincided' with him – 'the right kind of Doctor', as he previously put it in *Torchwood* – presumably to avoid damage to the time-lines.

A particularly significant exchange occurs a little later in the same episode, when the Doctor and Jack talk on opposite sides of a protective door as Jack works to complete a vital task in a room filled with radiation that to anyone else would be lethal. The Doctor admits that he 'ran away' on first realising, at the end of 'The Parting of the Ways', that Jack had become immortal – a disturbingly unnatural state, in the eyes of a Time Lord. He explains that his then companion Rose Tyler resurrected Jack, after he was exterminated by the Daleks, using the power of the time vortex, and inadvertently made him immortal in the process ... By the end of this discussion, the two men have effectively cleared the air between them and achieved a reconciliation.

The closing minutes of 'Last of the Time Lords' see the Doctor, Martha and Jack back in Roald Dahl Plass. Jack has decided to return to his responsibilities defending the Earth with Torchwood and pass up the opportunity to resume his travels in the TARDIS; 'I kept thinking about that team of mine,' he notes – perhaps recalling that the Doctor's arch-enemy the Master claimed in 'The Sound of Drums' to have sent them off on a wild goose chase to the Himalayas.[14] Having repaired Jack's vortex manipulator at the end of 'Utopia', and augmented it with a teleport capability as seen in 'The Sound of Drums', the Doctor now fixes it so that both these functions are disabled again, saying: 'I can't have you walking around with a time-travelling teleport. You could go anywhere; twice – the second time to apologise.' When Jack asks, 'And what about me? Can you fix that? Will I ever be able to die?', the Doctor replies, 'Nothing I can do. You're an impossible thing, Jack.' Masking his obvious disappointment with a quip, Jack gives the Doctor and Martha a farewell salute, recalling the one that he and his namesake exchanged at the end of the *Torchwood* episode 'Captain Jack Harkness'. There is a sting in the tail, though, when he pauses to consider how he will age and reveals that, as a 'poster boy' of the Boeshane Peninsula, where he lived as a kid prior to becoming 'the first one ever to be signed up for the Time Agency', he was sometimes referred to as 'the Face of Boe'. This, along with the fact that

---

14 Details of the Himalayas mission were later given in a report by Owen placed on the official *Torchwood* website. The team from Torchwood Three were apparently called in by UNIT to investigate a time rift, linked to the one in Cardiff, discovered part-way up the K2 mountain in Pakistan, where there were suggestions of activity connected to Abaddon, the creature killed at the climax of 'End of Days'. The team arrived at the site by helicopter and Toshiko set up equipment to probe for rift activity. This caused a doll with Jack's face to pop up from the snow – a literal 'Jack-in-the-box' – and this in turn triggered an avalanche that almost trapped the team on the mountainside. The report concluded: 'The whole thing was a set-up. Gwen tried to get some answers about who'd reported the activity, but suddenly nobody seemed to know anything. So we decided to head back home, although suddenly there wasn't an available transport, so we spent two days waiting. On our way back, they told us Harry Saxon had won the election, then he murdered the American President, then he was shot dead by his wife. A week really is a long time in politics.'

he cannot be killed, seems to suggest that he will one day become the wise old creature seen in the earlier *Doctor Who* episodes 'The End of the World', 'New Earth' and 'Gridlock', who is said to have lived for millions if not billions of years and who finally dies of old age after giving up the last of his life force to save the population of New New York at the end of the latter episode (old age presumably being the one thing that can, in the end, cause him to expire). Could Jack really be destined to become a huge, wizened head suspended in a glass life-support tank? For the time being, in the absence of any firmer evidence either in *Doctor Who* or in *Torchwood*, this has to be a moot point.

'Last of the Time Lords' ends with Martha leaving the TARDIS as well, to resume the life that was interrupted when she first met the Doctor at the beginning of Series Three of *Doctor Who*. Two days after the episode's 30 June debut transmission, however, the BBC issued a press release confirming that – as first reported in a *Daily Mirror* scoop on 29 June – Agyeman would soon be reprising her popular role. This read in part:

> The production team has now confirmed that the character is set to make a triumphant return in the fourth series [of *Doctor Who*]. Freema, who gained rave notices for her portrayal of Martha Jones, is also set to join the cast of *Torchwood*, where she will continue to play the character in three new episodes before returning to *Doctor Who* in the middle of the fourth series. *Doctor Who* executive producer and head writer Russell T Davies said: 'Series Three has gained outstanding reviews and Freema has been a huge part of that success, gaining rave notices for her portrayal of Martha. Now we are taking the character of Martha into brand new territory with a starring role in *Torchwood*.' Freema said: 'I can't wait to start [recording] on *Torchwood* and the new series of *Doctor Who*. It's a huge new challenge for me and I'm delighted Russell has decided to expand the character of Martha Jones.' The announcement leaves a vacant space in the TARDIS, and a new companion for the Doctor, who will join the new series for the entire 13-week run, will be announced shortly.

With Jack on his way back to the Hub, and Martha now due to meet up with the team for a multi-episode guest appearance, the scene was well and truly set for the start of *Torchwood*'s second series.

CHAPTER FOUR: RETOOLING THE FORMAT

On 25 October 2006, at which point the second series of *Torchwood* had not even been formally commissioned, and indeed the first series had only just started transmission and had not yet finished production, Russell T Davies and his team – headed by fellow executive producer Julie Gardner, producer Richard Stokes and co-producer and lead writer Chris Chibnall – had a preliminary round-table meeting in Cardiff to discuss storylines for the next run and decide which aspects of the show they wanted to keep the same and which they wanted to vary. One advantage they had was that whereas there had been relatively little opportunity for advance planning on Series One – which, in order to meet the scheduled transmission dates, had been rushed into production much more quickly than would normally be the case for a new show – this time they were under less intense pressure and had the chance to take stock and consider their options. The recording period on Series Two would also, as things transpired, be a few weeks longer than the mere six months allowed for Series One, and there would be more time available for post-production work to be carried out. The reason for this was that Series Two would begin transmission not in October, as Series One had, but the following January, giving a production cycle of 15 months rather than a year. As it seemed odds-on that there would also be a third series of *Torchwood*, to be produced in 2008 for transmission in 2009, the team could even start thinking about commissioning scripts to be held in reserve for that subsequent run.[15]

The main thing that Davies and his colleagues identified as being in need of adjustment for Series Two was the character interactions within the Torchwood team, as Chibnall recalled in an interview for Issues 8 and 9 of the genre magazine *DeathRay*, published in December 2007 and January 2008 respectively: 'Taken as a whole across the first series, the characters were too spiky toward each other. We always assumed it would be implicit that they liked each other, that they got on and that they loved their jobs, but what we learned is that you can never say that enough on screen … It's an adult show, and you don't want to iron out all the creases from the characters, … [but] at the same time you also have to bring warmth and heart to it … Because you're dealing with end-of-the-world scenarios frequently, things are going to be tense all the time, and you have to work hard at keeping your team unified. Having said all that, part of our 13-episode arc across the first series was to deliberately show the temptations that are laid in front of our people, and it was about them slowly coming together as a team … I think in retrospect you see the mistakes the characters make piling up. There [were] probably some scenes missing, … where they kiss and make up. We never showed that. We never showed why these people weren't sacked for some of the stuff they did, or showed strongly enough that these are the perils of working for the organisation. What we wanted was human and fallible heroes; that was crucial to the show. And the only way you can work out how fallible or not you can make them is by trying it … I think the graphic equaliser balance was a little off on Series One … but equally it's not a show where there's always going to be a happy ending. On Series One we

---

15 Former *Doctor Who* script editor Andrew Cartmel would be one of the writers commissioned to provide some prospective Series Three scripts in 2007.

were discovering the tone as we went.'

Reflecting on this issue in conversation with journalists at the Series Two press launch (see Chapter Six), Russell T Davies commented: 'That's the one thing we got wrong last year, the thing that just slipped a groove. I kept talking about the [crews of the] *Enterprise* [in the *Star Trek* franchise], really ... They all have faith and trust in each other, and when *Star Trek* really works, they play that brilliantly, like in that "Yesterday's Enterprise" episode [of *Star Trek: The Next Generation*]. The whole of "Yesterday's Enterprise" is about an act of faith; it doesn't matter about the spaceships and time loops. Just to get a team together that have that amount of trust is much more interesting drama than polarising them.'

To address this perceived deficiency in Series One, it was decided that Captain Jack's team should be shown to be more harmonious and cohesive in Series Two, with fewer episodes focused on just certain of the regular characters at the expense of having all five working together as a unit; and that there should be a greater sense of fun, adventure and romance injected into the stories. This would amongst other things entail the hitherto less-heavily-featured characters, specifically Toshiko and Ianto, being brought more into the limelight. Gareth David-Lloyd later reflected on this development of Ianto's character in an interview first published on the website of genre magazine *SFX* on 8 January 2008: 'He's on missions a lot more, he's driving the SUV a lot more, he's doing a bit more fighting ... He's given a lot of responsibilities that he didn't get in the first series, and it's all part of that team getting closer together, growing into each other, getting tighter knit. Everyone's aware of each other's duties, and if one person can't do it, then the next person steps in – and Ianto does on many occasions step in to do somebody else's job. And he has very much found his own role as a sort of researcher, [responsible for] logistics, and someone who can just break things down to their simple form rather than going the long way round it.'

In addition to this adjustment of the main character interactions, a conscious effort would be made in Series Two to ensure that the Cardiff time rift, and the 'flotsam and jetsam' coming through it, were central to all the stories, to avoid the absurdity of a succession of alien hazards being drawn to Cardiff seemingly by chance, as had happened previously in episodes such as 'Day One' and 'Greeks Bearing Gifts'.

One thing that would not be changed, however, was the 'threat of the week' approach adopted in Series One, which was considered to have worked well. 'For me,' Chibnall told *DeathRay*, 'the joy of the first series was the surprise element – we had all these different stories, and the audience never knew what they were going to get. But as programme-makers, you never know what might be controversial and what might be popular until it's been broadcast. The whole journey is a constant surprise ... What did work well for us was the fundamental choice of having a self-contained story of the week, every week. We're carrying that forward. I think the more emotional stories, such as the two Catherine Tregenna [scripted] episodes "Out of Time" and "Captain Jack Harkness", really showed the series at its best. We're looking to achieve that sort of impact in as many episodes as possible in the new series. But at the same time, some of the big high-concept things like "They Keep Killing Suzie" ... also worked. What's best is when we have one big single idea at the heart of each episode, whether it be the [resurrection] glove or three people from the 1950s showing up. We've worked very hard on the second series making sure that every episode has one big hook that you can then explore the fallout from.'

Interviewed by Joe Nazzaro for Issue 359 of the American science fiction magazine *Starlog*, published in October 2007, John Barrowman commented: 'There are always birthing and teething problems [on a new show], but over the course of the first year, I think we found out what they were. So we've tried to take them on board and iron them out during the second season.' Responding to Nazzaro's suggestion that the show's content had been toned down part-way through Series One because young *Doctor Who* fans were known to be tuning in, the actor added: 'It had nothing to do with kids watching, because it's an adult drama ... It isn't our responsibility to change things; it's the parents' responsibility to stop their kids from watching. One of the reasons that certain things were toned down a little bit was ... the budget. Special effects, the blood and gore, the medical stuff – you have to pay an extortionate amount for all of that. So we saved money for certain things toward the season's end. If anything, in Series Two, we're back to pushing the envelope. We don't swear as much as we did, which [was decided on partly] because we knew [the show] was going to be sold to the [USA]. So we didn't tone [*Torchwood*] down for the children; we toned [it] down for the American audience.'

In an interview first published on the *SFX* website on 10 January 2008, producer Richard Stokes also commented on the issue of swearing, and indicated that there would be a further reduction in this for Series Two: 'Partly because we're now at 9.00 pm on BBC Two, there has to be that understanding that we should appeal to a slightly broader audience, and the crossover between a family audience watching *Doctor Who* at 7.00 pm and a BBC Two show at 9.00 pm is probably gonna be slightly broader than [it was for] a 10.00 pm show on BBC Three.' In another interview, this one in Issue 166 of *SFX* itself, dated February 2008, Stokes added that there were also purely artistic considerations in play here: 'It's that thing where you write a script, everyone's happy with it, everyone signs off and you [record] it ... and you watch it in the edit and go, "Ooh, actually that moment just feels very slightly gratuitous." I mean, we haven't sat down and said, "We're gonna say 'fuck' less"! We've just been slightly more harsh on ourselves when we've read the script, saying, "Do we really need that? Does it actually make the scene better to do that?"'

As for the characterisation of Captain Jack, Chibnall told Issue 223 of *TV Zone*, dated Christmas 2007: 'I think the first thing to say is that, in Series Two, Jack has plenty of *joie de vivre*; there's not a *Torchwood* Jack and a *Doctor Who* Jack; we don't look at it like that. The thing we look at is the journey of the character and the emotions of the character, and having been killed and brought back to life and then essentially dumped back on Earth – or dumped himself back on Earth – Jack in Series One is troubled, conflicted, searching for something that he can't find, coming to terms with his immortality. There are a lot of things there that actually cause that character to be troubled. Should we have lightened him? Yes, in retrospect. But we also had to find out what the character is capable of and where he works and where he doesn't. Often fans of shows like to see what they know, and our job as writers and actors and directors is to take things into new territories and see how that works ... But by the end of Series One, Jack has completed that journey, he's found the Doctor again, so coming back into Series Two, you know from *Doctor Who* he's got his mojo back ... In Series One he's learning how to be a leader, he's learning how to live on Earth, how to deal with all the problems that are being thrown at him, so in a way it would have been unfair not to portray the character in that way. I think in the execution of it, if we'd had a little more time, we'd have stepped back and said it just needed a few more jokes and [a little more] lightness.'

Series Two would also see *Torchwood* becoming more willing, or perhaps less nervous, to embrace its *Doctor Who* connections, notwithstanding its different target demographic. This would be most obviously apparent in the three-episode crossover guest appearance of the Doctor's most recent, and hugely popular, companion Martha Jones; an idea formulated by Davies as early as the autumn of 2006, during the first weeks of production on *Doctor Who*'s third series. And just as Jack had undergone a distinct character progression in moving from one show to the other, so too would Martha, as Freema Agyeman reflected in an interview published in Issue 226 of *TV Zone*, dated March 2008: 'There have been some changes. We don't know how much time has passed since she stepped off the TARDIS to being in *Torchwood*, but enough time that she's established in [a] new job [as medical adviser to UNIT]. Things have changed in her life; she has got somebody in her life now, so obviously that's indicative of how her relationship with the Doctor is going to be when she meets him again [in Series Four of *Doctor Who*]. She's very much moved on and outgrown him, I think. She's happy with her life, but obviously she left her phone [with the Doctor], so she knows that she still has that connection, should she need it. But otherwise, she's carrying on with this life that she's created, and is happy with.'

The groundwork having been done to establish the revised tone and approach to characterisation desired by the show's high-level creative chiefs, all was now ready for Series Two of *Torchwood* to go into production.

CHAPTER FIVE: INTO PRODUCTION

The first titbits of behind-the-scenes news about Series Two began to emerge early in 2007. In an interview published on 1 February on the Total Sci-Fi website, writer Peter J Hammond hinted that he had been commissioned to provide a script, in the wake of his well-received Series One contribution 'Small Worlds'. This was confirmed in Issue 380 of *Doctor Who Magazine*, published on 1 March, which also reported that Chris Chibnall would be returning to supply three episodes, Catherine Tregenna two, Helen Raynor one and Russell T Davies one. The intention at this stage was that Davies would write the opening episode, as he had the previous year; in the end, however, his other commitments, mainly on *Doctor Who*, would make this impracticable – even though the opening episode would not, on this occasion, be in the first block to go before the cameras – and the task would fall instead to Chibnall, whose tally of scripts would thus rise to four. It was at one point intended that Tregenna would contribute three episodes and Raynor two, but their allocations were reduced as other writers were brought in.

On 25 February, Davies, Chibnall and Julie Gardner were all in Brighton to attend an annual BBC Worldwide showcase designed to interest overseas broadcasters in buying the rights to BBC programmes. As well as meeting a number of potential buyers for *Torchwood*, they took the opportunity to have script meetings with Hammond and two other potential writers, Phil Ford and Joseph Lidster.

The production base for Series Two, as for Series One, was BBC Wales' Upper Boat studios in Tonteg Road on the Treforest Industrial Estate, Pontypridd, Mid Glamorgan, eight miles from the centre of Cardiff. The first round-table tone meeting for the new run of episodes began at midday on 5 April; Davies, writing in Issue 382 of *Doctor Who Magazine*, published on 3 May, recalled: 'Our first tone meeting of the new series. Lordy God! Which means it's an epic, discussing everything from scratch – clothes, hair, dialogue, Hub, the new corridor, SUV, the lot. ("How come Jack Bauer's earpiece is invisible, but Torchwood's are huge?"[16]) Let alone the actual scripts, which demand the recreation of a certain 20th Century period, as well as ... well, that would be telling, but it's not an era we've tackled before.[17] I'm not sure anyone has! All very exciting, but Julie [Gardner] and I have to leave them at 17.00.'

Pre-production work continued throughout April, with designer Ed Thomas overseeing a makeover of the standing set of the Hub interior, which amongst other things entailed the creation of two new areas: a hothouse where the boardroom used to be and a completely new boardroom. The latter was conceived as being situated inside a large pipe somewhere in the depths of the Hub and was constructed in part from elements used previously for the set of the *Valiant* in the *Doctor Who* episodes 'The Sound of Drums' and 'Last of the Time Lords'.[18] The show's regular freelance contractors such as prosthetics expert Neil Gorton of Millennium

---

16 Jack Bauer is the lead character in the US series *24*. The discussion reported by Davies here resulted in a decision to make the Torchwood team's earpieces much smaller, and in most cases invisible, in Series Two.

17 The era referred to by Davies here was the 51st Century, which would be seen in the episode 'Adam'.

18 In fictional terms, the implicit assumption would be that a certain amount of reconstruction work was required following the damage done to the Hub at the end of the Series One finale 'End of Days'.

Effects meanwhile got down to work on their first contributions to the upcoming run of episodes.

Studio recording eventually got under way on Monday 30 April under the direction of Andy Goddard, who had been responsible for 'Countrycide' and 'Combat' the previous year. The first significant location work took place the following week, a few establishing shots in and around Cardiff having been recorded a little earlier while the cast were engaged in script read-throughs and rehearsals.

Occasional news items continued to filter out as production progressed. Perhaps the most notable of these was an 18 June report on the James Marsters Live website revealing that Marsters – famous for his role as Spike in *Buffy the Vampire Slayer* and *Angel*, two of the shows that had inspired Davies in his creation of *Torchwood* – would be guest-starring in the series. Early July meanwhile saw another writer being named: J C Wilsher, best known for his acclaimed police drama series *Between the Lines* (BBC One, 1992-1994). Then, on 16 July, the BBC put out its own first press release for Series Two. Headed '*Torchwood* to air on BBC Two' – confirming the previously-announced move of the show from its original BBC Three home – this read:

> Captain Jack Harkness (John Barrowman), Gwen (Eve Myles), Owen (Burn Gorman), Tosh (Naoko Mori) and Ianto (Gareth David-Lloyd) return as the close-knit team of investigators solving alien and human crimes as they delve into the underworld of modern day Cardiff.
>
> The high-octane storylines, [recorded] in and around Cardiff, include Torchwood's encounter with a rogue Time Agent; a tragic time-slip from World War One; and a memory-thief who uncovers long-forgotten secrets among the entire team.
>
> Making a special guest appearance in the first episode is James Marsters who starred as Spike, the punk-goth vampire, in *Buffy the Vampire Slayer* and *Angel*.
>
> Commenting on his role in *Torchwood*, James says: 'I am a huge fan of *Doctor Who* and *Torchwood* so it was me who knocked on their door.
>
> 'I am really excited about the character I am playing. I can't say too much about him, except he is naughty and a bit of a psychopath.'
>
> Later on in the run, Alan Dale makes a star appearance. Alan is currently appearing in *Ugly Betty* as Bradford Meade and he is well known for his roles in *The OC, Lost, The West Wing* and as Jim Robinson in the Australian hit soap *Neighbours*.
>
> He said: 'I am thrilled to be working on *Torchwood* and delighted to be in England again. I am a huge fan of British television drama.'
>
> Another familiar face among the surprise guest stars is *Doctor Who*'s gorgeous companion Martha Jones (Freema Agyeman) who brings her time-travelling expertise and medical skills to the team halfway through the series.
>
> She says: 'I'm really looking forward to working with the *Torchwood* team and can't wait to start [recording].
>
> 'It's a huge new challenge and a wonderful opportunity to develop and expand the character of Martha Jones.'
>
> Russell T Davies said: '[Recording] is well underway in Cardiff, and we're aiming

to make the show bigger and bolder than ever, as we move to our new home on BBC Two.

'It's too early to start giving things away, but we've got some amazing guest stars, fearsome new aliens, and compelling new storylines that will push the Torchwood team further than ever before.'

The 13-part series is written by Chris Chibnall, Catherine Tregenna, Helen Raynor, James Moran, Joseph Lidster, Peter J Hammond, J C Wilsher and Matt Jones.

Created by Davies, with Chris Chibnall as co-producer and lead writer, the first series, which aired on BBC Three last year, achieved the channel's highest ever ratings – with an audience of 2.5 million for the first episode.

Torchwood is executive produced by Russell T Davies and Julie Gardner, Head of Drama in BBC Wales. The producer is Richard Stokes.

A number of print and online news outlets ran stories based on this press release, most of them also publishing a close-up photograph of Captain Jack with Marsters' character, later revealed to be called Captain John Hart – the first official publicity image to be made available for the new series. These included the BBC's own website, www.bbc.co.uk, which in the Wales section of its News pages published a report headed '*Buffy* star's joy at *Torchwood* job', complete with excerpts from the quotes by Marsters, Dale and Agyeman.

On 27 July, during a John Barrowman guest spot on Channel 4's *The Friday Night Project*, viewers enjoyed a brief tour of parts of the Hub set and saw a short behind-the-scenes clip of the camera rehearsals for a scene from Series Two's opening episode. This involved Captain John holding Gwen hostage while the other Torchwood team members aim their guns at him.

Maintaining the momentum of advance publicity, the BBC issued a further press release almost exactly a month after the previous one, on 15 August. This focused on Agyeman's three-episode guest stint on the show. Headed 'A new face for *Torchwood* and a new look for Martha', and accompanied by the first publicity shot of Martha with the Torchwood team, it read in part:

Martha Jones … is back and reunited with Captain Jack Harkness … when she teams up with Torchwood … to help them solve a series of mysterious deaths in Cardiff.

Pictured here as she steps into the Hub for the first time, a more grown-up and worldly-wise Martha brings her medical knowledge and the expertise learnt during her travels with the Doctor to help Torchwood do battle against an alien threat.

Freema Agyeman says: 'Martha has grown up a lot since *Doctor Who*. She's now a fully qualified doctor and a bit hardened by life experiences. When she finds out that Captain Jack needs her help, she joins Torchwood for a while. She continues to develop her knowledge of alien intelligence, but this time keeping her feet on the ground.

'These will be invaluable skills to take back with her on future adventures with the Doctor. She outgrew the Doctor, in a sense, and so the next time they meet it will be in a more professional capacity. I'm so proud of her journey and who she has become.

'And for me as an actress, it's a great new challenge to be able to broaden and expand Martha as she develops in other directions for this more adult series. The

Torchwood team are fabulous to work with and have made me very welcome.'

Creator of *Torchwood*, Russell T Davies, says: 'Freema is a wonderful actress and we want to give her the chance to add another dimension to Martha. She is going to cause some waves in the team – especially as she joins Torchwood at a point when everything is going to change for one of them.'

Again, this press release was seized upon by the media to form the basis of a number of news stories over the days that followed.

Although there was still some five months to go before Series Two would actually reach the nation's TV screens, excitement was already beginning to build.

THE PRODUCTION WRAPS

Whereas on Series One, recording and post-production of the final episodes had not been completed until after the first had actually been broadcast, on Series Two the production wrapped well in advance of transmission. A farewell party was thrown for the cast and crew in Cardiff on the evening of Wednesday 21 November 2007. A blooper reel was shown, John Barrowman gave a speech, Gareth David-Lloyd's band Blue Gillespie played a set, and a DJ provided music throughout the rest of the evening. It had been anticipated that all recording for the series would be finished by that date; in the event, though, there were still a few pick-ups left to be shot, which meant that some of the team had to return to work the next day! This was by no means the first time that the Series Two production schedule had caused problems for cast and crew members. 'To be honest, it was like going to hell and back,' recalled John Barrowman in an interview published on 11 January 2008 on the website of the *Express & Echo* local newspaper of Exeter, Devon. 'It was disorganised and chaotic. And that's not to say people didn't work very hard, because the production team, camera crew, wardrobe, everyone worked extremely hard and really battened down the hatches, but for some reason, midway, it just went awry. At some points we were doing four episodes at once, which is why it was chaotic.' Within a couple of days of the wrap party, however, recording for Series Two had finally been completed, and all that remained to be done were some final pieces of post-production work.

PART THREE: THE SERIES AIRS

CHAPTER SIX: TOWARD TRANSMISSION

As work on *Torchwood* gradually wound down at the show's Upper Boat production base, Issue 222 of the genre magazine *TV Zone*, which hit the newsstands on 14 November 2007, whetted fans' appetites for the upcoming series with some sneak preview photographs of the new areas of the Hub set. Then, on 20 November, a BBC press release for BBC Two's Winter/Spring 2008 season contained an entry for *Torchwood*, revealing a few more snippets of previously-unpublished information:

> *Torchwood*, the award-winning drama created by *Doctor Who* writer Russell T Davies, returns for an even bigger and bolder series with Captain Jack Harkness (John Barrowman) and his alien-fighting team, premiering on BBC Two.
>
> Captain Jack, Gwen (Eve Myles), Owen (Burn Gorman), Toshiko (Naoko Mori) and Ianto (Gareth David-Lloyd) – the team of investigators solving alien and human crimes in the underworld of modern-day Cardiff – face high-octane adventures which push their resolve and friendships as never before.
>
> Joined by Freema Agyeman (*Doctor Who*'s Martha Jones) for three episodes and with guest stars Richard Briers (*Monarch of the Glen*), Alan Dale (*Ugly Betty*, *Neighbours*) and James Marsters (*Buffy the Vampire Slayer*), they journey from contemporary Cardiff to the 51st-Century, and back to the First World War.
>
> On their travels, Torchwood battle fearsome new aliens; a rogue Time Agent; a tragic time-slip from the Great War; and a memory thief who uncovers long-forgotten secrets among the entire team.

One point that this press release inadvertently highlighted was that, whereas in its original home on BBC Three *Torchwood* had been justifiably regarded as one of the channel's flagship programmes, with its move to BBC Two it had become just one of a long list of new shows due to be launched in the forthcoming season. In other words, it had gone from being a big fish in a small pond on BBC Three to being a small – or perhaps medium-sized – fish in a big pond on BBC Two. Possibly as a consequence of this, the promotional effort devoted to it was much lower-key – and far less expensive – this time around. While Series One had benefited from huge billboard and side-of-bus adverts, cinema trailers, specially-shot 'viral video' teasers posted online, and preview screenings of the first episode for lucky groups of fans in three city-centre cinemas, Series Two was afforded none of these things. Where Series Two had the advantage, however, was that the viewing public were, of course, already familiar with *Torchwood* by this point, whereas before Series One began it had been – Captain Jack aside – an unknown quantity. Arguably, therefore, there was less need for a high-profile promotional campaign on this occasion, and media and public interest could be maintained simply through the BBC's succession of press releases and the publicity they generated.

The next of these press releases appeared on 3 December, tying in with a Series Two launch event at the Rex Cinema in Soho, London, where a by-invitation-only audience of journalists was given a preview screening of the first episode, its title now revealed as 'Kiss Kiss, Bang Bang', introduced by Controller of BBC Two Roly Keating and with Russell T Davies, John Barrowman and other members of the regular cast in attendance for interviews – some of which were video-recorded by the journalists concerned and subsequently made available to view online. The episode was, by all accounts, very well received. Genre magazine *SFX*, in a piece posted later the same day on its website, reported, 'It had an audience of jaded media hacks guffawing with delight for 50 minutes. Some of the choicest humour is self-deprecating, with the programme subtly acknowledging its absurdities; there are delicious one-liners referencing Torchwood's status as "the world's least secret secret organisation", and Jack's penchant for standing around on the edge of rooftops … The opening scene (which involves a fish …) is hilariously outlandish, and there's also a lovely gag that *Star Wars* fans will appreciate. Russell T Davies said he wanted season two to have more fun, and they've delivered it in spades.' Headed '*Torchwood* premieres on BBC Two in New Year' – although the actual date and time of transmission were still being kept under wraps at this point – the press release read in part:

Torchwood … bursts back on our screens in mid-January 2008, this time premiering on BBC Two.

And this time it's bigger and bolder with more fun, adventure and excitement for the alien-fighting team …

…

In response to audience demand, younger fans will now have the opportunity of watching a specially edited pre-watershed repeat.

Roly Keating, Controller BBC Two, says: 'We're delighted that *Torchwood* is joining BBC Two.

'We know from the success and popularity of *Heroes* that there's a growing appetite for smart, high-quality, sci-fi drama on the channel, so *Torchwood* is a perfect fit.

'I'm also pleased to announce that, due to popular demand from families and younger viewers, we will be showing a special pre-watershed repeat so everyone can enjoy the new series.'

Making a special guest appearance in the first episode is James Marsters as Captain John … Captain John and Captain Jack go way back and have 'history'.

When [Captain John] appears through the rift under Cardiff looking for Captain Jack, not only does he disrupt Captain Jack's homecoming but the whole team, city and world are suddenly placed in danger.

The new series promises an exhilarating mixture of adventure, heartbreak, humour and surprise and pushes the team's resolve and friendships as never before.

…

[Torchwood] encounter alien sleeper cells; save a stranded creature from human exploitation; meet a tragic soldier from the First World War; and encounter a memory thief who exposes long-forgotten secrets among the entire team.

…

Richard Briers, Nerys Hughes and Ruth Jones (*Gavin and Stacey*) … appear in various roles.

Russell T Davies says: 'This series pushes the Torchwood team further than ever before. They are joined by some incredible guest stars who are really going to cause waves. It's adventurous, thrilling and packed full of surprises.'

Torchwood, which was shot in HD and will also be shown on the BBC HD channel, is [recorded] in and around Cardiff by BBC Wales.

BBC Wales Controller Menna Richards says: 'The first series of *Torchwood* was a huge hit with audiences. We're extremely proud that it's produced in Wales. And its success is a reflection of the huge wealth of talent and creativity that exists here. We're delighted that it's returning to our screens for another series full of action, humour and excitement.'

The 13-part series is written by Chris Chibnall, Phil Ford, Peter J Hammond, Matt Jones, Joseph Lidster, James Moran, Helen Raynor, Catherine Tregenna and J C Wilsher ...

There will be a new exciting online reality game and exclusive behind the scenes footage on bbc.co.uk/torchwood.

Again the press release was accompanied by a new promotional image for Series Two – or, rather, two images, as the one initially placed on the BBC Press Office website was strangely taken down and replaced with a different one later the same day. Both images showed the five Torchwood team regulars dramatically posed against a white tunnel background (actually photographs of a pedestrian tunnel at Poplar DLR station in London) and attired in new-style costumes, mainly in black but with plum-coloured shirts for Owen and Ianto and a matching blouse for Toshiko, designed to give them a slightly slicker, more uniform image for Series Two.

Of all the new revelations here, undoubtedly the most surprising was that there would be an edited, pre-watershed repeat of each Series Two episode for the benefit of family audiences – as there had been for *Buffy the Vampire Slayer* on its BBC Two broadcasts. This innovation was reported enthusiastically on the BBC's own children's news magazine programme *Newsround* but gave rise to concerns amongst established *Torchwood* fans, some of whom feared that it would preclude Series Two from dealing with subject matter as dark as that featured in Series One, while others fretted that it would entice more young children, and particularly those who were avid *Doctor Who* fans, to tune in to a show that, even with the edits, would still be inherently unsuitable for them. It would later emerge however that, although it had been under discussion for some time, the decision to go ahead with pre-watershed versions had not been taken until quite a late stage of the series' scripting, and had thus not influenced its basic content at all, so at least the first of these concerns would prove unfounded. In addition, as Davies and Barrowman made clear at the press screening, there would be no toning-down of the show's gay content. 'One thing that won't be cut out [for the pre-watershed versions] ... are the same-sex relationships,' reported the *Stage*. '"[They're] just a part of everyday life," noted John Barrowman before series creator Russell T Davies joked that he should get off his soapbox.' Chris Chibnall meanwhile told *SFX*: 'We've been talking about [doing pre-watershed versions] all year and it's something the BBC were very keen on, to get the show out to a wider audience. Actually when we broke it down and looked at the episodes, it was surprising how little we'd have to cut. Most of the stuff that we take out is stuff that children could imitate, and because we're in a slightly heightened fantasy world, there is less stuff that's imitable. It's all a question of cutting away at the right time, to be honest. It's the same story, there [are] not going to be any major differences. There were a couple of scenes where we shot differing versions of a line with swearing in it, but there [are] not many instances – there's not much swearing at all [in the new series].'

The clear suggestion in the press release that BBC Two chiefs were looking to *Torchwood* to appeal to – and hopefully retain – the large numbers of viewers won by the channel's now-concluding run of *Heroes* was reinforced when, on Wednesday 6 December, the first on-air trailer for Series Two was screened immediately prior to the US import's season finale.[19] The trailer presented a 20-second montage of clips from the two shows, cleverly edited together so as to suggest that *Heroes'* Peter Petrelli (played by Milo Ventimiglia) was phoning *Torchwood's* Captain Jack to give him a message. Ending with the voiceover announcement 'The heroics continue with *Torchwood* Series Two, January on BBC Two', this effectively represented a 'passing of the baton' between the two shows. The trailer was subsequently rerun a number of times and placed on the BBC's YouTube channel and on the official *Torchwood* website – at www.bbc.co.uk/torchwood – which was relaunched on 4 December with a new look for Series Two, designed by the Cardiff-based agency Carbon Studio, and with the Series One content removed.[20] Not surprisingly, the strong expectation amongst fans was that *Torchwood* would take over *Heroes'* regular 9.00 pm Wednesday slot early in the new year.

On 9 December, eagle-eyed fans spotted a couple of brief *Torchwood* clips amongst a montage of trailers on the BBC HD digital channel – which would again be screening each episode of the new series simultaneously with its terrestrial channel debut. One was a shot of the Torchwood team members walking in a group toward the camera – taken from the closing sequence of 'Kiss Kiss, Bang, Bang' – and the other a shot of Jack removing an object from the wall safe in his office in the Hub while Gwen looks on – a sequence not ultimately included in any transmitted episode.

On 14 December, the BBC Press Office's regular release of forthcoming programme information – brought forward by a week from its usual schedule because of the forthcoming holiday season – listed 'Kiss Kiss, Bang Bang' as airing in the week beginning 12 January, but still withheld the actual date and time. It also gave the first brief details to be published about the episode's plot:

> Captain Jack is reunited with the Torchwood team as they face a rogue Time Agent. The mysterious Captain John Hart, played by James Marsters (*Buffy the Vampire Slayer*), is determined to wreak havoc, and needs to find something hidden on Earth. But with Gwen's life in danger, and cluster bombs scattered across the city, whose side is Jack on?

---

19 It would actually be more accurate to refer to this as the first on-air trailer *in the UK*, as BBC America had already run a Series Two trailer in the USA, albeit made up almost entirely of clips from Series One (see Chapter Nine).

20 To the disappointment of some fans, the second official *Torchwood* website, the Torchwood Institute System Interface, which had been presented as if it were the website of a real-life Torchwood organisation, was not continued for Series Two – the address, www.torchwood.org.uk, now simply redirected to the main site.

This was followed a week later by similar details for the second episode, 'Sleeper':

When a burglary turns into a slaughter, Torchwood suspect alien involvement, as the award-winning drama created by *Doctor Who* writer Russell T Davies continues. Who is Beth, and can she be as innocent as she seems? However, when the investigation escalates into a city-wide assault, Captain Jack realises that the whole planet is in danger.

Christmas Day brought another on-air trailer for Series Two, transmitted immediately after the *Doctor Who* special 'Voyage of the Damned' on BBC One. This consisted of a 40-second montage of clips from the episodes up to and including 'A Day in the Death', with introductory captions stating 'Alone they're only human. Together they're Torchwood' and the closing voiceover announcement '*Torchwood*, coming soon to BBC Two'. A short teaser consisting of the show's 'T' logo and the official website address also debuted on this date on BBC Three, and was rerun frequently over the days that followed.

As the year drew to a close, a rather implausible report in the 26 December edition of the *Sun* suggested that a *Torchwood* role was on the cards for Australian actress and singer Dannii Minogue, who had recently been a regular celebrity judge on the hit ITV1 talent show *The X Factor* and whose sister Kylie had just been seen in 'Voyage of the Damned'. 'I'd love it if Dannii appeared in *Torchwood*,' John Barrowman was alleged to have said. 'She has an edge, and I know she's a fan of the show.'

The following day, the debut transmission slot for Series Two was finally confirmed by the BBC to listings magazines and websites: 9.00 pm on Wednesday 16 January 2008.

CHAPTER SEVEN: INTO TRANSMISSION

Torchwood trailers continued to be shown during selected programme breaks, mainly on BBC Two and BBC Three, throughout the first two weeks of January 2008. The longest of these – a 60-second extended version of the one seen after 'Voyage of the Damned' on Christmas Day, including one clip from as late a story as 'Adrift' – first surfaced between two episodes of the animated US series *Family Guy* transmitted in late-evening slots on New Year's Day on BBC Three. A slightly revised version, again including a number of previously unscreened clips, premiered two days later on BBC Two. A 20-second promo specifically for 'Kiss Kiss, Bang Bang', once more including some previously unseen material, first appeared on BBC One, BBC Two and BBC Three during the evening of 2 January, from which date all the trailers started including a closing caption giving the debut transmission day, Wednesday 16 January.

On 7 January, the official *Torchwood* website put up a short news item on 'Kiss Kiss, Bang Bang', which read in part:

Torchwood's Captain Jack Harkness … faces a dilemma when rogue Time Agent Captain John Hart … wreaks havoc on Cardiff in the first episode of the new series – should he kiss him or kill him?

Torchwood creator and executive producer Russell T Davies said: 'The sparks fly for Captain Jack when Captain John hits town. There is a lot of history between them. It could go either way!'

Also on 7 January, the BBC released online a preview clip from 'Kiss Kiss, Bang Bang'. Lasting almost four minutes, this was a slightly edited version of the episode's opening, pre-titles scenes with the Blowfish, concluding with Captain Jack asking his Torchwood colleagues 'Hey kids, d'you miss me?' The following day, a further clip, this time of almost two-and-a-half minutes' duration, was made available through BBCi's 'red button' interactive TV service. This consisted of the sequence where Captain Jack drives to Bar Reunion in the SUV and kisses and fights with Captain John while the other Torchwood team members follow in a taxi. A day later, yet another clip turned up, this time on the website of the US listings magazine *TV Guide*, showing Captain Jack introducing Captain John to Gwen, Owen, Toshiko and Ianto in the wrecked bar. On 10 January, the latter clip (with just a few seconds' difference in its start and end points) also appeared on the official *Torchwood* website, as did a compilation of snippets from the website's forthcoming 'Up Close' series of behind-the-scenes mini-documentaries; this included a number of shots of the show's stars larking about between takes on set and location, with John Barrowman even aping John Culshaw's exaggerated impression of Captain Jack from the *Dead Ringers* sketches (see Chapter One). Another new clip was placed on BBC America's *Torchwood* website on 11 January. This one lasted almost two minutes and consisted of the important sequence toward the end of the episode where Captain John learns that the diamond he's been seeking doesn't exist, finds himself in deadly danger when an explosive device attaches itself to his chest, and responds by taking Gwen hostage. By this point, fans had started to joke that if the BBC continued to make new previews available on a daily basis, virtually the whole of 'Kiss

Kiss, Bang Bang' would already have been seen in clip form before it made its on-air debut!

In some respects, however, despite the succession of news releases and the plethora of trailers, clips and behind-the-scenes snippets, Series Two continued to fare less well than Series One in terms of advance promotion. Of particular note, there was no *Radio Times* front cover heralding the show's arrival this time around, and although a preview article was included inside the magazine's 12 to 18 January edition, it was not as extensive as the previous year's; it consisted of just a short interview with John Barrowman and a piece comparing *Torchwood* with ITV1's *Primeval*. 'Kiss Kiss, Bang Bang' was recommended as one of 'Today's Choices' on the programme pages for 16 January, but reviewer Mark Braxton seemed not entirely convinced, commenting: 'As with the first run, there's a certain heartlessness that undermines the slick action and impressive visuals. But there are encouraging signs that the characters will be more likeable this time around.' This established a pattern for *Radio Times* coverage of *Torchwood* over the course of the following weeks: there would be only one more tie-in feature article – a 'One Final Question' interview with Freema Agyeman coinciding with her *Torchwood* debut in 'Reset' – and although almost every episode would be promoted as one of 'Today's Choices' for the day of its BBC Two debut transmission, the accompanying text by Braxton would generally be lukewarm in tone or, at best, damn with faint praise, making one wonder why the editor could not have assigned the task of writing these pieces to someone who actually liked the show.

On the morning of 16 January itself, Eve Myles and Naoko Mori made a guest appearance on the BBC's *Breakfast* programme. Yet another new preview clip was shown – this one, lasting almost a minute and a half, from slightly later in the scene in the bar, where Captain John tells the Torchwood team about needing to find the three 'toxic canisters' – along with short sections from the already-familiar sequences of the Blowfish driving the sports car and of Gwen, Owen, Tosh and Ianto talking about Jack in the taxi. The two actresses spoke about the appeal of *Torchwood*, the new pre-watershed edits of the episodes, the pleasures of working with John Barrowman and the differences between the first and second series.

'Kiss Kiss, Bang Bang' was finally transmitted, just a couple of minutes later than scheduled, at 9.02 pm on BBC Two that evening, preceded by a specially-prepared continuity clip in which the picture was supposedly broken up by interference through which a *Torchwood* logo and a red-tinted snippet from the show became briefly visible – a precedent that would be followed for all the subsequent BBC Two screenings.[21] The episode was then repeated at 11.30 pm on BBC Three. When the overnight ratings figures became available the following day, the news was good: 3.70 million viewers had tuned in to the BBC Two transmission, a 14.8% share of the total TV audience at that time, while 0.25 million had watched the repeat. The programme had been the highest-rated of the day on BBC Two, and the eighteenth most-watched on all channels. On 18 January, the Appreciation Index (AI) figure for the BBC Two screening was revealed: a very good 84, meaning that it had also been one of the most enjoyed programmes on TV that day. When, in due course, the final ratings figures were published, revised upwards to include those who had recorded the programme to watch later the same week, they were 4.22

---

21 For the first episode, the clip used was of the large Mayfly creature later to be seen in 'Reset'.

million for BBC Two and 0.35 million for BBC Three, making a combined total of 4.57 million. While this was about two million short of the total achieved by Series One's opening double-bill of 'Everything Changes'/'Day One', it was still an excellent performance by any standards.

There was another factor to be taken into account here, too: whereas the Series One episodes had generally had five additional BBC Three repeats within the week of their debut transmission, each of which had contributed a modest amount to the total audience figure, the Series Two episodes would have only one additional repeat, but on BBC Two, in the new, pre-watershed edited format. When the pre-watershed version of 'Kiss Kiss, Bang Bang' went out at 7.00 pm on 23 January – a week after the debut transmission, whereas for most subsequent episodes the interval would be only a day – it won an audience of 1.19 million viewers, pushing the combined total up to an even better 5.76 million. This was despite the fact that people in Scotland and Northern Ireland were unable to tune in to the pre-watershed version (unless they subscribed to a cable TV service that carried the English and Welsh BBC channels) as – to the annoyance of many – it was dropped in favour of local programming in their regions.[22]

Furthermore, viewers this year had an additional opportunity to watch each episode, at a time of their own choosing, in either complete or edited format, via the BBC's iPlayer service; and *Torchwood* quickly established itself as one of the most popular programmes on this pioneering online video player. Indeed, according to figures released by the BBC on 20 February, 'Kiss Kiss, Bang Bang' was the third most-watched programme on the iPlayer since its marketing launch on Christmas Day 2007, at a time when the service was attracting up to 1.3 million unique viewers a week. In addition, for a charge of £1.89, each of the transmitted episodes could be downloaded to a video iPod or iPhone from the Apple iTunes service, which was now beginning to carry a range of BBC programming under a recently-agreed deal. Simon Danker, director of digital media for BBC Worldwide, was quoted as saying, 'We want to give audiences a wide variety of options on how and where to view their favourite BBC shows'.

It may not have hit the headlines in quite the same way as it had the previous year, when it had broken digital channel ratings records, but there was no doubt that *Torchwood* had got off to a great start with its second series.

Press reaction to 'Kiss Kiss, Bang Bang' was also almost entirely positive. The following review by Tim Teeman in the 17 January edition of *The Times* was fairly typical:

> The brilliant thing about *Torchwood* [is that] everyday Cardiff hums alongside psychotic blowfish and time loops. In between the dizzying action, there are gorgeous shots of its orange street-lit arteries. Captain Hart tried to tempt Jack into a life of space crime: 'We should be up there among the stars,' he cooed – and you imagined them in a Philippe Starck-designed space pod.
>
> But Captain Jack was more attracted to Ianto. Captain Hart tried and failed to murder Captain Jack, then Gwen was again in danger. To save her, the Torchwooders had to also save Captain Hart, by now with a flashing clamp on his chest, who muttered some dark thing about Captain Jack's past and evaporated.

---

22 See Appendix D for a more detailed discussion of the Series Two ratings.

Even though John Barrowman is somehow utterly annoying – immortal? please no – his relationships with his team (frustrated love with Gwen, crush on Ianto) mean that those of us who don't really understand what they're chasing or fighting at least get all the soppy bits. Fast, funny and daring, *Torchwood* is also significantly sharper than its prime-time BBC One cousin, *Doctor Who*.

The *Sun*, meanwhile, was more inclined to focus on the steamy kiss between Captain Jack and Captain John, in a report in its 18 January edition:

> *Buffy* villain Spike reveals that his guest-spot on *Torchwood* had his girlfriend hot under the collar.
>
> James Marsters, best known for playing vampire Spike in *Buffy the Vampire Slayer* and its spin-off *Angel*, appeared as a guest in *Torchwood* this week.
>
> And his character Captain John got in a steamy man-on-man kiss with hero Captain Jack, played by John Barrowman.
>
> 'I had never kissed a man on film before, but my girlfriend said it was always a fantasy of hers that I would kiss another man,' he said. 'Luckily, she was there. She thought it was really hot.'

Shortly after the debut transmission of 'Kiss Kiss, Bang Bang', late on the evening of 16 January, the official *Torchwood* website was updated to launch the first 'mission' in a new online game, written by Phil Ford and designed by Carbon Studio, supposedly designed to recruit new Torchwood operatives, for which those visiting the website had been invited to register over the preceding few days. Further missions would follow on a regular basis after each of the next ten episodes, the final one appearing on the evening of 21 March.[23] The Digital Spy website reported on 31 January:

> *Torchwood* fans can take part in a new interactive adventure that ties in with the broadcast of the second series on BBC Two.
>
> The online game, hosted on bbc.co.uk/torchwood, features cast members Gareth David Lloyd, Eve Myles and Naoko Mori. It is written by Phil Ford, who penned four episodes of *The Sarah Jane Adventures* and an upcoming episode of *Torchwood*.
>
> Although the game functions as a separate entity, the specially-shot footage is designed to be consistent with developments in the current series throughout its 13 episode duration.
>
> Ford stated: 'You may find that there are elements of the episode that you've just watched which may crop up in each weekly mission. It's a good idea to watch the episodes very carefully in this season because you never know what in the background may turn up and be relevant to the story online.'

---

23 See Appendix B for more details

On 17 January, Eve Myles made a live appearance on the ITV1 daytime talk show *Loose Women*, but the conversation was fairly inconsequential, the presenters appearing to know little about their guest and still less about *Torchwood*. Of far more interest was a 27-minute-long radio show entitled *Torchwood All Access*, broadcast at 1.33 pm on 19 January on BBC Radio Wales and also accessible online, both live and for seven days afterwards, at www.bbc.co.uk/wales/radiowales. With a format similar to that of the established series of irregular *Doctor Who – Back in Time* documentaries, this had host Julian Carey presenting an overview of *Torchwood*, with audio clips from 'Kiss Kiss, Bang Bang' and interview quotes from Russell T Davies, Eve Myles, production designer Edward Thomas, Rhys actor Kai Owen and Gareth David-Lloyd. Reflecting on the *Torchwood* set-up, Davies commented: 'It's about a bunch of bisexuals living under Cardiff fighting aliens … You don't get that in many shows, really! For what is a very formatted genre show, it's also quite un-definable and quite barmy, and I love that!'

Judging from the success of 'Kiss Kiss, Bang Bang', it would seem that many viewers agreed.

CHAPTER EIGHT: THE SERIES IN PROGRESS

From the second episode, 'Sleeper', a regular pattern was established for transmission of the early episodes of Series Two: the BBC Two debut screening would be at 9.00 pm on a Wednesday evening; there would be a BBC Three repeat later that same evening; and – in England and Wales, at least[24] – the edited, pre-watershed version would be shown on BBC Two at 7.00 pm the next day, immediately followed by the first airing of the associated instalment of *Torchwood Declassified* – which had also been re-commissioned for a second series.[25] This seemed to be a popular schedule with the viewing public: the ratings remained strong and consistent in these slots – showing barely a dip even when up against the strong opposition of a live England -v- Switzerland football match on BBC One at 8.00 pm on 6 February 2008 – with a total audience of around five million per episode. This was an impressive achievement, and one that was not lost on the press. In a piece published at the beginning of February, David James of the *South Wales Echo* wrote:

> It's not just the aliens fleeing in terror.
>
> Cardiff-set sci-fi series *Torchwood* has blasted its way straight to the top of BBC Two's ratings.
>
> Despite some criticism of its fruitier storylines, newly-released official figures show the second series' first episode recorded 1 million more viewers than anything else on BBC Two that week.
>
> In its first week on the terrestrial channel, 4.2 million people watched John Barrowman's team of alien investigators see off a threat from *Buffy* star James Masters' rogue Time Agent.
>
> That figure does not include the 1.1 million people who watched the child-friendly pre-watershed version and the 250,000 who saw the BBC Three repeat.[26]
>
> Insiders at BBC Wales' Llandaff headquarters, where the show is produced, are pleased with the figures and are already turning their minds to consider a third series.
>
> A source said: 'The average for the slot on BBC Two is 2.8 million. *Heroes* averaged 2.3 million. So [*Torchwood*] is doing incredibly well.'
>
> ...
>
> Overnight figures for episodes two and three show the adult-themed sci-fi drama is holding on to its 14 percent audience share, pulling in 3.4 million and 3.2 million viewers before the number of people who record it to watch later are added.

---

24 BBC Two Scotland and BBC Two Northern Ireland would continue to drop the pre-watershed versions from their schedules, and often the *Torchwood Declassified* episodes as well. From 'Meat' onwards, however, the schedule in Scotland would be brought into line with that in England and Wales.

25 See Appendix C for more information on *Torchwood Declassified*.

26 As noted in Chapter Seven, the actual figures were 4.22 million for the initial BBC Two transmission, 1.19 million for the pre-watershed version and 0.35 million for the BBC Three repeat – slightly higher than suggested here.

Given this level of success, it was generally assumed that the same transmission pattern would be maintained for the remainder of the 13 episode run. In the event, however, with the sixth episode, 'Reset', which saw Martha Jones make her first *Torchwood* appearance, there came a significant turn-around: this episode debuted not on BBC Two but on BBC Three, in the late Wednesday evening slot that under the previous schedule would have been occupied by the BBC Three repeat of the fifth episode, 'Adam'. A revised pattern was thus established, with each new episode now debuting on BBC Three in the late Wednesday evening slot, being repeated on BBC Two at 9.00 pm the following Wednesday and then having its pre-watershed BBC Two screening at 7.00 pm the next day.[27]

To many fans, this change – which coincided with, and was probably designed to give a boost to, a general relaunch of BBC Three – was a surprising turn of events, in that it effectively represented a reversion to the Series One norm of episodes debuting on BBC Three before being repeated on BBC Two, arguably making something of a nonsense of the show's much-vaunted elevation to the terrestrial channel for its second run. While for the most part it seemed to have little impact on the ratings – the BBC Three audience for each episode went up, but the BBC Two audience went down by about the same amount, leaving the total the same at around the five million mark – it did have the unfortunate consequence that 'Adam' was omitted altogether from the BBC Three run and thus had only the two BBC Two screenings – one unedited, one edited – with an inevitable dip in the total number of viewers in that particular instance. There was a more positive knock-on impact on *Torchwood Declassified*: its sixth episode was given two airings rather than the usual one, after the unedited and edited BBC Two transmissions of 'Reset' respectively; and a couple of later episodes would also be accorded similar treatment.

This, though, was by no means the end of the scheduling changes affecting Series Two. The unedited BBC Two screening of the eleventh episode, 'Adrift', came not a week after the BBC Three debut but only two days, on 21 March – the Good Friday bank holiday. The twelfth episode, 'Fragments', was then shown on BBC Three later the same evening, meaning that two new episodes had debuted in the space of just one week. The following week saw 'Adrift' receive its edited BBC Two airing on Tuesday 25 March and 'Fragments' its unedited one on Friday 28 March. 'Fragments' then had its edited BBC Two transmission on Thursday 3 April. Concluding the initial run of Series Two, the final episode, 'Exit Wounds', debuted on BBC Two – a last-gasp reversion to what was supposedly *Torchwood*'s then home channel – on Friday 4 March. Its edited BBC Two repeat was due to air on Tuesday 8 April, along with the associated *Torchwood Declassified* mini-documentary, but in the event this fell victim to a last-minute postponement to the following Tuesday in order to make way for a documentary about Diana, Princess of Wales, an inquest into whose death had just concluded. Like 'Adam' before it, 'Exit Wounds' was left out of the BBC Three run altogether.

With all this chopping and changing, even the show's fans found it hard to keep track of when the last few episodes were due to air, let alone more casual viewers. Some speculated that

---

27 BBC Two viewers in Northern Ireland saw 'Reset' a day later than those elsewhere in the UK, as it was postponed to make way for live coverage of an awards show.

the schedulers were trying to avoid *Torchwood* clashing with BBC One's 'ultimate job interview' show *The Apprentice*, and BBC Two's accompanying *The Apprentice: You're Fired*, when they returned for new series on Wednesday 26 March; others wondered if the aim was to ensure that the last episode went out before Series Four of *Doctor Who* began on 5 April. Whatever the reason, though, if the BBC was hoping to establish *Torchwood* as an 'appointment to view' programme, this was surely not the way to go about it, with a succession of hard-to-follow alterations to the date and time of the appointment! In light of this, it was no great surprise when, for 'Adrift', the total audience dropped below four-and-a-half million for the first time during Series Two. Possibly because of this downturn, however, the final two episodes were both heavily trailed on all the main BBC channels – easily the most significant on-air promotion the show had received for some weeks – and the ratings then rallied somewhat. 'Fragments' was also the BBC iPlayer's fourth most-watched programme of the entire first quarter of 2008; and early indications were that 'Exit Wounds' would attract an even greater number of online viewers.

Still better news was in store when the Appreciation Index (AI) figure for the initial BBC Two transmission of 'Exit Wounds' became available a few days later: it was an astonishing 90, higher than *Torchwood* had ever achieved before, and indeed higher than any episode of *Doctor Who* had ever achieved on its terrestrial-channel debut transmission. Capping a run of impressive figures in the mid- to high-80s, this demonstrated beyond a shadow of a doubt that, with its second series even more so than with its first, *Torchwood* had scored a huge hit with the general viewing public.

Hand in hand with this success came a significant increase in the number of licences being granted by BBC Worldwide to companies keen to produce tie-in merchandise (see Appendix A for further details). Of particular note was the launch by Titan Magazines of *Torchwood: The Official Magazine*, the first issue of which was published on Thursday 24 January. In line with many contemporary marketing campaigns, this was publicised not only by way of print adverts, which were run in various other Titan titles, but also online, with a promo placed on the video-sharing website YouTube and a group established on the Facebook social networking website. As a BBC-endorsed publication, *Torchwood: The Official Magazine* was able to present a wealth of exclusive content, including, in its second issue, the first official confirmation of the titles for Series Two's last six episodes.

The early months of 2008 also saw *Torchwood* picking up several more award nominations for various Series One episodes. It was shortlisted in four categories – Best Drama Series (for 'End of Days'), Best Costume (for 'Captain Jack Harkness'), Best Original Soundtrack (for 'End of Days') and Best Actress (Eve Myles, for 'End of Days') – in the annual BAFTA Cymru awards; and 'Captain Jack Harkness' was amongst the five nominees in the Best Dramatic Presentation, Short Form category of the Hugo Awards, presented since 1953 by members of the World Science Fiction Convention. Series One as a whole was also nominated in the Best International Series category of the Saturn Awards, given by the Academy of Science Fiction, Fantasy & Horror Films since 1972. When the BAFTA Cymru ceremony was eventually held on 27 April, at the new venue of the Millennium Centre in Cardiff, the show failed to match its impressive tally of successes the previous year, but did win in one category: that of Best Costume. The Hugo and Saturn Award winners would not be announced until a little later in the year.

While Series Two was actually being transmitted, it received little additional promotion from the BBC. No further press releases were put out, aside from the weekly programme information bulletins issued by the Press Office for all BBC shows, and although the official website continued to be regularly updated, only one further preview clip was made available online – an extract of just over two minutes' duration from 'Exit Wounds', showing Captain Jack chained up in the Hub at the mercy of Captain John, which was uploaded on the BBC's YouTube account on 28 March. *Torchwood* consequently featured only sporadically in media stories during this period. On 7 February, the *Guardian* was the first source to reveal the intriguing news that a one-off made-for-radio *Torchwood* drama was being lined up for transmission on Radio 4 as the centrepiece of a themed run of programmes to mark the inauguration of the world's largest particle accelerator – the Large Hadron Collider – at the CERN laboratory in Switzerland later in 2008. Four days later, the Sci-Fi Wire website reported that *Torchwood* had been honoured with a special Gaylactic Spectrum Award; these awards, first presented in 1999, recognise distinguished works of science fiction, fantasy and horror that explore gay, lesbian, bisexual or transgender themes. Also on 11 February, listings magazine *TV & Satellite Week* published on its website – at www.tvandsatelliteweek.blogspot.com – a set of 11 exclusive, specially-posed shots, taken by their photographer Dan Goldsmith, of Freema Agyeman on the Hub set. 'Reset' guest star Alan Dale meanwhile guested on Channel 4's daytime *Richard & Judy* chat show on 12 February; his *Torchwood* role was discussed, and a clip from the episode was shown.

A far more substantial news story, however, appeared on the SciFi Pulse website on 4 March. Headed 'Major Changes Ahead for *Torchwood* & *Doctor Who*', this read in part:

> On *Torchwood*, things are going to change massively. Leaving the show are Burn Gorman (Owen Harper), Naoko Mori (Toshiko) and John Barrowman (Captain Jack Harkness), though it is likely that Barrowman will return now and then as Captain Jack in a recurring capacity.
>
> Joining the team as a full time member as of Series Three will be Freema Agyeman who will step in as Martha Jones and take over the day to day running of Torchwood from Captain Jack. Remaining with the show will be Eve Myles as Gwen Cooper.
>
> Another big change for *Torchwood* is the format of the show. Up until now the series has been aimed at a more grown up audience, and has been sold as a science fiction series for adults. This has allowed it plenty of latitude with regards to sexual innuendos and humour. Some of the humour may stay, but it will be dumbed down somewhat so as not to alienate the younger audience members.
>
> A third season of *Torchwood* has indeed been commissioned, but thus far only for five episodes as opposed to the usual 13. Which is something that has many in the industry somewhat puzzled, especially considering that the show is performing better than *Doctor Who* in the USA.
>
> The above changes to *Torchwood*'s format are so it can be shown in the Saturday evening slot that is usually occupied by *Doctor Who*. Producers at the BBC are looking to *Torchwood* to act as a buffer between seasons of *Doctor Who*.
>
> So when *Doctor Who* isn't on the air, *Torchwood* will be there to fill that void in

time and space that fans have when waiting an entire six months for the *Doctor Who* Christmas special.

This story at first attracted considerable scepticism, but when at least part of it appeared to be confirmed by the shocking deaths of Owen and Toshiko at the end of 'Exit Wounds', fans were left wondering how much of the rest would also prove to be correct. It was starting to seem that *Torchwood* would never be quite the same again …

CHAPTER NINE: SERIES TWO HITS AMERICA

Keen to capitalise on the huge success it had enjoyed with Series One of *Torchwood* (see Chapter Two), BBC America was the first broadcaster outside the UK to add Series Two to its schedules, with an announced start date of Saturday 26 January 2008 – only ten days after the BBC Two debut transmission. The first BBC America trailer for Series Two began running at the beginning of December 2007, although this consisted almost entirely of clips from Series One. A more *bona fide* trailer, presenting a minute-long montage of clips from the first half of Series Two, debuted on 19 December, during a commercial break in a *Life on Mars* episode, and was then rerun numerous times over the following days, as was a shorter teaser version. The channel also placed some publicity images from the first few Series Two episodes on its *Torchwood* website. HDNet meanwhile built up anticipation for its own, high definition screenings of Series Two, due to begin on 11 February, by rerunning the whole of Series One on New Year's Day.

The American press's love-affair with *Torchwood* continued into 2008. Reviewers were effusive in their praise of the Series One DVD box set, released on 22 January, while preview-writers were full of enthusiasm for the launch of Series Two, a number citing *Torchwood* as an oasis of quality in a television landscape seriously denuded by the then-ongoing strike by American screenwriters. National publications such as *USA Today* and *Newsday* raved about the show, while regional newspapers right across the continent, from the *Los Angeles Times* in the west to Pennsylvania's *Erie News-Times* in the east, recommended 'Kiss Kiss, Bang Bang' to their readers, often in glowing terms. Typically enthusiastic was Joanne Weintraub of the *Milwaukee Journal-Sentinel*, who wrote in the 19 January edition:

> *Torchwood* (8.00 pm Saturday, repeated at 11.00 pm, BBC America) returns for a second season with the long-awaited episode in which the ridiculously dashing Jack Harkness (John Barrowman) locks lips with a former partner turned nemesis played by James Marsters, better known as the legendary Spike of *Buffy the Vampire Slayer*. Marsters' character – a bisexual flirt, dirty fighter and total piece of work – drops tantalising hints to the Torchwood crew about Jack's shady past. All in all, smashing stuff.

Maureen Ryan of the *Chicago Tribune* was equally positive in her 24 January preview piece:

> Even the mildest fan of outer space adventures should enjoy the return of the cheeky British series *Torchwood*.
> ....
> It's a show that is made for grown-ups, yet it wrings a great deal of enjoyment from the traditional building blocks of mainstream sci-fi TV. It has ambition and attitude, but it doesn't sneer at the conventions of the genre.
> ...
> At one point in ['Kiss Kiss, Bang Bang', Captain John] Hart makes a reference to

Star Wars, at which point I nearly experienced brain failure. Spike from *Buffy* on a *Doctor Who* spinoff mentioning *Star Wars*? What a cool gift basket for geeks.

…

But *Torchwood*, for all its sarcasm and energy, is not just a silly romp about aliens. The members of the team can't speak about their strange and dangerous work to anyone, which leads to a great deal of loneliness, and Harkness is full of hidden secrets. Creator Russell T Davies has done a good job of giving many *Torchwood* stories an emotional resonance that extends well beyond chasing the monster of the week.

In a dreary winter TV landscape in which smart, witty escapism is in short supply, *Torchwood* stands out.

A number of US journals ran interviews with members of the regular cast. The *Pittsburgh Post-Gazette* spoke to Eve Myles, for instance, while the Sci-Fi Channel's Sci-Fi Wire website had some quotes from Burn Gorman. Online, the *iF Magazine* website – at www.ifmagazine.com – also presented interviews with Myles and Gorman, and with Gareth David-Lloyd. In a piece published on 31 January, Gorman commented insightfully on the character progression that Owen had undergone up to the start of Series Two:

'If I'm honest with you, the scripts [for Series One] came in maybe two or three weeks before we started shooting the episodes. When I was first introduced to the rest of the *Torchwood* team, we rehearsed for a few days and then we got shooting on episode one and episode two, but in terms of the character, I had absolutely no idea where it was going. Owen was involved in some fairly dysfunctional stuff as a part of the team. He's a bit of an ass, really, let's be honest, and he's arrogant and says the wrong thing at the wrong time. So as an actor I tried to look for things in him that would redeem him as a member of Torchwood; for example, he's really passionate and dedicated to his job as a doctor. He's taken the Hippocratic Oath and he takes it very seriously. I also think that as a member of the team, he is able to go into morally grey areas that others can't. Captain Jack is the hero figure and he can't get into certain situations. I had difficulty with some of the stuff Owen did, but at least he's a very human character. Like all of us, he messes up big time, but at the end of [Series One] he is genuinely apologetic and really sorry and wants to start over again. Jack sort of says that he's okay and can remain a part of the team, and that's the best thing that could happen to him. I hope that in Series Two he's a changed man.'

Several other US newspapers, including the *San Francisco Chronicle* and the *Arizona Republic*, published longer articles on the show, most of them reproducing a syndicated Associated Press story that read in part:

Attention, fans of quick-witted, Brit-flavoured science fiction television: Captain Jack is back.

'He's still the same Jack but he's a little more lighthearted,' says John Barrowman, who plays cheeky charmer Captain Jack Harkness on *Torchwood*, BBC America's flirty, fast-paced series.

'He's resolved a lot of his issues,' Barrowman says of his time-travelling, alien-hunting hero who wears World War Two-era togs and cannot die. 'He's got a new sparkle in his eye.'

...

As always, Torchwood operates outside the law and the British government. It stands tall against all manner of monsters, including a recurring cast of nasty, sewer-dwelling Weevils.

But Jack and crew still find time for office romance and ill-fated, inter-species love affairs – of the same- and opposite-sex sorts.

'Omnisexual is the science-fiction word we like to use,' says Barrowman, who sounds very American, both on- and off-camera. Born in Scotland, he grew up in Illinois.

'In the sci-fi setting we can talk about things that you probably couldn't talk about on a regular night-time drama,' the 40-year-old Barrowman says.

'I think audiences just get Jack because he's honest,' he says. 'To finally see a character who doesn't care who he flirts with, I think is a bit refreshing.'

...

All of Jack's cohorts are just as hormonal as he is.

'Yes, it is a science-fiction soap opera,' says [Eve] Myles, who is Welsh.

Last season Gwen hopped into Owen's bed despite her devotion to her clueless live-in lover, Rhys.

'It was completely out of character for Gwen,' Myles says. 'But that's what good drama is all about. You don't want to spoon-feed a sci-fi audience. You want to challenge them. So none of these characters [is] safe.'

In the future, Gwen 'does the best she can' with monogamy, Myles says. 'But it's a case of anything is possible with the Torchwood bunch.'

There was yet more press comment on 'Kiss Kiss, Bang Bang' in the days after it made its BBC America debut, as a number of newspapers printed reviews. The *Chicago Sun-Times*, the *Orlando Sentinel* and the New Jersey *Sun-Ledger* were amongst those heaping praise on the series-opener.

As with Series One, each episode of Series Two had small edits made to it by BBC America to bring it down to the length needed to fit an hour-long slot with commercial breaks and to remove instances of coarse language. One of the most heavily cut was 'Sleeper', although curiously the shouted insult 'Oi, fuckflap!' was left in, presumably because it had been misheard or overlooked by those responsible for carrying out the edits. Shown in the commercial breaks during the episodes were a series of short *Inside Look* inserts featuring specially-recorded interviews with the show's regular cast members; all these inserts were also made available to view on the channel's *Torchwood* website – at www.bbcamerica.com/content/262/index.jsp – which was given a general makeover for Series Two.

The positive press coverage continued as the series progressed. One of the few dissenters was *Entertainment Weekly*'s Ken Tucker, who wrote in a 29 February review on the magazine's website:

> *Torchwood* can be jolly, if winceable, fun, but it's also tonally weird. The cheesy special effects (the alien-meat creature's mouth clapped shut like a ventriloquist's dummy) and cheesier heroic proclamations ('The 21st century is when everything changes, and Torchwood is ready!') make the series seem aimed at kids. Yet there's also lots of bloodletting and rather explicit sex, along with florid, romance-novel subplots, such as team scientist Toshiko falling madly in love with a cryogenically frozen World War I soldier. The series' attempts to cross *X-Files* monster suspense with *Buffy*-style wisecracking just come off as endearingly goony: Jack interrogates an alien by bellowing, 'Why do you give off electromagnetic waves? Why?!' And apparently in the UK, it is inherently amusing to locate Torchwood HQ and the time-space rift that sets loose so many alien subplots in the bleak-looking town of Cardiff, Wales; I gather this is comparable to, say, locating *Lost* in a Paramus, NJ, park. As with P G Wodehouse novels and Robbie Williams songs, you have to be either British or adolescent to commit to this stuff; for the rest of us, it's a head-scratching lark.

Far more representative were the views of Ian Grey of the CityPaper Online website, who on 26 March wrote admiringly of the parallels between *Torchwood* and *Buffy the Vampire Slayer*:

> [James] Marsters' appearance is both a reminder of just how much *Torchwood* already owes *Buffy* – for obvious instance, the alien-spewing rift is a sci-fi take on *Buffy*'s demon-spewing Hellmouth – and a preview of just how smartly it would appropriate from Whedon's world, which, in a weird/wonderful bit of intertextual alchemy, has allowed Davies' show to become more indelibly, well, *Torchwood*-like. Like Buffy herself, Gwen struggles to keep her life as a normal person and world saver separate. Toshiko has expanded from a dangerously archetypical 'Asian' – all cool competence and raised Spock brows – into *Torchwood*'s Willow surrogate, the show's super-cute, smart, intrinsically open-souled centre.
>
> But geeky citations aside, what *Torchwood* most effectively assimilates from Whedon are supernatural nasties who function as metaphors for the characters' inner demons, along with a sweetly humanistic wallow in the gang's existential big pains. In that way that renders the science fictional literary, Jack's horrifically traumatic youth is revealed; his response to it explains why he *needs* to help people. A parallel-universe episode offers the anxious, socially inept Owen hiding under his semi-douchebag skin. And Toshiko finally meets a man she can love – a WWI soldier suffering from [post-traumatic stress disorder] – but her painful duty to the greater good trumps romances, and so much for that.
>
> And so fused in a cauldron of its characters' essential loneliness, the *Torchwood* crew, as in most great TV, coheres into a alternative viable family. Beyond that, the

current season shows that beneath its bisexual snogs and smart quips, *Torchwood* is about difference, empathy, and striving to do the right thing in an indifferent world while knowing you'll inevitably be getting it wrong half the time and learning to forgive yourself for doing so. And so *Torchwood* now isn't just delightful; it's kind of essential, inspirational even.

With positive media coverage such as this, and a reported audience of up to 750,000 watching each episode on debut transmission, BBC America were understandably delighted with *Torchwood*'s continued strong performance for them. 'It's been our highest-rated show ever,' confirmed network President Grant Ancier in comments reported on the website of industry journal *Variety* on 8 February 2008. 'And because it's not playing on another network first, we get the brand credit for it, which is very important to BBC America in terms of how to be viable to consumers, advertisers and cable operators.'

At the end of April, all episodes of Series One and Two of *Torchwood* were included in an initial list of programmes made available by BBC America for download via the US iTunes service, for a very reasonable price of $25.87 per series.[28] As in the UK, this proved extremely popular. On 1 May, the Macworld website reported:

BBC America began selling TV series in the US this week, launching with the following titles: *Torchwood*, *Little Britain* and *Robin Hood*. It appears the content has struck a nerve in the US, with the BBC now seizing three of the top ten TV seasons places on the iTunes Store in the US. *Torchwood* is at numbers four (Series Two) and five (Series One) on the top ten list while *Little Britain* takes third place in Apple's own top ten, which is itself generated on the basis of sales. Interestingly, none of the BBC's TV shows have ranked among the top ten series in terms of individual episodes, suggesting that the US audience, at least, is purchasing entire series of the BBC shows – clearly a very strong start.

It seemed that *Torchwood* was assured a receptive US market for as long as the BBC continued to produce it.

---

28 Curiously, in both the UK and the US, the episode 'To the Last Man' was erroneously listed as 'Last Man Standing' on the iPlayer service.

CHAPTER TEN: THE SECOND SERIES ENDS …
AND A THIRD IS CONFIRMED

As Series Two reached its highly dramatic conclusion with no announcement forthcoming from the BBC regarding a follow-up, *Torchwood* fans were feeling increasing anxiety about the show's future. Would there be a Series Three? And if so, what form would it take? One source of this anxiety was the concerns that John Barrowman had expressed regarding the hectic production schedule on Series Two (see Chapter Five), which some feared might dissuade him from continuing as Captain Jack. Interviewed for the Off the Telly website at the Series Two press launch back on 3 December 2007, Barrowman was asked point blank if he intended to stick with the role. 'Erm … I don't know,' was his guarded reply. 'I don't know if I'll get tired, but it depends how things work around me … I haven't made any decisions yes or no. We don't know if a third series will happen or not … If we do get the go-ahead, I really have to sit down and think about it … It's not the commitment, because I love Cardiff. I bought a house there, for goodness sake! But, honestly, this last series was a bit of a nightmare at times … Because of bad scheduling. Because of production things going wrong, and people not being organised. It was hard on all of us – us as a team. Me and other artistes. The production crew and everyone had to give free time back. Can you imagine going into a grocery store, paying for half of your groceries and … asking for the rest free? Only in this business would that happen. That's what I mean – we love the show so much, the crew love it, we're all passionate about it. We're willing to do that … You'll accommodate so much, then you have to get it sorted out. It was really tough towards the last few months. You know, we just dug our heels in and got it done. But things like that would have to be worked out. And that's being totally honest and professional.'

These comments were hardly reassuring for the fans. Ending on a more encouraging note, however, Barrowman added, 'I'd play Jack for the next 10 years if you asked me to.' This more positive slant from the actor was reflected in an interview published on 25 January 2008 on the Sci-Fi Wire website: 'If I was asked to do Jack for the next five or six years, I would do it with a big smile on my face, because I absolutely love playing him. When the time comes for us to close the page on *Torchwood* and Jack Harkness, I'm also then happy to do that when that decision is made. But I think it's got a bit of a life out there. Let's hope we get [Series] Three, Four and, hopefully, Five.'

At the forefront of many fans' minds, though, was the SciFi Pulse website's 4 March story indicating that, although there would indeed be a Series Three, there were big changes in store for the show. (See Chapter Eight.) The gist of this appeared to be backed up on 4 April – the day of the debut transmission of 'Exit Wounds' – when the *Daily Star* also reported that Series Three would consist of only five episodes, to be broadcast over the space of a single week, and that this was due in part to Barrowman's limited availability. It was unclear, however, whether this story was independently sourced, or whether it was simply based on aspects of the SciFi Pulse one.

Appearing in concert in Gateshead on Friday 11 April, Barrowman told members of the audience that he would be unable to take any more starring roles in London's West End for the foreseeable future as he would be otherwise occupied making Series Three of *Torchwood*, and possibly Series Four as well. This appeared to bode well for the show's future, but a further sign of major changes ahead was that both co-producer Chris Chibnall and producer Richard Stokes had decided to leave the BBC and take up new posts on the in-development ITV1 police series *Law and Order: London*. Chibnall's departure from *Torchwood* was announced in January, while Stokes's was first revealed in Issue 4 of *Torchwood: The Official Magazine*, published on Thursday 17 April.

On a more positive note, Issue 4 of *Torchwood: The Official Magazine* also revealed a little more about the forthcoming Radio 4 *Torchwood* episode, which had been recorded over two days back in March. This 45-minute, self-contained story would be set some time after 'Exit Wounds' and would involve Jack, Gwen and Ianto, still coming to terms with the loss of Owen and Toshiko, being summoned to CERN by Martha Jones – a further *Torchwood* guest appearance by Freema Agyeman – to investigate a series of strange disappearances at the facility. Transmission was expected to be sometime in June or July, but the exact date had still to be confirmed.

On Saturday 26 April, the first ever *Torchwood* convention, organised by James Marsters Live and dubbed The Rift, was held at the Porchester Hall in the Bayswater area of London, where an audience of over 300 attendees was entertained by an impressive line-up of guests: actors James Marsters, Eve Myles, Gareth David-Lloyd and Kai Owen and, on a panel moderated by author and radio presenter Keith Topping, producer Richard Stokes and writers James Moran, Joseph Lidster and Phil Ford.

Rumours about the show's future continued to circulate amongst fans. According to some, the supposed five-episode Series Three would be transmitted on BBC One – a first for *Torchwood* – and would see Martha Jones and another former TARDIS traveller, Mickey Smith (Noel Clarke), joining Captain Jack in Cardiff as permanent replacements for Owen and Toshiko. This would follow directly on from the conclusion of Series Four of *Doctor Who*, which – or so some thought – would see a whole host of familiar faces coming to the Doctor's aid, including not only Jack but also, making their *Doctor Who* debuts, Gwen and Ianto.

Fanning the flames of speculation, Russell T Davies commented in an interview for the May 2008 edition of the gay lifestyle magazine *Attitude*: '[*Torchwood*] is coming back. Hmm … What am I allowed to say? You will have seen the horrific events at the end of Series Two by the time this comes out. It's terrible, tragic and changes everything, and we got it right. Having said that, there is a big change ahead, a big, big format change. Same show, but completely revamped. I just can't say yet. [The show is] ridiculously huge in America, but not bigger than *Doctor Who* as people keep saying. [BBC America] are livid with us for making the changes. We'll do what we want!'

Appearing on the 6 May edition of BBC Two's celebrity cookery game show *Ready Steady Cook*, John Barrowman again seemed to confirm that *Torchwood* would be returning for a third run, but likewise said that it would be 'very different'.

In his 'Production Notes' column in Issue 396 of *Doctor Who Magazine*, published on 29 May, Davies stated that as of 1 May a new producer had been appointed – although no name was revealed – and that scripts were coming in.

The official word that everyone had been waiting for finally came on 3 June in the form of a statement given by Julie Gardner to the website of the US listings magazine *TV Guide*, which reported:

> Tired of all the rumours surrounding *Torchwood*'s future, TVGuide.com went directly to the rift, er, Cardiff, Wales, to learn if the truth was out there.
>
> Well, 'Woodies (or Torchies, if you prefer), scripts for Series Three are currently being developed and filming should start in the middle of August for airing on BBC One in the spring of 2009. Best news of all, John Barrowman will return as the dashing bi-sexual adventurer. Though keeping more details close to the vest, executive producer Julie Gardner vows that fans 'will be pleased with the casting'. That better mean Eve Myles is returning!
>
> Fans, however, may not be so happy with the mere five hours slated for next season. 'We've decided to do a five-part mini-series, one big story that will run during one week,' says Gardner, adding, 'I wanted to make a really big noise about the show.'
>
> So far, the BBC has only green lit these five hours, but there could be more, we're told. When (or even whether) BBC America will run the mini-series has yet to be decided.

This report was subsequently picked up and summarised by the ITV Teletext service, bringing it to the attention of many UK viewers for the first time. Then, on 11 June, *Torchwood: The Official Magazine* quoted on its Facebook page a confirmatory message it had received from Gardner, which read: 'As you know, plans for a third series have been underway for a long time, and we now have a new producer and a new director in place, as well as brand new scripts all ready to go. It's the longest and most ambitious story we have ever made, so be prepared for some shocks and surprises! Life at Torchwood is never quiet or easy, and the whole of Captain Jack's world is about to be turned upside down!' It was also suggested that Davies would himself be writing at least some of the five scripts.

The revelation of the identities of the new producer – Peter Bennett – and director – Euros Lyn – came just a few days later, on 16 June, in a news item on the official *Torchwood* website. Gardner was quoted this time as saying: '[Russell and I] are thrilled to be bringing *Torchwood* back for a third series. The new series promises to be a gripping and surprising TV event and we're certain the audience will love the team's exciting, roller-coaster adventures.' Bennett had previously had a number of assignments as a first assistant director on both *Doctor Who* and *Torchwood*, amongst many other first, second and third assistant director credits dating right back to the mid-1970s, while Lyn had also had previous *Doctor Who* experience, as the director of nine episodes spanning from 'The End of the World' in Series One to 'Forest of the Dead' in Series Four and including the Christmas special 'The Runaway Bride', although he had not previously worked on the spin-off.

Although pleased to know that there would indeed be a Series Three, *Torchwood* fans were generally disappointed by the confirmation of the drop to five hour-long episodes – adding up to only just over half the running time of Series One or Series Two – and mystified by the stated intention to screen these over the space of a single week. While many speculated that, as suggested in some of the earlier press reports, the reduced episode count was due to limited availability on Barrowman's part, the main reason was actually a logistical one: with only four *Doctor Who* specials scheduled to be made in the 2008-2009 financial year instead of the usual full series, it was no longer possible to justify having two full production crews operating simultaneously at BBC Wales's Upper Boat studios as had been the case over the previous two years.[29] Instead, there would be just one crew, which would make the first of the *Doctor Who* specials in April, Series Two of *The Sarah Jane Adventures* between April and August, the truncated Series Three of *Torchwood* between August and December, and the remaining three *Doctor Who* specials between January and March (all dates approximate). The good news, however, was that with a full fifth series of *Doctor Who*, plus another special, due to be made in the 2009-2010 financial year, a second production crew would then be reinstated at Upper Boat, which would also pave the way for a full fourth series of *Torchwood*, probably consisting of ten hour-long episodes, to be made for transmission in 2010, along with a third series of *The Sarah Jane Adventures*. As for the decision to transmit the five-episode Series Three over a single week, in a planned 9.00 pm time slot, the rationale for this was partly to test the waters for a permanent promotion of *Torchwood* to BBC One, and partly, as Gardner had told the *TV Guide* website, to create a memorable piece of 'event television'. For the BBC One schedules to be cleared for an hour each evening from Monday to Friday of a single week to make way for a special run of one particular drama would be a very rare occurrence[30], and a sure sign of the BBC's faith in *Torchwood*. Although it would mean that the series was over and done with within the space of just five days, it should be something that, with suitably high-profile promotion, would really stick in the viewing public's minds; and of course there would be many other opportunities to see the five episodes through repeats, the iPlayer service and the inevitable DVD release. So while it seemed that 2009 would be in some senses a 'gap year' for *Torchwood* – as for *Doctor Who* – the show's long-term future still looked bright.

---

29 The decision not to make a full series of *Doctor Who* in this financial year was due mainly to the BBC's wish to leave a transition period for Russell T Davies to hand over his showrunner duties to Steven Moffat – a change that would ultimately impact on *Torchwood* as well. It also however had the welcome consequence for the BBC of easing their financial position, as budgets were tighter than had been hoped for following the latest round of licence fee negotiations with the government.

30 This transmission pattern was actually tried out for the first time with the five-part thriller serial *Criminal Justice*, transmitted from Monday 30 June to Friday 4 July 2008 in that same time slot.

PART FOUR: THE FICTION

CHAPTER ELEVEN: TORCHWOOD TIMELINE

In most cases, the events depicted in *Torchwood* are not explicitly dated on screen.[31] It is however possible to deduce when they take place, based on evidence from the transmitted episodes and from other BBC-sanctioned sources such as the show's official website and the tie-in novels and audio CDs. The dating of contemporaneous events in *Doctor Who* and *The Sarah Jane Adventures* is also relevant, given that these are set in the same fictional universe and there are character crossovers between all three shows.

Presented below is a timeline of significant events, in chronological order, in which the entries derived directly from *Torchwood* are indicated in bold and those derived from *Doctor Who* or *The Sarah Jane Adventures* are in plain text. This is followed by a section of notes giving full explanations and justifications for the dating of events – certain aspects of which have been the subject of much debate and even controversy amongst fans – and expanding on various aspects of Torchwood history.[32]

The title given for each entry in the timeline is that of the episode, book or audio story in which the events described are seen to occur or, if they are not seen but recounted, that in which they are recounted. The letter in brackets indicates the corresponding entry in the Notes. Dates that are approximate or subject to a degree of uncertainty are preceded by the symbol '~'.

To avoid overcomplicating matters, events in Captain Jack's life prior to the point when he became immortal at the end of the *Doctor Who* episode 'The Parting of the Ways' are not listed here[33]; for the same reason, his long 'round trip' to 27 AD and back in 'Exit Wounds' is omitted (although it is referred to in the notes where relevant). (See Chapter Twelve for a full biography of Captain Jack.)

DATE	EVENT	EPISODE	
1869	Jack returns to Earth from the Game Station in 200,100.	'Utopia'	(a)
December 1869	The time rift in Cardiff is briefly opened.	'The Unquiet Dead'	(a)
1879	Queen Victoria decides to establish Torchwood.	'Tooth and Claw'	(a)

31 In some cases, indeed, dates have been deliberately obscured on screen in order to avoid adding to potential continuity problems. An example of this is the date on the flyer advertising Nikki's missing persons meeting in 'Adrift'.

32 More detailed discussion regarding the dating of events in Series One of *Torchwood* and in Series Three of *Doctor Who* can be found in, respectively, *Inside the Hub: The Unofficial and Unauthorised Guide to Torchwood Series One* and *Third Dimension: The Unofficial and Unauthorised Guide to Doctor Who 2007* (both Telos Publishing, 2007). However, it should be noted that, since the latter book was published, I have revised my opinion regarding the timescale of Harold Saxon's rise to power.

33 It is assumed that the 'Small Worlds' flashback scenes of Jack in Lahore in 1909 fall into this category.

1899	Jack is recruited to work for Torchwood Three on an 'uncontracted', i.e. freelance, basis by its leader, Emily Holroyd, and another operative, Alice Guppy. There is a submarine docked in the Hub.	'Fragments'	(b)
1901	Alice Guppy is still working for Torchwood Three, as is a man named Charles Gaskell. Jack is still carrying out Torchwood missions.	'Exit Wounds'	(c)
1918	Torchwood Three is now led by a man named Gerald, and his operatives include Harriet Derbyshire, Douglas Caldwell, Lydia Childs and Dr Charles Quinn, as pictured in a group photograph. Possibly because of his freelance status, Jack is not in the photograph and does not know all the circumstances surrounding the freezing of soldier Tommy Brockless.	'To the Last Man'	(d)
~1925	Jack is performing in a travelling show as part of a mission – possibly for Torchwood, possibly not – to uncover the mysterious Night Travellers.	'From Out of the Rain'	(e)
January 1941	An out-of-time Jack and Toshiko briefly visit the era of the Blitz and meet the man whose identity Jack adopted as his own.	'Captain Jack Harkness'	(a)
August 1941	Torchwood Three is led by a woman named Dr Matilda B Brennan – Tilda for short. She dislikes Jack, who is still freelancing for the organisation. Her agents include Gregory Phillip Bishop, a young male receptionist named Rhydian and a young, red-haired female driver named Llinos King. Brennan and Bishop are both killed at this time by alien light energies.	The Twilight Streets	(a)

~November 1943	Jack meets Estelle Cole in London and falls in love.	'Small Worlds'	(f)
1953	Torchwood agents at this time include two men named Cromwell and Valentine. Jack is known to Cromwell.	*Trace Memory*	(g)
1983	The security firm H C Clements is acquired by Torchwood.	'The Runaway Bride'	(a)
1997	Torchwood shoot down a Jathaa Sun Glider over the Shetlands. It is subsequently taken to Torchwood Tower in London.	'Army of Ghosts'	(a)
December 1999	Jack takes charge of Torchwood Three after the previous leader, Alex Hopkins, murders four other team members and commits suicide on New Year's Eve.	'Fragments'	(h)
~Autumn 2004	Toshiko joins Torchwood Three.	'Fragments'	(i)
March 2005	An attempted invasion by the Nestenes is foiled by the Doctor.	'Rose'	(j)
Spring 2005	Owen's fiancé Katie Russell is killed when a surgeon tries to remove a 'brain tumour' that turns out to be an alien parasite.	'Fragments'	(k)
7 February 2006	Ianto starts work at Torchwood One, having formally joined the organisation the previous year.	*Trace Memory*	(l)
February 2006	Owen joins Torchwood Three.	'Fragments'	(m)
March 2006	Slitheen infiltrate Downing Street. Toshiko poses as a medic to cover for a hung-over Owen when Torchwood are called in to examine a space pig – in reality a decoy created by the Slitheen.	'Aliens of London'/ 'World War Three'	(n)
September 2006	The time rift in Cardiff is temporarily opened.	'Boom Town'	(o)
December 2006	There is a Christmas invasion by the Sycorax. Torchwood One use weapons scavenged from the Jathaa Sun Glider to shoot down the Sycorax ship on the orders of Prime Minister Harriet Jones.	'The Christmas Invasion'	(p)

~February 2007	Just after Harriet Jones's downfall, Harold Saxon makes his first public appearance and joins the Government as Minister of Communications, launching the Archangel satellite network.	'The Sound of Drums'	(q)
~February 2007	The Krillitanes take over Deffry Vale School.	'School Reunion'	(r)
~August 2007	A General Election is forthcoming, and the UK is in political turmoil.	'Love & Monsters'	(s)
~August 2007	Torchwood One is destroyed in the Battle of Canary Wharf.	'Doomsday'	(t)
~ August 2007	**Ianto joins Torchwood Three.**	**'Fragments'**	**(u)**
September 2007	**Gwen joins Torchwood Three.**	**'Everything Changes'**	**(v)**
September–December 2007	**The Torchwood Three team undertake numerous missions.**	**'Day One', 'Ghost Machine', *Border Princes, Another Life, Slow Decay,* 'Cyberwoman', 'Small Worlds', 'Countrycide', 'Greeks Bearing Gifts', *Hidden.***	**(w)**
December 2007	**Suzie is resurrected and dies again.**	**'They Keep Killing Suzie'**	**(x)**
December 2007	**Eugene Jones dies.**	**'Random Shoes'**	**(y)**
December 2007	**The *Sky Gypsy* arrives in Cardiff via the time rift.**	**'Out of Time'**	**(z)**
December 2007	Harold Saxon, now Minister of Defence, orders the shooting down of the Racnoss spaceship.	'The Runaway Bride', 'The Sound of Drums'	(aa)
December 2007	**Jack and his team break up a Weevil fight club.**	**'Combat'**	**(bb)**
~January 2008	**Jack and Toshiko slip back in time to January 1941.**	**'Captain Jack Harkness'**	**(cc)**
~January 2008	**The rift is again temporarily opened and Abaddon emerges, but Jack defeats the creature. Jack then vanishes from the Hub.**	**'End of Days'**	**(dd)**
~August 2008	An invasion attempt by the Bane is foiled.	'Invasion of the Bane'	(ee)

~September 2008-January 2009	The events of Series One of *The Sarah Jane Adventures* occur.	'Revenge of the Slitheen', 'Warriors of Kudlak', 'Eye of the Gorgon', 'Whatever Happened to Sarah Jane?', 'The Lost Boy'	(ff)
~September 2008	The Royal Hope Hospital is temporarily transported to the Moon.	'Smith and Jones'	(gg)
~September 2008	A General Election is held and Harold Saxon wins. He sends the Torchwood Three team (minus Jack) on a wild goose chase to the Himalayas.	'The Sound of Drums'	(hh)
~September 2008	US President Winters is assassinated by the Toclafane.	'The Sound of Drums'	(ii)
~September 2008	Jack returns to Roald Dahl Plass.	'Last of the Time Lords'	(jj)
~September 2008	**Jack rejoins his Torchwood Three team.**	**'Kiss Kiss, Bang Bang'**	**(kk)**
~September 2008	**An alien sleeper cell is activated.**	**'Sleeper'**	**(ll)**
~September 2008	**Tommy Brockless is revived for his annual check-up.**	**'To the Last Man'**	**(mm)**
~September 2008-March 2009	**The Torchwood Three team undertake numerous missions.**	*Something in the Water, Trace Memory, The Twilight Streets*, 'Meat', 'Adam', *Everyone Says Hello*, 'Reset', 'Dead Man Walking', 'A Day in the Death', 'Something Borrowed', 'From Out of the Rain'	(nn)
~September 2008	**Jonah Bevan disappears into the rift.**	'Adrift'	(oo)
December 2008	A replica of the Titanic flies over Buckingham Palace.	'Voyage of the Damned'	(pp)
~March 2009	**Gwen Cooper searches for Jonah Bevan.**	'Adrift'	(qq)
~ April 2009	**The Torchwood team, minus Gwen, are caught in an explosion.**	'Fragments'	(rr)
~ April 2009	**Cardiff is devastated by 15 bombs. Owen and Toshiko die foiling a plot by Jack's long-lost brother Gray.**	'Exit Wounds'	(ss)

NOTES

(a) Date specified in episode or novel.

(b) Some of the officially-licensed *Torchwood* trading cards give the date of Jack's introduction to Torchwood as 1899, and there is plentiful evidence from other sources to support this. Jack begins working for Torchwood some time after its formation in 1879, but before 1900, as the young girl who reads his Tarot cards in his 'Fragments' flashback tells him that the century will turn twice before he is reunited with the one he is looking for, i.e. the Doctor, which happens at the conclusion of 'End of Days' in the 21st Century. In the 1999 segment of 'Fragments', the then team leader Alex Hopkins comments that Jack has had 'a century's service as field operative'. It is also confirmed in Jack's 'Exit Wounds' flashback that he is already working for Torchwood by 1901. A diary entry placed on the official *Torchwood* website and apparently written by Alice Guppy gives the date when she signed her contract to join Torchwood Three as Tuesday 13 September 1898. She had formerly been a thief, and was in prison when recruited by Torchwood. Mrs Emily Holroyd's previous partner in Torchwood (and it is implied there was only one) is said to have 'succumbed to a "Mutative Infection" and metamorphosed into the new Queen of a snake-like race', as a consequence of which Emily was 'obliged to burn him to death'.

(c) Date specified on screen. It must be late in the year, probably November or December, as the time-displaced Jack says that he needs to be frozen for '107 years', and the main events of 'Exit Wounds' occur around April 2009; if it was any earlier in 1901, he would presumably round up rather than down and say '108 years' instead. An entry on the official *Torchwood* website indicates that Emily Holroyd was still in charge of Torchwood Three in 1901.

(d) Date specified on screen. The names of the team members, seen in a group photograph glimpsed on screen in 'To the Last Man', are given in an entry on the official *Torchwood* website, along with brief biographies. Gerald's surname is uncertain: it is stated as Carter in the website entry but as Kneale on one of the *Torchwood* trading cards; possibly one or other of these was an alias that he used while on missions. According to the website biography, he joined Torchwood (branch unspecified) at age 24, around 1899, and controversially transferred to Torchwood Cardiff as its leader in the wake of an event referred to as the '1907 schism'. He retired from active service after holding himself personally responsible for the death of Harriet (circumstances unspecified) in 1919 but continued to act as a consultant until his own death in 1942. Harriet Derbyshire was recruited by Torchwood directly from Oxford, where she had been educating herself in Physics. She was based at Cardiff to study the time dilations caused by rift activity. Her death on active service in 1919 came at the young age of 24. She was granted a posthumous degree by Oxford in 1920 after the university changed its rules to allow women to graduate. Douglas Caldwell – who is curiously also referred to in his biography as 'Hill', suggesting another possible alias – was a draughtsman in the Royal Engineers. He originally met Carter in 1908 and was recruited by Torchwood when the First World War broke out. Initially stationed in Cardiff, he transferred to London in 1930 and was well known for his work on cloaking shields. He died in 1957. Lydia Childs was the team's secretary, recruited from Torchwood London partly due to her local knowledge, having been raised in Cardiff, and partly due to her outstanding organisational skills and excellent memory. She died in 1941. Dr Charles Quinn was put into quarantine by Torchwood after falling victim to an alien parasite at the age of 13. His life was saved through the work of a Torchwood surgeon, Dr Jan Van Nellen, but he was then kept under observation for some years and educated by Institute staff. On gaining his doctorate he was recruited to the organisation and made some significant studies of alien anatomy before taking on a teaching role. He was killed in a Second World War air raid. In 'To the Last Man', Ianto implies that the members of this team all died young, but these website biographies would seem to contradict that, except in Harriet's case – although he gives her age at death as 26 rather than 24. Could the '1907 schism' referred to in Gerald's biography account for the fact that Jack does not have full knowledge of Torchwood Cardiff operations in 1918, and that Gerald leaves sealed orders regarding Tommy Brockless's ultimate fate …? Another possibility is that Jack is away from the Hub on a long-term mission. Or perhaps, given his freelance status, he is away fighting in the Great War; in conversation with Gwen, he alludes to the Battle of Passchendaele (1917) and the Battle of the Somme (1916) and says 'I was there' (although this could be a reference to a point in his life when he was in the Time Agency or when he was earning his living as a conman, before he met the Doctor).

(e) No date is given on screen, but the 1920s is clearly the correct era for black and white film to have been shot of the type of travelling show that Jack joined as 'The Man Who Couldn't Die'; he says that it was '80 odd years' ago. A ticket, placed on the official *Torchwood* website, for the – presumably contemporary – Joshua Joy Travelling Show, in which the Night Travellers performed, is dated 5 March 1925. Jack reveals that he was sent to investigate rumours of the Night Travellers, but when Ianto asks who sent him, he replies 'Long story'. If it was a Torchwood mission, it seems strange that he would not simply say so – and strange that Ianto would not already know about it – which raises the possibility that it was actually a mission for some other organisation or person. This reinforces the suggestion in 'To the Last Man' that Jack may have ceased working for Torchwood for a period during the early part of the 20th Century. Against this, however, is Alex Hopkins' comment in the 1999 segment of 'Fragments' (see note (b)).

(f) It is stated in dialogue that Jack met Estelle at the Astoria Ballroom in London 'a few weeks before Christmas'. Although no year is specified on screen, letters placed on the official *Torchwood* website during Series One indicated that the two subsequently parted company in February 1944. This suggests that they met just before Christmas 1943.

(g) Details of Charles Arthur Cromwell's career are given in the novel *Trace Memory*. Born in 1915, he served in the Royal Navy between 1938 and 1941, in MI6 between 1941 and 1945 and in Torchwood – presumably Torchwood Three throughout – between 1945 and 1975. He came out of retirement on 14 February 2006 to advise Torchwood One on the case of Michael Bellini, with which he had been involved between 1953 and 1967, and was killed at Torchwood Tower on that date by the alien Vondrax. Details of Valentine's career are unknown, but sometime after

1953 he defected to the USSR and worked for their Torchwood equivalent, known as KVI. He was shot and killed by Jack in a Cardiff warehouse in 1967.

(h) Date specified on screen. Alex's surname is given in entries on the official *Torchwood* website. These include a 'stock take' by Owen of the bodies held in cryogenic storage in the Hub, in which it is stated that Alex and his team occupy five bays – implying that he had four team members, who were all killed. The bodies of two men and one woman are seen in 'Fragments', but it is possible that there is another, unseen, victim elsewhere in the Hub.[34] It is indicated in another memo that Hopkins was the first to suggest the acquisition of an SUV with 'Torchwood' printed on the side.

(i) It is stated in 'Greeks Bearing Gifts', set in autumn 2007, that Toshiko has been with Torchwood for three years. She must therefore have joined in autumn 2004 – just missing the annual defrosting of First World War soldier Tommy Brockless, as in 'To the Last Man', set around September 2008, she is present for the fourth time at this event, the previous three having presumably come around September 2005, September 2006 and September 2007.

(j) The missing persons posters seen in 'Aliens of London' give the date of Rose's disappearance at the end of 'Rose' as 6 March 2005.

(k) Owen's flashback in 'Fragments' begins with the caption '4 years earlier'. As 'Fragments' can be dated to around April 2009, this means that the earliest scene in the flashback must occur around April 2005. Owen and his fiancée Katie are making preparations for their wedding and have sent out invitations, and Owen tells a medical colleague 'I promised her a summer wedding'.

(l) The exact date when Ianto started work at Torchwood One can be deduced from information given in the novel *Trace Memory*. In the 'Fragments' flashback detailing Ianto's arrival at Torchwood Three, which must be set around August 2007, he is said by Jack to have joined Torchwood One two years earlier, which would be about six months before the date indicated in *Trace Memory*. This suggests that there was a delay of a few months between Ianto being recruited to the organisation

---

34 Other former Torchwood personnel mentioned as 'notables' in Owen's stock take are Phillip Lyle, Alice Guppy, Harriet Derbyshire, James Lees, Terry Marriott, Sharmila Seth and Suzie Costello. Of these, only Alice, Harriet and Suzie have been seen on screen. It is unclear what eras the others come from, although it is implied that Phillip has been there the longest, as – along with a 'silicate beast' – he is 'the only one left from the old cryogenics system'. It is possible that the names are listed in chronological order. (Alex and his team come between Sharmila and Suzie.) Could Phillip have been Emily Holroyd's original partner, who was burned to death? The omission of Emily's name from Owen's list (although she is mentioned in the stock take in a different context) suggests that she escaped being frozen in the Hub. The total number of bays allocated to former Torchwood personnel is 27, meaning that there are the bodies of up to 15 additional operatives stored there (allowing for the possibility that some of the bays may be empty), their names not being included in Owen's list of 'notables'.

and actually starting work, perhaps to allow for security checks to be carried out.

(m) Toshiko states in 'Exit Wounds' that the space pig incident as seen in 'Aliens of London', which takes place around 6 March 2006, came in Owen's second week as a member of the Torchwood team. This means that his recruitment to the team must have occurred at the end of February 2006, and that the events depicted in his 'Fragments' flashback, which begins around Spring 2005, must span a period of nine months or so. It is possible that he is retconned by Jack immediately after his fiancée's death – in the subsequent scene where he is seen to be hospitalised, presumably in a psychiatric ward, he appears to have forgotten what has happened, asking where Katie is – but then overcomes the effects of the drug (as Gwen did in 'Everything Changes'). When he next meets Jack, it is in the cemetery where Katie is buried, and there are fresh flowers on the grave, implying that the funeral has only recently taken place; it must therefore have been delayed for some time after Katie's death, perhaps due to the need for an autopsy or even an inquest, with the outcome no doubt fixed by Torchwood. (Death during surgery is one of the specific circumstances in which an inquest can be ordered in the UK.)

(n) Stated in dialogue to occur 12 months after 'Rose'. The circumstances that led to Tosh covering for Owen are revealed in 'Exit Wounds'.

(o) The events of this episode are stated in dialogue to take place six months after those of 'Aliens of London'/'World War Three'. The opening of the rift presumably causes some damage to the Hub, requiring subsequent repairs (by workmen who are then retconned, perhaps?). As confirmed in the novel *The Twilight Streets*, Jack puts Torchwood operations on lockdown to make sure that he and his team stay out of the way of his younger self, who arrives in Roald Dahl Plass with the ninth Doctor in the TARDIS, in order to avoid damage to the time-lines.

(p) Takes place the Christmas after 'Boom Town'.

(q) Journalist Vivien Rook indicates a photograph of Harold Saxon and says, 'This is his first honest-to-god appearance, just after the downfall of Harriet Jones. And at the exact same time, they launched the Archangel network.' Since Harriet Jones's downfall did not occur until after Christmas 2006 – when, as Prime Minister, she ordered the destruction of the Sycorax spaceship – Saxon can be assumed to have 'gone public' around February or March 2007. Briefly visible on screen, a magazine article held up by Rook and headed 'Archangel in the Heavens' refers to Saxon as Minister of Communications and reads in part: 'His rise has seen the disintegration of the established political system. Leaders of all three major parties – and even some Scottish Nationalists – defected to his banner of unity, bringing most of their parties with them.' This indicates a major political shake-up in the UK at this time. It is unknown who initially succeeds Harriet Jones as Prime Minister.

(r) Takes place after 'The Christmas Invasion', the events of which are referred to in dialogue. It is school term time and the trees are in bloom.

(s) The main events depicted in 'Love & Monsters' span a period of several months between March and about August 2007: the character Victor Kennedy arrives on 'a Tuesday night in March'; two years are said to have passed since the Auton attack seen in 'Rose'; the Christmas just gone was when the Sycorax attack of 'The Christmas Invasion' occurred; and Jackie Tyler has yet to cross to the parallel universe as depicted in 'Doomsday'. In a scene toward the end of the episode, Kennedy is seen reading an edition of the *Daily Telegraph* with headlines including 'Saxon leads polls with 64 per cent', 'Election Countdown: Four more months of government paralysis' and 'Fourth minister resigns: so who's running the country?'. This suggests that a General Election is forthcoming, and that it is the one in which Harold Saxon will ultimately come to power – the 'polls' referred to are presumably opinion polls. The phrase 'Four more months of government paralysis' could be taken to suggest that the Election is due to take place in about four months' time, suggesting a December 2007 or possibly January 2008 date for it. However, this is too open to interpretation to be conclusive, and other evidence suggests a date about nine months later than that. It seems strange that the Election would be anticipated in the press as long as a year in advance; possibly, however, it is expected to take place right at the end of the current government's term of office, in which case this would make sense. Alternatively, the Election might be postponed for some reason – such as the crisis depicted in 'Army of Ghosts'/'Doomsday' or the general political turmoil precipitated by Harold Saxon.

(t) The Battle of Canary Wharf is mentioned in dialogue in 'Everything Changes', so 'Doomsday' must occur before that. As 'Everything Changes' can be dated to around the end of September 2007, the most likely dating for 'Doomsday' is August 2007. Jack has severed Torchwood Three's ties with Torchwood One – as recalled in 'Fragments' – and, after the destruction of the old regime, remakes it in honour of the Doctor – as stated in 'The Sound of Drums'.

(u) Occurs shortly after the destruction of Torchwood One in 'Doomsday' and before Gwen joins Torchwood Three in 'Everything Changes'.

(v) The death of Suzie in 'Everything Changes' occurs three months before her resurrection in 'They Keep Killing Suzie', as stated in dialogue in the latter episode. 'They Keep Killing Suzie' is set around late December 2007, so 'Everything Changes' must be take place around late September 2007. It is completely dark outside when a clock gives the time as 8.35 pm.

(w) These events must all occur between 'Everything Changes' and 'They Keep Killing Suzie'. The novel *Border Princes* is set in mid-October.

(x) Set shortly before 'Random Shoes'.

(y) Set shortly before 'Out of Time'. Eugene's death is stated in dialogue to come 14 years after he lost the final of the Interschool Maths Competition 1992. If that final took place at the end of December 1992, during the Christmas holidays perhaps, the interval would be just less than 15 years.

(z) Owen states in 'End of Days' that the *Sky Gypsy* disappeared back into the rift – as seen at the end of 'Out of Time' – on 24 December. This confirms other indications in 'Out of Time' that it is set at Christmas time.

(aa) As stated in dialogue in 'The Runaway Bride', these events take place a year after those of 'The Christmas Invasion'. It is then confirmed in dialogue in 'The Sound of Drums' that Harold Saxon at some point became Minister of Defence and first came to prominence in that role (although he was already well known) when he ordered the shooting down of the Racnoss spaceship. It is also stated that he helped to design the UNIT skybase *Valiant*.

(bb) Set after 'Out of Time'. Documents placed on the Series One version of the official *Torchwood* website date the deaths of two of the characters in 'Combat' to 2007, so these events must take place some time between Christmas and New Year's Day.

(cc) The 21st Century scenes of 'Captain Jack Harkness' are set between 'Combat' and 'End of Days'. The General Election is in prospect, as some 'Vote Saxon' posters are seen.

(dd) 'End of Days' follows directly on from 'Captain Jack Harkness'. Jack goes missing some months before Harold Saxon sends the other Torchwood team members off on a wild goose chase to the Himalayas at the time of the General Election, which can be dated to around September 2008. The 13 production-team-supplied Captain's Blog entries for Series One on the BBC America *Torchwood* website span a period from 'Week 34' to 'Week 51'. The entry written in the aftermath of the events of 'Out of Time', set at Christmas 2007, is dated 'Week 48'. Assuming this is the first week of January 2008, this would make 'Week 34' the last week of September 2007 – consistent with the dating suggested above for 'Everything Changes'. 'Week 51' would then be the last week of January 2008. A police missing persons poster placed at one point on the Series One version of the official *Torchwood* website states that Jack was last seen in 'early February'. The weight of evidence would thus seem to suggest that Jack disappears from the Hub at the very end of January or the very beginning of February 2008.

(ee) 'Invasion of the Bane' must occur at least 18 months after 'School Reunion', as Sarah Jane states that K-9 has been in a safe in her attic for 'a year and a half', sealing off a dangerous black hole created in a Swiss laboratory. A digital clock seen at one point in Maria Jackson's bedroom gives the date as 11 January. However, Maria and her father have only just moved into their new house, so the clock cannot have been plugged in for more than a few hours and might not have been set to the correct date. The weather in the exterior scenes would not be consistent with a January dating.

(ff) 'Revenge of the Slitheen' is set shortly after 'Invasion of the Bane' and at the start of a new school year, i.e. in September. In 'The Lost Boy', Luke is said to have been 'lost' for five months, which probably means that this is set five months after 'Invasion of the Bane'.

(gg) Occurs three days before the General Election, as implied by dialogue in 'The Sound of Drums'. This must be after the start of Series One of *The Sarah Jane Adventures*, as in the alternate timeline of the *Doctor Who* episode 'Turn Left', Sarah Jane is said to be present at the Royal Hope Hospital with her son Luke and her friends Maria and Clyde. A notice seen on the back of a hospital door in one shot refers to 'Sizing for new uniforms' taking place during the weeks 'Mon 22 Sep – Fri 26 Sep' and 'Mon 29 Sep – Friday 3 Oct'. The weather and appearance of the trees in the exterior scenes are consistent with a September dating.

(hh) The Doctor suggests that the Master arrived on Earth 18 months earlier. In addition, journalist Vivien Rook says '18 months ago, [Harold Saxon] became real ... just after the downfall of Harriet Jones.' As Harriet Jones's downfall probably occurred around Febraury or March 2007, in the wake of the events of 'The Christmas Invasion', this would be consistent with the General Election occurring around September 2008.

(ii) Occurs just after Harold Saxon becomes Prime Minister. Jack is then chained up on board the *Valiant* for a whole year, but this is subsequently 'wiped out' – except for him and for others who are on board the ship – when time is rolled back to the point just after Winters' assassination, as stated in 'Last of the Time Lords'. It is uncertain what befalls the other members of the Torchwood team during 'the year that never was'.

(jj) It is unclear exactly how much time passes between the Master being defeated and Jack returning to Roald Dahl Plass, but it is unlikely to be more than a day or two, as Martha then goes home to help her family recover from their traumatic experiences and does not resume her travels with the Doctor. Although Jack is seen running toward the entrance to the Hub, it is clear from 'Kiss Kiss, Bang Bang' that he is not immediately reunited with his Torchwood team members at this point – possibly they are still making their way back from the Himalayas, or out on a mission. The Captain's Blog entries on the BBC America *Torchwood* website indicate that in the team's absence he spends a few hours checking mission logs and e-mails in the Hub. In the scene where Martha phones Thomas Milligan at the hospital where he works, a whiteboard on the wall behind Milligan shows what appears to be a chart divided into monthly columns on which figures have been entered up to October. It is possible that this shows targets or working patterns for the month ahead.

(kk) Jack probably seeks out his Torchwood colleagues very soon after the closing scenes of 'Last of the Time Lords'. It is clear that some months have passed since his disappearance at the conclusion of 'End of Days', as the team have adjusted to coping in his absence.

(ll) Set sometime between 'Kiss Kiss, Bang Bang' and 'To the Last Man'.

(mm) Tommy Brockless is revived once a year, and Gwen has not seen him revived before, so the events of 'To the Last Man' must occur less than a year after she joined Torchwood. The date is specified on screen as Friday 20th, but the month is not given.

(As it is well established that dates in the *Doctor Who/Torchwood* universe fall on different days of the week than in ours, the fact that it is a Friday does not afford any assistance.)

(nn) These events must all occur between 'To the Last Man' and the post-titles scenes of 'Adrift'. The novel *Trace Memory* is explicitly set between 'To the Last Man' and 'Meat'. In 'Meat', Rhys says that Gwen has taken 'about a year' to admit that she doesn't really work in 'special ops' for the police, suggesting a late-2008 dating. In 'Adam', the infiltrator Adam deceives the rest of the team into believing that he has been working with them for three years, and later enters the recruitment date '07/05/05-0000' into his fake personnel file on the Hub's computer – which, assuming that this means 7 May 2005, confirms a mid-2008 dating for this episode (although not necessarily as early as May, as the 'three years' would not be precise). 'Reset' is obviously set some months after 'Last of the Time Lords', as Martha has had time to become established in her new job as a UNIT medic and begin a relationship with Tom Milligan (although she is not yet wearing an engagement ring as in Series Four of *Doctor Who*). 'Dead Man Walking' follows directly on from 'Reset', and 'A Day in the Death' takes place three days later.[35] *Everyone Says Hello* is set before Gwen gets married and before Owen is killed, and must therefore come before 'Reset'.

(oo) Jonah is said to be 15 years old when he disappears, and his date of birth is established in the episode to be 15 February 1993. This means that the opening, pre-titles scene of 'Adrift' must take place some time after 15 February 2008. It must also take place some time after Jack's return in 'Kiss Kiss, Bang Bang', because he is later revealed to have visited the scene an hour after the disappearance. Gwen's investigation begins seven months and 11 days later, and this is probably around April 2009. Taken together, these facts place the disappearance around September 2008.

(pp) The Christmas after the one seen in 'The Runaway Bride'.

(qq) The main events of 'Adrift' probably take place not long before those of 'Fragments', around March or April 2009. The weather and the clothing worn by people in the exterior scenes are consistent with this. Although Gwen at one point refers to Jonah as being a 15 year old, and he would have turned 16 on 15 February 2009, not too much can be read into this as it is natural that she would still think of him as being the age he was when he disappeared.

---

35 Recorded on the official *Torchwood* website are a number of dated e-mails, sent and received by members of the Torchwood team and Martha Jones, that appear to relate to events of the early Series Two episodes. However, as the dates given are completely inconsistent with all other evidence, it can only be assumed that these indicate when the e-mails reached the website (by whatever mysterious means the website usually receives details of episodes set in the future!) rather than when they were written. Some support for this may be found in the fact that they are in columns headed 'Date received'. Also, in an exchange of e-mails between Gwen and Owen about the latter's report on the wild goose chase mission to the Himalayas, Gwen's initial e-mail has a *later* 'Date received' (10 January 2008) than Owen's subsequent reply (18 December 2007), which would seem to rule out these being the dates on which they were written.

(rr) Toshiko's flashback in 'Fragments' begins with the caption '5 years earlier'. As the events in the flashback lead up to her recruitment to Torchwood Three in Autumn 2004, after a period of imprisonment by UNIT, this means that 'Fragments' must occur some time before Autumn 2009. Ianto's flashback in the same episode begins with the caption '21 months earlier'. As this details his entry into Torchwood Three, which can be placed fairly precisely around August 2007, this allows the dating of 'Fragments' to be narrowed down still further to around April or May 2009. It is light outside at 6.03 pm but dark by 6.28 pm, which makes April a more likely dating than May.

(ss) Follows directly on from 'Fragments'. The 13 Captain's Blog entries for Series Two on the BBC America *Torchwood* website are dated simply 'Week 1' to 'Week 13', which could be taken to suggest that the events of this series span only 13 weeks. However, this is inconsistent with the evidence presented on screen, and there are suggestions that these entries – unlike those for Series One – have been written not at the time when the events actually occurred, but later on, in retrospect. There would, for instance, have been no opportunity for Jack to have written the entry detailing the events of 'Fragments' before he became caught up in those of 'Exit Wounds'. In the entry referring to the incident seen in 'Adam', Jack writes: 'Have been falling behind with these archive notes. I'm sure I had more stuff written down; guess it's all lost inside the two days we're missing.' If, as suggested in note (dd) above, 'Week 51' is the last week of January in the Torchwood dating system, then – assuming a 52-week yearly cycle is observed – 'Week 1' would be the second week of February. This may indicate that the Captain's Blog entries for Series Two were written by Jack over a 13 week period from the second week of February 2009 to the second week of May 2009, by which point he would have caught up with the backlog. (It admittedly seems odd that any dating system should choose the second week of February as 'Week 1', but perhaps this has some special significance in Torchwood history; possibly, for instance, the Torchwood Institute was inaugurated in the second week of February 1879.)

CHAPTER TWELVE: MAIN CHARACTER BIOGRAPHIES

Presented below are biographies for all the main *Torchwood* characters, based on information derived from the televised episodes and from other production-team-sanctioned sources such as the official *Torchwood* website and the tie-in novels. The principal sources for each entry are listed in brackets at the end of that entry. Where these sources are contradictory or ambiguous, attempts have been made to suggest explanations.

CAPTAIN JACK HARKNESS (JOHN BARROWMAN)

Jack Harkness – as he is now known[36] – was born in the 51st Century and grew up in a small colony on the Boeshane Peninsula with his father, Franklin, his mother and his brother, Gray. When he was a young boy, the colony was attacked by a race of horrible, howling alien invaders. Gray became separated from Jack, abducted by the creatures and tortured, and Franklin was killed. Jack became a 'poster boy' for the Boeshane Peninsula and was nicknamed 'the Face of Boe'. He fought in a war against a race of terrible creatures – presumably the same ones that abducted Gray – and, as a prisoner, witnessed them torture a young comrade who was his best friend. He later claimed to have become adept at torture himself. He spent years searching for Gray, but without success.

Jack was the first one from the Boeshane Peninsula to be signed up to an organisation called the Time Agency. As a Time Agent, he was able to travel in space and time using a vortex manipulator device worn on a leather wrist-strap. He was named 'Rear of the Year' in 5094. His one-time partner in the Time Agency was the equally-omnisexual Captain John Hart – also an alias, apparently adopted in direct response to Jack's – with whom he had a romantic liaison while they were trapped together for two weeks, which stretched to five years, in a time loop.

Jack ultimately quit the Time Agency after they wiped a two year period from his memory; it is unknown why they did this, or what happened during that period. He then turned to earning his living as an intergalactic conman. Probably during this time, he served as an officer with the British Army in Lahore in 1908-1909, although this was actually a cover for him to carry out a plot – overseen by someone else, identity unknown – to steal a consignment of diamonds from a nearby diamond mine. In the course of perpetrating another con in London at the time of the Second World War – this one involving an attempt to lure a Time Agent there and trick him into buying a supposed Chula warship that was actually an ambulance – he adopted the identity of an American flight officer, Captain Jack Harkness, altering the man's records to conceal the fact that he was actually killed in action on 21 January 1941 while voluntarily attached to the Royal Air Force's 133 Squadron in Cardiff.[37] It was at this point in his life that he met the Doctor,

---

36 Although he is referred to by his parents only as 'son' in the flashback scenes in 'Adam', it is possible that Jack is actually his real name, as Gray calls him that when they are eventually reunited in 'Exit Wounds' and would seem to have no reason to use an alias. Another possibility suggested by some fans is that his real name is 'Son' or 'Sun', and that this is actually what his parents are saying rather than 'son'.

37 Jack's uniform is that of a Group Captain, the equivalent rank to Captain in the RAF.

then in his ninth incarnation, and companion Rose Tyler. He reformed and spent some months travelling with his new friends in the TARDIS. This led to a fateful encounter with the Daleks on the Game Station, formerly known as Satellite 5, in the year 200,100, in the course of which he was exterminated by the creatures, only to be resurrected by Rose, who had temporarily acquired godlike powers.[38] As a result, he became immortal.

Jack managed to escape from the Game Station using his vortex manipulator. He arrived back on Earth in 1869, where the device burnt out and became useless for further time travel. He first discovered that he was immortal on Ellis Island in New York in 1892. Hoping that the Doctor might be able to reverse this condition, he then based himself near the time rift in Cardiff, knowing that the TARDIS would periodically materialise there in order to 'refuel'. In 1899, after being told by a young Tarot card reader that he would have to wait for the century to turn twice before he found the one he was looking for, he began to carry out missions on a freelance basis for the Cardiff branch of Torchwood (termed Torchwood Three), an organisation established by Queen Victoria in 1879 to protect the British Empire against the supposed threat posed by the Doctor and other such 'phantasmagoria'. He probably had a break from working with Torchwood Three for a period of some years around 1915-1925, and fought in the Great War. He at one point got married, to a woman whose identity is currently unknown. Later, he fought in the Second World War. In London in 1943, he met and fell in love with another woman, Estelle Cole, but wartime circumstances soon forced them to part.

At midnight on New Year's Eve 1999, Torchwood Cardiff – located in a base termed the Hub beneath Roald Dahl Plass – was placed in Jack's charge by its previous leader, Alex Hopkins, who then committed suicide, having already murdered the other members of the team as he believed they were not ready for the changes to come in the 21st Century. Jack proceeded to establish a new team, recruiting over the course of the next seven years Suzie Costello, Toshiko Sato, Owen Harper, Ianto Jones and – after Suzie, like Alex, committed murder and then suicide – Gwen Cooper. Jack had his long-awaited reunion with the Doctor after the TARDIS materialised outside the Hub in 2008 and he was able to hitch a lift to the planet Malcassairo near the end of the universe. There he learned that his immortality was irreversible. He subsequently returned to Earth with the Doctor and Martha Jones, only to be imprisoned by the Master aboard the skybase *Valiant* for a whole year before the Doctor was able to defeat his nemesis and time was rolled back. The Doctor then returned Jack to Roald Dahl Plass, where he decided to rejoin his Torchwood team defending the Earth.

In 2009, Jack had an unhappy reunion with his brother Gray, who blamed him for the years of torture he had endured and, with the unwilling assistance of Captain John, sought to exact revenge. Jack was taken back in time to 27 AD and buried under the ground on which Cardiff would later be built. He remained there until 1901, when he was found and dug up by his Torchwood colleagues of that era – who, at his insistence, then placed him in cryogenic storage in the Hub in order to avoid him meeting his younger self, who was fortunately absent on a

---

38 Jack must have encountered the Daleks before, perhaps when he was a Time Agent, as he recognises their spaceships as soon as he sees them in the *Doctor Who* episode 'Bad Wolf'.

mission at the time. He awoke some 107 years later, back in 2009.[39] Toshiko and Owen were killed before Gray was finally thwarted, leaving Jack and his remaining colleagues, Gwen and Ianto, to pick up the pieces and start again.

It is possible, given his boyhood nickname, that Jack later aged to the point where he became the Face of Boe, a similarly near-immortal creature consisting of a huge head in a fluid-filled transparent life-support tank, also known on the integrated planets of Cep Cassalon as 'the Creature that God Forgot'.[40] The Face of Boe gave birth to a number of children, including three sons and three daughters during the Fourth Great and Bountiful Human Empire around the year 200,000; all six of these Baby Boemina lived a normal lifespan of 40 years.[41] He ultimately died of old age after bequeathing the last of his life-force to save the population of New New York in the year 5,000,000,053. It is possible, however, that Jack and the Face of Boe are not one and the same: his nickname may, for instance, have been a joke, consciously referring to the real Face of Boe. This is made more likely by the fact that the Face of Boe is said to have been present 'when the stars of Andromeda were still nothing but dust' and by the fact that he does indeed appear to have been already known about in the community where Jack grew up.

(Principal sources: *Doctor Who*: 'The End of the World', 'The Empty Child'/'The Doctor Dances', 'The Long Game', 'Boom Town', 'Bad Wolf'/'The Parting of the Ways', 'Gridlock', 'Utopia', 'Last of the Time Lords'; *Torchwood*: 'Everything Changes', 'Countrycide', 'Captain Jack Harkness', 'Kiss Kiss, Bang Bang', 'Adam', 'Something Borrowed', 'From Out of the Rain', 'Fragments', 'Exit Wounds'; official *Torchwood* website and Torchwood Institute System Interface; and the book *Doctor Who: Monsters and Villains* (BBC Books, 2005).)

GWEN COOPER (EVE MYLES)

Gwen Elizabeth Cooper is the daughter of Geraint and Mary Cooper.[42] She began her career as a PC in South Wales Police Force, working in Cardiff. She was partnered for a time with PC Andy Davidson, with whom she may have had a brief romantic relationship in 2005. However, she was in love with Rhys Williams, an employee of a local haulage firm, whom she had first

---

39 It should be noted that a number of different-aged versions of Jack are present on Earth simultaneously at various points during the 20th and 21st Centuries. In January 1941, for instance, there are as many as four: i) the conman version that the Doctor and Rose meet in the *Doctor Who* story 'The Empty Child'/'The Doctor Dances'; ii) the post-'The Parting of the Ways' version, again from *Doctor Who*, who is currently working for Torchwood in that time period; iii) the version who has slipped back in time from 2008 with Toshiko in 'Captain Jack Harkness'; and iv) the version who is in cryogenic storage in the Hub. Thankfully, they all manage to avoid bumping into one other!

40 The Face of Boe is said in the *Doctor Who* episode 'The End of the World' to hail from the Silver Devastation; and in the later episode 'Bad Wolf' this is implied to be in the Isop Galaxy. This may therefore be the location of the Boeshane Peninsula.

41 If a throwaway remark he makes in 'Everything Changes' is to be believed, Jack has previously been pregnant at least once in his normal humanoid form.

42 Gwen's date of birth is given in the first issue of *Torchwood: The Official Magazine* as 16 August 1978, but this appears to be an unreliable source as far as Torchwood personnel information is concerned (see below).

met while they were at college, and they moved into a flat together. After being recruited to Torchwood Three, she had an affair with Owen Harper, although that ended after just a couple of months. She also felt a strong attraction and deep affection for Captain Jack, and refused to give up on him after he appeared to have been killed by the fearsome beast Abaddon. When Jack revived and then vanished from the Hub, she took over from him as leader of the team. She also got engaged to Rhys. After Jack's return a few months later, following his reunion with the Doctor, she effectively became his second-in-command. She also insisted on going through with her marriage to Rhys, despite having been made pregnant by a bite from a Nostrovite shape-shifter. She continued to use her maiden name for work purposes after her marriage.

(Principal sources: *Torchwood*: 'Everything Changes', 'Out of Time', 'Kiss Kiss, Bang Bang', 'Something Borrowed', 'Adrift'.)

OWEN HARPER (BURN GORMAN)

Owen hails from Plaistow in London's East End.[43] He had a difficult relationship with his mother: on his tenth birthday, she spent the whole day screaming, saying, 'I love you, because you're my son, but that doesn't mean I have to like you.' He decided to become a doctor after his father died suddenly at home one day from an aortic aneurysm. He lost his virginity at the age of 15 in a stationery cupboard at school. When he turned 16, his mother packed his bags to throw him out of the family home, prompting him to tell her, 'That is the nicest thing you've done for me in years, mother.'

Having trained in medicine and qualified around March 2001, he worked as a doctor at Cardiff Hospital, including in the A&E Department. He fell in love with another junior doctor, Katie Russell, and they got engaged. Then tragedy struck as Katie fell ill with what was first thought to be early-onset Alzheimer's Disease and then a brain tumour but was later revealed to be an alien brain parasite. This ultimately killed Katie when a surgeon attempted to remove it. Owen may have been initially retconned by Captain Jack, who intervened and took Katie's brain back to the Hub, but if so, he managed to overcome the drug's effects and recall what had happened. Around six months later, after he encountered Jack again at the cemetery where Katie was buried, he was recruited to work as Torchwood Three's medic.

He had affairs with both Suzie Costello and Gwen Cooper but then fell in love with Diane Holmes, a pilot whose plane had been transported through the rift from 1953. He was left distraught and near-suicidal when Diane took off again and flew back into the rift. Defying Jack's authority, he joined with the other team members in opening the rift, having been deceived into believing that this might lead to him being reunited with Diane. In doing so, he came close to bringing disaster upon the world in the form of the fearsome beast Abaddon. Jack subsequently

---

43 Owen's date of birth is given as 14 February 1980 in a personnel record briefly visible on a computer screen in the Hub in 'Exit Wounds' and also in the first issue of *Torchwood: The Official Magazine*. It is possible, however, that this is incorrect, as in 'Dead Man Walking', set in the summer of 2008, Martha says that he is 27 years old, not 28. Toshiko's equivalent personnel record also appears to be wrong, and Ianto's date of birth as given in *Torchwood: The Official Magazine* is probably incorrect (see below), casting further doubt on the reliability of these sources.

forgave him, however, and they were reconciled.

Owen then became more stable and was on the point of embarking on a relationship with Toshiko Sato when he was shot and killed during the course of a mission. He was revived by Jack with the use of an alien 'resurrection glove' but remained in some senses dead, having no heartbeat, blood circulation or capacity to heal himself, and being unable to breathe or digest food and drink. Having gone through a period of adjustment to his new circumstances, he resumed his work as a member of the Torchwood team. However, in the course of dealing with the consequences of an attack on Cardiff masterminded by Jack's brother Gray, he was trapped in a meltdown at the Turnmill Nuclear Power Plant and presumably suffered a final death as the chamber he was in was flooded with deadly radiation.

(Principal sources: *Torchwood*: 'Countrycide', 'Greeks Bearing Gifts', 'They Keep Killing Suzie', 'Out of Time', 'Combat', 'End of Days', 'Adam', 'Reset', 'Dead Man Walking', 'A Day in the Death', 'Fragments', 'Exit Wounds'; and the novel *Slow Decay*.)

TOSHIKO SATO (NAOKO MORI)

Toshiko Sato, known as Tosh to her friends, was born in London in July 1975.[44] Her family moved to Osaka in their native Japan when she was two, then back to the UK in 1986. Her grandfather worked at Bletchley Park during the Second World War, and celebrated his eightieth birthday in January 2008.[45] Her parents were in the Royal Air Force. She gained impressive qualifications at university, and was snapped up to work in a Government science think-tank when she was 20 years old. In the summer of 2004, when she was employed at the Ministry of Defence's Lodmoor Research Facility (possibly the same think-tank as before), an unidentified group kidnapped her mother and thereby blackmailed her into giving them classified information and equipment. UNIT troops foiled this scheme, arrested Toshiko and locked her up in a small cell in a grim prison facility. The troops also rescued her mother, who was subsequently retconned by Captain Jack to make her forget the whole experience, but this appears to have been the last time that Toshiko ever saw her, and she probably died shortly afterwards. In recognition of her technical brilliance, Toshiko was recruited by Jack to work for Torchwood Three, as an alternative to remaining permanently imprisoned by UNIT.

---

44 In 'Greeks Bearing Gifts' the alien known as Mary says that Toshiko was born in 1975, and later that her birthday is in July, and is not contradicted by her on either occasion. In a personnel record briefly visible on a Hub computer screen in 'Exit Wounds', however, her date of birth is recorded as 18 September 1981, and this is also the date given in the first issue of *Torchwood: The Official Magazine*. Possibly Toshiko used her technical skills to amend her personnel record and – out of vanity? – make it appear that she was about six years younger than was actually the case. Alternatively, perhaps Adam amended some of his newfound colleagues' records in 'Adam' and this was not spotted and corrected afterwards. In 'To the Last Man', she tells Tommy Brockless, by way of explanation for why she reacted awkwardly when he kissed her, 'I'm a bit older than you'. Given that he is 24 years old (disregarding the time he has spent in cryogenic suspension in the Hub), this is arguably more consistent with a 1975 birth date for Toshiko, as a 1981 birth date would make her only around two years older than him – surely no impediment to them having a relationship.

45 Bletchley Park was a secret code-breaking establishment.

She served as a member of the team in Cardiff for the next five years and proved highly dedicated to her work. She had a number of doomed romantic relationships, but secretly loved Owen Harper. She was ultimately shot and killed by Jack's brother Gray. Her body was presumably placed in cryogenic storage in the Hub.

(Principal sources: *Doctor Who*: 'Aliens of London'; *Torchwood*: 'Greeks Bearing Gifts', 'Captain Jack Harkness', 'End of Days', 'Fragments', 'Exit Wounds'.)

IANTO JONES (GARETH DAVID-LLOYD)[46]

Ianto Jones was born on 19 August 1983.[47] He grew up in Cardiff and his father, a master tailor by profession, would often take him to see films at the Electro Cinema. At school he was an able student but not exceptional. He received a minor conviction for shoplifting in his teens. He had a succession of temporary jobs but was essentially a drifter until he joined the Torchwood Institute in London around February 2006 as a junior researcher. His girlfriend was a fellow Torchwood One employee, Lisa Hallett, and his mentor was Rupert Howarth, head of the Biochemical Research Division. When the Battle of Canary Wharf ended, Lisa was left part-converted into a Cyberman. Ianto rescued her from the building and secretly took her to Cardiff, where he persuaded Captain Jack to allow him to join Torchwood Three. While he was courteous, efficient and loyal on the surface, he had a hidden agenda: he placed Lisa in the basement of the Hub and dedicated himself to finding a way to cure her, even if that meant putting the lives of all his colleagues – and possibly the whole world – in danger. These efforts proved in vain, and Lisa was ultimately killed by the other members of the team. Ianto was left grief-stricken, although Jack allowed him to keep his job. The two men also embarked on a sexual relationship, this having been brewing ever since they met.

Ianto's role in Torchwood Three was initially that of a general administrative assistant to his colleagues – he liked to think that no-one knew more than he about the organisation – but as time went by he became increasingly involved in missions as a fully fledged member of the team.

(Principal sources: *Torchwood*: 'Cyberwoman', 'They Keep Killing Suzie', 'Sleeper', 'Something Borrowed', 'From Out of the Rain', 'Fragments'; the novel *Trace Memory*; and comic strip story *The Legacy of Torchwood One!*.)

---

46 Gareth David-Lloyd has stated in interviews that his *Torchwood* character was originally to have been called Idris Hopper. This is intriguing, because Idris Hopper was a minor character – personal assistant to Margaret Blaine, or rather the Slitheen disguised as Margaret Blaine – in the Series One *Doctor Who* episode 'Boom Town', where he was played by Aled Pedrick. Did Russell T Davies originally intend that this minor *Doctor Who* character should transfer to become a more major one in *Torchwood*, just like Toshiko …? When David-Lloyd was cast, the character was renamed Ianto Jones after the part the actor had played in Davies's *Mine All Mine* (although in the latter, his first name had been spelt 'Yanto'). Idris Hopper has since reappeared in the *Torchwood* novel *The Twilight Streets* by Gary Russell.

47 This date is stated by Jack on screen in 'Fragments' and so is presumed to be correct. It does however contradict the 2 December 1982 date of birth given for Ianto in the first issue of *Torchwood: The Official Magazine*, and – bearing in mind that the 'Fragments' scene is a flashback recalled by Jack – it is just possible that he is misremembering.

RHYS WILLIAMS (KAI OWEN)

Rhys Alun Williams, son of Barry and Brenda, met his future wife Gwen Cooper when they were students at college. They first kissed in a supermarket, and Gwen nicknamed him 'Rhys the Rant' after he lost his temper in a queue. They fell in love and moved into a flat together. An affable, down-to-earth man, Rhys initially worked as a transport manager for Luckley's, a firm of printers. Then, in the summer of 2008, shortly after he and Gwen got engaged, he secured a more senior position as Cardiff manager of the Harwood's Haulage company, which also has offices in Ipswich, Sheffield and Carlisle. Gwen initially kept him in the dark about the nature of her job but was eventually forced to reveal that she caught aliens for a living. This was after Torchwood was called in to investigate a scheme involving the illicit transportation of alien meat in a Harwood's lorry. Rhys subsequently became mixed up in a number of other Torchwood operations, assisting the team to the best of his abilities, not least when Gwen was made pregnant by a Nostrovite shape-shifter the day before their wedding. He remains unaware of Gwen's earlier affair with Owen Harper, but knows that her former colleague PC Andy Davidson still has – unreciprocated – romantic feelings for her.

(Principal sources: *Torchwood*: 'Everything Changes', 'Kiss Kiss, Bang Bang', 'Meat', 'Adam', 'Something Borrowed', 'Adrift', 'Fragments'.)

PART FIVE: THE FACT

CHAPTER THIRTEEN: MAIN CAST
BIOGRAPHIES

JOHN BARROWMAN (CAPTAIN JACK HARKNESS)

John Barrowman was born on 11 March 1967 in Glasgow, Scotland. He grew up in his native city until, when he was aged eight, his family emigrated to live in the USA, in the town of Aurora, just south of Chicago, Illinois. He had always been keen on performing – both acting and singing – and pursued this interest during his education at Joliet West High School, Illinois, where he appeared in a number of student productions between 1983 and 1985. An early job was as a musical entertainer in a Nashville, Tennessee theme park called Opryland. He returned to the UK in 1989, initially to study Shakespeare at a London university, and his theatrical career really took off when he won a role opposite Elaine Paige in *Anything Goes* in London's West End. He also started gaining TV work during the 1990s, including as a regular presenter on the BBC children's series *Live and Kicking* (1993). Roles in the American series *Central Park West* (1996) and *Titans* (2000) followed, and more theatre work, including in a couple of productions on New York's Broadway. His starring roles in the theatre have come mainly in musicals, such as *Chicago*, *Sunset Boulevard*, *Miss Saigon*, *Evita*, *Beauty and the Beast* and *Phantom of the Opera*, although he has also had a number of non-singing parts, including in productions of *Rope* (1993) – during the run of which he met his long-time partner, architect Scott Gill – and *A Few Good Men* (2005). On the big screen he has appeared in the low-budget shocker *Shark Attack 3: Megalodon* (2002), in *De-Lovely* (2004), a biography of composer Cole Porter, and in Mel Brooks' *The Producers* (2005). He has sung on a number of original-cast soundtrack recordings of musicals, and has also released four solo CDs: *Aspects of Lloyd Webber* (1998), *Reflections from Broadway* (2000), *John Barrowman Swings Cole Porter* (2004) and *Another Side* (2007). When, in 2004, his agent was approached by casting director Andy Pryor about the possibility of him playing Captain Jack in *Doctor Who*, he was eager to take the role, having long been a fan. He was, in fact, the first regular to be cast in the revived show. So popular did he prove as Captain Jack that he was soon offered the opportunity to star in his own spin-off, *Torchwood*.

Since 2005, he has made frequent guest appearances on just about every entertainment show and celebrity quiz programme on British TV, cementing his position as one of the nation's most high-profile and popular stars. He performed in pantomime in *Cinderella* at the New Wimbledon Theatre over the 2005/2006 Christmas holiday season, and early in 2006 could again be seen on TV, in the variety shows *The Magic of Musicals* for the BBC and *Dancing on Ice* for ITV1. He also had a stint as a stand-in presenter on the ITV morning talk show *This Morning*. Later in 2006, he was one of the judges on the BBC One show *How Do You Solve a Problem Like Maria?*, about the search for a newcomer to star in a West End revival of the musical *The Sound of Music*. He was named Entertainer of the Year for 2006 by Stonewall and placed third in a Hottest Commodity poll in *Broadcast* magazine. On 27 December 2006, he and Gill became civil partners in a ceremony in Cardiff, the guests at which included his *Torchwood* co-stars and showrunner Russell T Davies. Further Christmas-season pantomime stints came in *Jack and the Beanstalk* at Cardiff's New Theatre in 2006/2007 and in *Aladdin* at the Birmingham Hippodrome in 2007/2008. In 2007, he amongst other things served as one of the judges on BBC One's *Any Dream Will Do*, a follow-up to *How Do You Solve a Problem Like Maria?*, this time designed to find a star for a new West End production of *Jason and the Amazing Technicolor Dreamcoat*

January 2008 saw the publication by Michael O'Mara Books of his autobiography *Anything Goes*, co-written with his sister, journalist and English professor Carole E Barrowman, which he promoted with a short signing tour of bookshops. During the on-air run of *Torchwood* Series Two, he again served as a judge on the latest BBC One talent-search show, *I'd Do Anything*, this time seeking newcomers to fill the roles of Nancy and Oliver in a West End revival of *Oliver!*, and continued to make various other TV guest appearances, including in an episode of BBC One's *Hotel Babylon* and on a number of occasions as presenter of the same channel's National Lottery Draw programme. In April 2008, he was seen as presenter of a new BBC One game show called *The Kids are All Right*, having recorded a successful pilot the previous year. He also undertook a short concert tour of UK cities.

EVE MYLES (GWEN COOPER)

Eve Myles was born in 1978 in the small South Wales mining village of Ystradgynlais and was educated at Ysgol Maes Y Dderwen School there, and then at the Royal Welsh College of Music and Drama in Cardiff, graduating in 2000 with a BA in Drama. Her TV credits prior to *Torchwood* included parts in *Score* (BBC Wales, 2001), *Tales from Pleasure Beach* (BBC Wales, 2001), *EastEnders* (BBC One 2003), *Colditz* (ITV1, 2005), as Gwyneth in the *Doctor Who* episode 'The Unquiet Dead' (2005) and, most notably, a regular starring role as Ceri Lewis in the BBC Wales drama series *Belonging* (2000-). She had a role in the movie *These Foolish Things* (2006), and on stage has appeared in Royal Shakespeare Company productions of *The Taming of the Shrew* and *Titus Andronicus* (2003) – for which she won an Ian Charleson award – and at the National Theatre in *Henry IV, Part I and II* (2005). Her favourite *Torchwood* episode to date is 'Countrycide'.

NAOKO MORI (TOSHIKO SATO)

Naoko Mori was born in 1975 in Nagoya, Japan. Her family moved to New Jersey, USA, when she was four, and it was there that she learned to speak English. They relocated again to Tokyo when she was ten and then to Surrey in the UK when she was 12. She started taking dance and singing lessons, and soon decided to pursue a career on the stage, joining the National Youth Music Theatre. At the age of 17, she became the first Japanese national to play a lead in London's West End, when she had a stint as Kim in *Miss Saigon*, opposite John Barrowman. Prior to her appearances in *Doctor Who* and *Torchwood*, she was best known for playing Mie Nishi-Kawa in the medical drama *Casualty* (1993-94) – which marked the start of her TV career – and Sarah (aka 'Titicaca') in the comedy series *Absolutely Fabulous* (1995-2003), both for the BBC. She also won parts in a number of other series, including *Thief Takers* (ITV1, 1997), *Bugs* (BBC One, 1998), *Psychos* (Channel 4, 1999), *Judge John Deed* (BBC One, 2001), *Spooks* (BBC One, 2002), *The Smoking Room* (BBC Three, 2004) and *Hiroshima* (BBC One, 2005), and in the movies *Hackers* (1995), *Spice World* (1997), *Topsy-Turvy* (1999) and *Running Time* (2000). On

20 November 2006 she began a run of several months in the role of Christmas Eve in the ribald puppet show *Avenue Q* at the Noel Coward Theatre in London's West End, which took her up to the start of her work on Series Two of *Torchwood*; she also appeared in the show's Royal Variety Performance segment on 4 December 2006.

BURN GORMAN (OWEN HARPER)

Although born in Hollywood, California, Burn Gorman was brought up in England from the age of seven by his British parents. He has since pursued parallel careers as an actor and a musician. He began acting in the theatre, and he has gone on to notch up numerous stage, radio, television and film credits. Prior to being cast in *Torchwood* his TV work included roles in *Coronation Street* (ITV1, 1998), *A Good Thief* (ITV1, 2002), *Funland* (BBC Three, 2005) and – perhaps most notably – as Guppy in *Bleak House* (BBC One, 2005). He has since appeared in *Sex, the City and Me* (BBC Two, 2007), in the *Marple* episode 'Ordeal by Innocence' (ITV1, 2007) and as scriptwriter Ray Galton in *The Curse of Steptoe* (BBC Four, 2008). On film he has had parts in, amongst others, the gangster movie *Layer Cake* (2004), the comedy/drama *Colour Me Kubrick* (2005), the light-hearted fantasy *Penelope* (2006) and cult Spanish director Alex de la Iglesia's thriller *The Oxford Murders* (2008). As a musician, he has performed at venues around the world and accompanied stars including Neneh Cherry and Groove Armada. He has also worked on videos for the Streets, is an expert breakdancer, and in 2003 won a BBC OneXtra award as Human Beatbox Champion. He is married and has one child.

GARETH DAVID-LLOYD (IANTO JONES)

Gareth David-Lloyd was born in the Welsh town of Bettws, Newport on 28 March 1981. He was educated locally at Monnow Junior School and Bettws Comprehensive School. After taking acting lessons at the Risca Leisure Centre, he joined the Dolman Youth Theatre and Gwent Young People's Theatre. He undertook more formal training in performing arts at Crosskeys College and, after a move to Reading, the Rep College. He won minor TV parts in *Absolute Power* (2003), *Casualty* (2003) and *The Genius of Beethoven* (2005) for the BBC and *Rosemary & Thyme* (2004), Russell T Davies's *Mine All Mine* (2004) and *The Bill* (2005) for ITV. He also took on further stage roles, including as Sebastian in *Twelfth Night* and Macheath in *The Threepenny Opera*. Ianto in *Torchwood* is, however, his highest-profile role to date. While recording Series One, he was also studying for a part-time degree in Philosophy with the Open University. His other credits include performing some audio-book readings of M R James ghost stories and co-writing the hard-hitting film *Wrecked* (2007). He sings and plays piano in a blues band called Blue Gillespie.

FREEMA AGYEMAN (MARTHA JONES)

Freema Agyeman was born in 1979 to an Iranian mother, Azar, and a Ghanaian father, Osei. She is one of three children, with an older sister, Leila, and a younger brother, Domenic. Her parents divorced when she was young, and she lived with her mother and siblings in a flat on the Woodberry Down housing estate in Finsbury Park, North London. She was educated at Our Lady's Convent in Stamford Hill and the Anna Scher Theatre School in Islington. Although as a child she had had ambitions to be a doctor and a marine biologist and had enjoyed science, she eventually chose English, Fine Art and Theatre Studies as her A Level subjects. She later studied at Middlesex University, graduating in 2000 with a BA (Honours) in Performing Arts and Drama, and also at Radford University in Virginia, USA. She had plans to work with children if her acting career stalled, but in fact she soon won a regular role as Lola Wise in the revived soap opera *Crossroads* (Carlton, 2001-2003), and this led on to further TV work, including in a 2004 episode of *Casualty* (BBC One, 1986-), a 2005 episode of *Mile High* (Sky One, 2003-2005), a 2005 episode of *Silent Witness* (BBC One, 1996-) and three episodes between 2004 and 2006 as a semi-regular in *The Bill* (ITV, 1983-). She also played the femme fatale Nana in the independent film production *Rulers and Dealers* (RDL Productions, 2006). Having auditioned unsuccessfully for the minor part of Sally in the *Doctor Who* Christmas special 'The Christmas Invasion' (2005), she made her debut in the show as Adeola Oshodi in 'Army of Ghosts' (2006) and immediately impressed the production team with her performance and personality. She was earning a living working shifts at a Blockbuster video rental store when, shortly afterwards, she was invited to audition for what she was initially told was a regular role in *Torchwood*. She eventually learned what part she was really being considered for – that of the companion in *Doctor Who* – when she was called back for a further, top-secret audition opposite David Tennant in producer Phil Collinson's Cardiff flat. She won the role, and went on to appear as medical student Martha Jones in every episode of Series Three of *Doctor Who*. Although Martha then parted company with the Doctor, she returned in three episodes of Series Two of *Torchwood* – allowing Agyeman to contribute to the spin-off after all – and in five episodes of Series Four of *Doctor Who*.

KAI OWEN (RHYS WILLIAMS)

Kai Owen was born on 4 September 1975 in Conwy, Wales. He worked in his family's butcher's shop from the age of 13, but went on to train in acting and musical theatre at the Mountview Academy in London, graduating in April 1998. His TV work prior to *Torchwood* included parts in *Treflan* (S4C, 2002) and *Casualty* (BBC One, 2003) and the starring role of David 'Shiner' Owen in the six-part serial *Rocket Man* (BBC One, 2005). He has also appeared in a number of plays in the theatre, including *Portrait of the Artist as a Young Dog* (2004), *A Chorus of Disapproval* (2006) and, perhaps most notably, co-starring as Ronnie in *Life of Ryan ... and Ronnie* (2006). His favourite *Torchwood* episode to date is 'Something Borrowed', although he also enjoyed having a more prominent role than usual in 'Meat'.

TOM PRICE (PC ANDY DAVIDSON)

Tom Price has worked extensively as a stand-up comedian and was a finalist in the *Daily Telegraph*'s Open Mic Awards in 2001 and both the ITV Take the Mic competition and the Paramount New Act of the Year competition in 2002. As an actor, he has had starring roles in the Channel 5 comedy sketch show *Swinging* and in three series of the BBC Radio 4 sitcom *Rigor Mortis*. He has also appeared several times in Edinburgh Fringe productions, including playing John Cleese in the Graham Chapman biography *A Very Naughty Boy*. He has worked as a presenter, too, including on BBC Three's *Destination Three* and MTV's dating game show

Senseless. He is often seen or heard in TV commercials, having promoted products including Nescafe coffee, Velvet Triple Soft toilet tissue, Trident chewing gum and PG Tips tea. He has his own website at www.tompriceless.com.

CHAPTER FOURTEEN: PRINCIPAL CREATIVE TEAM BIOGRAPHIES

RUSSELL T DAVIES (EXECUTIVE PRODUCER)

Russell T Davies was born in Swansea, South Wales, in 1963. (He in fact has no middle name: he started using 'T' as an initial in the 1980s in order to distinguish himself from an actor, journalist and broadcaster also named Russell Davies.) He was educated at Olchfa School, a huge comprehensive, and had an early involvement with the West Glamorgan Youth Theatre in Swansea. He then studied English Literature at Oxford University, graduating in 1984. His TV career began with posts as a floor manager and production assistant at the BBC, where in the late 1980s he also trained as a director and gained a presenting credit on *Play School* (1987). He produced the children's series *Why Don't You ...?* for BBC Manchester from 1988 to 1992, during which time he also started to work as a writer, gaining credits on *The Flashing Blade* (1989), *Breakfast Serials* (1990) and *Chucklevision* (1991). His writing career moved up a gear when he was responsible for the acclaimed BBC children's serials *Dark Season* (1991) – which he also novelised for BBC Books – and *Century Falls* (1993). In 1992, he moved from the BBC to Granada, where he produced and wrote for the popular children's drama *Children's Ward* (1992-1996). He also started to gain writing credits for family and adult programmes, including *Cluedo* (1993), *Families* (1993), *The House of Windsor* (1994) and *Revelations* (1994). He worked briefly as a storyliner and writer on the hugely popular *Coronation Street* (1996) and contributed to Channel 4's *Springhill* (1996). It was at this time that he had his first professional association with *Doctor Who* – having been a long-time fan of the series – when he wrote the *New Adventures* novel *Damaged Goods* (1996) for Virgin Publishing. The following year, he was commissioned to contribute to the ITV period drama *The Grand* (1997), and ended up scripting the whole series after a number of other writers dropped out. He subsequently left Granada and joined a company called Red Productions, where he had a major success as creator, writer and producer of *Queer as Folk* (1999-2000), a ground-breaking two-season drama series for Channel 4 about a group of gay men in Manchester, which also spawned a US remake. Since then, his career has gone from strength to strength, with writer and executive producer credits on *Bob and Rose* (2001) and *Mine All Mine* (2004) for ITV and *The Second Coming* (2003), *Casanova* (2005) and of course *Doctor Who* (2005-), *Torchwood* (2006-) and *The Sarah Jane Adventures* (2007-) for the BBC. He is now frequently cited as one of the most influential and powerful people in the British TV industry. In 2008 he was granted an OBE in the Queen's birthday honours for services to drama.

JULIE GARDNER (EXECUTIVE PRODUCER)

Julie Gardner was born in South Wales, near Neath, in 1969. Having gained a degree in English at London University, she began her working life as a teacher of English to secondary school pupils in Wales. In her mid-twenties, however, she decided that this was not the career for her, and she successfully applied for a job at the BBC, as the producer's secretary on the series *Our Friends in the North* (1996). She quickly ascended the ladder of promotion to script reader in the Serial Drama Department, then to script editor and then to producer, working on shows including *Silent Witness* (1996), *Sunburn* (1999) and *The Mrs Bradley Mysteries* (2000). In 2000, she left the BBC and took up a post as development producer at London Weekend Television. There she was responsible for dramas including a controversial modern-day retelling of Shakespeare's *Othello* (2001) and *Me and Mrs Jones* (2002). She was working on further ideas at LWT when, in 2003, she was head-hunted to become Head of Drama at BBC Wales. The new *Doctor Who* series gave her one of her first executive producer credits, and she has since gone on to fulfil a similar role on *Torchwood* and *The Sarah Jane Adventures*. Other projects she has overseen at BBC Wales include *Casanova* (2005), *Girl in the Café* (2005) and *Life on Mars* (2006-2007). On 21 September 2006 it was announced that she had been promoted to the post of the BBC's Head of Drama Commissioning, and would have special responsibility for implementing a cohesive independent drama strategy across the UK. She would however remain as Head of Drama, BBC Wales, for the foreseeable future, and would continue as executive producer of *Doctor Who*, *Torchwood* and *The Sarah Jane Adventures*.

RICHARD STOKES (PRODUCER)

Richard Stokes trained in picture editing at film school and gained early experience as third assistant director on some corporate videos. He then joined the BBC as a researcher, initially for light entertainment shows, before, in the mid-1980s, being recruited to BBC One's flagship soap opera *EastEnders*. He remained on *EastEnders* for several years, advancing to script editor, series editor and ultimately producer. After this, he produced *Murder in Mind* (2001-2002) and popular medical drama *Holby City* (2002), and then became an executive producer on the latter, on *The Inspector Lynley Mysteries* (2004) and on some single films, including *Magnificent 7* (2005). He narrowly lost out to Phil Collinson for the post of producer on *Doctor Who*, but was later offered *Torchwood* instead, which he readily accepted, joining the production in January 2006. Following completion of work on Series Two, he left the BBC to take up a job as producer of *Law and Order: London*, a Kudos Production for ITV1, based on the successful US series *Law and Order*.

SOPHIE FANTE (PRODUCER)

Sophie Fante was third assistant director on *Franz Kafka's It's a Wonderful Life* (1993), a BAFTA- and Oscar-winning short film made by BBC Scotland, and gained early movie credits as production co-ordinator on *Bent* (1997) and script editor on *One of the Hollywood Ten* (2000). She went on to work as a producer for the BBC on the third and fourth series of *Belonging* in 2002 and 2003, on five episodes of *Casualty* in 2005 and on the Catherine Tregenna-scripted drama *Stick or Twist* in 2006. Her first *Doctor Who*-related credits were as producer of the interactive adventure *Attack of the Graske* in 2005 and on the 'Tardisode' teasers for the Series Two episodes in 2006. She has been credited as producer alongside Richard Stokes on two *Torchwood* episodes, 'Random Shoes' and 'Adrift'.

CHRIS CHIBNALL (CO-PRODUCER, HEAD WRITER)

Chris Chibnall was raised in Lancashire and began his TV career as a football archivist and occasional floor manager for Sky Sports. He then took a succession of administrative jobs with different theatre companies including, between 1996 and 1999, the experimental group Complicite. He subsequently became a full-time writer, initially for the theatre, with credits including *Gaffer!* – a single-actor piece about homophobia in football, first staged in 1999 – and *Kiss Me Like You Mean It* – which premiered at the Soho Theatre in 2001 and has also been staged in a number of European venues, including Paris under the title *Un Baiser, Un Vrai*. On the strength of his play scripts, he was invited by the BBC to develop a period drama series for them. This became *Born and Bred* (2002-2005), which he not only created but also contributed to as consultant producer and lead writer throughout its four seasons. His other TV writing credits include episodes of *All About George* (2005) and *Life on Mars* (2006). During 2005, he was charged with developing the fantasy show *Merlin* for BBC One, but this was ultimately farmed out to the independent company Shine Productions. In January 2008, it was announced that he had taken a job as showrunner on *Law and Order: London*; this would preclude him from continuing as a *Torchwood* writer on Series Three.

BRIAN MINCHIN (SCRIPT EDITOR)

Brian Minchin was born in Aberystwyth, Wales, in 1987. He worked for several Welsh independent production companies and served as assistant producer or producer on a number of low-budget films, mainly for Sgrin Wales and ITV Wales, including *Down* (2003), which he also co-wrote, *Work in Progress* (2004) and *Dead Long Enough* (2005). He was script editor on BBC Wales's *Belonging* in 2005 before moving on to *Torchwood*.

GARY RUSSELL (SCRIPT EDITOR)

Gary Russell was born in Maidenhead, Berkshire on 18 September 1963. He began his working life as a child actor, winning notable TV roles in *The Phoenix and the Carpet* (BBC One, 1976), *The Famous Five* (ITV, 1978), *Dark Towers* (BBC One, 1981) and *Schoolgirl Chums* (BBC One, 1982). A lifelong *Doctor Who* fan, he edited his own fanzine, *Shada*, in the 1980s, and contributed to a number of others. This led to a new career as a freelance writer and editor. He contributed to the official *Doctor Who Magazine* and was its editor between 1992 and 1995; wrote a number of *Doctor Who* novels between 1994 and 2005; co-wrote with Philip David Segal the non-fiction book *Regenerations* (HarperCollins, 2001) about the 1996 TV movie; and was producer and occasional director of the Big Finish *Doctor Who* audio CD dramas between 1998 and 2006. He then joined BBC Wales, initially to administer product licensing for *Doctor Who, The Sarah Jane Adventures* and *Torchwood*. He acted as producer for the animated series *Doctor Who: The Infinite Quest* before starting work as a script editor, gaining his first on-screen credits in that capacity on Series Two of *Torchwood*. He has also written *Doctor Who – The Inside Story* (BBC Books, 2006), *Doctor Who – The Encyclopedia* (BBC Books, 2007), *The Sarah Jane Adventures: Warriors of Kudlak* (BBC Books, 2007), *Torchwood: The Twilight Streets* (BBC Books, 2008), *The Torchwood Archives* (BBC Books, 2008) and stories for IDW Publishing's *Doctor Who* comic book series, which launched in 2008. Outside of the *Doctor Who* world, his most notable work as an author has been on a number of non-fiction titles related to the series of movies based on Tolkein's *The Lord of the Rings*. These include: *The Lord of the Rings: Gollum:*

How We Made Movie Magic (Houghton Mifflin, 2003), co-written with Andy Sirkis; a range of books about the movies' art and design work, culminating in the 'best of' collection *The Art of The Lord of the Rings* (Houghton Mifflin, 2004); and *The Lord of the Rings: The Official Stage Companion: Staging the Greatest Show on Middle Earth* (HarperCollins, 2007).

LINDSEY ALFORD (SCRIPT EDITOR)

Lindsey Alford studied Psychology and Zoology and joined the BBC's Natural History Unit as a researcher on wildlife programming. She then transferred to BBC One's *Casualty*, progressing from researcher to storyliner to script editor over a period of several years. Moving to BBC Wales in 2006, she gained further script editor credits on *Doctor Who* ('Daleks in Manhattan'/'Evolution of the Daleks' and 'Human Nature'/'The Family of Blood') and the whole of the first series of *The Sarah Jane Adventures* before taking on that responsibility on the *Torchwood* episode 'Adrift'. She then became the principal script editor on Series Four of *Doctor Who*.

JAMES MORAN (WRITER)

James Moran was born in York. He got his first break as a writer by winning a Sci-Fi Channel competition with his script for the short film *Cheap Rate Gravity*, produced in 2002. He went on to write the successful movie *Severance* (2005). His *Torchwood* episode 'Sleeper' was his first TV work to be produced; he has since written 'The Fires of Pompeii' for Series Four of *Doctor Who* and scripts for forthcoming episodes of *Primeval* (ITV1), *Spooks: Liberty* (BBC Three) and *Law and Order: London* (ITV1). He has his own blog, at www.jamesmoran.blogspot.com, on which he has written extensively about his experiences working on both *Torchwood* and *Doctor Who*.

HELEN RAYNOR (WRITER)

After graduating from Cambridge University in the mid-1990s, Helen Raynor began her career in the theatre, as an assistant director and director for a number of companies, including the Bush Theatre, the Royal Shakespeare Company and the Royal Opera House. She then joined the BBC, where she became script editor of BBC One's daytime serial *Doctors* (2002-2004). This led on to a post as one of the initial two script editors on the new *Doctor Who* (2005-). She has also gained credits as a writer for the theatre (*Waterloo Exit Two*, Young Vic, 2003), for radio (*Running Away With the Hairdresser*, BBC Radio 4, 2005) and for TV (*Cake*, BBC One, 2006). In addition to her two *Torchwood* episodes, 'Ghost Machine' and 'To the Last Man', she has written four for *Doctor Who*: 'Daleks in Manhattan'/'Evolution of the Daleks' and 'The Sontaran Stratagem'/'The Poison Sky'. She contributed the *Doctor Who* short story *All of Beyond* to the anthology *Short Trips: Snapshots* (Big Finish, 2007).

CATHERINE TREGENNA (WRITER)

Cath Tregenna hails from Wales. She started out as an actress, winning minor parts in the film *Y Mapiwr* (1995) and the BBC series *Satellite City* (1996), before turning to writing. For BBC Wales she scripted episodes of *Belonging*, storylined *Pobol y Cwm* and developed (from an idea by former *Doctor Who* director Matthew Robinson) and wrote for the courtroom drama series *The Bench* (2001-). In addition to *Torchwood*, her other writing credits include episodes of

BBC One's *Casualty* (2003-2006) and *EastEnders* (2003), two series of the S4C show *Cowbois ac Injans* (2006-2007) (co-scripted with her brother Jon Tregenna) and the play *Art and Guff*, which debuted at London's Soho Theatre in March 2001.

J C WILSHER (WRITER)

John C Wilsher began his working life in academia. A job as a researcher at Lancaster University, monitoring the community impact of the city's Brewery Arts Centre, led to him taking some acting roles with the local amateur dramatics company. He wrote some material for a cabaret act with two other members of the company, and as this was well received, he decided to quit his researcher job and try to write professionally. He quickly gained commissions for radio – with *The Ghosts of the British Museum* (1978) – and TV – with *The Quiz Kid* (1979) – and this marked the start of a long and successful career in both media. He is known particularly for his work on police dramas, including ITV1's *The Bill*, on which he gained over 40 credits between 1989 and 2001. Probably his most notable achievement to date has been creating and writing for the award-winning series *Between the Lines* (1992-1994). He is a past President and Deputy Chair of the Writers' Guild of Great Britain.

MATT JONES (WRITER)

Matthew Jones was born on 5 August 1968. He wrote a regular column for *Doctor Who Magazine* in 1995 and made three contributions to Virgin Publishing's *Doctor Who* ranges: the short story 'The Nine Day Queen' in *Decalog 2: Lost Property* (1995) and the New Adventures novels *Bad Therapy* (1996) and *Beyond the Sun* (1997). In 1999 he broke into TV as script editor on Russell T Davies's *Queer as Folk* (Channel 4). This led on to him script-editing and writing one episode of *Love in the 21st Century* (Channel 4, 1999), writing episodes of *Children's Ward* (ITV1, 2000) and *Coronation Street* (ITV1, 2000), script-editing the first series of the award-winning *Clocking Off* (BBC One, 2000), and writing and producing the one-off drama *Now You See Her* (Sky One, 2001). In a succession of projects for Company Pictures, he was creator, writer and producer of the crime drama *Serious and Organised* (ITV1, 2003), executive producer and writer of the World War Two-set *P.O.W.* (ITV1, 2004) and executive producer of the 2004 series and producer of the 2005 series of *Shameless* (Channel 4). Prior to contributing to *Torchwood*, he wrote 'The Impossible Planet'/'The Satan Pit' for Series Two of *Doctor Who*.

JOSEPH LIDSTER (WRITER)

Joseph Lidster got into writing through his interest in *Doctor Who*. He scripted six stories for Big Finish's *Doctor Who* audio CD drama series – the earliest being the seventh Doctor story 'The Rapture' (2002) and the most recent a segment of the sixth Doctor portmanteau story '100' (2007) – and also wrote for their *Bernice Summerfield* and *UNIT* spin-off ranges and their *Sapphire and Steel* and *The Tomorrow People* series. In print, he contributed to and edited a number of the *Short Trips* anthologies of *Doctor Who* short stories, again from Big Finish. From 2005 he began to take on a number of *Doctor Who*-related projects for the BBC, including providing text for the show's tie-in websites, ghostwriting Martha Jones's MySpace blog during the on-air run of Series Three, penning an online prologue to the episode '42' and abridging the first three *Torchwood* novels and two of the new series *Doctor Who* novels for their BBC Audiobooks versions. His *Torchwood* episode, 'A Day in the Death', was his first TV credit. He has also written the BBC Audiobooks *Torchwood* story 'Shadows', due for release in September 2008.

PHIL FORD (WRITER)

Phil Ford gained his first TV writing credits in 1998 on episodes of ITV1's *Taggart, Coronation Street* and *Heartbeat*. He went on to contribute scripts to a number of other ITV1 series, including *The Bill* (2001), *Footballers' Wives* (2002), *Bad Girls* (2005-2006) and *Bombshell* (2006). It was, however, his work on *Gerry Anderson's New Captain Scarlet* (ITV1, 2005), for which he wrote the majority of the episodes, that caught the attention of Russell T Davies and his team. He was commissioned to provide the two-part stories 'Eye of the Gorgon' and 'The Lost Boy' for Series One of *The Sarah Jane Adventures* and was then elevated to head writer on Series Two. For *Torchwood*, he wrote not only the episode 'A Day in the Death' but also the 'alternate reality' online game presented on the official website; in addition, he has been commissioned to write one of the range of novels based on the show, entitled *Skypoint*. His other recent commissions include two episodes of the BBC One series *Waterloo Road* (2007).

PETER J HAMMOND (WRITER)

Peter J Hammond – sometimes credited as simply P J Hammond – took a course in art at the Hammersmith College of Arts and Crafts, studied drama at Goldsmith's College and penned a number of plays for BBC radio before beginning a long and distinguished career as a writer of popular British TV. In the 1950s and 1960s he contributed scripts to a considerable number of series, many of them police dramas or thrillers, including *Dixon of Dock Green* (1955), *Z Cars* (1962), *Thirty Minute Theatre* (1966), *Ramshackle Road* (1968) and *Special Branch* (1969). He also served as script editor of *Z Cars* for a year, in 1969/1970. In the 1970s, his credits included episodes of the popular telefantasy[48] series *Ace of Wands* (1971-1972), the soap opera *Emmerdale Farm* (1972) and the hard-hitting police series *The Sweeney* (1975) for ITV, and the nursing drama *Angels* (1975) and the police series *Target* (1977) for the BBC. More recently he has written for *Lame Ducks* (1984), *The Bill* (1992), *Dangerfield* (1996), *Wycliffe* (1997-1998) and *Midsomer Murders* (2001-), amongst others. He came close to contributing to Season 23 of the classic *Doctor Who* series in the mid-1980s, but his story, 'Paradise Five', was ultimately rejected. His most celebrated work came on the atmospheric ITV telefantasy series *Sapphire & Steel* (1979-1982), of which he was the creator and lead writer.

ASHLEY WAY (DIRECTOR)

36-year-old Cardiff-born Ashley Way started out as an assistant director on a number of largely-

---

48 Writer Phil Tonge, in an online article about BBC telefantasy, gave the following succinct definition of this term: 'Telefantasy is a term originally coined by French writers who wanted to avoid long-winded sub-categories for programmes such as say *The Avengers* ... Basically, if a programme contains elements of SF, horror, the supernatural, mythology and/or surrealism, then it can be deemed to be "telefantasy".'

Welsh-based film projects. These included *The Proposition* (1997), *Hooded Angels* (2000) and *Berserker* (2001) and a series of fantasy-orientated subjects directed by David Lister: *The Fairy King of Ar* (1998), *Dazzle* (1999), *The Meeksville Ghost* (2001), *Askari* (2001) – for which he also co-wrote the script and acted as associate producer – and *The Sorcerer's Apprentice* (2002). He wrote and directed the 2003 movie *Hoodlum and Son*. His TV credits include the South African-produced children's puppet series *Filligoggin* (2000) (co-directed with David Lister) and episodes of *Belonging* (BBC Wales, 2000-) and *Casualty* (BBC One, 2005-2006). His first contact with the *Doctor Who* world came when he directed the special interactive episode 'Attack of the Graske' in 2005. He then went on to direct the 13 online 'Tardisode' trailers for the Series Two episodes. Aside from his contributions to the latest series of *Torchwood* and *Belonging*, other recent directorial credits include the S4C production *Calon Gaeth* (2007).

COLIN TEAGUE (DIRECTOR)
Colin Teague's directorial credits include the feature films *Northwest One* (1999), *Shooters* (2002), *Spivs* (2004) and *The Last Drop* (2005), all of which apart from *Shooters* he also co-wrote, and episodes of *London's Burning* (ITV1, 2002) and *Holby City* (BBC One, 2003-2006). In addition to his four episodes of *Torchwood* – 'Ghost Machine' and 'Greeks Bearing Gifts' for Series One and 'Meat' and 'Adam' for Series Two – he has also directed the 'Invasion of the Bane' special for *The Sarah Jane Adventures* and three episodes of *Doctor Who* – 'The Sound of Drums' and 'Last of the Time Lords' for Series Three and 'The Fires of Pompeii' for Series Four – making him one of only two directors to date to have worked on all three series (the other being Alice Troughton).

ANDY GODDARD (DIRECTOR)
Andy Goddard began his career as a writer and director on the award-winning short film *Little Sisters* (1997), *Yabba Yabba Ding Ding* (Film Four 1999), *Kings of the Wild Frontier*: 'New Found Lands' (STV, 2000) (co-written with Ian Rankin) and *Rice Paper Stars* (BBC Scotland, 2000). He then focused increasingly on directing rather than writing, and was responsible for episodes of *G4CE* (CBBC, 2001), *Stacey Stone* (CBBC, 2001), *Taggart* (ITV1, 2003), *Casualty* (BBC One, 2003), *The Bill* (ITV1, 2003-2004), *Twisted Tales* (BBC Three, 2004), *Murphy's Law* (BBC One 2004-2005), *Hex* (Sky One) and *Wire in the Blood* (ITV1 2005-2006).

JONATHAN FOX BASSETT (DIRECTOR)
Jonathan Fox Bassett's directorial credits prior to *Torchwood* include episodes of *Teachers* (Channel 4, 2001), *20 Things to Do Before You're 30* (Channel 4, 2003), *Murder in Suburbia* (ITV1, 2005), a *Comedy Lab* pilot called *Skin Deep* (Channel 4, 2005), *Mayo* (BBC One, 2006), *The Inspector Lynley Mysteries* (BBC One, 2006) and the whole series *Live! Girls! Present Dogtown* (BBC Three, 2006).

MARK EVEREST (DIRECTOR)
Mark Everest started out as a writer, with a 1983 commission for the ITV children's drama strand *Dramarama*, but then turned to directing. He specialised in drama-documentaries,

including *Secrets of the Dead*: 'The Hidden Scrolls of Herculaneum' (Channel 4, 2001), *Seven Wonders of the Industrial World*: 'The Hoover Dam' (BBC, 2003) (which he also wrote, based on a section of the book by Deborah Cadbury), two episodes of *Space Race* (BBC Two, 2005) (one of which he wrote) and *Lost Cities of the Ancients*: 'The Vanished Capital of the Pharaoh' (BBC Two, 2006). His *Torchwood* assignment, 'Adrift', is his first straight drama credit on TV.

EDWARD THOMAS (PRODUCTION DESIGNER)
Edward Thomas took a foundation course in art and design after leaving school, and then studied at the Wimbledon School of Art, from which he graduated with a BA (Hons) degree in 3-D Design, specialising in theatre. He began his career as a designer on a wide variety of commercials and a number of theatrical productions, including *Turandot* for the Royal Opera Company at Wembley Arena, *Under Milkwood* for the Dylan Thomas Theatre Company and Shakespeare's *Twelfth Night* and *Cymbeline* for the Ludlow Festival. This was followed by work on numerous feature films, including over a dozen South African productions in the early 1990s and *The Mystery of Edwin Drood* (1993), *Resurrection Man* (1998), *Darkness Falls* (1999) and *The Meeksville Ghost* (2001). He also gained credits on a wide range of TV shows including, for BBC Wales, *Jones*, *The Coal Project* and, of course, *Doctor Who* (2005-), *Torchwood* (2006-) and *The Sarah Jane Adventures* (2007-). He has sometimes been credited as Edward Alan Thomas or simply as Ed Thomas, and is represented by the Creative Media Management agency.

PART SIX: EPISODE GUIDE

TORCHWOOD – SERIES TWO (2008)

SERIES CREDITS[49]

Created By: Russell T Davies
Producer: Richard Stokes, Sophie Fante (2.11)
Co-Producer: Chris Chibnall

MAIN CAST

John Barrowman (Captain Jack Harkness)
Eve Myles (Gwen Cooper)
Burn Gorman (Owen Harper)
Naoko Mori (Toshiko Sato)
Gareth David-Lloyd (Ianto Jones)
Kai Owen (Rhys Williams) (all except 3.06 and 2.10)[50]
Freema Agyeman (Martha Jones) (2.06, 2.07, 2.08)

PRODUCTION TEAM

1st Assistant Director: Nick Brown (2.01, 2.06), Marco Ciglia (2.02, 2.04), Richard Harris (2.03, 2.05, 2.07, 2.08), Rhidian Evans (2.09, 2.11, 2.13), Susanna Shaw (2.10, 2.12), Nick Britz (2.10, 2.12)
2nd Assistant Director: Lynsey Muir (2.01, 2.03, 2.05, 2.06, 2.07, 2.08), James DeHaviland (2.02, 2.04, 2.09, 2.11, 2.13), Pru Mettyer (2.10, 2.12)
3rd Assistant Director: Paul Bennett (2.01)
Location Manager: Nicky James
Assistant Location Manager: Iwan Roberts (2.05), Christian Reynish (2.10)
Unit Manager: Geraint Havard Jones (2.08)
Production Manager: Steffan Morris (all except 2.02, 2.04), Rhidian Evans (2.02, 2.04),
Production Co-ordinator: Hannah Simpson (all except 2.09, 2.13), Claire Thomas (2.09, 2.13)
Purchasing Assistant: Rhys Evans (2.08), Natalie Newbigging (2.11)
Continuity: Heulwen Jones (2.01, 2.06), Vicky Cole (2.02, 2.04), Llinos Wyn Jones (2.03, 2.05, 2.07, 2.08, 2.09, 2.11, 2.13), Vicky Cole (2.10, 2.12)
Production Secretary: Claire Thomas (2.04)
Runner: Brynach Day (2.04), Tom Evans (2.04), Lowri Denman (2.11), Sian Goldsmith (2.11)
Script Editor: Brian Minchin (2.01, 2.02, 2.03, 2.04, 2.05, 2.06, 2.10, 2.13), Gary Russell (2.07, 2.08, 2.09, 2.12), Lindsey Alford (2.11)
Script Assistant: Ross Southard (2.11)
Camera Operator: James Moss (2.01, 2.06, 2.10, 2.12), Martin Stephens (2.02, 2.03, 2.04, 2.05,

---

49 Where an episode number (or more than one) appears in brackets after a person's name in the listing, this means that they were credited only on the episode (or episodes) indicated. Otherwise, the person concerned was credited on all 13 episodes. Some production roles were credited only on certain episodes.

50 Although credited, does not actually appear in 2.02, 2.03 or 2.08.

2.07, 2.08, 2.09, 2.11, 2.13)

Camera Assistant: Mani Blaxter Paliwala (2.05, 2.08, 2.11)

Focus Puller: Chris Reynolds (2.01, 2.06), Rob McGregor (2.03, 2.07), Anna James (2.08), Terry Bartlett (2.11)

Grip: John Robinson (2.02, 2.05), Allan Hughes (2.07, 2.09, 2.13), Chris Hughes (2.11)

Gaffer: John Truckle (2.01, 2.06, 2.10, 2.12), Dave Fowler (2.02, 2.03, 2.04, 2.05, 2.08, 2.09, 2.11, 2.13)

Best Boy: Chris Davies (2.03, 2.06, 2.08)

Boom Operator: Kevin Staples (2.08), Martin Stephens (2.09)

Electrician: Alan Tippetts (2.06, 2.07), Tom Olley (2.06, 2.07), Tonty Ephgrave (2.06), John Budd (2.07)

Supervising Art Director: Keith Dunne

Standby Art Director: Beverley Gerard (2.01, 2.03, 2.05, 2.06, 2.10, 2.12), Lisa McDiarmid (2.02, 2.04), Kathy Featherstone (2.07, 2.08), Nick Burnell (2.09, 2.13), Matt North (2.11)

Art Department Assistant: Jackson Pope (2.04, 2.13)

Standby Props: Trystan Howell (2.08)

Props Master: Stuart Wooddisse

Set Decorator: Adrian Anscombe (2.01, 2.03, 2.05, 2.06, 2.09, 2.13), Kay Browne (2.07, 2.08), Claire Leytes (2.10, 2.12), Joelle Rumbelow (2.11)

Props Buyer/Production Buyer: Ben Morris (2.02, 2.11)

Construction Manager: Matthew Hywel-Davies

Graphics: BBC Wales Graphic Design

Costume Supervisor: Charlotte Mitchell (2.01, 2.03, 2.05, 2.06, 2.10, 2.12), Bobbie Peach (2.02, 2.04, 2.07, 2.08, 2.09, 2.11, 2.13)

Costume Assistant: Sara Morgan (2.02)

Make-up Supervisor: Claire Pritchard Jones (2.01, 2.03, 2.05, 2.06, 2.09, 2.10, 2.12, 2.13), Kate Roberts (2.02, 2.04, 2.07, 2.08, 2.11)

Make-up Artist: Andrea Dowdall (2.04), Emma Bailey (2.06), Kate Gardiner (2.10)

Stunt Co-ordinator/Arranger: Tom Lucy (all except 2.11[51])

Stunt Performer: Curtis Rivers (2.01)

Casting Associate: Andy Brierley

Assistant Editor: Matt Mullins (2.03, 2.04, 2.08, 2.11)

Post Production Supervisor: Helen Vallis, Chris Blatchford

Post Production Co-ordinator: Marie Brown (2.01, 2.03, 2.09, 2.13)

On-Line Editor: Mark Bright (2.04, 2.05, 2.06, 2.07, 2.08, 2.09, 2.10, 2.11, 2.12, 2.13), Jon Everett (2.05, 2.06, 2.11, 2.13), Matt Mullins (2.13)

Colourist: Mick Vincent (all except 2.02), Jon Everett (2.04)

Dubbing Mixer: Tim Ricketts (2.01, 2.06, 2.11), Peter Jeffreys (2.02, 2.03, 2.04, 2.05, 2.07, 2.08, 2.09, 2.10, 2.12, 2.13)

Supervising Sound Editor: Doug Sinclair

---

51 Credited twice on 2.04

Sound FX Editor: Howard Eaves (2.01, 2.02, 2.08, 2.09, 2.11, 2.13)

Casting Director: Andy Pryor CDG
Production Accountant: Ceri Tothill
Sound Recordist: Jeff Matthews (2.01, 2.02, 2.03, 2.04, 2.05, 2.11, 2.13), Dave Baumber (2.06, 2.07, 2.08, 2.09, 2.10, 2.12)
Series Designer: Julian Luxton
Costume Designer: Ray Holman
Make-Up Designer: Marie Doris
Theme Music: Murray Gold
Incidental Music: Murray Gold (2.01, 2.13), Ben Foster (2.02, 2.03, 2.04, 2.05, 2.06, 2.07, 2.08, 2.09, 2.10, 2.11, 2.12, 2.13)
Visual Effects: The Mill (all except 2.11)
Visual Effects Producer: Marie Jones (all except 2.11)
Vis Effects Supervisor: Barney Curnow (all except 2.11)
Special Effects: Any Effects
Prosthetics: Millennium Effects (2.01, 2.02, 2.04, 2.05, 2.06, 2.09, 2.10[52], 2.11, 2.12, 2.13)
Editor: William Webb (2.01, 2.06, 2.11), Mike Hopkins (2.02), Richard Cox (2.03, 2.05, 2.07, 2.08, 2.09, 2.13), Fergus MacKinnon (2.10, 2.12)
Production Designer: Edward Thomas
Director of Photography: Simon Butcher (2.01, 2.06, 2.10, 2.12), Mark Waters (2.02, 2.03, 2.04, 2.05, 2.07, 2.08, 2.09, 2.13), Toby Moore (2.11)
Production Executive: Julie Scott
Associate Producer: Catrin Lewis Defis
Executive Producer: Russell T Davies, Julie Gardner

A BBC Wales Production

---

52 Credited twice on 2.10

EPISODE GUIDE

In the episode guide that follows, no details are given for transmissions on the BBC HD channel, which were received by only a very small proportion of UK viewers. In general, however, each episode debuted on BBC HD at around the same time as it did on BBC Two or, as the case may be, BBC Three.

Viewers in Scotland and Northern Ireland were initially unable to see the pre-watershed BBC Two repeats of the episodes along with those in England and Wales, as these were dropped in favour of local programming in their regions. From 'Meat' onwards, however, this applied only in Northern Ireland, as Scotland then adopted the same schedule as England and Wales. The sixth episode, 'Reset', had its initial BBC Two airing a day later in Northern Ireland than in the rest of the UK.

All references here to credits in *Radio Times* relate to the listings for the BBC Two transmissions; there were no detailed listings given in the magazine for the BBC Three screenings.

Actual transmission times as well as scheduled ones are given for the unedited BBC Two screenings and the debut BBC Three screenings. These are not available in other instances, but the episodes invariably went out within a minute or two of their scheduled times.

Readers who have yet to see the episodes may wish to bear in mind that this guide is a comprehensive one that contains many plot 'spoilers'.

2.01 – KISS KISS, BANG BANG

Writer: Chris Chibnall
Director: Ashley Way

DEBUT TRANSMISSION DETAILS
BBC Two
Date: 16 January 2008. Scheduled time: 9.00 pm. Actual time: 9.02 pm.
BBC Three
Date: 16 January 2008. Scheduled time: 11.30 pm.
Duration: 47' 26"

Pre-watershed version
BBC Two
Date: 23 January 2008. Scheduled time: 7.00 pm.
Duration: 45' 50"

ADDITIONAL CREDITED CAST: James Marsters (Captain John Hart), Tom Price[53] (PC Andy), Menna Trussler (Old Woman), Paul Kasey (Blowfish), Crispin Layfield (Mugger), Nathan Ryan (Victim), Inika Leigh Wright[54] (Hologram Woman), Sarah Whyte[55] (Teenage Girl)

PLOT: Captain Jack rejoins his Torchwood team, killing an alien Blowfish they have been pursuing, just in time for the arrival through the rift of his former Time Agent partner Captain John Hart. John claims to be searching for three cylindrical radiation cluster bombs that threaten Cardiff, and the team agree to help him. The truth, however, is that the three 'bombs' contain parts of a device that he believes will enable him to locate a valuable Arcadian diamond that was owned by a woman he killed. It turns out that John has been tricked: once the device is assembled, completed with a pyramidal component taken from the pocket of the dead Blowfish, a hologram of the woman appears and reveals that there is no diamond; this is a trap she set for her murderer. A bomb rises up from the device and, attracted by his DNA, clamps itself immovably to John's chest. The Torchwood team have ten minutes to get him out of the city before the bomb explodes, but he handcuffs himself to Gwen. Gwen reasons that the only way to save the city now is for her to take John into the rift via the still-active crack through which he arrived. At the last minute, Owen injects John with a serum made up of blood taken from all the Torchwood team members, confusing the bomb and causing it to come free. Jack then throws it into the rift just before it

---

53 Credited in *Radio Times* but not on screen.

54 Not credited in *Radio Times*.

55 Not credited in *Radio Times*.

explodes. John also departs into the rift, but not before giving Jack the cryptic news: 'I found Gray.'

QUOTE, UNQUOTE

* Gwen: 'Excuse me. Have you seen a Blowfish driving a sports car?'

* Old Woman: 'Bloody Torchwood!'

* Jack: 'Hey kids. D'you miss me?'

* Jack: 'Captain Jack Harkness; note the stripes.'
  John: 'Captain John Hart; note the sarcasm.'

* Ianto: 'Why are you doing this?'
  John: 'We're a cosmic joke, Eye Candy. An accident of chemicals and evolution. The jokes, the sex, just cover the fact that nothing means anything, and the only consolation is money. So run, Ianto Jones.'

* John: 'Join me, Jack. Back in the old routine, we'd be emperors. How can you stay tied to one planet when there's thousands of worlds, sparkling with wonder? We should be up there, among the stars, claiming them for our own, just like before.'

DOCTOR WHO REFERENCES

* Toshiko: 'Where were you?'
  Jack: 'I found my Doctor.'
  Owen: 'Did he fix you?'
  Jack: 'What's to fix? You don't mess with this level of perfection.'
  Ianto: 'Are you going back to him?'
  Jack: 'I came back for you. All of you.'

* When Jack tells Gwen 'I saw the end of the world,' this is probably a reference to his having witnessed the destruction wreaked on the planet by the Master in 'Last of the Time Lords'. It could alternatively be an allusion to his having visited the dying days of the universe in 'Utopia'.

* Captain John tells Gwen that Jack was once a conman – a reference to his past occupation as seen in 'The Empty Child'/'The Doctor Dances'.

* Captain John is seeking an Arcadian diamond; Arcadia was previously mentioned by the Doctor in 'Doomsday'.

ALIEN TECH

- Captain John comes through the rift using his vortex manipulator, which is smaller than Captain Jack's but lasts much longer. He also uses it to project holograms, one of which Captain Jack receives as a message on his own equivalent, but not-fully-functional device. Quoting from a hologram message sent by Princess Leia in the movie *Star Wars*, Captain John jokes, 'Help me, Obi-Wan Kenobi, you're my only hope.'

- Toshiko has a new hand-held electronic scanner device with multiple functions, somewhat akin to a *Star Trek* tricorder, which will make further appearances throughout Series Two. Gwen is also seen using an identical device – or perhaps the same one – to detect Captain John's numerous hidden weapons on his entry into the Hub.

- In place of their large Bluetooth-style devices of Series One, the Torchwood team now have much smaller comms earpieces that are generally invisible to the naked eye, suggesting that they may actually be implanted beneath the skin; they are activated by a light touch to the ear, and respond with a beeping noise.

- The three 'radiation cluster bombs' are cylinders containing parts of a device that, when assembled, projects a hologram and then transforms into a powerful bomb that flies through the air and attaches itself immovably to Captain John's chest.

CONTINUITY POINTS

- Captain John demonstrates exceptional – possibly superhuman? – strength when he lifts a mugger off the ground with one hand and throws him off the top of a multi-storey car park.

- Captain John tells Captain Jack that the Time Agency has now been disbanded and that there are only seven Time Agents left, including them.

- Rhys phones Gwen to tell her he has got a new job as 'manager at Harwoods' – the haulage firm that will be featured later in the series in 'Meat'.

PRODUCTION NOTES

- Made with 'Reset' as part of Block 3 of production.

- This episode had the working titles 'Fresh Start' and 'Separation Anxiety'. The eventual title, 'Kiss Kiss, Bang Bang', was derived from a nickname given to James Bond and similar spy movies by the Japanese press in the 1960s, as acknowledged in the song 'Mr Kiss Kiss, Bang Bang' composed by John Barry and Leslie Bricusse for the 1965 Bond movie *Thunderball*. It has since been appropriated for numerous other songs, films and TV episodes, including a November 2000 instalment of the US series *Dawson's Creek*.

- This episode does not feature the standard opening clips montage used throughout the rest of Series Two.

- Captain Jack's arrival for his confrontation with Captain John at the appropriately-named Bar Reunion was shot outside a redressed entrance to a building in Mount Stuart Square, Cardiff, on 3 July 2007. The Medina section of the Tiger Tiger bar and restaurant in Greyfriars Road then became the interior of Bar Reunion for the fight scene and subsequent action, which was shot on 10 and 11 July. A container park at Barry Docks was the location used for the freight container scenes, taped on 16 July, with extra containers being added digitally by The Mill in post-production. The car park scenes were recorded on 18 and 19 July at the NCP car park in Wood Street just behind Cardiff Central railway station (not, as some viewers assumed, the same Tredegar Street car park seen in the Series One opener 'Everything Changes', which has since been demolished), with Torchwood examining the body of the man thrown from the roof in the adjacent Great Western Lane. The following day saw recording taking place in Schooner Way for the scene where Gwen drives John back to the car park in the SUV. The sequence of Jack taking John into the Hub via the 'entrance for tourists' in Roald Dahl Plass was taped in the early hours of the morning on 21 July, as were the scenes of the other Torchwood team members being driven in a London taxicab around the same area. The sequence of Jack and Ianto searching an office building was recorded at the British Gas offices in Helmont House, Churchill Way on 24 July. The rooftop confrontation between the two Captains and Jack's fall from the building – performed by John Barrowman's regular stunt double Curtis Rivers, suspended on a wire from a crane – were then completed at the same venue the following evening. The opening scene with the Blowfish in the sports car – a red Chrysler Crossfire – was shot in Merthyr Road, Whitchurch, starting at around 11.30 pm on 5 August. The traffic lights where the Blowfish stops to let a woman cross the road were just by the Bird's Fresh Fish shop. The pursuit of the sports car by the Torchwood SUV was then shot around the same area, including on Penlline Road, Kelston Road, Park Road, Pendwyallt Road and Pantwyr Road. The house where the Torchwood team confront the Blowfish was in the nearby Coryton Close. Recording on this date wrapped early at 3.00 am instead of the planned 4.00 am.

- The National Orchestra of Wales contributed to the incidental score of this and other Series Two episodes.

- The music playing in the Blowfish's car is the Prodigy mix of 'Release Yo' Self' by Method Man. The track heard when Captain John first arrives at Bar Reunion is 'Mao Tse Tung Said' by Alabama 3 from their *Exile on Coldharbour Lane* album of 1997, and that accompanying the fight between the two Captains is 'Song 2' by Blur from their self-titled album of the same year.

- The Blowfish character was given the nickname 'Hootie' during production – this was derived from the name of the American rock band Hootie and the Blowfish.

- A line cut from the final draft of the script would have had Captain Jack asking his team 'How were the Himalayas?', referring to the wild goose chase they were sent on by the Master, in his guise of Prime Minister Harold Saxon, as mentioned in the *Doctor Who* episode 'The Sound of Drums'.

- The notion of a rogue Time Agent foil for Captain Jack was first conceived during production of Series One, and the character was almost introduced toward the end of that first run, but ultimately held over for use at a later date in favour of other story ideas. After James Marsters contacted Russell T Davies's agent and expressed an interest in appearing either in *Doctor Who* or in *Torchwood*, the production team realised that he would be perfect casting for the role. Chris Chibnall then developed Captain John – whose surname was originally to have been Hammond – for inclusion in the opening episode of Series Two.

- James Marsters was initially disconcerted by John Barrowman's ribald antics on set between takes, but Barrowman soon put him at ease, and ultimately the two men got on very well. Marsters also formed a particularly good friendship with Gareth David-Lloyd.

- It was originally mooted that Captain John should arrive through the rift on a pan-dimensional surfboard of the type introduced in the *Doctor Who* episode 'Boom Town', but this idea was dropped as it was felt that it would look cooler if he simply walked out casually. The fight scene between the two Captains in the bar was intended to evoke the feel of the famous naked wrestling scene between characters played by Oliver Reed and Alan Bates in the 1969 Ken Russell movie *Women in Love*.

- When Naoko Mori first read the scripted line where Toshiko calls Captain John 'cute' she thought this must be a mistake, as it seemed out of keeping with her repressed character of Series One. She was reassured on learning that it was an intentional early indication of her coming out of her shell more in Series Two.

- Speaking at the Series Two press launch on 3 December 2007, Russell T Davies indicated that he had requested the inclusion of Captain John's lines revealing that the Time Agency had been closed down. 'Otherwise we had this offstage agency that we never knew anything about,' he was quoted as saying. 'They never featured, and we never did anything with it. And besides, I like that the Doctor is the only one who can travel through time. So with a few script lines, we sort the whole universe out.'

- Russell T Davies's original idea for Captain John's costume was to use a Grenadier Guard's uniform with jeans, but he and costume designer Ray Holman subsequently agreed that the uniform coat was too long and that its bright red colour and white details would not look right. Holman explained how the final jacket was arrived at in an interview for Issue 12 of *DeathRay*, published in April 2008: 'I went through all the other military jackets [at Angels costumiers] and eventually found a couple we could use: a short mess jacket in red, and another that had braiding on it. For the Captain John jacket I combined the two, so we had the cut of the mess jacket but covered in braiding. It's completely made up, there's no uniform like it, so I was free to pick any colour I wanted. I went for a darker red, with a dark blue on the collar and cuffs. I had three made up – one for James [Marsters], one for the stuntman, and one that was bigger, so that James could wear padding underneath for the fight scenes.'

- Gwen wears a T-shirt featuring an iconic image of the American rock band New York Dolls.

- When Captain John makes fun of the name Torchwood, saying 'Oh, not Excalibur …?', this is an in-joke, as *Excalibur* was an early working title for *Torchwood*.

- The fact that the explosion in the rift portal at the end causes time to jump back to the night of Captain John's arrival, assumed by some fans to be a significant plot point that would be picked up later in the series, was actually just a production contingency adopted because the changeable weather on location made it impossible for the closing scene to be completed during daylight.

- A brief clip from the series' fifth episode, 'Adam', is included in the scene where Captain John mentions Gray. This is from the flashback sequence in which the young Jack and Gray get separated on the Boeshane Peninsula, although only their hands are seen here and no other details are revealed at this stage.

- The name Captain John Hart was also used for a character in the *Doctor Who* story 'The Sea Devils' in 1972.

- The episode ends with a 'Coming Up …' trailer for the rest of the series.

- Cuts made to the episode for the pre-watershed version included shots of blood and gore and a reference to cocaine in the initial encounter with the Blowfish; the exclamation 'Shit!' in the scene where Captain John dangles a mugger from the roof of the multi-storey car park; references to Captain John having been through 'murder rehab'; Owen's line 'Bollocks to that, Tosh'; a shot of Captain Jack's apparently dead body arched over a bench at the base of the office building from which he has been thrown by Captain John; Captain John's suggestion of having an orgy; and various references to sex in the 'Coming Up …' trailer.

OOPS!

- Toshiko traces the three cylinders by cross-referencing radiation surges with rift activity ... but it later turns out that canisters are not radioactive after all.

PRESS REACTION

- 'Russell T Davies has been telling everyone who'll listen how *Torchwood* [Series Two's] secret ingredient is humour. And parts of ["Kiss Kiss, Bang Bang"] were very, very funny – from the opening sequence depicting a druggy, murderous Blowfish driving a sports car, and the numerous in-jokes: about Torchwood being the world's least secret secret organisation and Captain Jack's puzzling habit of standing on rooftops looking reflective. It was largely a hoot. Something about it was just more colourful [than Series One], down in no small part to the best thing about the opener: James Marsters. Davies has always admitted that the biggest reference point for *Doctor Who* was Joss Whedon's *Buffy the Vampire Slayer*, and *Torchwood* is Angel to *Who's Buffy* (dark spin-off with an immortal team leader, etc etc). Shamelessly and brilliantly, they basically transplanted Marsters' character from both series, vampire Spike, into their world. His English accent, red jacket and love of the bottle all survived the transition to Captain John Hart – a rogue Time Agent and former lover of Captain Jack, he stole every scene he was in.' Daniel Martin, Guardian Unlimited website, 17 January 2008.

- 'The new series of *Torchwood* didn't waste much time getting going. In the opening scene, a woman watched a fish-headed alien driving a sports car, with our heroes in hot pursuit. "Bloody Torchwood," she muttered – which I must say are my sentiments as well. Tucked away on BBC Three, the programme seemed harmless enough as a poor and even camper relation of *Doctor Who*. In the glare of BBC Two prime-time, it's revealed as both far too pleased with itself and surprisingly amateurish. It's also far too much in love with its main character, Captain Jack Harkness (John Barrowman), whose twin roles are to keep saving the day and to be fawned over by everybody else. Last night, some of the fawning even came from the main baddie, Captain John Hart (James Marsters), who was apparently thrown into the mix on the principle that one glamorous space-travelling bisexual isn't enough. Amid the leaden gags and ponderous reflections on Life Itself, there followed a fantastically ungripping plot where each of the Torchwood team in turn found themselves in peril – and escaped soon afterwards.' James Walton, *Daily Telegraph*, 17 January 2008.

- 'It's not only [Chris Chibnall's] best work for the series to date, but arguably the best episode the series has produced to date. From the opening gag (and the Blowfish is a magnificently incongruous and beautifully realised special effect) on, there's not a single line wasted, not a single pause for breath. Where last year the series defined itself against its stable mate by ramping up the violence, swearing and sex, this year it looks set to define itself as *Doctor Who* with the brakes off. The adult content is still there, make no mistake ...

but it feels much more integrated, much more natural to the content of the show. The producers have talked on several occasions about the fact that the first series was produced under tremendous time pressure, and the extra time, and new time slot, given to them for this series has obviously paid dividends. There's no massive reboot, no seismic change, the same elements are in place, but they feel far more cohesive, far more unique.' Alasdair Stuart, Firefox News website, 5 December 2007.

- 'Captain Jack snogging Spike from *Buffy* and *Angel*? Somebody's sci-fi fantasy has just been realised, I expect, but any hopes Series Two might serve less sex, less rubbish aliens and more credible drama are pretty much dashed by John Barrowman and guest star James Marsters being so pleased to see each other again. Marsters, keeping his on-off London accent and a jacket borrowed from Adam Ant, bursts in as roguish time agent Captain John Hart who used to be Captain Jack's partner. Here he slips in through the rift and asks the Torchwood team to help find artefacts hidden on Earth. Coming up later in the series, *Doctor Who*'s companion Martha Jones will be dropping in. But with its obsession with orgies and gadgets still hovering around the mentality of a 14-year-old boy, *Torchwood* still doesn't look like an adult version of *Doctor Who*. Cleaned-up, pre-watershed episodes will go out at 7.00 pm from next Wednesday. So Hart lusting after a poodle is likely to be cut ...' Uncredited, *Daily Mirror*, 16 January 2008.

- 'The first thing that shouts out right from the start of the new run of *Torchwood* is its newfound sense of humour. It's not that the scripts are necessarily any funnier, it's just that it's played with a *Buffy*-esque sense of laughter in the face of danger that was absent last year ... As Jack's fellow Time Agent ..., James Marsters effectively plays Spike with a slightly posher accent but, to be frank, to grumble about that would be like complaining that David Niven and Cary Grant lacked range. The characters are similar, but the differences are key, and are used to shine a light on Jack. All in all, massively improved, and if this is what the action episodes are going to be like this year, then when mixed in with the character pieces, *Torchwood* will finally have hit its stride.' Anthony Brown, *TV Zone* Issue 224, January 2008.

FAN COMMENT

- 'The team who in the previous series always acted like they might kill each other should they get stuck in a lift together for five minutes were finally looking and acting like a proper team – a team who like and care for each other and woe betide anyone who gets in their way. I really loved the little sequence of Jack watching them all work together like a well oiled machine at the beginning of the episode. Clearly Jack's absence caused them to bond and all the pettiness and hatred seem to have fallen away ... I thought Marsters really, really sold the concept of Hart as a man who was in his own way still very much in love with Jack. Jack is fairly dismissive of their relationship so you see it through Hart's eyes – and you never believe for a second that it was only a fling. They were together for five years and what they had was important enough to Hart that he's desperate to re-kindle it. I thought his line delivery of "He won't stay with you; we had something special" was quite heartbreaking in its conviction that Jack would choose him over his team. The look of horror and regret after he'd pushed Jack off the roof was also brilliantly done.' 'fairyd123', LiveJournal blog, 17 January 2008.

- 'Something that struck me about this episode was how messy the emotional stuff was – they weren't bottling up their feelings, but they didn't know quite what to do or say, so they stumbled a bit. The scene with Jack and Ianto in the office was so … man, it's so *Ianto* to have a thin crust of workmanlike efficiency over a core of deep hurt. His "Why are we helping him?" was so *plaintive*, and yet so quiet, almost like he wasn't expecting an answer … Jack's scenes with Gwen were interesting in a different way. He's always been trying to hold onto her at arm's length – not to let her go, but to keep her at a distance at the same time – and she's finally wised up to that, and she's not putting up with it anymore. Or at least, she doesn't *mean* to put up with it anymore. Time will tell whether her resolve holds when Jack's actually there to tempt her.' Katherine Farmar, LiveJournal blog, 17 January 2008.

ANALYSIS: 'Kiss Kiss, Bang Bang' gets Series Two of *Torchwood* off to a fine start. The opening pre-credits sequence, in which the Torchwood team in their SUV pursue a Blowfish in a sports car through the night-time streets of Cardiff, neatly encapsulates what the show is all about, combining fast-paced action with tongue-in-cheek humour and, when the coked-up Blowfish taunts its pursuers after being cornered in a suburban house, serving up some handy character profiles of Gwen, Owen, Toshiko and Ianto – all topped off with a bit of alien gore when Captain Jack makes his dramatic re-entry onto the scene and shoots the creature in the head. Brilliantly written by Russell T Davies – who supplied it as a lead-in to Chris Chibnall's script for the rest of the episode – and superbly realised by director Ashley Way and his crew, this serves as an excellent refresher course for those who followed the show during Series One and an ideal introduction for those who've come to it fresh. And that's just the first couple of minutes!

The Blowfish is actually one of *Torchwood*'s most well-depicted alien creatures, the fish-like head atop the smartly-suited human body again acting as a metaphor for the show's own trademark juxtaposition of the weird and the mundane. It is never explained how *Torchwood* come to be pursuing the creature, how it obtained its detailed knowledge of them or what exactly its connection is with Captain John, who has no such knowledge to start with, but this doesn't matter; it serves its purpose in the narrative, and its back-story can be left simply to the viewer's imagination.

Captain John himself is a fantastic addition to the show's mythos, acting as a dark, twisted reflection of Captain Jack in much the same way as the Master does of the Doctor in *Doctor Who* – and thus in the process reinforcing the existing parallels between Captain Jack and the Doctor. He also reveals by association a little more about Captain Jack's past as a Time Agent and suggests how he could have turned out had he not become a reformed character after his initial meeting with the Doctor. Much has been made of the production team's coup of getting

James Marsters to play the part. It is questionable just how well-known the actor really is to the general public in the UK; *Buffy the Vampire Slayer* was never much more than a cult hit here, generally getting audiences of around two-and-a-half million on its BBC Two screenings, and this is even more true of the other shows he has appeared in, such as *Smallville*. For the type of viewers who are particularly drawn to TV science fiction shows like *Torchwood*, though, his portrayal of the English-accented, platinum-blond vampire Spike is undoubtedly iconic. In 'Kiss Kiss, Bang Bang', he fully justifies his great reputation, giving a finely-judged performance that makes Captain John just similar enough to Spike to delight his established fans (helped by a couple of *Buffy*-esque lines in the script) and just different enough to keep things interesting and surprising. His weapons-bedecked, military-style costume – again a variation on the theme of Captain Jack's – helps to give him the air of a swaggering, devil-may-care buccaneer, but there are subtler aspects to his character too, both in the writing and in Marsters' playing of the part. His motivations come across as being personal and capricious rather than simply and stereotypically villainous, adding great depth to the character. A good illustration of this is the way that he views Captain Jack's unwillingness to join forces with him as a personal affront; a hurtful rejection by a former lover rather than a straightforward refusal to get drawn into a nefarious scheme.

Marsters brings great star quality and imposing physical presence to the part; attributes that are really prerequisites if an actor is to face off effectively against the larger-than-life John Barrowman in scenes such as the stand-out Western-influenced initial confrontation in Bar Reunion, where their kissing and fighting are evidently just different varieties of hot-and-heavy foreplay. The brief details revealed of their past together in the now-defunct Time Agency are intriguing, and outrageous devices such as the paralysing lip-gloss that Captain John wears to disable Gwen with a kiss are great fun, if not entirely logical – why does the poison not affect him too, or Jack on the two occasions when he kisses him? – or indeed original – the same idea has cropped up a number of times before, for instance in the 'Our Mrs Reynolds' episode of *Firefly*, another show from *Buffy the Vampire Slayer* creator Joss Whedon, and perhaps most notably in the *Batman* stories featuring Poison Ivy with her deadly kisses. At any rate, it is very good to know that this is not simply a one-off appearance by Captain John, and that he will be back again in later episodes – and hopefully as a semi-regular in future series as well.

A key aspect of 'Kiss Kiss, Bang Bang' is, of course, Captain Jack's resumption of his responsibilities at Torchwood after his sojourn with the Doctor in Series Three of *Doctor Who*. When he disappeared from the Hub at the close of 'End of Days', Gwen told the others, 'Something's taken him; Jack's gone,' raising the possibility that he has been abducted or otherwise spirited away against his will. It seems rather curious, then, that her first reaction on his return to the Hub is to shove him angrily and shout 'You left us, Jack!' Perhaps, though, they have already had a 'What happened to you?' type conversation, unseen by the viewer, on the way back from the encounter with the Blowfish. Anyhow, it is obvious that a fair amount of time has passed since Jack's disappearance, and Gwen has risen to the challenge and taken charge of the team in his absence. This makes it quite understandable that there should be some initial awkwardness between them, not only on a professional level when Jack blithely reassumes control and effectively usurps Gwen's authority – 'I was hoping for a little power struggle, resolved by some naked wrestling,' he quips – but also on a personal one when, in a quiet moment together, he discovers that she has got engaged to Rhys in his absence – 'Well, no-one else will have me,' she tells him, in a scene replete with sexual tension.

This all recalls the way that the relationship between Gwen and Jack evolved during Series One, from the mutual fascination of their initial meeting in 'Everything Changes', through her development of a strong attraction toward him, as seen for instance in the firing range sequence in 'Ghost Machine', to their eventual forging of a special bond of friendship, or perhaps even love, based on shared respect and trust – as demonstrated when, out of all the team members, it is Gwen that Jack asks to accompany him *en route* to his fateful battle with Abaddon in 'End of Days', and she who refuses to give up on him after he appears to have been killed, ultimately reviving him with a kiss. Indeed, on one level, Series One could arguably be seen as the story of that unfolding relationship between the two lead characters, complicated by Gwen's affair with Owen – now ended – and her attachment to Rhys – still very much ongoing. It is clear from 'Kiss Kiss, Bang Bang' that this will continue to be an important theme during Series Two.

Another significant advancement on the character front comes when, in a scene very nicely underplayed by both John Barrowman and Gareth David-Lloyd, Jack rather nervously invites Ianto out on a date, and Ianto rather awkwardly accepts. Clearly their relationship is now progressing beyond the purely sexual encounters strongly hinted at if not actually seen during Series One; and it is tempting to speculate that this is a sign of Jack consciously moving on in recognition of the fact that there is no longer any prospect of him pursuing an ongoing romance with Gwen, she having committed herself to Rhys – despite the arguably stronger feelings she still has toward Jack – and he being too principled a person to countenance coming between them. Again, this sets things up very nicely for further development later in the series.

The show's writers also seem to have spotted that David-Lloyd has a special talent for delivering dryly humorous lines with perfect comic timing, and 'Kiss Kiss, Bang Bang' features just the first of many wry interjections from Ianto that will prove a source of great amusement throughout Series Two – a good example being his comment to Jack, 'You're good on roofs,' a tongue-in-cheek reference to the Captain's predilection for surveying the city from high vantage points, as seen particularly during the early episodes of Series One.

Owen, too, seems to have undergone some significant character progression since we last saw him. Following Jack's forgiveness of his betrayal in 'End of Days', he appears altogether more stable, as if he recognises that he has been given a second chance in Torchwood and is determined to approach his work more seriously and professionally than before. Even his womanising seems to be a thing of the past: when Toshiko says to him at one point, 'Bet you'd normally be out on the pull, this time of night,' he replies, 'No. Bollocks to that, Tosh. Talk about diminishing returns ... I've done all that, haven't I? Where did it get me? You know, I need a proper woman ... Someone I've got something in common with, yeah?'

Perhaps the least obviously changed of all the regulars is Tosh, who is still not in a relationship with anyone and is still clearly wishing, in vain, that Owen will notice that she has feelings for him, as is most starkly apparent when, in a continuation of the above-mentioned exchange, Owen asks her 'Got anyone on the horizon, hmm?' and she hopefully replies, 'As you say, difficult to meet anyone I've got anything in common with, what with the things we see'. Even in her case, though, there are signs that she is coming out of her shell a little. She is visibly flattered by the attention that Captain John gives her – particularly when he suggests that she is 'the brains *and* the beauty' of the Torchwood team – and is even bold enough to describe him as 'cute'.

In production terms, 'Kiss Kiss, Bang Bang' serves as a perfect restatement of *Torchwood*'s distinctive visual style, with much of the action taking place at night in a variety of now-familiar Cardiff locations ranging from the glamour of the Roald Dahl Plass, with its imposing water tower fountain leading down (supposedly) into the Hub, to the brightly-lit arteries of the city streets as seen in a succession of sweeping aerial shots, to the soulless urban concrete of a multi-storey car park and a high-rise office building, to the bleak industrial settings of a cavernous warehouse and a mazelike dockside container park. The look is slick, dark and dramatic. Ashley Way's direction is his strongest yet for the show, following on from his excellent work on 'Captain Jack Harkness' and 'End of Days' in Series One. The pacing of the action is spot-on, and there are some genuine shock moments such as when Captain John viciously headbutts Toshiko and then perfunctorily shoots Owen – demonstrating that *Torchwood* remains thankfully unafraid to portray direct physical violence of a kind that would simply not be seen in other genre shows. The style of the Torchwood team's costumes has been tweaked slightly for this series – except in the case of Jack's 1940s retro attire – with more leather in evidence and the predominant blacks offset with touches of other colours, particularly pinks, purples and reds, giving them an even stronger and sexier image. The Hub set has also been given a makeover, no doubt necessitated in fictional terms by its partial destruction in 'End of Days', and looks better than ever, the most notable change being the addition of the impressive new boardroom.

The storyline involving Captain John's attempt to recover the three radiation cluster bombs, which turn out to be nothing of the sort, is fairly straightforward and even a little predictable – the viewer is never convinced for one minute that his motives are altruistic, and it is hardly surprising when he is thwarted at the end. There are also certain aspects of the plotting that don't stand up to too much scrutiny. When Captain John handcuffs himself to Gwen and swallows the key, for instance, there is a brief explanation provided as to why the team cannot simply cut off his hand in order to free her (although the dialogue in question shows signs of having been dubbed on in post-production, presumably when someone suddenly spotted this obvious flaw), but no thought given to the alternative possibility of them cutting off Gwen's hand – a drastic step, admittedly, but one that they would surely consider given that, at this point, it seems inevitable that she will otherwise be killed when the bomb clamped to Captain John's chest detonates. A severed hand can, after all, be reattached in hospital.

But the specifics of the storyline aren't really that important here; although simple, it's highly entertaining, and crucially acts as a framework enabling Chibnall to relaunch the show, reintroduce its premise and its characters and establish the new, less-angsty, more fun-fuelled tone decided upon for Series Two. It might not make much scientific sense that injecting Captain John with a cocktail of the team members' blood causes the bomb to become confused and detach itself, but it is a neat metaphor for the team working together in a newfound spirit of unity in order to achieve their aims; 'Torchwood DNA,' as Owen puts it. And that's what really matters in *Torchwood*; not the sci-fi trappings or the fantastic concepts, but the characters, their relationships and the real human drama at the heart of the stories. 'Kiss Kiss, Bang Bang' presses all the right buttons, and is as well-pitched and effective a series-opener as one could wish for.

2.02 – SLEEPER

Writer: James Moran
Director: Colin Teague

DEBUT TRANSMISSION DETAILS
BBC Two
Date: 23 January 2008. Scheduled time: 9.00 pm. Actual time: 9.03 pm.
BBC Three
Date: 23 January 2008. Scheduled time: 11.25 pm.
Duration: 48' 07"

Pre-watershed version
BBC Two
Date: 24 January 2008. Scheduled time: 7.00 pm.
Duration: 46' 21"

ADDITIONAL CREDITED CAST: Nikki Amuka-Bird (Beth[56]), Dyfed Potter (Mike[57]), Doug Rollins (David), Claire Cage (David's Wife), Sean Carlson (Mr Grainger[58]), Victoria Pugh (Mrs Grainger[59]), Luke Rutherford[60] (Burglar 1[61]), Alex Harries[62] (Burglar 2[63]), Dominic Coleman[64] (Police Officer), Paul Kasey (Weevil), William Hughes[65] (Boy[66]), Millie Philippart[67] (Girl), Matthew Arwel Pegram[68] (Driver), Derek Lea[69] (Paramedic)

> PLOT: Torchwood are called by the police to a flat in Cardiff where an attempted burglary has been repelled by the occupants, a young husband and wife, using seemingly unnatural strength: one of the burglars has been viciously killed and the other propelled through a window to sustain serious injuries on landing on a car roof

---

56 Surname given in dialogue as 'Halloran'.

57 Surname given on the official *Torchwood* website as 'Lyndon'.

58 First name given in dialogue as 'Patrick'.

59 First name given in an on-screen graphic on the Hub's computer as 'Emily'.

60 Not credited in *Radio Times*.

61 Name given on the official *Torchwood* website as 'Leonard Bull'.

62 Not credited in *Radio Times*.

63 Name given on the official *Torchwood* website as 'Gareth Hopkins'.

64 Not credited in *Radio Times*.

65 Not credited in *Radio Times*.

66 Name given in dialogue as 'Alex'.

67 Not credited in *Radio Times*.

68 Not credited in *Radio Times*.

69 Not credited in *Radio Times*.

five floors below. As the husband, Mike, has also been injured in the incident and needs hospital treatment, suspicion falls mainly on the wife, Beth, but she denies any knowledge of what happened. Jack is convinced that she is an alien in human form. He interrogates her and eventually subjects her to a mind probe. This reveals that, unknown even to herself, she is one of a group of alien sleeper agents left on Earth to lead normal human lives until the time is right for an invasion. Beth was prematurely activated when she was threatened by the burglars, which caused her arm to transform temporarily into a blade-like weapon. Torchwood attempt to place her in cryogenic suspension, but her implanted alien technology confounds the Hub's systems and she is able to escape. She visits her husband in the hospital, intending to say goodbye, but kills him when her alien persona temporarily reasserts itself. She is recaptured by Torchwood, but the uncovering of her true identity has by this point caused three other sleeper agents in Cardiff to activate. Two of these are killed when they carry out suicide bombings as part of a strategy to disrupt the city's emergency response capability. The remaining one then heads for a mine where, Toshiko discovers, the military are secretly storing ten nuclear weapons. Jack and Gwen follow with Beth and manage to kill him, thus thwarting his intention to set off the weapons. Torchwood then prepare for another attempt to put Beth into cryogenic storage, but she effectively commits suicide by pretending to threaten Gwen and thereby forcing the others to shoot her. The immediate danger is over, but it seems there are many other, currently dormant, sleeper agents still at large in the world …

QUOTE, UNQUOTE

- Police Officer: 'In my opinion, the husband did it. He was looking for trouble, expecting to be burgled.'
  Jack: 'Really?'
  Police Officer: 'Yeah. Look.' [Points to cricket bat on the floor.] 'No other reason I can think of for keeping sports equipment in the bedroom.'
  Jack: 'Oh, you should come round to my house for a game of hockey sometime.'

- Ianto: 'Mobiles, landlines, tin cans with bits of string, everything, absolutely everything. No phones. Phones all broken. Hello? Anyone there? No! 'Cos the phones aren't working.'

- Jack: 'Come on, have a little faith! With a dashing hero like me on the case, how can we fail?'
  Ianto: 'He is dashing. You have to give him that.'
  Owen: 'And what if they can't stop it?'
  Toshiko: 'They'll stop it.'
  Owen: 'Yeah, but if they can't?'
  Ianto: 'Then … it's all over.'
  Owen: 'Lets all have sex.'

Ianto: 'And I thought the end of the world couldn't get any worse.'

- Jack: 'Now, when are the others coming?'
  David: 'They're already here.'

DOCTOR WHO REFERENCES
- Mind probes have featured or been referred to a number of times in *Doctor Who* – perhaps most infamously in 'The Five Doctors', when a Time Lord Castellan reacts to the threat of being subjected to such a device with the deathless phrase, 'No, not the mind probe!'.

ALIEN TECH
- The mind probe is presumably an alien device.

- The Hub's cryogenic storage equipment is explicitly stated here to be of alien origin.

- Toshiko uses a device, possible alien, to generate an electromagnetic pulse and disable the transceiver in Beth's arm, and also in the process deactivate her force field. Gwen later uses the same device on the last sleeper agent, David.

CONTINUITY POINTS
- The sleeper agents have personal force fields, a nanometre thick just above the skin, that normally prevent anything from harming them. When Owen attempts to take a blood sample from Beth, the hypodermic needles snap; so too does a scalpel. Beth admits that she cannot recall ever having been ill. She gives off electromagnetic waves when under stress, causing lights to flicker and go out. When she is threatened, her true nature comes to the fore and her arm transforms into a vicious blade-like weapon. Her arm also has alien technology implanted within it, which gathers intelligence and transmits it to her home planet. The technology is capable of fooling the Hub's systems and causing false readings. Jack somehow has prior knowledge of the sleeper agents; he says, 'Official designation is Cell 114. They infiltrate planets, adapting their bodies, gathering intelligence, sometimes for years. Watching, until they're ready to take over … If we're lucky, [Beth's] the first. They send an advance guard to gather intel, given false memories so that they blend in.'

- An interesting question raised by this episode is to what degree the existence of aliens is accepted by the general public in the *Doctor Who/Torchwood* universe. Beth at one point says 'There's no such things as aliens', indicating that she at least does not believe in them (unless, of course, this is simply part of her sleeper agent programming). Back in 'Everything Changes', when Jack mentioned alien-related incidents such as the Battle of Canary Wharf, Gwen replied: 'My boyfriend says it's like a sort of terrorism. Like they put drugs in the water supplies – psychotropic drugs, causing mass hallucinations and stuff.'

Similarly, in 'The Runaway Bride', Donna Noble professes ignorance of the various recent alien incursions; she missed the Sycorax spaceship over London the previous Christmas as she had a hangover, and she failed to spot the attempted invasion by Cybermen during the summer as she was away on holiday, scuba diving in Spain. This suggests that, despite the seemingly overwhelming amount of evidence by this point that aliens have visited the Earth, there are still many people who do not accept the fact, either because they prefer to believe Government cover stories, however implausible, or because they are naturally sceptical or wilfully unobservant.

• Prior to his murder by the sleeper agent David, Patrick Grainger was leader of the Council in Cardiff and also the City Co-ordinator, responsible for taking charge in the event of major emergencies.

PRODUCTION NOTES
• Made with 'Meat' as part of Block 2 of production.

• Location recording for this episode took place between mid-June and early July 2007. The scenes in and outside Beth's flat were shot at Cymric House in Cardiff Bay on 4 July; in a subsequent report in the 25 August edition of the *Western Mail*, assistant location manager Iwan Roberts was quoted as saying, 'We needed a large apartment with high ceilings and a big bedroom for these scenes, so Cymric House was ideal.' In one of the scenes, a character falls out of the window, so the big windows facilitated this perfectly. What's more, the building looks really impressive from the outside, so it's a great backdrop.' Also on 4 July, the sequence of the ambulance paramedic activating as a sleeper agent was recorded outside the Mimosa bar and restaurant on Bute Street, while that of the young woman sleeper agent who abandons a baby in its pram was taped in Stuart Street. St Cadoc's Hospital in Lodge Road, Caerleon, Newport, was the location used for the sequences taking place at the (fictional) City Cardiff Hospital, the last of which, showing Jack, Gwen and Beth leaving the building and driving away in the SUV, was shot on 18 June. The subsequent scene of Jack communicating with the Hub by CB radio was taped on 23 June in Gabalfa Avenue. The most notable location work, however, took place on 1 July in Westgate Street, where the explosion in the (fictional) Telecommunications Switching Station & Mobile Switching Centre – in reality a disused building formerly occupied by the Inland Revenue – was recorded. A public warning about this was issued in advance by the police in view of the fact that the UK was on a heightened state of alert following a terrorist attack on Glasgow Airport the day before; this did not prevent the following day's edition of the *Sun* from printing a sensationalised account of the staged incident, under the heading 'Beeb bosses bang out of order'. Other sequences for this episode were recorded under the M4 link road bridge on Penarth Road (the fuel tanker stops and explodes); on the Imperial Park Bypass (the SUV races after the last sleeper agent); and at the disused MoD Caerwent facility in Caldicott, Monmouthshire (the scenes outside the nuclear storage base).

- The opening clips montage makes its first Series Two appearance at the beginning of this episode, having been re-edited to include some new material. Captain Jack's voiceover has also been changed. In Series One, he said: 'Torchwood. Outside the government, beyond the police. Tracking down alien life on Earth and arming the human race against the future. The 21st Century is when everything changes, and you've gotta be ready.' Now, he says: 'Torchwood. Outside the government, beyond the police. Fighting for the future on behalf of the human race. The 21st Century is when everything changes, and Torchwood is ready.'

- Beth's flat has the fictional address 114 Brodsky Gardens – could she have chosen to live there due to a subconscious recollection that she was part of the alien Cell 114?

- At one point early in the investigation, Owen calls Gwen 'Jessica Fletcher', a reference to the lead character of the US series *Murder, She Wrote*, which – including specials – ran from 1984 to 2003.

- This episode is the first to feature a new Hub corridor set, made up largely of reused elements from a sewer set originally constructed for the *Doctor Who* story 'Daleks in Manhattan'/'Evolution of the Daleks'.

- William Hughes, who plays the Graingers' son Alex in this episode, previously appeared as the young Master in a flashback sequence in the *Doctor Who* episode 'The Sound of Drums'.

- Script editor Brian Minchin felt that James Moran might be a good writer for *Torchwood* as he had seen the movie *Severance*, which Moran scripted, and admired it. Producer Richard Stokes also knew Moran, having approached him on the strength of *Severance* to discuss some potential science-fiction series ideas back before *Torchwood* was first commissioned.

- 'Sleeper' had the most severe cuts of any Series Two episode for its pre-watershed version. These included all of the stabbings, nearly all of the blood, Owen's suggestion 'Let's all have sex,' and a number of instances of coarse language, including 'Oi, fuckflap!' – an insult apparently never heard on TV before – directed by a motorist to a sleeper agent who has blocked the road with a petrol tanker, which he subsequently blows up.

- Scriptwriter James Moran has blogged quite extensively about his *Torchwood* experiences at www.jamesmoran.blogspot.com.

OOPS!

- Jack suggests that Beth's brief transformation into her true alien form when she attacked the burglars was an act of self-preservation. However, given that she has a personal force field that cannot be broken even by hypodermic needles or a scalpel, it is difficult to see what harm the burglars could have done her.

PRESS REACTION

- 'After being so jazzed by the lighter, more confident tone of last week's "Kiss Kiss, Bang Bang," I felt very frustrated with the first ten minutes or so of "Sleeper", which seemed to be backsliding to all the things I didn't like about last year: plots with minimal logic (in retrospect, Torchwood was right to look into this case, but at the time I had no idea why they were there), everyone yelling all the time, Jack reinserting the stick up his butt, etc. Who, I wondered, thought that doing a Guantanamo allegory was a good fit for this show? But then we discovered what Beth really was, and the episode began to click. When I described the basic plot of the episode in my column last week, someone said it sounded similar to [the storyline involving the character] Boomer in *Battlestar Galactica* Season One. And while there are parallels, "Sleeper" went more into the visceral horror of finding out you're not who you think you are, particularly those moments where Beth's body began operating independently from her mind. The scene in the hospital where she killed her husband without realising it sent chills down my spine, as did throwaway moments with the other sleeper agents, like the woman who let the baby carriage roll into traffic. I'm not sure I completely followed the rest of the story – Why would some of the other sleeper agents be willing to blow themselves up? How is that even possible with such a bad-ass force field? – but the episode moved quickly and there were enough moments of sheer terror to engage me as it went along. I still prefer the Jack of last week (or of *Doctor Who*), but this wasn't bad at all.' Alan Sepinwall, New Jersey *Star-Ledger*, 2 February 2008.

- 'Is it acceptable to torture aliens? Apparently so, if you're a member of Torchwood. After the burglary of a couple ends in murder, the gang whip out some nasty equipment to interrogate a woman (the superb Nikki Amuka-Bird) they suspect of being an extraterrestrial terrorist. The parallels we are supposed to draw are obvious, but it's heavy-handed and the scenes of torture sit uncomfortably with the general tongue-in-cheek tone of the series.' James Stanley, *Metro*, 23 January 2008.

- 'Never before has *Torchwood* struck such a winning blend of scares, tears and laughs. James Moran's script may use standard generic tropes like the sleeper agent, a concept recently deployed by *Battlestar Galactica*, but the execution is perfect and retains the unique identity of *Torchwood* ... The visual highlight of the episode, and possibly the series, occurs with a brilliant and terrifying montage sequence when the sleeper agents are activated around Cardiff. It echoes the iconic imagery of classic *Doctor Who*, when the monsters emerged from the sea, sewers or spacecraft to begin their invasion. Of particular note is a clever and horrifying twist on the famous Odessa Steps sequence from *Battleship Potemkin*, as the agent's pram rolls out of sight into a busy road with the horrifying consequences left for our imagination. The gore throughout the episode befits the show's post-watershed timeslot and contains classic body horror elements that David Cronenberg would be proud of.' Ben Rawson-Jones, Digital Spy website, 23 January 2008.

- 'Last year, *Torchwood* got away with some clumsy dramatic artifice by virtue of its energy and the fact it was a new show. This year, they'll have no such fall-back position, so it's rather disappointing to see so much good work on display in "Sleeper" – many moral questions and a genuine debate on prisoners' rights – being reduced in impact by a confused and rushed bloodbath of an ending … [The] character faults and occasional outré moments (the blood-splattered wife seemed particularly unnecessary) however don't equate to a failure of imagination. Just to a bit of taste.' Keith Topping, *TV Zone* Issue 225, February 2008.

FAN COMMENT

- 'After last week's semi-comic run-around, we're firmly in thriller mode. That's fair enough, but such a situation must be sufficiently solidly constructed to provide genuine tension. If you put your weight against any part of "Sleeper", it wobbles. Too often, the viewer is left trying to figure out aspects of the plot, instead of being immediately aware of the action. An established trait of the sleeper cell is that they have personal force fields, which protect them from physical harm. Yet half their number die off-camera as a result of explosions that they themselves have caused. Jack's exposition on the species does not mention any kamikaze strategy, so the viewer naturally assumes that all the sleepers are still proceeding with their plan, until their deaths are casually mentioned. By not taking the time to define the limits of the enemy, the writer forces the audience to spend their time slowly reasoning out what is obviously a very flexible set of rules. Instead of cheering Jack as he runs a sleeper agent over in the Mystery Machine, their thoughts are drawn to the amount of kinetic energy needed to damage the invaders. The most serious instance of this problem serves to seriously undermine the finale, as a bullet-proof alien is shot dead. There isn't actually a plot hole here – Beth had not actually succumbed to her true [alien] personality, and so would not have tried to reactivate her implant's force field. However, the effort that it takes to figure this out is enough to draw the audience away from the moment, making the conclusion a logic puzzle rather than a moving sacrifice. The trick with sci-fi plotting is to give just enough solid facts for events to superficially make sense. Here, there are just enough to confuse.' Julian Hazeldine, Noise to Signal website, 29 January 2008.

- 'Beth was an excellent character and well played. I was half expecting her ending and half not – at the start I thought she'd die by the end, but then I wondered if maybe they would freeze her and bring her back in a later episode … As for Gwen – hurrah! Finally she's the character her blurb says she's supposed to be. She's the heart of the operation and the human face. Her sympathetic and kind approach to Beth worked much better than Jack's ranting. Speaking of which, he was an utter bastard for most of the episode, and that felt a little out of sorts to me. Yes, I understand he's an ex-soldier and he's used to doing harsh things to get the job done, but I really didn't like his attitude at all. His shouting and bullying method of interrogation achieved nothing with a woman who was obviously terrified, his "I'm sorry" held no sympathy at all and I didn't like his smug look when he was proved right about her being an alien. They honestly made the usually overwhelmingly likeable Jack a bit of a wanker for most of the episode and that didn't sit well with me. I can understand him being very concerned but I can't see him showing no empathy at all for the woman – it only served to make him look less human than her. Especially when she used her alien powers not to do something nasty but to go and say goodbye to her husband (the tragedy of which I didn't see coming and was very well played).' 'doylefan22', LiveJournal blog, 24 January 2008.

* 'Colin Teague made some interesting directing choices, some of which I really appreciated, some of which seemed a little too much like he was confused and thought he was directing an episode of *Homicide: Life on the Streets*. [But], hey, you could over-emulate a lousier show, that's for sure, so at least he stuck with a good one. One of the things that I did like was the reflection motif. In Beth's flat, we see Jack's reflection in the mirror while he's talking to the cop; in [the Hub,] we see Jack's reflection in the [two way mirror in] Beth's cell while she's reacting badly to the news that she's a sleeper agent; ... then [we see] the exploded alien reflected in the SUV's side mirror after the confrontation. This whole episode is about putting a human face on the alien threat that Torchwood is tasked with eliminating. But we know that Jack himself is not quite human, not anymore – so does that make him an alien? What does this mean in terms of who Torchwood can let live/must kill? How dangerous is Jack himself?

Gwen: 'What makes us human? Is it our minds or our bodies?'

And the camera lingers on Jack. If it's our bodies, then Jack may be in some trouble. He's thought about this, too, and he's worried.' 'fodian', LiveJournal blog, 24 January 2008.

ANALYSIS: After the more rollicking approach ushered in for Series Two by 'Kiss Kiss, Bang Bang' – aptly described by the BBC Two continuity announcer on its initial transmission as 'punchier, pacier, funnier' – 'Sleeper' feels almost like a throwback to Series One. The opening scenes recall those of 'They Keep Killing Suzie', with the Torchwood team being brought in by the police to help out in the investigation of a bloody murder scene. From there on in, it's all pretty grim stuff, the only real humour coming in the form of some more of Ianto's now-characteristic dry interjections, brilliantly delivered by Gareth David-Lloyd. This is by no means a bad thing, just a rather surprising one, and gives the first indication that Series Two is not going to be quite as different in tone from Series One as might perhaps have been anticipated.

The high-level plot involving the alien sleeper cell, left in place to be triggered when the time is right for an invasion to be launched, is epic in scale, and the viewer gets a real sense of this toward the end of the episode when several of the sleeper agents become active and start to wreak havoc in and around Cardiff, causing much death and destruction – perhaps most memorably when one of them abandons a baby in its pram, which rolls into the road and is heard to be struck by a car, and then sets off a huge explosion in the city's telecommunications centre. These sequences are superbly realised by director Colin Teague and his team, and chillingly evoke the images of carnage and confusion associated with real-life suicide bombings and other terrorist incidents.

This highly topical concern of the threat of terrorism, and how to respond to it, is a key theme of James Moran's impressive debut TV script. Jack's forceful questioning of the terrified Beth, and later his unrelenting use of the mind probe on her, inevitably bring to mind the controversial interrogation techniques used by the US military to extract information from terrorist suspects at Guantanamo Bay. This is certainly not the cheeky, wisecracking Jack of 'Kiss Kiss, Bang Bang'; and, notwithstanding some comments from Ianto suggesting that the severity of his initial grilling of Beth is really just part of a 'bad cop, good cop' routine with Gwen, his willingness to resort to such harsh methods uneasily recalls his assertion in 'Countrycide' that he was once the 'go-to guy' for torture. More surprising still is that his insistence on proceeding with the use of the mind probe, even when it is clearly causing Beth extreme pain, encounters very little resistance from the other members of the team. Even Gwen, who was originally recruited to be the caring heart of Torchwood, goes along with Jack's uncompromising actions with scarcely a word of objection. Of course, Jack is ultimately proved correct in his suspicions when the mind probe breaks through Beth's conditioning and reveals her to be one of the alien sleeper agents. But does Moran really intend this to be an 'end justifies the means' endorsement of Guantanamo Bay-style methods? If so, it would be an unusually right-wing message for a show like *Torchwood* to promote. One ameliorating factor is that at least Beth is not forced kicking and screaming into the mind probe – which has a macabre resemblance to an electric chair, the effects of which are tastelessly mimicked by Ianto at one point – but appears, initially at least, to acquiesce to the use of the device, if only because she herself is now desperate to uncover the truth. Nevertheless, this whole sequence makes for very uncomfortable viewing.

The bayonet-like weapon into which Beth's arm transforms, after peeling open to reveal alien technology beneath its surface in a very effective invocation of body horror, recalls the metal arm-spike extruded by the T-1000 robot in *Terminator 2: Judgment Day* – the *Terminator* franchise having been acknowledged by Moran as a subconscious influence – and was originally intended to emerge from between the knuckles in the manner of that used by comic-book superhero Wolverine in Marvel's *The X-Men*. Conceptually, however, probably the closest parallel to Beth and the other sleeper agents is to be found in Ridley Scott's movie *Blade Runner*, based on Philip K Dick's novel *Do Androids Dream of Electric Sheep?*, in which the characters Deckard and Rachel appear to all intents and purposes human but are actually, unknown even to themselves, android replicants. There are also echoes here of Richard Condon's 1959 spy novel *The Manchurian Candidate* and its film versions, of another Philip K Dick movie adaptation in Paul Verhoeven's *Total Recall*, and even of the Series Three *Doctor Who* story 'Human Nature'/'The Family of Blood' with its storyline about a man called John Smith losing his human identity as his true Time Lord persona is revealed; and Season One of the US series *Battlestar Galactica* from 2005 features an arc in which the apparently human Sharon 'Boomer' Valerii gradually comes to realise that she is actually a Cylon. It is this fascinating idea, that the sleeper agents are unaware of their own true nature and have hitherto been leading normal human lives, that is really the key to the drama in 'Sleeper' and the source of much of its impact. The epic high-level story is given a smaller-scale, more personal dimension in Beth and the devastating impact it has on her.

For this to succeed, it was crucial that the actress cast in the role of Beth should give a good performance, and thankfully Nikki Amuka-Bird rises to the challenge admirably, delivering a compelling portrayal of a woman who is literally losing her mind while also struggling to come to terms with the horrific murders she has unwittingly committed – not least that of her own husband, in a truly shocking scene at the hospital. So while, stylistically, the episode has all the trappings of a *Spooks*-style thriller, with its bloody killings, harsh interrogations, terrorist-style explosions and secretly-stored nuclear weapons, it also has a more intense, emotional aspect, which is where the real heart of the story lies. Again this recalls 'They Keep Killing Suzie', and seems to be a particularly effective template for *Torchwood* to follow.

The other stand-out performance by a guest actor in this episode comes from Doug Rollins as David, the sleeper agent who breaks his wife's neck, then murders Patrick Grainger – splattering Grainger's wife and children with blood in the process, in another memorably gory sequence – and finally heads for the disused mine with the aim of setting off the ten nuclear weapons stored there. Despite having relatively little dialogue, Rollins does a great job of portraying David's transformation from human to alien, and presents a really terrifying figure as he bears down remorselessly on the soldiers at the military base and massacres them with his arm-weapon, all with a fearsome expression of alien evil on his face. David's final warning to Jack that the others of his kind are already present on Earth is also absolutely chilling, and sets things up nicely for a possible sequel at some future date.

As far as the regulars are concerned, it is arguably Gwen who gets the best share of the material this time around. Just as in 'They Keep Killing Suzie' she was paired for much of the action with Suzie, here she is paired with Beth; and it is in the way that she responds to the woman's tragic situation that her empathic nature does ultimately come to the fore. The rapport that grows between the two women, as Gwen does all she can in the circumstances to comfort and reassure Beth, is one of the most affecting aspects of the whole episode. Eve Myles gives, as always, a terrific performance here, skilfully conveying the conflict that Gwen feels between on the one hand her sympathy for Beth and on the other hand her recognition that the woman poses a real threat that has to be contained by Torchwood.

While on the subject of Gwen, a tantalising clue as to just how far her relationship with Jack has gone comes with the following exchange of dialogue, as Beth is about to be subjected to the mind probe:

Beth: 'Will it hurt?'
Jack: 'Yeah.'
Beth: 'Your bedside manner's rubbish.'
Gwen: 'You should see his manners in bed. They're atrocious. Apparently. So I've heard.'
Ianto: 'Oh they are. I remember this one …'
Jack: 'Ahem!'

The obvious implication of this seems to be that not only has Ianto slept with Jack, which comes as no surprise, but so too has Gwen, which is far more of a revelation – to the viewer at least, if

133

not to the other members of the team, who show no visible reaction, even though they surely cannot be taken in by her lame attempt to pass off as hearsay her knowledge of how he behaves in bed. Again this presents intriguing possibilities for potential future exploration – and if nothing else adds further grist to the mill for the fan-fiction writers.

If Moran's script has a shortcoming it is that it sometimes leaves room for confusion over the sleeper agents' attributes, capabilities and, particularly, degree of invulnerability. When, for instance, it is revealed that Beth's alien implants have fooled the Hub's computers into giving false readings, it is initially unclear whether this applies just to the readings suggesting that she was frozen when in fact she was not, or whether it extends also to the readings indicating that her transceiver and force field have been deactivated. (As things turn out, it appears that the former is the case.) Some fans have even suggested, a little cynically perhaps, that this is the second episode running in which it would seem, from the information provided, that a major problem could be solved simply by Torchwood cutting off a character's arm – in this case Beth's, as that is where all her alien implants and weapons are sited. But this is a bit like that hoary old joke about being able to defeat the Daleks by putting a flight of stairs in their way; the viewer has to take it as read that it can't really be as simple as that, even if there is nothing in the programme to prove otherwise.

In terms of production values, 'Sleeper' is virtually faultless. There are a few shots in which the sleeper agents' prosthetic arm attachments look decidedly false, but that is a minor quibble. Overall, the quality of the direction, design and effects work is well up to that of the script, making for an excellent overall package. The strong start to Series Two continues.

2.03 – TO THE LAST MAN

Writer: Helen Raynor
Director: Andy Goddard

DEBUT TRANSMISSION DETAILS
BBC Two
Date: 30 January 2008. Scheduled time: 9.00 pm. Actual time: 9.00 pm.
BBC Three
Date: 30 January 2008. Scheduled time: 11.00 pm.
Duration: 50' 28"

Pre-watershed version
BBC Two
Date: 31 January 2008. Scheduled time: 7.00 pm.
Duration: 50' 26"

ADDITIONAL CREDITED CAST
Anthony Lewis (Tommy[70]), Roderic Culver (Gerald), Siobhân Hewlett (Harriet[71]), Lizzie Rogan (Nurse), Ricky Fearon (Foreman)

PLOT: A young First World War soldier, Tommy Brockless, has been kept in cryogenic suspension in the Hub since 1918, when he was taken by Torchwood from his bed at St Teilo's Military Hospital after a fracture in the rift briefly caused that era and some future one to erupt into each other. Torchwood know that one day Tommy will have a part to play in sealing the fracture and thus averting disaster, but they are not sure when or how. Tommy is woken on one day each year for a medical check-up, and Toshiko has become friendly with him. On the occasion of his 2008 revival, ghostly apparitions start to appear at the now-deserted Hospital, and Torchwood realise that this is when the rift fracture occurs, triggered by the building's imminent demolition. A box containing sealed orders from the Torchwood of 1918 automatically opens, and Jack learns that Tommy has to go back in time and resume his place at the hospital, taking with him a rift key with which to seal the fracture – despite the fact that he will suffer a recurrence of the shellshock for which he was originally being treated, and will be shot by a firing squad three weeks later for supposed cowardice. Despite the heartache it causes her, Toshiko persuades Tommy to go back to 1918 and fulfil his heroic destiny.

---

70 Full name given in dialogue as 'Thomas Reginald Brockless'.

71 Surname given in dialogue as 'Derbyshire'.

QUOTE, UNQUOTE

- Toshiko: 'Iraq.'
  Tommy: 'Seems like there's always a war somewhere.'
  Toshiko: 'It's not exactly a war.'
  Tommy: 'Looks like one. The first year they woke me up, 1919, they told me it was all over. We won. "The war to end all wars," they said. Then three weeks later you had the Second World War. After all that. Do you ever wonder if we're worth saving, the human race?'

- Toshiko: 'So, what do you want to do now?'
  Tommy: 'Well, we could go back to mine, but there's only room for one and its bloody freezing.'
  Toshiko: 'You want to come back to my place?'
  Tommy: 'I'm hardly rushing you. You've known me four years.'
  Toshiko: 'Four days.'

- Tommy: 'Why me? You're no better than the generals. Sitting safely behind the lines, sending us over the top. Any one of you lot could go, but you're not, are you? You're sending me.'
  Jack: 'You belong here.'
  Toshiko: 'I'm sorry.'
  Tommy: 'I have been shoved from pillar to post all my life, by the Army, by Torchwood.'
  Jack: 'Hey, hey!'
  Tommy: 'All this time I've had, it means nothing.'

DOCTOR WHO REFERENCES

- Tommy's comment 'So I'll be saving the world in some pyjamas' recalls the Doctor doing just that in 'The Christmas Invasion'.

- Harriet Derbyshire's name recalls that of Delia Derbyshire, one of the pioneering founders of the BBC's Radiophonic Workshop, who realised the distinctive *Doctor Who* theme music in 1963.

ALIEN TECH

- The Torchwood of 1918 have a portable device for detecting rift activity.

- Toshiko says 'Torchwood have used alien cryogenics since Victorian times,' confirming suggestions to this effect in earlier episodes.

- Owen and Toshiko attach a series of circular rift monitor devices to the walls of the Hospital ward. These emit a repeated beeping noise when the time shift becomes active.

- It is unclear where the rift manipulator key comes from. It looks antique in design and may have been already held by Torchwood in 1918, and subsequently recovered by them from Tommy after he used it to seal the rift fracture. However this suggestion opens up the possibility that it is itself a paradox.

- Torchwood have a helmet-like device that enables a psychic projection of the wearer to be sent into the mind of another person if injected with a sample of that person's blood and if that person's precise location in time is known.

CONTINUITY POINTS
- In 1918, Torchwood Three was led by a man named Gerald. One of his agents was a woman named Harriet Derbyshire.

- Tommy says that he was born on 7 February 1894 in Blackley, Manchester, and was a private officer in the 10th West Yorkshire Regiment. He was the only son of Constance May Bassett, who died in 1900, and Thomas Campbell Brockless, who died in June 1931, aged 57, of a heart attack.

- The last time Tommy was revived, Toshiko told him that she intended to learn to play the piano and to speak Spanish. She has done neither of these things in the year since then, having typically been too wrapped up in her work, although she has bought a Spanish book – prompting Tommy to comment, 'Oh aye? You made of money?', reflecting the fact that books were still regarded as luxury items in 1918.

- Toshiko has obviously moved to a different, larger, flat since Series One.

PRODUCTION NOTES
- Made with 'Adam' as part of Block 1 of production. This was at one point intended to be the fourth episode on transmission.

- One of this story's working titles was 'Soldier's Heart' – an American Civil War term for shellshock. The final title alludes to a famous First World War order given by Field Marshal Douglas Haig on 11 April 1918 that included the words: 'Every position must be held to the last man: there must be no retirement.' It was this policy – also mentioned by Harriet Derbyshire in the opening scene – that led to shellshocked servicemen being sent back to the front after just a short period of recuperation.

- Early drafts of the script had Tommy asking after Suzie Costello, who would have been present the last time he was defrosted.

- The closing titles include the credit: 'Thanks to the British Red Cross for Permission to Use the Red Cross Emblem.'

- The scenes of Toshiko and Tommy on Penarth Pier were recorded, in between heavy rainfalls, on 9 May 2007. This was the first significant location work done for Series Two. Also recorded this day were the sequences in Toshiko's flat, at a house in Palace Road, Cardiff. The shots of Toshiko and Tommy in Harbour Drive by Cardiff Bay, and of Toshiko and Owen looking out over the Bay in the final scene, were captured the following day. Cardiff Royal Infirmary was the location for the scenes set in the fictional St Teilo's Military Hospital, which were taped between 12 and 18 May. The pub where Toshiko and Tommy play pool was The Eli Jenkins on Bute Street.

- Helen Raynor staked her claim to do an episode centred around Toshiko at the very first Series Two script meeting. A big inspiration for the story was a short fictional document written by James Goss for the Torchwood Institute System Interface website created by bbc.co.uk for Series One of *Torchwood*. Goss recalled the circumstances in a 29 January 2008 posting on his blog, Skip's Acorn Treasury: 'Just over a year ago, I was one of the writers on the BBC's fictional *Torchwood* website (along with TV's Helen Raynor and TV's Joseph Lidster), coming up with silly fictional things from Torchwood's history. One of these stories was about how Torchwood kept a man frozen in the cellar. They'd defrost him once a year, give him a day out, and then pop him back in the freezer. No-one knew why he was there, they were just waiting for his time to come. The script editor of the site was Helen Raynor, who said rather kindly, "That's a good idea, you should do something with that." A few months later, we're sat in my flat … Helen is casting around for ideas for her next *Torchwood*. I pipe up about the man in the freezer. Helen says something terribly polite, and that she'd like to look into it as an option, if I wouldn't mind … A few days later I get a curiously legal e-mail from a script editor on *Torchwood* asking about contracts, rights and contributors on the *Torchwood* website. I reply formally, adding at the bottom, "If this means what I think it does, then yes I did, yes you own it, and I'm delighted."' Another of Raynor's inspirations for the story was her interest in the issue of World War One soldiers who were executed for cowardice when they were suffering from what would now be recognised as shellshock.

- The music playing in the scene where Toshiko gets ready to go to work at the beginning of the episode, and again in the scene where she walks away at the end, is 'One of These Mornings' by Moby, featuring the vocals of Patti Labelle, from his 2002 album *18*. The track heard in the bar where Toshiko and Tommy have a drink and play pool is 'She's Got You High' by Mumm-Ra, a single taken from their 2007 debut album *These Things Move in Threes*. Also heard is 'Squares' by the Beta Band from the 2001 album *Hot Shots II*.

- The pre-watershed version of this episode had only minimal cuts – fewer than any other.

OOPS!

- There is a continuity error in the scene where Toshiko and Tommy playfully tussle on the pier: Toshiko is seen to drop her shoulder-bag twice.

- Tommy pronounces the name of his home town Blackley as 'Black-lee', whereas it should be pronounced 'Blake-lee'.

PRESS REACTION

- 'Don't be put off by our saying this, but we've got a bit of a filler episode here. You know, the kind of stand-alone story that could basically have been shoehorned in almost anywhere in this series or the last? Characters don't change a jot and any big, series-wide storylines don't get touched on. It's a filler. But that's far from a bad thing when the filler in question is quite this smart and neatly scripted. This is a pocket love story, something sweet and fleeting … It's also a moment in the spotlight for the team's underused techno geek Toshiko … It's a spot-on episode, played with fine understatement by both [Naoko] Mori and [Anthony] Lewis. It's good to see the former getting some chunkier material to use, but it's the latter's shellshocked man out of time who truly gives the science fiction story a heart.' Ceri Thomas, *London Lite*, 30 January 2008.

- 'Captain Jack Harkness – who should never, ever be confused with the 1928 Wembley Wizard and subsequent *Sunday Post* football columnist of the same name – swanks around like a big lump. In addition, Toshiko falls for a handsome British soldier, Tommy, trapped out of his time; a chap who unwittingly holds the key to saving the entire world. Within an old hospital haunted by ghosts from 1918, a crisis foreseen by Torchwood 90 years ago is about to reach its climax. Modern Cardiff may be consumed by a violent and hellish vortex, causing literally almost a pound's worth of damage!' David Belcher, the *Herald*, 30 January 2008.

- 'There were some nice little touches, such as the ghosts that the nursing staff had seen turning out to be Gwen and Jack – two times bashing into each other, you see – and the fact that every time Tommy wakes up there seems to be another war on. But it just wasn't quite enough to satisfy – the emotional heart of the story didn't hit home nearly as hard as it could and should have done.' Anna Waits, *TV Scoop* website, 31 January 2008.

- 'Sometimes the final shot can stay with you forever. Think about the moving final image of Francois Truffaut's *Les 400 Coups* or Harrison Ford's ambiguous expression at the end of *Blade Runner: The Director's Cut*. [The episode's] closing tracking shot of Toshiko, as she walks away from Owen, is another example of a resoundingly triumphant ending that conveys so much via the simple image. Toshiko's face, in this short sequence, bears all the emotions of the episode as her countenance flits from a smile about the happy moments she shared with thawed soldier Tommy, sadness and regret at sending him back to his death, uncertainty about her own future – all underlined with a sense of her blossoming as a woman. It is poignant [and] touching and actress Naoko Mori and writer Helen Raynor deserve a great deal of credit for reaching such dramatic heights.' Ben Rawson-Jones, Digital Spy website, 30 January 2008.

FAN COMMENT

- 'The anti-war message was handled just perfectly. Jack's own experiences weren't glossed over and the horror he still feels over the firing squads was balanced perfectly with the realisation that he had to send Tommy back to face that. Once again, we see Jack making the difficult decisions here, but unlike in the first season, the team have grown up enough to recognise that these decisions are necessary. I loved the scene in the bar and the comparisons drawn between the war in Iraq and the other wars that have taken place over the last century. Tommy's question of whether or not we're worth it was a nice nod back to Tosh and the disillusionment she had with the world at the end of "Greeks Bearing Gifts". And on the subject of continuity, both Owen and Ianto were handled excellently here. Owen with his advice to Tosh coming from his own experiences with Diane. Ianto speaking of the death of Harriet, who was the same age as Lisa when she died.' 'marvola', LiveJournal blog, 31 January 2008.

- 'It was a beautiful character study of Tosh, who up until now has been without a doubt the most overlooked and under-characterised of the Torchwood team. It was hard not to fall in love with Tosh in this episode. She's so lonely that she looks forward to the day that Tommy gets defrosted to the extent that she excitedly rings the day on her calendar and wants to look her foxiest for him. As Tommy pointed out, she wasn't conscripted into Torchwood but she has allowed it to consume her to the extent that all she is is her work. She makes plans she'll never follow through and buys books she knows she'll never read. Torchwood is her home and her prison and she's let herself get into a comfy rut ... And then along comes Tommy – who knows who she is and what she does and is probably the only person in Tosh's life ever to call her a "daft lass". No wonder she falls so hard for him. My heart just melted when she confessed that she had been worried that he was going to see her growing old. But as with all great love stories, it can never go anywhere and ultimately Toshiko has to become like the generals Tommy despises and send him off to his death. And even though it kills her to do it – she still does it. Tosh never suggests that actually they could run away together, never once tells Tommy that no he doesn't have to go back to 1918. Because she's forced during the course of the episode to grow up and she knows what's truly at stake – it's an interesting comparison to Gwen who was quite willing to rip the world to shreds and fuck the consequences when Rhys died [in "End of Days"].' 'fairyd123', LiveJournal blog, 31 January 2008.

ANALYSIS: In 'To the Last Man', writer Helen Raynor has returned to the ghost story theme of her earlier script 'Ghost Machine' and cleverly combined it with one of the key elements of another highly-regarded Series One episode, Catherine Tregenna's 'Captain Jack Harkness' – specifically, the element of a timeslip leading to a doomed love affair between a member of the Torchwood team and a serviceman from a past war who is destined to die. The atmosphere of Tregenna's episode, with its ghostly manifestations in a disused dance hall, is also neatly recaptured here, as Torchwood investigate a spate of similar apparitions in an abandoned hospital. There are, though, sufficient differences between the two episodes to save this from being simply a rehash of a tried-and-trusted formula.

The episode opens superbly with a sequence set in 1918, in which we see for the first time two Torchwood agents of a bygone era. These are Gerald and Harriet, excellently portrayed, by Roderic Culver and Siobhàn Hewlett respectively, with the just the sort of upright manner and cut-glass diction one would expect from people holding such positions of authority at that time – although, when Gerald says to the hospital nurse 'Well, you're a very brave girl' and Harriet clears her throat reprovingly, there is a pleasing hint that this earlier Torchwood leader shares a little of his 21st Century counterpart's inclination to flirt! The dramatic ending to this 1918 sequence, as Tommy – also played very well throughout by Anthony Lewis – asks 'Who are you?' and Gerald replies 'We're Torchwood', whets the appetite perfectly for events to come.

The idea of Torchwood reviving Tommy once a year for a medical and a day out, then refreezing him in the Hub until such time as he is needed, provides an excellent basis for the story; and it was a shrewd move on Raynor's part to appropriate this from a short piece originally written by James Goss for the fictional *Torchwood* website created for Series One. It is only in the way the idea is developed that, unfortunately, things go a little awry. The fundamental premise – that Torchwood have kept Tommy in cold storage for 90 years so that when the foreseen rift fracture occurs he can slip back to 1918 and thereby, with the aid of a rift key, stitch time together again – is sound enough, and must have taken a good deal of thought to work out. It is all the more frustrating, then, that the ingenuity shown here is not matched in other aspects of the plotting. For one thing, the viewer is expected to swallow the completely unbelievable coincidence that Tommy's date with destiny just happens to come on exactly the same day as he is defrosted for his latest annual check-up. Then there is the absurd implication that he has been cured of his shellshock by being frozen in the Hub but immediately succumbs to it again – and at the same time conveniently loses all his memories of Torchwood – on his return to 1918; an aspect of the story that could perhaps have been better explained by reference to post-traumatic stress disorder. Equally contrived is the notion of sealed instructions having been left by Gerald in an old tin box with a temporal lock primed to open at precisely the right time, which raises all sorts of awkward questions, such as why the instructions needed to sealed rather than simply placed on the incident file for future reference, why Jack does not already know what happened in 1918 given that his association with Torchwood pre-dates that, and how Gerald and his colleagues came to have the ability to create the temporal lock – which, despite its scientific-sounding name, is really just a sort of magical device that would not look out of place in a Harry Potter movie. Worst of all is the sequence toward the end where Toshiko is injected with a sample of Tommy's blood so that she can have a telepathic conversation with him in 1918 and remind him that he needs to turn the rift key. Not only is this completely nonsensical but it also involves Owen coming up with a last-minute solution involving an injection of blood for the second time in the space of three episodes. Moreover, it is totally unnecessary, as the fact that the rift is splintering offers all the justification that is needed for Toshiko to be able to communicate with Tommy as one of the ghostly apparitions established earlier on, which would have made for a far neater resolution to the story.

On the evidence of this, and of her contributions to *Doctor Who*, it would seem that Raynor is a writer who is not particularly adept at story construction and consequently has a tendency to resort to implausible contrivances to try to make her plots hang together. Where 'To the Last Man' is concerned, though, this is much less of a problem than would normally be the case, as the real appeal of this episode lies not so much in the details of its plot as in its emotional story of the relationship between Toshiko and Tommy, and of the impact this has on the other members of the Torchwood team

The annual revival of Tommy sets up an intriguing difference of perspective between him and Toshiko in terms of how they view their burgeoning romance. Whereas for him it has been only four days since they first met, for her it has been four years. The fact that she still reacts very awkwardly when he takes the initiative and kisses her – despite obviously finding him desirable and having even made a special effort to dress attractively for him (although unfortunately the smock-like purple dress she has chosen to wear over her trousers is a bit of a fashion disaster) – speaks volumes about the difficulties she continues to have with relationships, after her disastrous liaison with the alien infiltrator Mary in 'Greeks Bearing Gifts' and her pining for Owen throughout Series One. Even Tommy is moved to observe, 'I'm hardly rushing you'. One can only wonder how many more years it would have taken her to pluck up the courage to make the first move, had he not beaten her to it. As the events of the story unfold, however, and she learns that Tommy has to return to 1918 and almost certainly face death before a firing squad, she really comes into her own, taking the young soldier back to her flat for what will be their first and last night of passion together. It also says a lot for her that, when it comes to it, she does not flinch from doing her duty for Torchwood, convincing Tommy that he must go back to his own time despite the terrible consequences of this for him and the heartbreak for her. This recalls how Gwen refused to allow her friendship with Beth to deflect her from taking the right course of action in 'Sleeper' and further illustrates the greater spirit of unity and responsibility within the Torchwood team in Series Two, in marked contrast to the litany of dissent, recrimination and betrayal seen in Series One. Having said that, it is difficult to see what real choice Toshiko had, as time would have been thrown into chaos had Tommy not gone back and fulfilled the purpose for which he was frozen in the first place.

The mellowing of Owen continues with a very nice scene in which he tells Toshiko that he is concerned about the possibility of her getting hurt if she has to say goodbye to Tommy – surely an oblique reference to the hurt that he himself suffered when he lost Diane in 'Out of Time' – while the ongoing development of the relationship between Jack and Ianto is highlighted as the viewer for the first time sees them share a truly passionate kiss, initiated by Ianto after Jack says: 'Being here, I've seen things I never dreamt I'd see, loved people I never would have known if I'd just stayed where I was, and I wouldn't change that for the world.' Jack is again shown having to take a tough stance in this episode, insisting that Tommy has no option but to go back to 1918 and complete the task that has been set for him; but he nevertheless comes across rather more sympathetically here than in 'Sleeper', as a strong leader who is not unmoved by Tommy's plight but is obliged to act for the greater good.

Another stand-out aspect of the episode is Andy Goddard's typically taut direction, no better demonstration of which is to be found than in the wonderfully spooky scenes in the deserted hospital. Particularly effective are the sequences in which Gwen investigates the building on her own, encountering at various times the ghostly apparition of a one-legged, pyjama-clad patient who advances on her on his crutches, a present-day team of demolition men – the sudden appearance of whom gives the viewer a real start of surprise – and a 1918 nurse who, it transpires, actually sees *her* as a ghost and indignantly shouts at her that she shouldn't be there. This is spine-chilling stuff, and really succeeds in giving these parts of the episode an authentic ghost story atmosphere. Also worthy of note is the fact that Goddard uses hardly any CGI work on this episode, almost all of the visual effects being achieved in-camera using more conventional techniques, again contributing to the traditional ghost story feel.

Things come full circle as the episode approaches its dramatic conclusion and the viewer is given effectively a rerun of part of the opening sequence with Gerald and Harriet from Torchwood 1918, this time from a different perspective, now knowing exactly why they are taking Tommy from his hospital bed and what is to become of him. There is a fantastic shot here as, on ushering Tommy out of the ward, Gerald glances back over his shoulder and sees the same man – either 90 days older or 90 years older depending on how one looks at it – coming in with the rift key to resume his place in the bed. It is presumably at this moment that Gerald realises what needs to be done, so sealing Tommy's fate.

Once Toshiko has had her implausible psychic conversation with Tommy and convinced him to turn the key, setting time to rights, the episode plays out with a poignant closing sequence in which she packs his things away in the Hub, acknowledges Jack's thanks and is then joined by Owen as she looks out over the expanse of Cardiff Bay, reflecting that all this still exits only because of Tommy's bravery. The final shot of her walking away, a tumult of conflicting emotions playing across her face, is absolutely heart-rending, and a further testament to the superb acting skills of Naoko Mori.

But this is not just a spooky ghost story-cum-tragic romance; it also has a more serious intent in drawing attention to the terrible injustice done to those shellshocked British servicemen of the First World War who were branded cowards and sent before a firing squad – an issue about which Raynor clearly has strong feelings. There has been a certain amount of debate over the true scale of this calumny – Captain Jack implies that more than 300 shellshock sufferers were shot, whereas it seems that this was actually the total number of British and Commonwealth servicemen executed for all crimes, only a proportion of which would have been shellshock-related – but quibbling over the precise numbers really misses the point. The irrefutable fact remains that many shellshocked servicemen did suffer this fate during the First World War, and Raynor is to be applauded for highlighting what can only be considered a shameful episode in British military history – as was recognised in 2006 when the government issued posthumous pardons to all concerned in response to a campaign headed by the Shot at Dawn group, which Raynor is reported to support.

All told, despite the shortcomings in its plotting, 'To the Last Man' is an episode that really plays to *Torchwood*'s strengths, combining entertaining science fiction concepts with affecting character drama and an important point to make about a weighty real-life issue.

2.04 – MEAT

Writer: Catherine Tregenna
Director: Colin Teague

DEBUT TRANSMISSION DETAILS
BBC Two
Date: 6 February 2008. Scheduled time: 9.00 pm. Actual time: 9.00 pm.
BBC Three
Date: 6 February 2008. Scheduled time: 11.00 pm.
Duration: 50' 15"

Pre-watershed version
BBC Two
Date: 7 February 2008. Scheduled time: 7.00 pm.
Duration: 49' 33"

ADDITIONAL CREDITED CAST
Colin Baxter (Policeman), Patti Clare (Ruth), Garry Lake (Vic), Gerard Carey (Greg[72]), Matt Ryan (Dale[73])

PLOT: A Harwood's Haulage lorry crashes and the police call in Torchwood to investigate its mysterious load, which turns out to be a consignment of alien meat. The meat is being cut from the hide of a huge 'space whale' creature, kept chained up by a gang of small-time crooks in a warehouse, and transported in Harwood's lorries to an abattoir, from where it finds its way into food for human consumption. Rhys, the manager of Harwood's in Cardiff, initially comes under suspicion from Torchwood, but it turns out that he was unaware of the illicit scheme. Gwen finally admits to Rhys what she does for a living, and he then helps Torchwood to gain access to the gang's warehouse. The villains are eventually overpowered and retconned, but Owen is forced to give the 'space whale' a lethal injection of drugs after it breaks free of its chains. Jack reluctantly agrees to Gwen's demand that Rhys should be allowed to keep his memories of what has happened.

QUOTE, UNQUOTE
- Ianto: 'Pizza's arrived. Presumably it will be a late one.'
  Owen: 'What did you get me?'
  Ianto: 'Usual: meat feast.'

---

72 Surname probably 'Harris', as the firm responsible for the alien meat scam is stated in dialogue to be called 'Harris and Harris', and Greg and Dale are also said to be brothers.

73 See previous footnote.

Owen: 'Lovely.'

- Gwen: 'Have you ever eaten alien meat?'
  Jack: 'Yeah.'
  Gwen: 'What was it like?'
  Jack: 'He seemed to enjoy it.'

- Gwen: 'He is not driving us in.'
  Rhys: 'They're expecting me. You lot can hide in the back of the van.'
  Gwen: 'What is this, *Scooby-Doo*? Absolutely no way is he getting involved!'

- Toshiko: 'So, after we stun-gun the workers, we put the creature out of its misery.'
  Jack: 'No. We're gonna save it. Stabilise it, wait for the rift to open, and send it back.'
  Ianto: 'I guess we'll have to look after it in the meantime.'
  Toshiko: 'Tell me exactly how we're going to use it to arm ourselves against the future?'
  Owen: 'We could always hide behind it.'

- Jack: 'I'm in the wrong job.'
  Ruth: 'We have got job vacancies.'
  Jack: 'Oh, maybe you could fit me in?'
  Ruth: 'I'd be delighted to.'
  Jack: 'Would I need a licence for trucking?'
  Ruth: 'Yes, it takes four weeks, and then you can go long distance.'
  Jack: 'That wouldn't be a problem.'

DOCTOR WHO REFERENCES
- None

ALIEN TECH
- None.

CONTINUITY POINTS
- Rhys's shocked reaction on learning that Gwen catches aliens for a living could be taken as further evidence that in the *Doctor Who/Torchwood* universe the existence of aliens is still disbelieved by some members of the general public even in 2008 (see discussion under 'Sleeper'). His comment to Gwen about Torchwood, 'Are you sure they're not some kind of weird cult?', even *after* he has seen the 'space whale' in the warehouse, is indicative of a strong resistance to accepting the truth on this. On the other hand, his incredulity could be interpreted as being due, at least in part, to the apparent absurdity of the idea of a concentration of alien activity in, of all places, Cardiff. Alternatively, could Torchwood have put a mild dose of retcon in the Cardiff water supply at some point, say after the events of 'End of Days', affecting people's memories of previous alien incursions …?

- Owen says that the alien meat contains high levels of chloride, suggesting that the creature lives in water: 'I reckon it came through the rift into the sea and it's beached itself.' It was originally smaller, explaining how it could be transported to the warehouse, but has been growing ever since: 'So the protein chains are regenerating despite the mutilation, so not only is it replenishing its own flesh, but it's increasing it, giving them a brand new meat supply.'

PRODUCTION NOTES

- Made with 'Sleeper' as part of Block 2 of production.

- This episode had the working title 'Another Working Day'.

- Location recording took place in and around Roald Dahl Plass on 3 July 2007 for a number of scenes from this episode, including the one toward the end where Gwen and Rhys, the latter with his arm in sling, sit together on Mermaid Quay and kiss, the earlier one where Rhys secretly observes Jack and Gwen by the water tower fountain, and the sequence of the Torchwood team in the back of the white Harwood's Haulage transit van, which was being rocked about by the crew from out of vision to simulate the motion of driving. The meat processing plant holding the 'space whale' was actually a warehouse near Roath Dock, Cardiff Bay. The Imperial Park Bypass was used for some of the road scenes.

- The concept of the alien meat coming from a trapped 'space whale' was suggested by Russell T Davies. Contrary to the assumption of some commentators, writer Catherine Tregenna did not intend the story to promote vegetarianism, and she is not a vegetarian herself. She was simply keen to write an episode that was more action-orientated than her two character-driven Series One contributions, although subsequently she acknowledged that one of the main themes turned out to be the 'love triangle' between Gwen, Rhys and Jack.

- The argument between Gwen and Rhys, culminating in her finally telling him that she catches aliens for a living, was partly improvised by Eve Myles and Kai Owen.

- The book Jack is glimpsed reading in his office in the Hub is a genuine 1950s pulp science fiction novel entitled *Scavengers in Space* by Alan E Nourse.

- This was one of the more heavily-edited episodes of the series for its pre-watershed repeat. Some of the particularly gory scenes were excised; the 'Have you ever eaten alien meat?' exchange between Gwen and Jack was removed; and the dialogue in the big argument between Gwen and Rhys was changed, with the two instances of 'Piss off!' being omitted and Rhys's 'You fucking him, or what?' redubbed to a rather lame 'You seeing him, or what?'.

OOPS!

- Rhys's hands are tied behind his back by the crooks, but when he is shot, he flings his arms out in front of him. (Perhaps like Ianto, but unseen by the viewer, he has managed to free himself from his bonds while the crooks have been distracted?)

PRESS REACTION

- '*Torchwood* continues its Club 18-30 style approach to sci-fi with a story involving an illegal alien meat supply. The heavy-handed analogy to factory farming falls flatter than the innuendo, but there is fun to be had as Gwen is rumbled by her fiancé Rhys, who has been wondering where she spends all those late nights. He asks what she does for a living, to be told "I catch aliens!" There's not really a good comeback to that, is there?' James Stanley, *Metro*, 6 February 2008.

- 'There may be a few too many local jokes worked in for anyone who hasn't spent a lot of time in South Wales, but still this episode manages to cram in both the light-hearted – Captain Jack surely couldn't squeeze even one more purple-veined lump of innuendo into his dialogue, could he? – and the deeply personal and philosophical, without either knocking the legs out from under the other … The musings about the nature of what humans do to animals are fairly obvious (though no less well handled) but it's the Gwen/ Rhys stuff that sticks with you. Chunks of it owe a glaring debt to *Men in Black* – a scene where the pair sit on a bench gazing at the sky as Rhys wonders what else is out there could have been nicked wholesale from the Will Smith movie – but the understated affection between the couple eases you over the rough spots.' Ceri Thomas, *London Lite*, 6 February 2008.

- 'At last! That was the message that pumped through my brain as I watched Gwen and Rhys tearing down the walls of their illusions and lies, and revealing what's been going on behind them all this time. At last, something for Kai Owen to get his teeth into instead of hovering around in the flat picking up crumbs of plot. At last, some really good acting. At last, some believable dialogue. And at last, a story that was well conceived, realised and paced. With this episode, at last *Torchwood* came of age. That's not to say there weren't some minor mishaps along the way, and you can't ignore the fact that the alien was the most unbelievable creation we've yet seen (it looked even more wooden than the whale in the original 1956 version of *Moby Dick*), but these were minor quibbles in what was easily the best *Torchwood* story so far.' John Beresford, *TV Scoop* website, 6 February 2008.

- 'Another "mission statement" for *Torchwood* Series Two seems to be giving the characters who didn't come to life in the first run some decent material. So after turning Ianto into a one-liner machine, it's Rhys's turn, as he shows he's got every bit as much to him as his girlfriend (more in some ways, as he doesn't even have the police back-up) … Kai Owen rises to the challenge once given the material, … matching John Barrowman point for point in his own series. As a way of twisting the series' dynamics, it's a strong [idea], and while the CGI effects for the alien creature aren't entirely convincing, they're good enough to hold water.' Anthony Brown, *TV Zone* Issue 226, March 2008.

FAN COMMENT

- 'The good characters in *Torchwood* are never the look-at-us super-secret alien hunters, they're the ordinary people like PC Andy and Beth. And Rhys. Dropping Rhys into the Torchwood set-up achieves a level of realism never, ever attained by the usual team. For once, it's actually believable. And Cath Tregenna does good things with Gwen and Rhys's relationship, too. We particularly love the more subtle stuff, like the way Gwen instantly sticks up for Rhys when it turns out he's involved … We also love the fact that they've corrected the howling stupidity of Rhys being the last person in Cardiff to know what Gwen does for a crust. It's long overdue, and had Gwen retconned him at the end we would have formed a posse, hunted the writer down and dropped some overripe blueberries down her favourite dress. It could be, and hopefully will be, an interesting new direction for the two of them instead of the Rhys miffed/Gwen apologising and lying rut we've been stuck in since episode one. It's really, really nice. Shame all that's a bit undermined by the ongoing dumb character notes that are forced in. Gwen's demonstrably close relationship with Rhys just doesn't fit with those godawful scenes with Jack supposedly dripping with sexual tension. Yes, you can love someone and fancy someone else, and even love two people at once, but when you're frantic with worry that someone you love's in danger, you're unlikely to be distracted by someone grabbing your wrist and breathing heavily into your face, even if that someone is John Barrowman. (It's not surprising that Rhys picks up on that, since it's so flamin' obvious, but we also like that he doesn't think of suspecting Owen for a second. Well, you wouldn't, would you?)' Uncredited reviewer, androzani.com website, undated.

- 'This is the fourth episode out of four where we've had a classic plot from the Giant Book of Classic TV and Film Plots. The first was "conning the con man", the second was "undercover sleeper agent", the third was "fix the time paradox", and the fourth starts out as a standard detective story that morphs into a standard "sneak into the enemy fortress and take it from the inside" story. (I'm not dissing classic plots. They're classic for a reason. They work.) It's the fourth episode out of four where the plot has only served as a prop to hang the character interactions on, which have been of a very high calibre thanks to the dialogue and the acting. And it's the third episode out of four where Owen pulls out the solution (in most cases literally) that saves everybody at the last minute. The recurring theme of "humans are the worst monsters of all" was picked up again. It … appeared in *Torchwood* before in "Countrycide" and "Combat". In some ways this story was even more disturbing than "Countrycide". You could distance yourself from the horror of "Countrycide" by saying that cannibalism was unlikely to occur on that scale, with that many people involved. But no such distance was possible in "Meat", where it was entirely believable that a handful of humans with more greed than compassion would butcher an alien for profit. It's no different butchering a space whale than butchering a real whale … In addition, you actually got to see the butchering go down, which most people find unappetising. The "home" theme showed up again in the form of "You can't go home again." This turned out to be true not just for the space whale but also for Jack. He came back wanting everything to be the way it was before he left, with only himself having changed. But real life isn't like that. First Ianto informed him that they weren't going back to what they had before, and here Gwen does the same in no uncertain terms.' 'crabby_lioness', LiveJournal blog, 7 February 2008.

ANALYSIS: There have, perhaps surprisingly, been quite a few stories involving alien 'space whales' or similar, in all media. The *Star Trek* franchise, for instance, has featured a number of such creatures, and the movie *Star Trek IV: The Voyage Home* (Paramount, 1986) implied that Earthly whales have an alien connection. In animation, space-faring whale-like entities have appeared in such diverse productions as a 1965 Belgian movie called *Pinocchio in Outer Space* and an episode of the American children's cartoon series *Courage the Cowardly Dog* (Cartoon Network, 1999-2002). Video games, comic books, radio shows, music videos and novels have all contributed their own entries to this curious sub-genre. There is even a (little known) psychedelic blues band called Space Whale. *Doctor Who* almost got in on the act in the early 1980s when writers Pat Mills and John Wagner came up with a story entitled 'Song of the Space Whale'. Originally pitched to the production team in 1980, this was not finally rejected until 1985, by which point it had undergone many rewrites and Wagner had jumped ship. Whether or not Russell T Davies had that earlier abandoned project in mind when he decided to commission a *Torchwood* story featuring a 'space whale' – or 'giant alien manatee' as Jack refers to it at one point – is unknown, but his idea turned out to be something of a mixed blessing. While it gave Catherine Tregenna a good jumping off point for the development of her very-well-written script, it posed the show's CGI creators at The Mill a tough challenge that, for once, they weren't fully successful in meeting.

It's not so much the shape of the CGI creature or the texture and detailing of its skin that fail to convince, but the way it moves. This means that while it actually appears highly impressive in those shots where it is motionless on the floor of the warehouse, staring forlornly at people with its huge, limpid eye, in those where it starts to rear up and thrash about it does have an unfortunate tendency to look a bit like a puppet. Clearly a great deal of time and effort went into the creation of this effect – as detailed in the accompanying *Torchwood Declassified* mini-documentary, in which it is revealed that Davies vetoed more elaborate initial design ideas on the basis that an exotic-looking creature would be exploited for its appearance rather than simply its meat – so maybe its failure to live up to the viewer's expectations just goes to show that there is a limit to what can be credibly achieved using CGI – unless, perhaps, one has a feature-film budget to play with.

This one less-than-wonderful aspect aside, though, 'Meat' is well up to *Torchwood*'s usual very high standards in terms of production values. From the convincing realism of the opening sequence of the police cordoning off the lorry crash site to the nerve-racking suspense of the Torchwood team's daring raid on the warehouse – a bleak industrial setting ideally suited for use as a location on the show – it delivers a powerful dramatic punch, with characteristically assured direction throughout from Colin Teague.

One of the most notable aspects of Tregenna's script, and one of the most pleasing too, is the unusually large slice of the action it gives to Rhys, a character that didn't look to have too much to him initially but really came into his own as Series One progressed, due in large part to the spot-on performance of the perfectly-cast Kai Owen. Thankfully the production team thought twice about their original plan to have him killed off in 'End of Days', leaving the way open for him to return and play a rather more prominent role in Series Two; and the wisdom of this can be clearly seen here. One of the most memorable, and quotable, scenes of the entire 13-episode run is that in which, after a brilliantly-extemporised argument, Rhys finally learns what exactly it is that Gwen does for a living – 'Aliens? In Cardiff?' – and thus, for better or for worse, gets exposed to the murky and dangerous world of Torchwood. As Tregenna herself has observed, this opens up what is ultimately the most interesting narrative territory explored in 'Meat' – specifically, the triangle of relationships between Rhys, Gwen and Jack. Even more so than the moving plight of the abused alien creature, it is this that gives the story its real emotional resonance.

At first there is suspicion on all sides: Rhys is suspicious of Gwen's relationship with Jack – at one point coming right out and asking her, in anger, 'You fucking him, or what?' – and Jack is suspicious of Rhys's possible involvement in the alien meat scam; understandably so, given that Tregenna has cleverly set up a series of situations that, seen from Torchwood's perspective, make him appear decidedly guilty. As events unfold and it becomes clear that Rhys has actually just been trying to get to the bottom of what is going on, some initial locking of horns between the two men – 'This is quite homoerotic,' comments Jack in an amusing aside – gives way to the development of a degree of trust, to the extent that Rhys is allowed to play a crucial role in Torchwood's second attempt to gain access to the villains' warehouse. There is another great scene between the two men here as, on the road together in the cab of a Harwood's lorry, they express their mutual admiration for Gwen and effectively indulge in a bit of male bonding, with Rhys again getting some choice lines: 'I just wish you would've been uglier. You're not gay, by any chance, are you?'. By the end of the episode, Jack has even been persuaded – albeit by way of an ultimatum from Gwen – not to retcon Rhys, trusting him to keep the secrets he has learned about Torchwood.

Gwen, for her part, is torn between the two men, in more ways than one. She is adamant that Rhys cannot be guilty of any wrongdoing, even though at first his actions seem highly suspicious even to her, and is fiercely protective of him when, later on, Jack accepts his suggestion that he should take part in the raid on the warehouse. At the end of the episode, she tells Jack that she would rather leave Torchwood than allow Rhys to be retconned. Clearly she loves her fiancé deeply. At the same time, though, there are obvious signs that she continues to find herself strongly attracted to Jack. When, during Torchwood's initial investigation of the warehouse, Jack pins her up against a wall to restrain her from rushing in after Rhys, the sexual tension between them is palpable. More telling still is the later scene in the Hub where, while kissing Rhys, Gwen looks over his shoulder directly at Jack, turning what started out as a gesture of affection toward her fiancé into a teasing come-on to the man it seems she wishes she was *really* kissing.

It is this element of moral ambiguity that makes Gwen such a great character. Given that she was originally introduced as an audience identification figure, recruited by Jack to bring heart to the Torchwood team, it would have been all too easy for her to have been portrayed as a one-dimensional paragon of virtue, but thankfully the show's production team and writers have avoided that potential trap and taken the more realistic approach of giving her some distinct human failings, making her arguably the most complex and interesting of the five regulars. Chief among those failings is her undoubted tendency toward egotism, which sometimes manifests itself as self-righteousness and occasionally even as selfishness, as seen most obviously in her highly questionable treatment of the ever-devoted Rhys – particularly in Series One, when she had her affair with Owen and, in a memorably shocking scene in 'Combat', confessed this to Rhys only to admit that she had retconned him and simply wanted to hear him say that he forgave her. Even here, in 'Meat', she displays gross hypocrisy in her indignant reaction to Rhys's suggestion that she might have been unfaithful to him with Jack – 'All I ever asked was you trust me,' she says – conveniently overlooking the fact that she has indeed been unfaithful to him, certainly with Owen and possibly, if the hint in 'Sleeper' is to be believed, with Jack as well. The redeeming factor, though, is that she recognises these failings in herself – as shown, for instance, by the heart-rending scene in 'Combat' where, having been unsuccessful in eliciting the forgiveness she sought from Rhys, she sits alone in the Hub sobbing over a takeaway pizza – and seems intent on striving to do better in future. In the light of this, her confrontation with Jack at the end of the episode, when she makes clear that, if it came to it, she would choose her life with Rhys over her job with Torchwood, takes on a symbolic significance – which Jack seems to realise, as his reaction indicates a distraught acceptance on his part that he has effectively lost Gwen to Rhys, and that there is no longer any prospect of a romantic relationship between them, and the semblance of a normal life that would represent for him, if indeed there ever was.

While they generally remain more in the background of this episode than their colleagues, Owen, Toshiko and Ianto all nevertheless get some excellent scenes here as well, further demonstrating Tregenna's adeptness at handling the show's regular characters. There are some great exchanges between Toshiko and Owen, as Toshiko tries subtly – and not so subtly – to let Owen know how she feels about him. 'Maybe the answer is to go out with someone who knows what you do?' she hints, only to get the reply, 'Look around you Tosh; only we know what we do.' Later, she sweetly brings him a plate of cheese and pickle sandwiches, and asks 'Do you fancy a game of pool sometime?', which he obliviously interprets not as an invitation to go on a date but as a suggestion that they set up a Torchwood tournament. Can he really be so blind to what is really going on, or is he simply trying to rebuff her advances in as gentle a way as possible? This is left as a moot point here. Ianto, meanwhile, gets to deliver some more dry one-liners, the best being his hilarious 'We could release a single' in response to Toshiko's observation that knowledge of how the 'space whale' grows could enable them to 'feed the world' – which is actually a fair point on her part, as there is no indication on screen that the villains are giving the creature vast quantities of food, suggesting that its constantly-replenishing bulk is coming out of nowhere. As in 'Countrycide', Ianto also gets to play a full part 'in the field', as Torchwood carry out their raid on the warehouse; but here, unlike in that earlier episode, he shows a newfound resourcefulness in the face of danger, moving stealthily around the warehouse and disabling villains with a taser gun – a clear testament to his growth both as a member of the Torchwood team and as a regular in the show itself. The dark raincoat he wears in these scenes is also exactly right for his character, and a great piece of costuming.

The raid on the warehouse is really the climax of the episode, generating an atmosphere of mounting tension as the Torchwood team break in and stealthily search the building but are ultimately discovered and held at gunpoint by the villains – who, although perhaps a little nondescript, fulfil their function in the story well enough. There is some further interesting material for Jack here as, having earlier insisted against his team's wishes that they should keep the 'space whale' alive until such time as an opportunity arises to send it back through the rift, he now shows an unexpected degree of empathy for the creature – gently touching its wounded side and asking 'What have they done to you, my poor friend?' – arguably revealing a more sensitive side to his nature than has ever been seen before. It is not Jack who finally saves the day, though, but Rhys and Owen; Rhys by stepping into the path of a bullet intended for Gwen – an act of pure selflessness that thankfully sees him only wounded, and that surely seals his place in Gwen's heart – and Owen by injecting the 'space whale' with a lethal concoction of drugs when it breaks free from its restraining chains and things have clearly gone too far for it to be saved.

'Meat' is an episode that perfectly combines a crime-based science-fiction plot with some intense emotional drama, and as such can be considered quintessential *Torchwood*.

2.05 – ADAM

Writer: Catherine Tregenna
Director: Andy Goddard

DEBUT TRANSMISSION DETAILS
BBC Two
Date: 13 February 2008. Scheduled time: 9.00 pm. Actual time: 9.00 pm.
Not shown on BBC Three as part of original run.
Duration: 50' 35"

Pre-watershed version
BBC Two
Date: 14 February 2008. Scheduled time: 7.00 pm.
Duration: 49' 02"

ADDITIONAL CREDITED CAST
Bryan Dick (Adam), Demetri Goritsas (Jack's Father[74]), Lauren Ward (Jack's Mother), Jack Montgomery (Young Jack), Ethan Brooke (Gray), Rhys Myers (Young Adam), Paul Kasey (Weevil), Jo McLaren[75] (Murdered Woman)

PLOT: Adam Smith, an alien entity who survives by feeding himself into and corrupting people's memories, infiltrates the Torchwood team and convinces them that he has been one of their number for the past three years. Under his influence, Owen becomes timid and geeky, while Toshiko becomes self-assured and sexy. Ianto realises that something is amiss when he finds that his diary contains no mention of Adam. Adam, however, wipes this from Ianto's mind and gives him the false belief that he has murdered three young women. Jack, who in turn has had deeply-buried memories of his long-lost brother Gray reawakened by Adam, refuses to accept that Ianto is a serial killer. Checking the Hub's security camera recordings, he discovers the trick that Adam has played on them. He locks Adam in a cell and gives each member of the team an amnesia pill to make them forget the past 48 hours. He then takes a final pill himself, erasing Adam altogether.

QUOTE, UNQUOTE
- Toshiko: 'What's that?'
  Owen: 'It's a screen-cleaner. I thought you might like it. Do you … do you like it?'
  Toshiko: 'Just what I need. A small rodent looking at me while I work. I think I'll call it Owen.'

---

74 Name given in dialogue as 'Franklin'.

75 Not credited in *Radio Times*.

- Owen: 'If it was our anniversary. I wouldn't disappear. In fact, I would, er … cherish you.'
Toshiko: 'Ahh, Owen.'
Owen: 'Yeah, no, no. Really, really I would. In fact, I wouldn't let you out of my sight, Tosh. Because I love you.'
Toshiko: 'What?'
Owen: 'Yeah, there we are, I've said it. I love you. Yes, um, I always have, actually, ever since we started working together, and in fact I, um, actually ache for you. You know, physically. When you're in the room, I just want to reach out and touch you and …'
Toshiko: 'Owen!'

- Adam: 'You can't shoot me! You made me live! And you always remember what you killed, don't you, Jack?'

DOCTOR WHO REFERENCES

- In one of the shots of the revised opening clips montage for this episode (see 'Production Notes' below), the Torchwood team are seen breaking out some weapons from the Hub's armoury; these are guns previously used by the human Dalek army in 'Evolution of the Daleks'.

- Adam is said to have come from 'the void', which may be the same void from which the Daleks emerged at the end of 'Army of Ghosts'.

ALIEN TECH

- Jack runs a test on Ianto with 'the best lie detector on the planet'. This device, which in appearance somewhat recalls the Voigt-Kampff machines from the movie *Blade Runner*, is presumably alien in origin.

CONTINUITY POINTS

- Rhys and Gwen met at college and had their first kiss in a supermarket.

- Jack says of his 51st Century home on the Boeshane Peninsula: 'We lived under threat of invasion. They came without warning. We thought they'd pass over us, like they always did. But they didn't. Not that day … The most horrible creatures you could possibly imagine. Their howls travelled before them.'

- Adam states that if Jack takes the amnesia pill at the end, he will lose all memory of his father: 'He will cease to have existed for you.' It is uncertain, though, whether this is indeed the case, or whether Jack loses just his last happy memory of them being together, which Adam had in any case corrupted. Certainly he still recalls Gray, as is confirmed later in the series.

PRODUCTION NOTES

- Made with 'To the Last Man' as part of Block 1 of production. This was initially intended to be the tenth episode on transmission; Russell T Davies decided to bring it forward to fifth on the day that shooting began, necessitating some rapid rewriting of certain scenes and the substitution of an engagement ring for a wedding ring on Gwen's finger. The early mention of Gwen having been away in Paris with Rhys was originally supposed to be a reference to their honeymoon.

- This episode had the working title 'Memory Adam'.

- The first scene to go before the cameras for Series Two was the one where Gwen returns to her flat and, not recognising Rhys due to Adam's tampering with her memories, holds him at gunpoint. This was recorded on 30 April 2007.

- The scene of Toshiko and Adam on the bed in the former's flat was recorded on the same date, 9 May 2007, and at the same location, a house in Palace Road, Cardiff, as those of Toshiko and Tommy at the flat for 'To the Last Man'. Coney Beach and Merthyr Mawr Warren in Bridgend were the locations used for the Boeshane Peninsula; recording took place there around 22 May. The side of the Waterguard pub on Harbour Drive, Cardiff Bay, doubled for the outside of Jack's home, where the scenes of his father dying were shot on 23 May. The sequence of Jack and Ianto preparing to go on a Weevil hunt and Jack having a vision of the young Gray watching him was taped on 29 May in Talbot Road, Cardiff, as was the shot of Jack arriving in the SUV outside Gwen's flat. The scene of Jack emerging from the sewers to be met by Adam was recorded at Cardiff Docks, while the venue for the night-time confrontation between the two men over Jack's reawakened memories of Gray was a basketball court in Canal Park, Butetown.

- The standard opening clips montage was revised for this episode only to incorporate various shots of Adam, tying in with the idea that he has convinced everyone that he has been part of the Torchwood team for the past three years.

- Writer Catherine Tregenna devised the back-story involving Jack's brother Gray, which was then fed into other episodes of the series, most notably 'Exit Wounds'.

- A scene cut from the finished version of the episode had Owen, after normality was restored at the end, phoning his mother. This is one of the deleted scenes included on the Series Two DVD box set. The intended back-story, as explained to Burn Gorman, was that Owen's father left home when he was young, and that his mother blamed him for this, shining further light on the reasons for the hard exterior to his character.[76]

---

76 This would contradict the novel *Slow Decay*, in which it is stated that Owen's father died when he was young, and that this was what inspired him to become a doctor.

- The music track playing over the scene where Gwen and Rhys playfully tussle on the bed in their flat at the start of the episode is 'I Love You, You Big Dummy' by Magazine, from their 1979 album *Secondhand Daylight*. The one heard in the sequence where Toshiko and Adam are on the bed at her flat is 'Christiansands' by Tricky from his 1996 album *Pre-Millennium Tension*.

OOPS!

- Unlike the Torchwood team members, Rhys is not retconned to erase his memories of Adam, who came to his flat with Jack after Gwen called for assistance. This presumably leaves open the possibility that a small part of Adam remains in existence at the end of the episode. (On the other hand, Adam never touched Rhys and gave him false memories, as he did the others, so perhaps he really has gone for good.)

PRESS REACTION

- 'Continuing the pattern of increasingly strong stories of this series, I found it easy to forgive the small idiosyncrasies of this one. Even the CCTV-assisted revelation of Adam's guilt didn't feel contrived or overly rapid. What made the whole thing real, and lifted it above the occasionally vapid stories that the first series was prone to, was the chance to get behind the characters; to see something of their vulnerabilities and humanity and, in the case of Jack, to learn about his childhood, his family, and his early loss. For once we didn't need oodles of sfx or alien hardware. Just a small, intricately carved wooden box, some sepia-tinted false memory flashbacks, and a damned good story. What's more, to a man (or woman), the cast proved that given the right material they've got what it takes to deliver a compelling performance. No surprises that this story was written by Catherine Tregenna, who also wrote last week's "Meat". Both among the best, if not *the* best, episodes of *Torchwood* to be aired so far. More from her, please!' John Beresford, *TV Scoop* website, 13 February 2008.

- 'A few niggles. I find it icky whenever Jack becomes a Christ figure, blessing the team with his forgiveness. And Barrowman's occasional tendency to turn it up to 11 is problematic in a story with as much opportunity for histrionics as this one. That aside: a decent episode. It's jam-packed, and all the plot strands are gripping, illuminating or funny. We've never been given such a large chunk of Jack's back-story before (at least, not in this show), and everyone benefits from the way the script builds the show's mythology and fleshes out the characters.' Ian Berriman, *SFX* Issue 168, April 2008.

- 'After the space whale shenanigans of last week, this is a clear step up and a continuation of the show's long, proud tradition of having impressive guest stars aboard. Bryan Dick is a perfect fit, in many ways an unsettlingly perfect fit, and his Adam is a calm, assured, funny young man who's a real asset. Apart from the small point that he's an alien whose body consists entirely of their memories, of course. Dick does a great job of transitioning from plausible team mate to flamboyant maniac to desperate bargaining, and his scenes with Jack, in particular the contamination of Jack's memories of his family, are electric. Barrowman has been on good form for a while now and here he's clearly relishing playing off someone who is a match for him in every conceivable way. The final confrontation between them, despite being little more than two men, one of them in a cell, talking, has more tension and drama to it than any of the scenes with the "Beast" at the end of the previous season.' Alasdair Stuart, Firefox News website, 15 February 2008.

FAN COMMENT

• 'The big boardroom scene where everyone resets themselves with their defining memories was a bit heavy handed. Actually, a lot. But, it had some good moments, like with Tosh remembering her maths class and also her first flat and not having a flat-warming party. For some reason, those moments got to me more than hearing about Ianto's recollection of Lisa or the fact that Owen has mother issues (of course) … I don't really get *how* Adam came to be amongst them in the first place. I know he had that box, but the mechanics of how he went from not there to being there never felt all that well-explained to me. I also didn't see how he got into Jack's memory at the end if he wasn't touching Jack. Wasn't that the only way he could insert or remove memories? Also, does Jack really not remember his family? I didn't really get how forgetting Adam would mean forgetting his only happy memory of his past. Jack really doesn't remember without Adam being there? Is this just repression on Jack's part? I couldn't quite tell. Overall, I enjoyed this episode. It wasn't what I was hoping for, but I thought it was good with some very different sort of directing than I've seen on *Torchwood*. Almost avant-garde-ish during the whole Adam and Ianto sequence that kept cutting from the Hub to that alley.' 'joonscribble', LiveJournal blog, 13 February 2008.

• 'I'm not sure what the hell I'm supposed to think about the Tosh/Adam scenes in this episode. I got the impression that Tregenna wanted the audience to think that by messing with her memories Adam gave Tosh something rather wonderful. He made her super confident (and super bitchy!) and gave her the gift of knowing what it felt like to love and be loved and cherished in return, and [the implication was] that by [being made to] forget Adam, Tosh suffered a great loss. Adam put the whammy on Tosh and had sex with her. I'm sorry, but without wishing to be all screeching feminist about it, am I actually supposed to view that as anything other than rape? Adam messes with Tosh's memories, makes her lose her inhibitions and they have sex. Just because the mechanism that influenced Tosh is a mumbo-jumbo sci-fi concept rather than say Rohypnol doesn't make the act anything other than sexual assault. This is the second time *Torchwood* has shown a bizarrely cavalier attitude to sexual assault, and given that Burn Gorman recently admitted that he has taken no end of stick for the date-rape spray in ["Everything Changes"] you'd think they would have learnt their lesson.' 'fairyd123', LiveJournal blog, 14 February 2008.

ANALYSIS: Given that the *Torchwood* production team and writer Catherine Tregenna are all avowed devotees of *Buffy the Vampire Slayer*, it seems likely that the immediate inspiration for 'Adam' was the episode 'Superstar' from the US show's fourth season – the season that, perhaps not entirely coincidentally, featured a recurring cyber-demon villain named Adam. In 'Superstar', the normally peripheral character Jonathan Levinson takes centre stage by casting a spell that affects the regulars' memories and makes them believe that he is the leader of their group; a plot that has obvious parallels in 'Adam'. Even the show's standard opening title sequence was re-edited for that episode to include images of Jonathan instead of Buffy; an idea appropriated by the *Torchwood* team for their version. However, this is by no means the only example a telefantasy show featuring an episode along these lines – other examples include 'Conundrum' from Season Five of *Star Trek: The Next Generation* and 'The Fifth Man' from Season Five of *Stargate SG-1* – and it could be considered almost a staple of the genre now. It has, indeed, already formed the basis of one previous *Torchwood* story, not on TV but in the tie-in novels range: in Dan Abnett's *Border Princes*, the character James Mayer – an alien in human form – infiltrates the Hub in much the same way as Adam does in Tregenna's script; a similarity that is almost too close for comfort given that many *Torchwood* viewers will have read Abnett's novel, or heard the audiobook version of it, prior to seeing the episode.

One significant difference between 'Adam' and its *Buffy the Vampire Slayer* precedent is that its treatment of the central premise is far darker and more harrowing in terms of its impact on the regulars. This is most obviously so in the case of Ianto, who is made to believe that he is a twisted psychopath responsible for stalking and murdering a number of young women on the night-time streets of Cardiff. It would be tediously repetitive to praise the regular cast members each time they give a strong performance in an episode, as they are all consistently superb throughout Series Two, but Gareth David-Lloyd really excels here in portraying Ianto's anguish and despair on being fed these horrendous false memories by Adam, and his self-loathing on asking Jack to lock him up in the cells as a monster. One of the great things about *Torchwood's* development over the course of its first two series has been the gradual elevation of Ianto from a glorified butler and tea boy (even the early idea of him serving as the team's chauffeur having been dropped after it was discovered that David-Lloyd had not at that point passed his driving test) to a fully-fledged member of Captain Jack's team, on a par with the others – at least in the fans' eyes, if not in the BBC's billing or contract terms, as the actor has jokingly bemoaned in interviews.

There is actually, as in 'Meat', some excellent material for all five regulars here, further cementing Tregenna's reputation as one of the show's very best writers. Burn Gorman and Naoko Mori get to act out an amusing personality-swap for Owen and Toshiko as the former becomes meek and nerdy while the latter is transformed into a confident, assertive sex-bomb, apparently in a relationship with Adam for the past year. This is perhaps taken a little too far when Owen suddenly starts wearing glasses and Toshiko discards hers – surely Adam's powers affect only their memories, not their eyesight as well? – although this could be just a vanity thing: maybe Owen always needs glasses but, unlike Toshiko, normally avoids wearing them, or uses contact lenses instead, and the positions have now been reversed? That aside, the role-switch is very well done, with Gorman and Mori both demonstrating excellent versatility in convincingly portraying radically different versions of their usual characters. In one scene, Owen even attempts to ingratiate himself with Toshiko by bringing her a plate of sandwiches – a neat reversal of the incident in 'Meat' where Toshiko brings Owen sandwiches and suggests they go on a date.

For Gwen, meanwhile, the major consequence of Adam's interference is that she for a time loses all her memories of Rhys. This affords some great scenes not only for Eve Myles but also, for the second episode in succession, for Kai Owen. The confrontation in their flat, where Gwen pulls a gun on Rhys as she believes him to be a stalker, makes for a very effective contrast to the opening sequence of them happily larking about on the bed; and when Jack arrives in response to her panicked call, there is even a brief resurfacing of some of the mistrust between him and Rhys that seemed to have been resolved in 'Meat', as Rhys at first understandably suspects that Jack may have drugged Gwen to cause her to forget about him. The subsequent process of Gwen becoming reacquainted with Rhys, initially via a camcorder message in which he recalls how they originally met, and then in person as they go shopping for groceries and eventually, as if for the first time, go to bed together, gives a sweet insight into their relationship, and in a more interesting and unusual way than through the use of flashbacks.

Last but by no means least, Jack is forced by Adam to re-experience traumatic childhood memories of the loss of his younger brother Gray, giving the viewer a fascinating glimpse into his life on the Boeshane Peninsula and answering at least some of the questions posed by Captain John's cryptic mention of Gray in 'Kiss Kiss, Bang Bang'. Just how objectively accurate these memories are, or how tainted by Jack's profound sense of guilt, is open to debate – he starts off by saying that Gray let go of his hand, but later subtly changes this to saying that he let go of Gray's – but this certainly represents the most revealing look yet into Jack's early years in any televised episode, either of *Torchwood* or of *Doctor Who*.

This episode also showcases Jack's qualities as a strong but sensitive leader of his team. It is his faith in Ianto that leads him to discover the trick that Adam has played on them, as he refuses to accept that his lover is capable of the sadistic murders he believes himself to have committed, even though this means disregarding the contrary indications of a supposedly matchless lie detector. Then he acts as counsellor-cum-confessor to the whole team as he gathers them around the table in the Hub's boardroom and, with the aid of a hypnotic image displayed on a screen, gets them to recall defining moments of their lives and thereby reclaim their true identities prior to taking an amnesia pill to erase their false memories of Adam – a quite extraordinary sequence, with distinct religious overtones, in which amongst other things Gwen makes the revealing admission to him, 'I love [Rhys], but not in the way I love you'. Finally he withstands Adam's attempts to weaken his resolve by offering him, and then corrupting, further long-buried memories of his family – again evoking a religious theme, that of resistance to temptation – and effectively erases the interloper from existence by taking an amnesia pill himself.

The Boeshane Peninsula flashbacks are significant not only because of what they reveal about Jack's background but also because, in production terms, they represent *Torchwood*'s first attempt at depicting an alien planet. This is simply but effectively done, making good use of some suitably bleak sand-dune locations in the vicinity of Cardiff, which along with the sand-coloured desert outfits worn by the population recall the planet Tatooine from the *Star Wars* movies, helping to lend these scenes something of a epic quality. A popular fan theory is refuted here, though, as it is clearly implied that the unseen creatures that attack Jack's home world are large flying beasts emitting fearsome screeches, whereas some had postulated that the monsters he battled in his youth were the Daleks.

Adam is an intriguing entity, very well portrayed by Bryan Dick. He is said to have languished for years in the void until the unique memories of the Torchwood team – and particularly of Jack – gave him substance. Other than that, however, his nature and origins are left tantalisingly unspecified. Also unclear is his precise connection to the mysterious wooden puzzle box that the Torchwood team are seen trying to open. At the end of the episode, Jack finds a 'key' to this box in a plastic evidence bag marked with Adam's name – although by that stage he no longer knows who Adam is – and finally manages to open it, revealing that it contains nothing more than a small quantity of sand. Is this all that remains of Adam; a physical manifestation of, as he says, the last good memory he ever had – or, rather, stole – of the sand dunes of the Boeshane Peninsula? Perhaps fittingly, this is left to the viewer's imagination.

All told, 'Adam' is another fine entry in a series that is by this point proving to be consistently strong.

2.06 – RESET

Writer: J C Wilsher
Director: Ashley Way

DEBUT TRANSMISSION DETAILS
BBC Three
Date: 13 February 2008. Scheduled time: 9.50 pm. Actual time: 9.52 pm.
BBC Two
Date: 20 February 2008.[77] Scheduled time: 9.00 pm. Actual time: 9.01 pm.
Duration: 46' 23"

Pre-watershed version
BBC Two
Date: 21 February 2008. Scheduled time: 7.00 pm.
Duration: 45' 55"

ADDITIONAL CREDITED CAST[78]
Alan Dale (Copley[79]), Jacqueline Boatswain (Plummer), Jan Anderson (Marie[80]), Rhodri Miles (Billy[81]), Michael Sewell (Mike), John Samuel Worsey[82] (Policeman)

PLOT: The Doctor's former companion Martha Jones, now working as a medical officer with UNIT, visits the Hub as part of an investigation into a spate of suspicious deaths. It transpires that the victims have all been killed by a hit-man employed by the PHARM, a medical research organisation for whom they were acting as paid volunteers in tests of a new drug called Reset, which can return the body to a healthy state and thus eliminate diseases previously considered incurable. The drug is being secretly drawn from a captive alien Mayfly creature and has the unfortunate side-effect of introducing the creature's eggs into the unwitting volunteers' bodies. The eggs develop into larvae that eventually kill the volunteers and emerge to find new hosts, within whom they develop into their adult form, again with fatal consequences. The hit-man has been covering up evidence of this. Torchwood gain access to the PHARM, shut it down and put all its captive alien tests subjects out of their misery.

---

77 Postponed to 21 February 2008 in Northern Ireland.

78 In *Radio Times*, the cast were credited not in the listings for the debut transmissions, but in the one for the BBC Two pre-watershed repeat.

79 Full name given on a Hub computer screen as 'Dr Aaron Copley BSc PhD DSc'. However, when Jack later calls him 'Dr Copley' he says 'Professor, actually'.

80 Surname given on a screen in the Hub as 'Thomas'.

81 Surname given in dialogue as 'Davis'.

82 Not credited in *Radio Times*.

The PHARM's director, Professor Copley, shoots Owen before he in turn is shot by Jack. Both Copley and Owen are killed.

QUOTE, UNQUOTE

* Jack: 'Suddenly, in an underground mortuary on a wet night in Cardiff, I hear the sound of a nightingale. Miss Martha Jones.'

* Gwen: 'Who'd assassinate a student?'
  Martha: 'Student Loans Company.'
  Gwen: 'Yeah, yeah. I think you just cracked it.'

* Copley: 'For god's sake, we're on the same side!'
  Jack: 'No! Combating hostile aliens is one thing, but this is slavery, exploitation, a war crime!'

DOCTOR WHO REFERENCES

* The door leading into Ianto's fake tourist information office has pasted over one of its windows a copy of the front page of the edition of the *Western Mail* bearing a picture of Cardiff's one-time mayor Margaret Blaine, aka Blon Fel Fotch Pasameer-Day Slitheen, from the *Doctor Who* episode 'Boom Town'. Although glimpsed in a number of previous *Torchwood* episodes, this is seen most clearly here as Martha arrives at the beginning.

* 'Martha's Theme', composed by Murray Gold for Martha's appearances in *Doctor Who*, is quoted a number of times by Ben Foster in his incidental music for this episode.

* The UNIT organisation was created by writer Derrick Sherwin for his 1968 *Doctor Who* story 'The Invasion' and has featured many times since. Its full name, United Nations Intelligence Taskforce, is not given here: showrunner Russell T Davies decided that this should no longer be used in *Doctor Who* or its spin-offs after the real-life United Nations allegedly complained about a fictional UNIT website set up by bbc.co.uk to promote the show. Although the United Nations cannot prevent its name being used in a fictional context in a TV drama, Davies stated that he did not want to risk young fans getting into trouble with the organisation if, for instance, they set up their own websites referring to UNIT by its full name. (In Series Four of *Doctor Who*, UNIT would be renamed the Unified Intelligence Taskforce.)

* There are numerous allusions made to the events of 'The Sound of Drums'/'Last of the Time Lords'. Jack asks after Martha's family and she says that they are 'getting better'. He also describes himself and Martha as the 'end of the world survivors club' and, in a clear reference to the Doctor, asks 'Do you miss him?' Martha replies: 'No. I made my choice. Maybe sometimes. A tiny bit, tiny, tiny. Then I come to my senses again.' Speaking to

Professor Copley, Jack says, 'I had a bad experience with a politician recently' – probably meaning his encounter with the Master, in his guise as Prime Minister Harold Saxon. When the suggestion arises that she should go undercover to infiltrate the PHARM, Martha notes, 'Come on, Jack, I've been in worse places, and you know it.' Jack tells Owen, 'Trust me, she's more than capable. I'd rely on Martha if the world was ending; in fact, I did.' When Ianto cautions Martha not to draw attention to herself, she notes, 'Be invisible; I can do that.'

- Martha is now a medical officer for UNIT. She says: 'This woman from UNIT rang, out of the blue, said I was just what they needed, that I'd come highly recommended by an impeccable source.' Jack points skywards and asks, 'You mean …?' – again an obvious reference to the Doctor – and she replies 'Well, who else would have done it?' 'He must have thought he owed you a favour,' notes Jack. 'I guess we all do.'

- Martha tells Owen that she and Jack were 'under the same Doctor'.

- Samantha Jones, the alias adopted by Martha when she attempts to infiltrate the PHARM, is the name of one of the Doctor's companions from BBC Books' Eighth Doctor Adventures tie-in range. This is appropriate, as Martha's entry into the TARDIS at the end of 'Smith and Jones' and the idea of her feeling unrequited love for the Doctor during Series Three of *Doctor Who* both had parallels in Samantha's story from the novels.

ALIEN TECH

- Owen is learning how to use a hand-held alien instrument that he has dubbed the 'singularity scalpel' in the belief that it was designed for surgical purposes – although there has apparently been some debate about this. He masters its use just in time to save Martha's life with it.

- The special contact lenses that Martha is given to wear use alien technology. They are powered by body heat and so work only when being worn. They act as a camera, and can also be used to send text messages to the wearer, and even audio signals in the case of an emergency. They communicate with the wearer's sensory neuro-receptors, bypassing the auditory system. The signals cannot be intercepted because, according to Ianto, the technology 'exploits a solution to the EPR paradox' – which relates to, as Martha puts it (displaying a perhaps surprising knowledge of physics), 'quantum entanglement of remote particles'. The lenses are disabled by a radiation surge, the source of which appears to be the adult Mayfly creature that approaches Martha.

CONTINUITY POINTS

- Jack says of UNIT: 'Intelligence, military, cute red caps. The acceptable face of intelligence gathering on aliens. We're more *ad hoc* – but better looking.'

- Ianto says of the PHARM: 'Well, the public image is innocent enough. Private-Public Partnership between the government and a consortium of the pharmaceutical companies, researching and developing cutting-edge bio-technology.' Toshiko adds: 'Their IT systems are way more cutting-edge than they need to be, plus they've got seemingly unrestricted security clearance'. The acronym PHARM stands for Pharmacology, Health And Research Medicine, according to a website page displayed on a screen in the Hub. The organisation's real remit, as described by Professor Copley's assistant Plummer, is to 'farm captive aliens for the exotic chemical products they metabolise'; from a Weevil, for instance, they obtain 'some pesticides and a quite powerful chemical defoliant'. An adult alien Mayfly is the source of Reset, which the PHARM predict will one day be 'bigger than penicillin'.

- Jack references the opening line 'I am a camera' from Christopher Isherwood's novel anthology *The Berlin Stories*, adapted as a play under the title *I am a Camera* by John Van Drutenin in 1951 and as a movie under the same title by John Collier in 1955, and implies that Isherwood once said this to him while they were 'cruising the Kurfürstendamm' together – this having been the heart of the gay scene in Berlin in the early part of the 20th Century. It is unclear if this occurred during Jack's early life as a Time Agent or a conman or since he became immortal and arrived on Earth in 1869. Jack also quotes Isherwood as having said, 'It's not the getting in, it's the getting out.'

- Professor Copley tells Martha that the PHARM have never seen lymphocytes like hers in a human being, although aliens are a different matter. Her blood cells have mutated under the effects of radiation that marks her out as having travelled in time and space. This has given her a 'uniquely effective immune system'.

PRODUCTION NOTES

- Made with 'Kiss Kiss, Bang Bang' as part of Block 3 of production.

- Freema Agyeman's name was added to the opening credits for this and the following two episodes.

- The scene where Toshiko and Owen chase a Weevil into a warehouse was shot at Georgia Pacific GB Ltd – formerly the British Tissues Hangar – on Llandow Trading Estate in Llandow. The hospital where Martha and Owen visit the woman Marie was the District Miners' Hospital in Caerphilly. The sequence of Gwen and Owen visiting Heath Park to inspect the body of the murdered student Barry Leonard was actually shot in Heath Park.

- The sequence where Martha first sees the large Mayfly as it comes around a corner followed by security guards was directed by producer Richard Stokes from Ashley Way's storyboards, as Way was unavailable at the time.

- Freema Agyeman's first recording day on *Torchwood* was 24 July 2007.

- Chris Chibnall was very keen to have J C Wilsher contribute an episode to *Torchwood* as he was a big fan of his earlier work on shows such as *The Vice*. Once approached, Wilsher readily agreed. At the time when he wrote his initial drafts of the script, this was not intended to be one of the three episodes in which Martha would appear, and it was Ianto rather than Owen who was supposed to be killed at the end, prior to being resurrected in the following episode. The brief was then changed – in the latter respect because Russell T Davies thought it would be more interesting to give this storyline to Owen, in view of his more outgoing nature and his medical knowledge of the workings of the human body – and during the course of rewrites Wilsher was also asked to build up a flirtation between Owen and Martha, in order to make the death scene more poignant. The exact manner of the death was the subject of much discussion. Wilsher was keen that it should be abrupt and essentially meaningless, to reflect what often happens in reality; in this, he was inspired in part by scenes he recalled seeing in the US series *Hill Street Blues* and *The West Wing* where, in both cases, a regular character was killed off in a random way in the course of a shop being robbed. His initial idea was that Plummer should kill Owen with the alien singularity scalpel as he tried to shield Martha from the device, but this was ultimately changed to have Copley shoot him with a gun, in order to give it more of a real-word feel. The writer had been asked to beef up Copley's role in general after Alan Dale had been cast to play the part.

- In devising the alien Mayfly creatures, Wilsher was inspired in part by an Algis Budrys science fiction story he recalled reading in which aliens accidentally bring a virus to Earth and are imprisoned to be used as a source of a vaccine for it. He told the official *Torchwood* website: 'I wanted something that was a lethal parasite from a human point of view, but in itself an innocent and rather appealing creature – which we realise by the end is itself an exploited victim. An insect that grew from a parasitic larva into something alarmingly big seemed to do the job.'

- Alan Dale's agent put him forward for a role in *Torchwood* because James Marsters, who was also a client of his, was enjoying himself so much on 'Kiss Kiss, Bang Bang'.

- The music track that Ianto is listening to in the fake tourist information office when Martha arrives is 'Freakin' Out' by Graham Coxon from his 2004 album *Happiness in Magazines*. The one heard as Martha and Owen work together in the Hub is 'Feel Good Inc' by Gorillaz from their 2005 album *Demon Days*.

- The website trialsportaluk.co.uk, for people wishing to register as clinical trial volunteers, was created by BBC Wales Graphics for this episode and does not exist in reality.

- In the edits made for the pre-watershed version of this episode, a shot of Billy Davis's guts exploding as Owen accidentally releases the alien Mayfly from him with the singularity scalpel was replaced with a shot of Jack's reaction to the incident, which was not seen in the unedited version.

OOPS!

- The PHARM test subject Meredith Roberts' birth date is given as 11 January 1962 and Owen says that he was 45 years old, implying that the date is somewhere between 11 January 2007 and 10 January 2008. This must be an error, as there is copious evidence that the episodes at this point in Series Two are set later in 2008. (See Chapter Eleven.) (Possibly maths was not Owen's strong subject in school ...?)

PRESS REACTION

- '[Martha's arrival] kicks off a surprisingly cheery trip into conspiracy-theory land, with a good dose of espionage caper thrown in for good measure. [Freema] Agyeman brings a lighthearted vibe that nicely brightens up some of *Torchwood*'s darker corners. Batting veiled references to their adventures with you-know-Who back and forth with Captain Jack ... and generally out-freaking the rest of the team by seemingly knowing their leader even better than they do, Martha slots right in ... The best bit is that having Martha here doesn't feel like a cheat, like the spin-off having an identity crisis and running back to the daddy show for comfort. It might have last season, but not now – settled and sorted, *Torchwood* oozes confidence these days.' Ceri Thomas, *London Lite*, 20 February 2008.

FAN COMMENT

- 'In this series Torchwood has been working as a close-knit family. In almost all ways that's good. But most families have agreements with each other not to discuss certain things. Take the scene in "Kiss Kiss, Bang Bang" where the team ask Jack where he's been and he replies, "I found my Doctor." Notice what doesn't happen next? No-one asks Jack who he means, and this is a room full of professional nosy people. Look at their faces. They all know Jack means "the Doctor", Torchwood's #1 target. But this is Jack, their leader, their father figure, standing in front of them. In all their minds Jack's needs come before some antique vendetta, so they say nothing. Now look at the scene where Owen asks Martha how she met Jack. She hesitates and tells him, "We were under the same Doctor." Owen asks no more on that subject. Look at his face. He knows exactly who she means, and in spite of his great curiosity, the unspoken family agreement keeps him from asking more. But Martha isn't party to any family agreements and can ask the questions the others won't. Because of Martha's innate charm and because Martha is trusted by Jack, their father figure, Martha's questions are answered, and the audience learns things we would not have learned otherwise. Jack is giddy to see Martha again and she is nearly giddy as well. He trusts her implicitly, but at the same time she is not part of his Torchwood family and not bound by the same agreements. She is part of another family, the companions' family, and he can talk to her about parts of his life that he doesn't feel comfortable sharing with the others. He can also step out of the father figure role around her, and you can see this burden melting off his shoulders when she's around.' 'crabby_lioness', LiveJournal blog, 15 February 2008.

- 'I loved this episode and found it plausible too. In terms of the team, there was cohesion and delegation. There was competence, good use of tech, a little hubris and some rather nice moments of comeuppance. In terms of a nod to world-building, I got a real sense of the pervasive problem of alien infestation, and that worked for me far more than the team sweeping up what the rift-tide dragged in. I can easily believe that New Labour would turn a blind eye while wealthy pharmaceutical companies experiment on aliens in the hope of finding humanity's panacea – at the right price. It's utterly plausible and so subtly written that the [revelation of] the underlying threat comes down to a student cured of diabetes. A small moment in which the otherworldly possibility intrudes on the normal and changes everything. And that has always been what *Doctor Who* is about. Which is why I can say that Freema's guest appearance isn't the only reason that this episode is covered by the fingerprints of the show that came before. Nor is it down to the references to the Doctor. Jack is obviously standing in for the Time Lord in this episode – both in the overt belief he has in Martha and her ability and in [his] convictions when he says that he won't condone alien torture – and to my mind that's apt. Why? Well, mainly because the Jack Harkness who leads Torchwood is the man he is because of his misadventures with the Doctor, as well as being who he is because of the years spent on the slow road. He's utterly plausible as long-lived and multi-faceted in this. "Reset" is, to my mind, the closest Barrowman has come in a while to fully *being* Jack Harkness. And I applaud. And marvel and lament that he doesn't have a chance to work consistently with the same directors that can coax such a performance from him. Thank you Ashley Way – can we please keep you?' 'Boji', LiveJournal blog, 15 February 2008.

ANALYSIS: The much-vaunted arrival of Martha Jones in the Hub comes in a first-time *Torchwood* contribution from experienced scriptwriter J C Wilsher that brings a subtly different vibe to the show. Wilsher's expertise in writing police procedurals is very evident here as Jack's team, assisted by Martha, carry out their investigation of the PHARM, their systematic examination of the medical and other evidence recalling at times the familiar characteristics of forensic crime dramas such as the US hit *CSI: Crime Scene Investigation*. This is an especially fast-paced episode, too, a succession of short-and-sharp scenes being fired at the viewer with machine-gun rapidity; and when Martha goes undercover at the PHARM, it takes on something of the feel of an espionage thriller.

This is not simply a case of style over substance, either, as there are also some interesting ideas at the heart of the story. It could for instance be argued that the PHARM's aims are, in some respects, not too dissimilar to Torchwood's own. Jack's assertion that whereas Torchwood are protecting the Earth against aliens, the PHARM are torturing and exploiting them, is only partly persuasive. The Weevil held captive amongst the alien test subjects in the PHARM's experimental facility uncomfortably recalls Torchwood's own resident Weevil, nicknamed Janet, locked in a tiny cell in the Hub in conditions that would surely be considered cruel if applied to a zoo animal; and at the end of the episode, the only freedom that Torchwood can give the test subjects is death.

The life-cycle of the alien Mayfly is also well worked-out – if, as Wilsher has acknowledged, a little reminiscent of that of the titular creature of Ridley Scott's classic movie *Alien* (1979) – although the fact that human subjects are tricked into acting as unwitting hosts for the eggs by being given a supposedly beneficial medical treatment is rather similar to the alien-eggs-in-diet-pills plot of the Andy Lane-penned *Torchwood* novel *Slow Decay* – which, coming in the wake of the parallels between 'Adam' and *Border Princes*, makes one wonder if the production team really did turn to the novels as a source of inspiration when planning this series.[83, 84]

Martha is just the latest in a long line of the Doctor's companions to become associated with Torchwood – Rose, Mickey, Donna and of course Jack have all previously joined the organisation, albeit the parallel universe version of it in Rose's and Mickey's cases and the H C Clements subsidiary in Donna's case – and she slots smoothly into the team in the Hub, quickly developing a good rapport with the regulars. Her past with the Doctor and Jack is acknowledged, and arouses curiosity in the others, but neither that nor the fact that she is effectively muscling in on their territory is allowed to become a source of conflict – a wise production choice, as it would have reflected badly on the Torchwood team's professionalism had they shown themselves unable to work harmoniously alongside this VIP visitor from UNIT. In fact, Martha even gets to exchange some gossip with both Ianto, who memorably describes Jack's sexual 'dabbling' as 'innovative … bordering on the avant-garde', and Gwen, who shares a joke with her about them being the only two people on the planet not to have had sex with Jack – although Eve Myles' cleverly nuanced delivery of these lines ('No, no … not at all') suggests that Gwen is being less than honest here!

The idea of Martha having joined UNIT as a medical officer is a sensible one that fits her established character and allows for her to have a continued involvement with alien phenomena, paving the way for her planned return to *Doctor Who* part-way through Series Four. Freema Agyeman gives, as always, a highly engaging performance, showing all the qualities that made her so popular as a companion but at the same time suggesting a degree of growth and added maturity, as signalled also by her more sophisticated hairstyle and attire and by the fact that she is now in a committed relationship – a clear indication that she has moved on from the frustration of her unrequited love for the Doctor.

It is absolutely fitting that Martha should be the one entrusted with the crucial but dangerous task of infiltrating the PHARM's headquarters – as Jack notes, she has come through far harder challenges in the past – and the special contact lenses she is given to use, transmitting audio and video signals back and forth between her and the Hub, are an ingenious and well-realised gimmick – although in plot terms it is rather too convenient that they suddenly stop working

---

83 It is rumoured that the working title for a story at one point pencilled in to be the Series Two finale, but later dropped, was 'Spaceship Under Bay', which recalls a central aspect of the third of the original batch of tie-in novels, Peter Anghelides's *Another Life*.

84 *The Glittering Storm*, one of the original audiobooks in *The Sarah Jane Adventures* range, also has a plot bearing some similarities to that of *Slow Decay*.

at a crucial moment, and there is also the mystery as to why Torchwood have apparently never thought to use them on any of their other missions, when they would surely have been equally useful.

Agyeman aside, the major guest star for this episode, playing the PHARM's director Professor Aaron Copley, is New Zealand-born Alan Dale, famous originally for his long-running role as Jim Robinson in the Australian soap opera *Neighbours* and more recently for a string of appearances in many successful US dramas including *The West Wing*, *24*, *The OC* and *Ugly Betty*. Dale brings just the right quality of gravitas and authority to Copley to make him a fitting adversary for Torchwood, as seen to particularly good effect in the excellent scene where he indulges in some testosterone-fuelled verbal sparring with Jack on their first meeting. This is no one-dimensional villain, either: it is clear from his biographical details on the Hub's computers and from Owen's sincerely-expressed admiration of his achievements that Copley is a highly accomplished and respected scientist; and Dale's conviction in the role succeeds in conveying the impression that he genuinely believes that what he is doing at the PHARM is justified in terms of the greater good. The viewer is put in mind here of Jack's implicit ends-justify-the-means rationalisation for certain of his actions, such as his harsh treatment of Beth in 'Sleeper', and again given cause to wonder if Torchwood's methods are really all that different from the PHARM's.

Production-wise, the episode maintains *Torchwood*'s usual exemplary standards. After the slightly disappointing appearance of some of the CGI work on 'Meat', The Mill really redeem themselves here, making an absolutely superb job of realising the Mayfly creatures in their various stages of development and achieving a number of other highly impressive effects. Ashley Way's dynamic direction nicely complements the urgency of Wilsher's script and brings good performances from all the supporting cast members. Some of the body-horror scenes, which feature quite prominently in the script, are actually quite graphically-depicted and shocking, a good example being Owen's disastrous attempt to destroy a Mayfly growing within Billy Davis, the PHARM's hit-man, by using the 'singularity scalpel' – an alien instrument that again seems to owe a debt of inspiration to the tie-in novels series, the first three entries in which all featured a hand-held Bekaran scanner device with a similar capability to display, for medical purposes, images of the inside of a person's body through their clothes and skin. Toshiko's subsequent plan to have Davis's corpse propped up in the driver's seat of the Torchwood SUV to trick the PHARM's security guards into letting the vehicle into their site is particularly macabre – 'Oh, you are warped on the inside,' comments Ianto – and recalls a similar idea, albeit used more for comic effect, in the 1989 movie *Weekend at Bernie's*.

No discussion of 'Reset' would be complete without mention of the dramatic final scene, with Owen being shot and killed by Copley – a development that comes right out of the blue and is genuinely shocking, particularly for those viewers who do not already know that, owing to events in the following episode, this is not actually the last they will see of the character. The fact that Martha has hooked up with the team, and would be capable of taking over as Torchwood's resident medic, makes it seem all the more plausible that this really is Owen's swansong. His death is given particular poignancy by the fact that he has been showing clear signs over the course of Series Two of conquering his emotional demons and becoming more at ease with himself and his colleagues, culminating in this episode in his amiable flirtation with Martha and, even more so, his final recognition and acceptance of Toshiko's invitation to go out on a date with her – which should, admittedly, have sounded warning bells, as embarking on a relationship with Toshiko seems to be tantamount to the kiss of death, judging by the fates of Mary in 'Greeks Bearing Gifts', Tommy in 'To the Last Man', Adam in 'Adam', and now Owen too. This unexpectedly powerful ending is really the icing on the cake of another excellent episode.

2.07 – DEAD MAN WALKING

Writer: Matt Jones
Director: Andy Goddard

DEBUT TRANSMISSION DETAILS
BBC Three
Date: 20 February 2008. Scheduled time: 10.00 pm. Actual time: 10.02 pm.
BBC Two
Date: 27 February 2008. Scheduled time: 9.00 pm. Actual time: 9.02 pm.
Duration: 48' 16"

Pre-watershed version
BBC Two
Date: 28 February 2008. Scheduled time: 7.00 pm.
Duration: 47' 23"

ADDITIONAL CREDITED CAST[85]
Skye Bennett (Little Girl), Paul Kasey (Weevil), Joanna Griffiths (Nurse), Ben Walker (Jamie Burton), Lauren Phillips (Hen Night Girl), Golda Rosheuvel (Doctor[86]), Janie Booth[87] (Hospital Patient), Rhys Ap William[88] (Police Officer),

PLOT: Jack locates and retrieves another alien resurrection glove and uses it to bring Owen back to life. The resurrection is permanent, but Owen's body no longer functions normally. Worse still, it acts as a conduit, allowing a spectral entity, Duroc, to emerge from the darkness. In order to manifest permanently on Earth, Duroc needs to claim the lives of 13 people. Martha is unnaturally aged by the glove when it clutches her face. The Torchwood team take her to the nearby St Helen's Hospital for treatment, and Duroc also arrives there, intent on harvesting the lives it needs from amongst the patients. Owen realises that only he can defeat Duroc, as he is already dead and it cannot affect him. He engages the entity in a hand-to-hand struggle, and it is banished back to the darkness. Martha then returns to her normal age.

QUOTE, UNQUOTE
- Martha: 'How many are there?'
  Ianto: 'Two. Well, they tend to come in pairs. We fished the first one out of the harbour last year.'

---

85 In *Radio Times*, the cast were credited in the listing for the BBC Two debut transmission.

86 Name given in 'Exit Wounds' as 'Angela Connolly'.

87 Not credited in *Radio Times*.

88 Not credited in *Radio Times*.

- Owen: 'You've stopped flirting with me. I mean, it's all right; I wouldn't flirt with me in my condition either, but, er … Is it still necrophilia if I'm conscious?'

- Martha: 'You have the power to bring people back to life, and you never told UNIT. Why?'
  Jack: 'They would have wanted to use it.'

- Owen: 'I can't sleep, I can't drink and I can't shag. And they are three of my favourite things.'
  Gwen: [Rushing to hug him.] 'Owen.'
  Owen: 'I'm not the same, Gwen. I came back different. Hollow. Like I'm missing something. And I do not wanna be like this.'

- Martha: 'It must be Death, because it's stolen my life.'

- Ianto: 'I have searched for the phrase "I will walk the Earth and my hunger will know no bounds", but I keep getting redirected to Weight Watchers.'

DOCTOR WHO REFERENCES
- None, although it seems possible that Duroc may have some connection with, or even be an alternative form of, the Fendahl from 'Image of the Fendahl'.

ALIEN TECH
- The alien resurrection glove, found by Jack in the disused St Mary's Church, is apparently the pair of the one seen in the Series One episodes 'Everything Changes' and 'They Keep Killing Suzie'. It is however slightly different in appearance and markedly different in effect. The subject is resurrected permanently but has no heart, lung or digestive function and experiences a build-up of alien energy that ultimately leads to the emergence of Duroc on Earth. The glove starts moving of its own accord and attacks the Torchwood team, causing Martha to be greatly aged when it clutches her face. It is destroyed by a gunshot from Owen.

- Toshiko uses a hand-held device to scan Jack and explains its function by saying, 'The filament filter detects biochemical energy'. The fact that she detects no such energy shows that Owen is not draining energy from Jack as Suzie drained energy from Gwen in 'They Keep Killing Suzie'.

- Martha places on Owen's wrist a device, possibly alien in origin, to monitor changes in the energy spreading through his body. The output of this can be displayed on the Hub's screens.

- Toshiko again calls into service a device previously seen in the Series One episodes

'Everything Changes', where she used it to scan the pages of an unopened book and download them onto her computer, and 'Cyberwoman', where it was said to be capable of opening any lock within 45 seconds. Here she uses it as a translator of alien languages, saying 'This has never let us down before' – possibly a wry comment on the object's apparent multi-functionality.

CONTINUITY POINTS

- Martha states that it is 9.30 pm at the start of the episode, and that Owen was killed approximately an hour earlier. The action takes place over the course of that night. Martha also states that Owen is 27 years old (although other evidence in the series would tend to suggest that he may actually be 28 – see Chapter Twelve). He is said to be Torchwood officer 565, but the significance of this number is unclear.

- The Tarot girl says that she has been looking forward to seeing Jack again, implying at least one and probably more previous meetings between them.

- The code to access the Hub's alien morgue is given by Owen as '231165'. As originally scripted, it was to have been '231163' – an in-joke reference to the date, 23 November 1963, on which *Doctor Who*'s first episode was transmitted.

- Jack says that he once dated Marcel Proust, the famous French novelist of the late 19th and early 20th Centuries.

- In order to get released from a police cell, Jack calls out: 'Torchwood authorisation: Harkness, Jack, 474317.'

- Owen wryly describes himself as 'King of the Weevils, maybe even the Weevil Messiah', recalling unfounded fan speculation that he would eventually change into a Weevil himself after being bitten by one of them in 'Combat'.

- The Weevils, seen here for the first time *en masse*, all wear identical boiler suits and shoes. This suggests that they already have these on when they arrive in Cardiff through the rift, from wherever they originate. In the early episodes of Series One, the boiler suits worn by the Weevils were of a different design and had a 'Torchwood' logo on them, which would seem to imply that when captured by Torchwood the creatures are – or were then, at any rate – given replacement clothes.

- According to documents discovered by Gwen, in 1479, the people of St James – which would later become Cardiff – built a wall around the town to protect themselves from the plague. One young girl died, but the priest of St Mary's Church – the same church from which Jack retrieved the glove – miraculously brought her back to life. Unfortunately, she did not come back alone, but brought Death with her. Death needed to take 13 souls before it had a permanent hold on the Earth, but only 12 died. It was 'faith' that prevented it claiming the thirteenth. Faith is later discovered by Ianto to have been the name of the young girl, who was able to defeat Death – which is how the people of that era saw Duroc – because she was already dead.

- The Torchwood team do not know how long the 'colossal amount' of energy absorbed by Owen will continue to sustain him. It could be 30 years, or 30 minutes.

PRODUCTION NOTES

- Made with 'A Day in the Death' as part of Block 4 of production. The scene where Jack arrives at the club to meet the young Tarot card reader is an insert directed by Mark Everest from Block 7 of production.

- This episode had the working title 'Death Comes to Torchwood'.

- The scenes of the hen night, and of Jack's meeting with the Tarot girl, were shot on 17 August in a club in Greyfriars Road in central Cardiff. The NCP multi-storey cark park on Wood Street – previously featured in 'Kiss Kiss, Bang Bang' – was the location used for the scenes with Jack, Owen and the Weevils, recording taking place mainly on levels 4 and 5. This was done on 20 August, as was the scene of Jack and Owen getting arrested by the police, the location for which was again Greyfriars Road. The sequence of Jack at the church where he finds the resurrection gauntlet was shot at St Matthew's Church in Dorothy Street, Trallwng, Pontypridd on 21 August. The exteriors and some interiors of the (fictional) St Helen's Hospital Cardiff were recorded from 27 to 29 August at the Optometry and Visual Sciences Department of Cardiff University in Maindy Road. The lobby scenes, where Owen battles Duroc, were done on 28 August. Further hospital interiors were shot on 31 August at the Royal Glamorgan Hospital near Llantrisant. Additional recording took place on Greyfriars Road on the same date. The sequence of Owen aimlessly walking the streets was taped outside the Steam Bar, part of the Hilton Hotel, in the Friary.

- The music heard in the scene of Owen in the bar is 'Awfully Deep' from British-Jamaican rapper Roots Manuva's 2005 album of the same title.

- In early drafts of the script, Jack interrogated a Hoix – a type of creature first seen in the *Doctor Who* episode 'Love & Monsters' – in order to determine the location of the second resurrection glove. The Tarot girl seen in the final version was not originally intended as a recurring character but was brought back by Chris Chibnall in the 1899 segment of 'Fragments'. The fact that the girl has obviously not aged between the two eras ties in with Matt Jones's original conception of her as a mysterious character who was much older than she seemed; he had wanted her to be seen with a glass of whiskey and a cigar, but this was judged by executive producer Julie Gardner to be inappropriate. A Hoix ultimately appeared later in the series, in 'Exit Wounds'.

- The episode was originally to have dealt more fully with the themes relating to the soul and life after death; this material was cut prior to recording as the script was overrunning. Jones came up with the idea of Duroc needing to collect 13 lives as a way of setting up a 'ticking clock' and adding greater urgency to Torchwood's battle against the entity. His intention was that it should be uncertain whether the entity was actually Death itself or a creature from another dimension that had been mistaken for the Grim Reaper. He approached writing for the resurrected Owen from the point of view that the character was experiencing a period of bereavement following his own death, progressing from desperate denial to a mature acceptance.

- The arcane words that Owen speaks when possessed are 'Melenkurion abatha, duroc minas mill khabaal', which are taken from *The Chronicles of Thomas Covenant, the Unbeliever*, a trilogy of novels by Stephen R Donaldson; in the novels, they are a blessing calling on the benevolent magical force of Earthpower. Toshiko's translator device reveals the phase to mean 'I shall walk the Earth and my hunger will know no bounds.' It is Owen who identifies the entity that has passed through him as Duroc, equating to Hunger.

OOPS!

- The Tarot girl tells Jack that a church was built on top of the resurrection glove after people found out what it could do. He then goes to retrieve the glove – but how does he know which church the girl meant, and why is the glove not in fact buried beneath it but hidden in a box ...?

- It seems highly unlikely that Jack and Owen, having been arrested for fighting in a bar, would be locked up in the same cell at the police station. (Has Jack already tipped the police officers off that he is from Torchwood before the point where he calls out to them and demands to be released ...?)

PRESS REACTION

- 'As little bits and pieces from Series One come together, you wonder how long something like this plotline has been simmering at the back of the producers' minds. It's a pity to see Freema Agyeman sidelined as the Martha trilogy turns out to be the Owen trilogy (and her ageing feels as if it's been crowbarred in to give her something to do, with its arbitrary resolution undermining the impact of the very real deaths featured elsewhere), but giving this storyline to Burn Gorman rather than anyone else is definitely a good call. He keeps the darkness simmering in the early, comical scenes of Owen heading out on the town and discovering the limitations of his condition, so that the arrival of the personification of Death (nicely nebulous special effects, if not 100 percent convincing) feels part of the same episode rather than a sudden twist.' Anthony Brown, *TV Zone* Issue 227, May 2008.

- '[It's] a mess, heavy-handed and clunky, showing Owen literally grappling with Death, as if we hadn't got the subtext. It's an episode where everything is thrown into the pot, and the result is that it feels like several episodes crammed into one; we get a plot ripped straight from the *Buffy* episode "Life Serial", as Owen brings something back with him from the afterlife, along with the nitty-gritty of what being dead means ... and random other elements thrown in for little reason. It's a strange episode, reaching for profundity and quasi-Biblical doom (the latter serviced much better in *Doctor Who's* "The Satan Pit"), and is overshadowed by "A Day in the Death".' Jes Bickham, *DeathRay* Issue 12, April 2008.

FAN COMMENT

- 'This sequel of sorts to "They Keep Killing Suzie" is all its predecessor was, and more ... Regular Davies-co-worker Matt Jones proves his worth yet again with this solid piece of drama. Where "Suzie" terrorised us with its zombie lead, here we are encouraged to feel great pity for Owen and his colleagues. Despite similar themes, the character interplay is different enough that it seems to be a completely different story. Although the initial premise is flawed (after the problems with Suzie, why would Jack choose to bring back Owen?) this is quickly forgotten as Myles and Gorman turn in star performances once more ... [But] what of the future? With Owen now undead, we essentially have two immortal characters in the show. This can only end one of three ways: either Owen will be written out entirely (no!), a big reset switch will be pulled (no!!!) or in a surprise twist Jack will be killed, and in his final breaths tell Owen to become the Face of Boe and warn a mysterious traveller that he is not alone. Well, that's my theory anyway ...' Arthur Penn, Torchwood Guide website, undated.

- 'Frustratingly, "Dead Man Walking" flirts with greatness before it pisses it up the wall. I loved the idea of Jack bringing Owen back so he could get the code to a filing cabinet (however, you have to wonder about Torchwood's security protocols at this point), and I honestly thought they were going to drag Owen back for an utterly perverse last-gasp goodbye ... Maybe the episode title was designed to throw us off the scent. Maybe this would be the twist to end all twists. Now *that* would have been inspired. What we actually got was a perfunctory, vague, plot-hole-ridden Spooky Do. Owen was clearly only dead in the sci-fi sense of the word; just ask Spock, Sheridan and Starbuck ... Forget alternative dimensions, Death looked like he'd shuffled in from a completely different programme. One of those *Supernatural/Charmed/Ghost Whisperer/Fit Chick With Magical Powers* type programmes that are still riding the tails of *Buffy the Vampire Slayer*. Ah, *Buffy*. Her shadow looms ever larger over this season; from the Church of the Evil Weevils to the tarot card bollocks and a girl called Faith, this episode felt like a trip back to the 1990s. However, when *Buffy* dealt with the ramifications of someone dying and coming back "wrong" it did it as a musical number. And it still displayed more gravitas and profundity that this throwaway fluff.' Neil Perryman, Behind the Sofa website, 2 March 2008.

- 'Jack's always had a certain ambiguity, with a very specific idea of how the greater good should be served. Giving up that child to the aliens in "Small Worlds" being a prime example. Except on this occasion Jack brought Owen back from death because he could, without as far as we could tell knowing what the consequences would be. Which might have been fine had his actions not ultimately led to the deaths of 12 people. This puts us in the position of having to sympathise with heroes who've dropped off the moral compass, become the boogey man (or woman), and I'm not sure that we can, or should have to. Perhaps I'm just touchy, and I know this has nothing to do with wanting my heroes to be whiter than white ... You could argue that the Torchwood team did exactly what any human being would do, ignoring the wider picture and making the most of the tools available in order to save a colleague. Except, y'know, 12 people. What about *their* families and friends, eh? We should applaud the writers for trying to be different, for attempting to put the audience on the back foot, since they've put us in the position of having to root for characters who have been doing the kinds of things that villains have a tendency to do; in other words, Torchwood reverted to type and became exactly the organisation the Doctor wrinkled his nose at in "The Sound of Drums". Notice that in the middle of everything Martha (in about the only scene that justified her presence in the episode) tore a strip off her pal, thereby keeping her on the right side of right, almost ring-fencing her from responsibility.' Stuart Ian Burns, Behind the Sofa website, 29 February 2008.

• 'It was interesting to see in this episode just how much Jack's year on the *Valiant* has changed him. Before he went away he killed Lisa and Mary without blinking and he was quite happy to put Suzie down again ... And yet Owen dies and he point blank refuses to let him go. He seeks out the second "risen mitten" even though he knows the havoc that the first one wrought and uses it on Owen over the objections of his team mates ... And Jack didn't bring Owen back so that the team could say goodbye or so that he could prepare him for death. He brought him back simply because he could not bear to lose a member of his team so soon after all he's been through. It's the same fear of losing those around him (presumably amplified by the loss of his father and Gray) that made him act like a moronic frat boy in "Meat" when he was faced with the potential loss of Gwen. But this is so much worse – by bringing Owen back for his own selfish reasons (even if they are motivated by love) he has condemned him to a half life ... I thought the Owen resurrection scene was brilliant. Gallows humour at its very best. Loved that they didn't choose to show an Owen who had been changed by his near death experience into being a gentler person. In death, Owen was still enough of a bastard to call Gwen on her overly sentimental ways, dissing her attempts to say goodbye by pointing out that he only had two minutes to live – sheer brilliance. Jack asking for the morgue code was practical and weirdly hilarious. And Toshiko's declaration of love was beautifully played – especially the "Oh fuck" moment that immediately followed when she realised that Owen wasn't going anywhere just yet.' 'fairyd123', LiveJournal blog, 21 February 2008.

ANALYSIS: The roots of 'Dead Man Walking' can be traced back to the end of the Series One episode 'They Keep Killing Suzie' where, following the destruction of the alien resurrection glove first introduced in 'Everything Changes', Jack says 'The resurrection days are over, thank god' and Ianto replies 'Oh, I wouldn't be too sure. That's the thing about gloves, sir. They come in pairs.' This exchange of dialogue was inserted into the script by Russell T Davies specifically with a view to the possibility of having another episode featuring a resurrection glove at some point in the future, and led in turn to the development of the idea that one member of the Torchwood team, originally intended to be Ianto, should be killed off part-way through Series Two and brought back in an 'undead' state using the second glove.

Matt Jones was the writer charged with the task of expanding this idea into a full storyline, and in doing so he clearly drew inspiration from traditional images of Death personified as a skeletal form shrouded in a dark cloak, often depicted with a scythe as the Grim Reaper – a figure sometimes associated with Satan, as featured in the same writer's earlier *Doctor Who* two-parter 'The Impossible Planet'/'The Satan Pit'. This representation of Death is also familiar from the iconography of Tarot cards, as cleverly referenced by Jones in the scene where Jack obtains the location of the second glove from a mysterious young girl who does a Tarot reading for him, revealing in the process that he is actually depicted on one of the cards in her deck, wearing armour and holding a sword – an intriguing development replete with potential for further exploration in some future episode, particularly as she says 'You'll owe me a favour'. Death is the thirteenth trump card in most Tarot decks, and Jones's incorporation of the notion that his entity, Duroc, needs thirteen victims in order to manifest fully on Earth ties in neatly with the more general mystical significance of that number in relation to witches' covens and the like. This whole aspect of the storyline could also be seen as a reworking of the ideas presented in Chris Boucher's 1977 *Doctor Who* story 'Image of the Fendahl', in which the Fendahl is similarly described as being literally death itself and likewise needs 13 victims – a core plus 12 acolytes – in order to achieve corporeal existence.

Another intriguing revelation is that, surprisingly, the Weevils not only know about the resurrection glove but treat it with reverence, and cower before Owen once he is brought back to life through its use. Or is 'brought back to life' the correct term here? This is arguably one of the less well thought-out aspects of the story: even after he is restored to consciousness, Owen is still continually referred to as being 'dead' – as reflected in the title of the episode – when according to the modern medical definition, which equates death with an absence of brain activity, that clearly is not the case. Admittedly the term 'clinically dead' is still used to describe someone who, although not brain dead, has no heart or lung function, which actually fits Owen's situation very well; but, even then, there are some obvious inconsistencies here: if he has no blood circulation or metabolism, as implied by the fact that his system cannot process food or drink, why does he still retain his normal skin colour and show no signs of decomposition?; and if he cannot pass breath in and out of his lungs, how is it that he can still speak? It is all very well to put these things down to the mysterious 'energy' with which he has been infused by the glove, and quite understandable that the production team should want to avoid having him wear special make-up (a logistical nightmare) or exhibit the bodily degeneration of a stereotypical zombie (a terrible cliché), but this does nevertheless give the impression that the depiction of his diminished state has been approached in a rather half-hearted manner. In fact, when it comes down to it, what Owen is having to come to terms with and adjust to here is not really death at all, but a rather unique form of physical impairment – and one that is arguably a lot less debilitating than many of those that people with disabilities have to cope with in the real world.

One surprising aspect of the storyline is that Freema Agyeman is given relatively little to do in it. When fans first heard that she would be making a three-episode guest appearance in *Torchwood*, most assumed that the focus of those episodes would be very much on her character. It turns out, though, that while that is indeed the case in 'Reset', it is Owen who takes centre-stage in 'Dead Man Walking', and will do so again in the following episode. In fact, one gets the distinct impression that Martha has been more or less shoehorned into 'Dead Man Walking', and that things would be little different if she were not present at all. The subplot involving her being unnaturally aged by the resurrection glove – courtesy of some surprisingly below-par make-up effects work – only to recover her youth at the end, sits awkwardly with the rest of the story and shows all the signs of having been written in simply to avoid her being sidelined altogether from the action.

There are some other curiosities here too. The episode opens with Martha preparing to perform an autopsy on Owen's body – a surprising instance of Torchwood sticking to the letter of the law in cases where death is not from natural causes – and, astonishingly, it seems that the rest of the team intend to stand around and watch while she does it. The Tarot girl says that the glove had a church built on top of it, and yet when Jack goes to retrieve it from the now-disused church, he seems to be aware that he will find it not under the ground but in a box in a hole in the wall – in the light of which, one can only surmise that the group of Weevils seen sleeping there must have dug it up at some earlier point and placed it in the hole as an object of worship, amongst all their other collected 'treasures'. And although this second glove is supposed to be the pair of the first – an idea that could perhaps have been held back for use in a later series, as coming so soon after 'They Keep Killing Suzie' it risks accusations of a lack of originality – it has a subtly different design and operates in a quite different way, reviving permanently rather than for just two minutes, not needing to leech energy from the user via a circuit incorporating a 'life knife', and ultimately of course causing the resurrected individual to act as a conduit through which Duroc can emerge from 'the darkness' and terrorise the Earth.

The concept of there being 'something in the darkness' is, on the other hand, wholly consistent with what was established in 'They Keep Killing Suzie'; and although many fans initially assumed that that was intended to foreshadow the appearance of Abaddon in 'End of Days', it actually makes far more sense that the 'something' in question should be, in effect, Death itself. It does indeed come for Jack, too, just as Suzie predicted that it would, as his is the first life it seeks to claim after it emerges from Owen, albeit that the attempt proves unsuccessful – a discovery that is made rather less predictable for the viewer than might otherwise have been the case by the clever way in which director Andy Goddard has chosen to present it, with an initially bewildering jump-cut from a shot of the smoke-like form of Duroc rushing towards Jack in the Hub's autopsy room to a shot of him suddenly coming back to life some time later in the passenger seat of the Torchwood SUV, parked outside the hospital; a turn of events that also indicates, rather amusingly, that Jack's team have by this point become accustomed to, and possibly even a little blasé about, the fact that he always returns from the dead.

This is just one of many excellent directorial touches from Goddard, and indeed the whole episode is packed with an incredible succession of well-written and memorably-realised scenes: Jack's unsettling encounter with the Tarot girl; his subsequent visit to the dilapidated St Mary's Church, where he has to creep through a huddle of sleeping Weevils in order to locate the glove; the weird, distorted shots of Owen in the darkness beyond death; Owen's encounter with the angel-costumed hen-night girl in the bar; the initially gross but then poignant exchange between Jack and Owen in the police cell; Owen's shocking transformations, causing him to utter an arcane incantation in an unnaturally guttural voice – again, shades of 'The Impossible Planet'/'The Satan Pit' – while his eyes turn jet black, an image reminiscent of the effects of the 'black oil' infection in a running storyline in *The X-Files*; the Weevils' pursuit of Jack and Owen through the multi-storey car park, ending with the eerie discovery that they now defer to Owen; the glove's sudden attack on the Torchwood team, in a sequence that recalls classic crawling-hand precedents such as *The Addams Family*'s Thing, Warner Brothers' 1946 movie menace *The Beast with Five Fingers* and *Doctor Who*'s 'The Hand of Fear', and contrives to be both scary and amusing at the same time; Duroc's remorseless passage through the hospital corridors; and Owen's surprising farewell-cum-distraction kiss for Toshiko, followed by his emotional conversation with the young leukaemia patient, Jamie, and climactic hand-to-hand struggle with Duroc, the latter evoking archetypal 'dancing with Death' imagery such as that featured on the cover of Paul Cornell's seminal *Timewyrm: Revelation* in Virgin Publishing's New Adventures range of *Doctor Who* novels.

There are a wealth of great character moments here, too, from Toshiko's admission that she loves Owen, and always has, when she thinks that the glove has given him only two minutes' more life, to Ianto's characteristically dry 'Ah, here we go again' when it becomes clear that the resurrection is going to be, like Suzie's, a more permanent one, to the sideways looks that Jack gives Ianto when he prepares to fend off the rampaging glove with a hockey stick – amusingly recalling his comment in 'Sleeper' about sports equipment in the bedroom – and many, many more besides.

The idea that Owen is able to defeat Duroc by virtue of the fact that he is already dead is quite fitting, and the revelation that this is also how the entity was overcome on its previous appearance back in the 15th Century, by a young girl named Faith who it seems had similarly been brought back to life through the use of the resurrection glove, raises the intriguing possibility that this is actually the Tarot girl's true identity.

The depiction of Duroc is very well achieved in production terms, the visual effects used for this giving it just the right sort of undefined quality, somewhere between the solid and the insubstantial. Martha's less-than-convincing old-age make-up aside, all other aspects of the production are also well up to standard, making this a great showcase for *Torchwood*'s trademark slick, sexy, *noir*-ish visuals.

In the final analysis, despite – or perhaps even partly because of – all the flawed and frankly mystifying aspects discussed above, this episode has so many great things going for it that it actually turns out to be just about the most enthralling of Series Two; definitely a case of the whole being far more than the sum of the parts. It's *Torchwood* on crack: ultra-dark and a little twisted; bizarre and unpredictable; full of audacious ideas and outrageous set-pieces; and altogether quite, quite brilliant. In other words, it's *Torchwood* at its very best.

2.08 – A DAY IN THE DEATH

Writer: Joseph Lidster
Director: Andy Goddard

DEBUT TRANSMISSION DETAILS
BBC Three
Date: 27 February 2008. Scheduled time: 9.50 pm. Actual time: 9.52 pm.
BBC Two
Date: 5 March 2008. Scheduled time: 9.00 pm. Actual time: 9.02 pm.
Duration: 47' 19"

Pre-watershed version
BBC Two
Date: 6 March 2008. Scheduled time: 7.00 pm.
Duration: 44' 54"

ADDITIONAL CREDITED CAST[89]
Richard Briers (Parker[90]), Christine Bottomley (Maggie[91]), Louis Decosta Johnson (Farrington[92]),
Brett Allen (Taylor), Gill Korlin (Webb)

PLOT: Owen meets a young woman named Maggie Hopley on the roof of a tall building from which she is planning to jump to her death. He tells her of his own death and resurrection; of how his encounter earlier that night with Henry Parker, an elderly and eccentric collector of alien artefacts who was on his deathbed, brought him to his lowest ebb; and of how The Pulse, a device from Parker's collection, 'sang' to him and ultimately helped him to realise that there is always a glimmer of light in the darkness that is worth carrying on for.

QUOTE, UNQUOTE
• Maggie: 'You're dead!'
  Owen: 'Yeah, I was brought back. Like Jesus, really, but without the beard, you know. Shit, I'm never going to have a beard. Not that I wanted one, you understand, but, you know, one day ...'

• Owen: 'I bet you're loving this, aren't you? It's like you've finally won.'
  Ianto: 'I didn't realise we were in competition.'
  Owen: 'Oh, come on. Even Tosh had more of a life than you used to, and now you're always

---

89 In *Radio Times*, the cast were credited in the listing for the BBC Two debut transmission.

90 Full name given in dialogue as 'Henry John Parker'.

91 Surname given in dialogue as 'Hopley'.

92 First name given in dialogue as 'Philip'.

out on missions, you're shagging Jack, and I'm stuck here making the coffee.'

Ianto: 'It's not like that. Me and Jack.'

Owen: 'Yeah, yeah. You and Jack. Gwen's getting married; Martha's got her bloke; god, even Tosh had Tommy. This is really *shit*!'

- Owen: 'For some reason, you want me. You know, I dunno why, but you always have. Always looking at me, watching me screw all those other women, your heart breaking, and now it's different. Because I'm safe now, aren't I, and it's all cosy, and it's romantic, and isn't it beautiful, you know.'
  Toshiko: 'You can say what you like, I'm not leaving you.'
  Owen: 'We'll of course you're not, because this is it, isn't it? This is the date that we were talking about. You know, you've got your beer, you've got pizza. You and me, it's just how you wanted it. All we need now is a sodding pool table!'
  Toshiko: 'Stop it! What's wrong with you?'
  Owen: 'I'm broken, Tosh!'

- Jack: 'Thirty-six minutes. Not bad.'
  Owen: 'You were watching?'
  Jack: 'Skinny guy in tight jeans runs into water? I was taking pictures.'

- Owen: 'I'm Dr Owen Harper, and I'm having one hell of a day.'

- Maggie: 'What do I do now?'
  Owen: 'You've got a choice. If you think that the darkness is too much, then go for it. But if there is a chance, there's just some hope … It could be having a cigarette, or that first sip of hot tea on a cold morning. Or it could be your mates. If there is even a tiny glimmer of light, then don't you think that's worth taking a chance?'

DOCTOR WHO REFERENCES

- A graphic of one of the Dalek tommy-guns from 'Evolution of the Daleks' can be glimpsed on a Hub computer screen in one scene, and a schematic diagram of a Cyberman on the wall in another.

- Toshiko eats a pizza from Jubilee Pizza, the company whose takeaway boxes were first seen in Utah in 2012 in 'Dalek'.

ALIEN TECH

- Henry Parker has a large collection of alien artefacts at his home. Most prominently featured of these is the one he has termed The Pulse, a small oval object glowing with red light, which he believes is keeping him alive. Owen quickly determines that this device is the source of the massive energy build-up that Torchwood have been monitoring, but ascertains that it is actually having no physical effect on Parker at all. It simply represents hope to him. He discovers that The Pulse is a reply to messages that NASA sent out into space in the 1970s in an attempt to communicate with alien civilisations. Owen says: 'It sang to me. It's a glimmer of light in the darkness. See, sometimes it does get better.'

CONTINUITY POINTS

- On testing Owen, Martha finds that there is no sign of muscle decay and he is in 'great shape'. If he continues to exercise, he will not atrophy, and will not even age. There is no sign of further cell mutation; he is 100 percent human.

- Martha's preferred beverage is a cappuccino with chocolate sprinkles.

- Parker is described as a Howard Hughes-like recluse who hasn't left his house since his wife died and hasn't been seen in public since 1986. He has hitherto been considered harmless by Torchwood. The alien artefacts he has purchased within the past year include a Dogon eye – as previously featured in 'Random Shoes', an episode to which 'A Day in the Death' bears some similarities – 'a pair of Ikean wings', some meteorites and an Arcateenian translation of James Herbert's novel *The Fog* – Arcateenian being the species of the alien Mary from 'Greeks Bearing Gifts', as identified in the 'Invasion of the Bane' special of *The Sarah Jane Adventures*. Parker knows a certain amount about Torchwood and thinks that Toshiko has 'very lovely legs'.

- Jack asks Gwen if there is any news on 'Banana Boat' and she says that he has been arrested in Lanzarote. This foreshadows events in the following episode, 'Something Borrowed', when 'Banana Boat' is revealed to be the nickname of Rhys's friend who is to be best man at his wedding.

- When Martha stitches up a gash in Owen's hand without anaesthetic, Owen says: 'I can't feel anything. I can't feel the needle or thread. I can't feel your hands on mine. I can touch things, I can hold them, I know they're there, but I just can't feel anything. I'm numb.'

- Owen, like Toshiko, has obviously moved to a different flat since Series One.

- Gwen has not asked Toshiko to be a bridesmaid at her wedding, a fact for which she has apologised.

PRODUCTION NOTES

- Made with 'Dead Man Walking' as part of Block 4 of production.

- The opening shot of Owen standing in the street as life goes on around him was taped in Wharton Street in central Cardiff, while that of him running through a park was done in Bute Park. His plunge into Cardiff Bay was taped on 16 August on Mermaid Quayside, just by the Pierhead building; the stunt was performed by Burn Gorman himself, wearing a wetsuit beneath his clothes. The shots of Owen under the surface were recorded in much warmer water, weeks later, in an indoor swimming pool at a private house in the village of Pontyclun in the Rhondda Valley. The scene of the Torchwood team (minus Toshiko) bidding farewell to Martha in Roald Dahl Plass was taped on 21 August (after the crew had returned from recording the church scenes for 'Dead Man Walking' in Pontypridd). The Glamorgan Building of Cardiff University on King Edward VII Avenue was used for the interiors of the Parker residence, shot on 28 August. The exteriors were shot at a private residence. The rooftop scenes featuring Owen and Maggie were recorded atop the Tower Building of Cardiff University's School of Psychology. Imperial Park Bypass was the road used for the flashback scene of the aftermath of the car accident in which Maggie's husband was killed.

- As Owen talks about his life at the beginning of the episode, brief clips are seen from 'Ghost Machine', 'Meat', 'Sleeper', 'Everything Changes', 'Out of Time', 'Reset' and 'Dead Man Walking'.

- This episode is set three days after 'Reset' and 'Dead Man Walking'.

- The music Owen listens to while alone and depressed in his flat is 'Atlas' by Battles, the first single from their 2007 album *Mirrored*. The programme he is seen watching on his TV is an instalment of the genuine BBC One property show *To Buy or Not to Buy*.

- Joseph Lidster viewed Parker as being, in effect, an elderly version of Owen, and approached his dialogue accordingly. He found the pivotal scene where the two men meet a particularly challenging one to write, and it went through several redrafts, with Richard Briers at one point requesting the reinstatement of some cut lines that he had particularly liked when first approached to play Parker. Lidster was keen to show Owen having to confront and come to terms with his new situation and his inability to die, so that he could then move on. He also wanted to portray Parker as an essentially benign character, to show that not everyone that Torchwood come into contact with is a threat or an enemy. The Pulse was originally to have given Parker hope by showing him an image of his dead wife, but it was ultimately felt that it would be more effective if he simply drew hope from the device itself. More of this scene was shot than was ultimately used in the finished episode; cuts were made during editing to give it maximum impact. As a Roman Catholic, Lidster did not subscribe to the *Torchwood* view of there being nothing but darkness after death, but saw the main message of his story as being to make the most of life.

OOPS!
- There is a lot of inconsistency over the issue of whether or not Owen can breathe, and if so to what extent. Clearly he does not *need* to breathe, but he must surely be capable of making his muscles push air in and out of his throat, otherwise he would not be able to

speak. He can also be seen breathing in some shots, and heard drawing the occasional sharp breath (unsurprisingly, given that he is being played by a live actor!). However, when he is underwater in the Bay, no air bubbles to speak of can be seen emerging from his mouth or nose, and later on he finds that he is incapable of performing artificial respiration on Parker. (Probably the best conclusion to be drawn from all this is that he *can* breathe, but only just enough to be able to speak, not enough to be able to do other tasks requiring greater lung power such as, say, blowing up a balloon.)

PRESS REACTION

- 'A variant on *It's a Wonderful Life* that avoids being the straight pastiche most series settle for, it's not perfect, but in its portrayal of the heartbroken Maggie, who's tried waiting for the pain to fade, tried moving on and waiting for life to get better, it is as stark and real a portrayal of depression as I've seen in some time. The blood and violence of the brutal flashback to her wedding day crash is an example of using shock to good effect, and if the ending's slightly unsatisfying – I'm really not sure that the alien music would be quite enough – it does capture that feeling of maybe, maybe, that allows people to get through another day.' Anthony Brown, *TV Zone* Issue 227, May 2008.

FAN COMMENT

- 'What a morose, sloppy and confused episode. Joseph Lidster certainly has an ear for dialogue – with some neat monologues, descriptive angst, and a few amusing jokes – while [Burn] Gorman did an impressive job making Owen believably depressed and tortured. Richard Briers also did a wonderful job with a shallow, one-note character, restricted to bed and introduced very late. But everything else flapped around – lurching from tedious to mystifying, with scenes stapled to a plot that didn't develop satisfyingly. "A Day in the Death" was a simple Owen-centric story that didn't make much sense, particularly because the Parker subplot was so badly integrated into the main story, and I'm still confused about what "The Pulse" actually was (beyond a dumb metaphor for "life" itself). Lidster laudably tried to reach for something emotive, human, complex and poignant – but it just wasn't compelling, well-structured, or very insightful. It basically played like a series of moments with Owen bouncing around between a young girl who wants to die (Maggie), a middle-aged man who can't die (Jack) and an old man who refuses to die (Parker). There was definitely an intriguing and intelligent storyline to be weaved between that threesome, given Owen's unique perspective on death, but this sadly wasn't it.' 'Dan', Dan's Media Digest blog, 28 February 2008.

- 'That was bloody good. And kind of an answer to the more depressing theme in last season. I mean, it's an episode about suicide, and you know how that would have ended last year. This year? Owen, of all people, finds a way through, talks her out of it. And since he was the one who tried it last year (arguably, if he didn't want saving) that fixes a whole lot. Not least being that any acts of heroism from here on out are not in fact suicide attempts. Owen as shadow for Jack continues [to be] fascinating. Live forever/die forever. But also the kill-them-a-lot treatment for suicidal feelings. Apparently having done it they get over it. This season has a great balance between (black) humour and all the action bits we got all last year. I like it a whole lot better.' 'beccaelizabeth', LiveJournal blog, 27 February, 2008.

- 'I was convinced that the writers were going to take the easy way out – that there was going to be an alien McGuffin hidden away amongst Richard Briers' character's belongings, a handy box of nanogenes perhaps, that would fix Owen right up … So for the twist to be that there is no twist – that Owen remained every bit as dead as he was at the beginning of the episode – was a bit of a shock. It's a hell of a ballsy move on the part of the production team … and I'm not quite sure where they're going to go with it, but you have to give them kudos for being different. I thought "A Day in the Death" was a wonderful episode. Considerably less barking than last week's, which also meant that it was marginally less fun, but it was far more emotionally satisfying … If "Dead Man Walking" was all about the power of death, "A Day in the Death" was all about the power of hope. How the tiniest glimmer of light can overwhelm an ocean of darkness. As such it could have been rather corny and sentimental but [it] was saved by another extraordinary performance from Burn Gorman. I thought the framing device of the world's worst therapy session was rather clever and certainly very different … Burn had fantastic chemistry with the actress playing the suicidal Maggie and they played off each other really well. I really liked how unsentimental their scenes were. There were no platitudes, no false hope, Owen didn't lie that one day Maggie was going to wake up and all of a sudden it wouldn't hurt anymore. Because life is just life. It can be incredibly cruel, and Maggie doesn't need or want Owen to pretend otherwise.' 'fairyd123', LiveJournal blog, 28 February 2008.

ANALYSIS: Death and loss have always been major themes of *Torchwood*, but never before has an episode been so completely given over to them as 'A Day in the Death'. This was a surprising production choice, in two respects. First, 'Dead Man Walking' had already, quite intentionally, shown Owen progressing from a state of self-pity and hopelessness to one of greater equanimity regarding his changed physical condition, leaving him with a renewed sense of purpose in his role as Torchwood's medic; 'A Day in the Death' arguably just has him go through that same process all over again, but this time makes it the entire focus of the episode. Secondly, devoting a second episode in a row to a story centred around Owen makes a bit of a nonsense of Martha's highly-anticipated three-episode crossover from *Doctor Who*, as she ends up taking a prominent role in only one of the three episodes, 'Reset', and being consigned to the background in the other two – a real wasted opportunity, and a gross under-use of Freema Agyeman's talents.

None of this, however, is any reflection on scriptwriter Joseph Lidster, whose TV debut this is, as he was simply given a brief and asked to follow it. The story he came up with bears certain similarities to Series One's 'Random Shoes', in that it is narrated by a dead man, told mainly in flashback and concludes with a life-affirming message of hope. That, though, is really where the similarities end, and 'A Day in the Death' is certainly the stronger of the two episodes, being better-structured, more thoughtful and frankly just better-written. Particularly clever is the way that Lidster initially leads the viewer to believe that Owen is on the roof for the same reason as Maggie – intending to jump off – and only at the end reveals that he has actually come to terms with his undead state and gone up there to try to talk her out of killing herself. Maggie's story, of having lost her husband, Brian, in a car crash on their wedding day, is a suitably harrowing one, and the shots of her in her blood-soaked wedding dress are highly dramatic, recalling similar imagery from Quentin Tarantino's *Kill Bill* movies. This, though, is not an episode that majors on action set-pieces or gory horror. Rather, it is a relatively low-key affair; an intense character study that offers the viewer a better insight than ever before into what makes Owen tick, and at the same time casts some interesting light on his Torchwood colleagues as they react in their various different ways to his changed circumstances.

Jack's decision to relieve Owen of his Torchwood duties until he has undergone a series of medical tests carried out by Martha at first seems rather harsh and surprising, although no doubt by-the-rulebook, as Owen is clearly no longer subject to any alien influence. It soon becomes apparent, though, that Jack's concern is not so much that Owen represents a continued threat to his fellow team members or to the general public, but that he poses a danger to himself, as he is obviously finding it harder than he initially anticipated to adjust to ongoing existence with his diminished physical capabilities. One particularly problematic aspect of this is that any injuries he sustains will never heal – as evidenced both when he accidentally cuts his hand open on a scalpel and when, in a fit of anger, he deliberately breaks one of his own fingers, as a consequence of which he will henceforth have to have a permanently bandaged left hand. There are some interesting parallels here between Owen's undead nature and Jack's own state of immortality, but also some significant differences, as Owen himself points out: 'You know, you get to live forever, I get to die forever. It's funny, that.'

There are some great scenes in this early part of the episode as Owen finds himself at a complete loss to know what to do with himself, not only at Torchwood, where he is reduced to taking over Ianto's coffee-making responsibilities – the priceless look of hurt and betrayal on Ianto's face when Jack first suggests this affording a rare moment of amusement in what is all told a pretty serious episode – but also at home, where he passes the time by watching some wallpaper TV and throwing out all the food, drink and toiletry products for which he no longer has any use. Toshiko's response to his predicament, visiting him at his flat and proceeding to drink a beer and devour a takeaway pizza while talking incessantly about the trivial irritations of her morning, might at first appear incredibly insensitive, but is actually a deceptively shrewd way of forcing him to face up to, and hopefully get over, the fact that, for those around him, life goes on as before. When, predictably, Owen loses his temper, snaps vindictively at Toshiko and rushes out, it is heartrending to witness, but gives the viewer a new admiration for Toshiko, who has obviously been prepared to expose herself to this incredibly hurtful tirade for the benefit of the man who, despite what has happened to him, she still clearly loves – as she reaffirms later on after Owen, believing that he may be destroyed for good, says his goodbyes to the team and apologises for how he has treated her.

The argument in the flat leads on to a particularly memorable sequence as Owen runs at breakneck speed through a park, along the waterfront and onto a pier and jumps straight into Cardiff Bay, where he remains underwater for 36 minutes before finally emerging to find

Jack waiting for him. As on a number of other occasions, particularly since their conflict and subsequent reconciliation in 'End of Days', one gets the impression here that Jack is acting almost as an older brother or even a father figure to Owen, looking out for him and protecting him. This is a turning point for Owen, a cathartic washing away of much of the angst and self-pity he has been feeling, somewhat akin to the similarly symbolic sequence where the Doctor's companion Ace leaps into the waters of Maiden's Point at the end of the 1989 *Doctor Who* story 'The Curse of Fenric'. Jack then agrees to reinstate Owen to Torchwood as, having no body heat, he is uniquely suited to take on their latest mission, slipping past an array of heat sensors in order to break into the home of eccentric recluse and alien artefact collector Henry Parker and investigate the source of some worrying energy spikes – although, as it turns out, they needn't have bothered breaking in at all, as they could just have sent Toshiko in a short skirt to fix up a meeting with Parker, judging from the admiration he expresses for her legs and the almost childlike curiosity he shows where Torchwood are concerned.

This subplot concerning Parker and his alien artefacts is not one that would be substantial enough to sustain an episode in its own right. Its value in 'A Day in the Death' lies purely in how it further advances Owen's story by bringing him into contact with Parker – an elderly reflection of himself, as Lidster saw it – and ultimately completing his rehabilitation. For any long-time *Doctor Who* fan, it is difficult to forgive Richard Briers for his atrocious performance as the Chief Caretaker in the 1987 story 'Paradise Towers', which by his own admission he saw simply as an opportunity to mess about and have a laugh. As Parker, however, he partly redeems himself, giving a sensitive and affecting performance as a rich but lonely old man terrified of death and clinging on grimly to his last hope, an alien device he has dubbed The Pulse. While it was probably a wise move on the production team's part to edit down significantly the material originally shot for the scene where Parker and Owen sit and talk in the former's mausoleum-like bedroom – although the unedited version, running to as long as 10 minutes and 44 seconds, can be seen in full as part of the deleted scenes package on the Series Two DVD box set – this is arguably the most crucial section of the entire episode. It is here that Owen really hits rock bottom, finding that he has insufficient breath in his lungs to resuscitate Parker when his heart fails, but then comes to realise through his contact with The Pulse that, whatever pale semblance of life he has been left with, it is still worth holding on to, as there is always a glimmer of light in the darkness.

There are a few aspects of the script that don't quite work. One that immediately comes to mind is a very convoluted joke where, in a discussion about Parker, Ianto mentions Tin-Tin, meaning a character from the Gerry Anderson puppet series *Thunderbirds*, in which Parker is the name of Lady Penelope's chauffeur, and Owen misunderstands him to mean Tintin, the hero of the comic book series *The Adventures of Tintin* by Hergé, and proceeds to suggest that the young adventurer, who was never seen with a girlfriend, was having sex with his dog – which all seems a bit random unless one understands the various references. This even gets drawn out into a sort of running joke when, later on, Jack gives Owen a T-shirt bearing an image of Tintin and his dog, Snowy, to wrap around his hand as protection against getting burnt when he disables the electricity generator at Parker's mansion. This is all rather strange, and one is tempted to wonder if it is actually an in-joke inspired by the fact that *Doctor Who* writer and future showrunner Steven Moffat was at that point in discussions to script a trilogy of movies about Tintin to be directed by Steven Spielberg and Peter Jackson for DreamWorks Pictures.

Martha's emotional farewell scene also falls a bit flat, as it is only three days since she first arrived at the Hub, and she has not played a particularly prominent role in either this episode or the last. Admittedly it would have been even odder had Toshiko been there too, as she hasn't had any one-on-one scenes with Martha since she arrived[93], but surely Jack could at least have given Martha a lift to the station – or wherever else she is going at that time of night, as she actually seems to be heading toward the Bay – rather than just let her walk off into the distance with a suitcase in each hand? Mind you, Jack seems distinctly taken aback and uncomfortable when Martha kisses him – her amusing excuse for doing so being 'Well, everyone else has had a go' – although he does quickly recover and say, 'You can *so* come back any time,' to which she replies 'Well, maybe I will, one day' – a portent of things to come in Series Three, perhaps?

Misfires like this are few and far between, though, and overall the script is a superbly assured one by Lidster that certainly does not seem like the work of a TV first-timer. He even manages to avoid depicting Parker's security guards as clichéd heavies, having one of them, Taylor, rush off in concern on learning that his wife is apparently in St Helen's hospital following a car crash – an effective but shockingly harsh lie that Gwen tells him as a diversion when Toshiko manages to patch a call through to his mobile phone – and the other two, Webb and Farrington, be so far removed from the 'shoot first, think later' stereotype that Owen is able to freak them out with his undead state and then knock then unconscious. The exchanges between Owen and Maggie on the roof are admirably economical and free of over-sentimentality, and the interweaving of the flashback scenes is smoothly and seamlessly done – no mean achievement. The revelation of the true purpose of The Pulse is also well achieved, and really rather moving. It is pleasing to note, too, that there are no easy answers offered to Maggie's problems – there is certainly no suggestion that Owen is planning to retcon her, despite the fact that she now knows quite a lot about Torchwood and its operations – and it is left to the viewer's imagination what she will do next, although the strong implication is that she will now decide against committing suicide and instead try to go on with her life, even with the enduring pain of having lost her husband.

One of *Torchwood*'s great strengths is that it has the ability, and the courage, to explore such sophisticated, adult themes in a genre context, and 'A Day in the Death' stands as a well-crafted and thought-provoking meditation on life and death from a humanist perspective.

---

93 Given Toshiko's unhappy history with UNIT, as subsequently revealed in 'Fragments', perhaps she wasn't keen on spending time with Martha …?

2.09 – SOMETHING BORROWED

Writer: Phil Ford
Director: Ashley Way

DEBUT TRANSMISSION DETAILS
BBC Three
Date: 5 March 2008. Scheduled time: 9.50 pm. Actual time: 9.50 pm.
BBC Two
Date: 12 March 2008. Scheduled time: 9.00 pm. Actual time: 9.02 pm.
Duration: 46' 17"

Pre-watershed version
BBC Two
Date: 13 March 2008. Scheduled time: 7.00 pm.
Duration: 45' 33"

ADDITIONAL CREDITED CAST
Nerys Hughes (Brenda[94]), Sharon Morgan (Mary[95]), William Thomas (Geraint[96]), Robin Griffith (Barry[97]), Collette Brown (Carrie), Danielle Henry (Megan), Ceri Ann Gregory (Trina), Jonathan Lewis Owen (Banana Boat), Morgan Hopkins (Mervyn), Valerie Murray (Registrar), Pethrow Gooden[98] (Shop Assistant)

PLOT: Gwen is involved in the hunting down and killing of a ferocious alien shape-shifter, during the course of which it bites her on the left arm. She wakes up the following morning, the day of her long-planned wedding to Rhys, to discover that she is heavily pregnant: the shape-shifter has implanted an egg in her. Gwen insists on going ahead with the wedding, arguing that the problem can be sorted out afterwards. Later, by autopsying the shape-shifter, Owen discovers that it is a Nostrovite, which means that its female partner will be searching for Gwen to rip the alien baby out of her when it is ready to be 'born'. The Nostrovite attacks the wedding guests, but Jack eventually blows it up, while Rhys, following Owen's instructions, uses the singularity scalpel to destroy the alien baby within Gwen. The wedding finally goes ahead, and at the reception Jack drugs all the guests with level six retcon to ensure that they forget the strange things they have witnessed.

---

94 Surname given in dialogue as 'Williams'.
95 Surname given in dialogue as 'Cooper'.
96 Surname given in dialogue as 'Cooper'.
97 Surname given in dialogue as 'Cooper'.
98 Not credited in *Radio Times*.

QUOTE, UNQUOTE

- Shop Assistant: 'Can I help you?'
  Ianto: 'Yeah. I'm looking for a wedding dress for a friend.'
  Shop Assistant: 'Of course you are, sir. You'd be surprised: we're quite used to men buying for "their friends".'

- Toshiko: [Referring to her dress] 'Do you like it?'
  Owen: 'Drop-dead gorgeous, Tosh; and I think I speak with some authority.'

- Brenda: 'What a lovely outfit. Such a brave choice for you.'
  Mary: 'And you were so made for green.'

- Gwen: 'You know, Tosh, it'll happen for you one day. There's always Owen.'
  Toshiko: 'I don't think so. "In sickness and in health, till death do us part" – it's going to sound like a bad joke, isn't it?'

- Jack: 'What is it with you? Ever since Owen died, all you ever do is agree with him.'
  Ianto: 'I was brought up never to speak ill of the dead. Even if they still do most of the talking for themselves.'

DOCTOR WHO REFERENCES

- A schematic diagram of a Cyberman can again be spotted on a wall in the Hub in one scene.

ALIEN TECH

- Owen uses a hand-held scanner to examine Gwen, thus discovering that she is carrying an alien egg.

- Owen has modified the singularity scalpel first seen in 'Reset' and instructs Rhys on how to use it to destroy the Nostrovite baby within Gwen. There is a device called a 'microtron' in the Hub that could have done the same job, but it weighs 'about two tons' and is thus not portable.

- Jack assembles a huge multi-part gun, probably of alien origin, that is kept in the back of the Torchwood SUV, and uses it to blow up the Nostrovite at the wedding.

CONTINUITY POINTS

- It is very difficult to kill a Nostrovite with bullets – particularly when it is consumed by the 'mother instinct'. The creatures are carnivorous, with a taste for human flesh, and have black blood. They owe their shape-shifting ability to an organ described as a 'Proteus gland'. They mate for life. The male carries the fertilised egg in a sack in its mouth and passes it on to a host with a bite. The mother then tracks down the host and rips the baby out of her.

- Banana Boat has apparently been reading a copy of the (fictional) magazine *Peach* – which he must have had in his flat for an unusually long time, as it is the same edition as was seen on sale in the supermarket in 'Out of Time', set over six months earlier. Rhys tells Gwen that Banana Boat was released by the Lanzarote police with a warning – a reference to his recent arrest on the island, as mentioned in passing in 'A Day in the Death'.

- Gwen's mother and father, Mary and Geraint Cooper, are seen for the first time in this episode, as are Rhys's, Brenda and Barry Williams. The Coopers live in Swansea.

- Ianto says that his dad was a master tailor who could 'size a man's inside leg measurement by his stride across the shop threshold'.

PRODUCTION NOTES
- Made with 'Exit Wounds' as part of Block 6 of production.

- This episode had the working title/descriptor 'The Wedding'.

- The sequence of Jack, Ianto and Owen setting off for Gwen's wedding in the SUV was recorded in Roald Dahl Plass on 25 October 2007. This episode's main location shoot, for the wedding and reception, was done over several days at the beginning of November at Margam Country Park in Margam, Port Talbot, in and around a renovated 18th Century building called the Orangery, which can indeed be hired for weddings and other events. The hotel exteriors and shots of the gardens of the wedding venue were taped in Dyffryn Gardens in St Nicholas, Vale of Glamorgan, while the hotel interiors were recorded partly at Court Colman Manor in Pen-y-Fai, Bridgend and partly in studio. Central Cardiff locations used included a men's public toilet in the Hayes and the churchyard of St John's Church in St John's Street, where recording took place on the evening of 19 November for the scenes of Gwen's pursuit of the shape-shifter, and Allison Jayne Ltd in the Friary, which was used for the shop where Ianto buys a new, larger wedding dress for Gwen.

- The tracks playing in the club where Gwen has her hen night are 'Filthy/Gorgeous' and 'Comfortably Numb' by Scissor Sisters from their eponymous first album of 2004 and 'Hole in the Head' by the Sugababes from their 2003 album *Three*. The music heard on Gwen's radio-alarm clock when she wakes to find herself heavily pregnant is 'Fire in My Heart' from the 1999 album *Guerrilla* by Welsh rock band Super Furry Animals. The records played at the wedding reception – where Ianto acts as DJ following the death of Mervyn – are 'You Do Something to Me' by Paul Weller from his 1995 album *Stanley Road* and the huge hit single 'Tainted Love' by Soft Cell from 1981.

- This episode, as the most humorous of the season, was deliberately scheduled amidst a number of particularly dark ones, to provide a respite and contrast.

- The episode opens with a flashback clip from 'Kiss Kiss, Bang Bang' of Gwen and Jack discussing Gwen's engagement. This features a few seconds of material edited out of the original episode: an extra line of dialogue from Gwen, 'I need stability, Jack; someone I can rely on,' and a shot of Jack reacting to this.

- The action takes place over about 24 hours, from a Friday evening to a Saturday evening.

- It was Eve Myles' idea that Gwen should compulsively eat gherkins in the scene just after she discovers she is pregnant; the script had had her simply drinking a glass of water at this point.

- Earlier drafts of the script had Jack retconning Gwen and Rhys as well as the wedding guests at the end of the episode and convincing them that the occasion had gone off without a hitch.

- William Thomas, who portrays Gwen's father Geraint in this episode, also played characters in the *Doctor Who* stories 'Remembrance of the Daleks' and 'Boom Town', making him the first actor to have appeared in all three of the classic series, the new series and *Torchwood*.

- One of the old black-and-white photographs that Jack looks at in the final scene is actually a promotional shot of John Barrowman taken some years earlier for his role as Billy Flynn in the musical *Chicago*.

- The cuts made to this episode for its pre-watershed version included, unsurprisingly, most of the 'death-by-oral-sex' scene in which the Nostrovite feasts on Mervyn the DJ.

OOPS!

- Jack says at one point 'You've heard of immaculate conception, haven't you?' In the Bible, however, this term refers not to the virginal conception of Jesus by Mary, as he seems to be implying, but to the sin-free sexual conception of Mary by *her* mother.

- There is no wedding photographer, and none of the guests is seen to have a camera, which would make this a very unusual wedding indeed. (Possibly, though, for security reasons, Gwen has stipulated in advance that she does not want anyone to take photographs?)

- There is a very noticeable continuity error in the scene where Gwen and Rhys run away from the wedding hotel while, back in the bedroom, Owen shoots the Nostrovite disguised as Jack. Gwen is holding up the skirts of her dress in one shot, so that it is easier for her to run, but not in the next.

PRESS REACTION

- 'The best episode of the series so far. Heck, probably the best episode of *Torchwood* ... Sweet, funny, exciting and with a belting cameo from Nerys Hughes (much loved by fans of *The Liver Birds* and *District Nurse*) thrown in for good measure, it's an absolute corker, even by the high standards of our favourite sci-fi indulgence.' Ceri Thomas, *London Lite*, 12 March 2008.

- '"Something Borrowed" aims somewhere near farce, with Gwen waking up pregnant on her wedding day. It's an engaging set-up, especially as we get more focus on Gwen and Rhys, whose relationship always rings true and is the most believable one in the show. But it's here that we feel *Torchwood*'s 50-minute episodes are an indulgence; this feels overlong and episodic, as the alien shape-shifter is encountered, escapes, is encountered, escapes, and so on. And she's dealt with by simply getting an enormous gun out of Torchwood's SUV. It's neither big nor clever, and the half-hearted and unconvincing subplot about Gwen and Jack loving each other rears its tedious head again. Bonus points for Rhys smacking Jack in the face, though. It's about time.' Jes Bickham, *DeathRay* Issue 12, April 2008.

FAN COMMENT

- 'I didn't have problems with their use of the wake-up-pregnant trope. It wasn't posited as a punishment for being sexual ... It could have happened to any live member of the team, [or] an innocent passer-by that chose to go to the loo at the wrong time, and it was structured as bite rather than rape in the actual attack. The fact that the bite-ee was Gwen worked as it had to, because waking up pregnant with an alien shape-shifter with a taste for human flesh was the maximum human drama choice ... She also didn't feel like a victim. She had too much agency and took enough of her own calls and steps toward saving herself to fall into that trap. While the fact that the others weren't castrated/dumbed down to boost her was a definite bonus ... How much do I love that they didn't fall into the mistake of making Tosh a bridesmaid? ... Tosh turning up with the practical things to help the situation and being there for Gwen made the two women closer and we got them talking in a way that really worked and felt organic ... [The] fact [that] the whole team worked together to help out [and] minimise the damage by staying away until it became essential not only made them look better as a team but also as people/characters that deserve the love ... The episode also managed enough light and humour in the wedding and the way people bitch and try to pull and get pissed and things go wrong that it added the necessary lightness after the Owen Death Arc while not forgetting the consequences of that, from Dead Man Dancing to Owen having only one fully functional hand so someone else had to press the buttons [on the singularity scalpel]. Mmm ... Consequences, I love 'em, and they've really kept those coming.' 'paratti', LiveJournal blog, 5 March 2008.

- 'I have no problem with people writing fanfic about Jack and Ianto and making them sexy and interesting and into an actual relationship if that's the sort of thing they want to read

– there's lots of potential in the pairing, and good fic has been written on a lot less, really. But do I actually see it in the show? Not really. That is, if we are meant to infer that Jack actually has feelings for Ianto, then the writers are doing a very poor job of showing it. I am not saying Jack doesn't love Ianto – he is part of his team, part of his family, and Jack loves them all in his own way … But take away the flirting and the stopwatches, and I get the feeling it isn't all that different from the affection and protectiveness he's shown for Tosh and Owen. Poor ikkle Welsh teaboy is going to get his heart-broken unless we get an unexpected 180° turn before the finale, and I am not sure I like where this is heading … Gwen all but offering undead Owen as a consolation prize to poor-Tosh-who-can't-get-a-man … What was the writer thinking? That's a horrible thing for Gwen to say – it's unfair to Owen, because being undead is bad enough without being offered as a pretend-boyfriend to your friend *by your ex-lover* – "Here, have this one – can't even get it up, but at least it's cured him of his manwhore ways, eh?"; and mostly it's just horrible to Tosh, because apparently she cannot possibly find a breathing man to make her happy and the idea here is "If you can't get the man of your dreams, settle for someone who'll have you," and, wow, if that's supposed to be subtext for Gwen/Rhys I am going to be really, really angry because I like Gwen/Rhys, damn it.' 'mon_starling', LiveJournal blog, 5 March 2008.

ANALYSIS: Coming in the wake of two exceptionally dark and serious episodes, 'Something Borrowed' brings a welcome change of tone and takes *Torchwood* further than ever before into comedy territory. The idea of having Gwen wake up heavily pregnant on the morning of her wedding day is really inspired and gives writer Phil Ford the chance not only to have a bit of fun with the show's regular characters but also to spoof soap-opera-style 'wedding from hell' storylines.

In interviews prior to transmission, Russell T Davies predicted that some fans would find the comedy excessive, but that really isn't an issue here at all, and the episode has actually proved a very popular one amongst fans. If anything, the question to be asked is whether or not the humour has been pushed quite far enough. There is, lurking at the heart of the episode, a more conventional *Torchwood* story about the team trying to prevent one of their number from being killed by a vicious alien shape-shifter, and this means that the viewer is occasionally troubled by sensible questions such as why Jack does not force Gwen to postpone her wedding, despite all her protests, and thereby save everyone present from being exposed to deadly danger – questions that might not have arisen had Ford gone for a still broader approach, perhaps even venturing into the area of farce. Director Ashley Way's lack of a significant track record in comedy is also rather apparent at times, as he does not always manage to extract maximum value from the humour that *is* in the script. This, though, is really just a minor quibble, and – as always where humour is concerned – to a large degree a question of personal taste.

For the first time in Series Two, Gwen is given centre stage in an episode, and Eve Myles takes full opportunity to show off her versatility, demonstrating some great comic timing and proving herself equally adept at handling this sort of material as she is the more action-orientated fare she is usually afforded in the show. Scenes such as the one where Gwen absentmindedly devours a jar of gherkins while snapping angrily at Owen and Jack – poking fun at the familiar pregnancy clichés of unusual food cravings and raging hormones – are hilarious; and the icing on the wedding cake comes when she shoots the Nostrovite with a gun concealed in her bouquet, making this the second episode in a row to evoke memorable imagery from Quentin Tarantino's *Kill Bill*.

Gwen is by no means the only member of the team to be gifted with some great comic material, either. Toshiko's razor-sharp put-downs of the cheesy advances she receives from Rhys's best man, the absurdly-nicknamed Banana Boat, are extremely funny, if perhaps a little uncharacteristic, and Ianto's dry humour is again very much to the fore, one of his best lines coming in the penultimate scene, when Jack tasks the team with carrying out a mop-up operation: 'That's what I love about Torchwood. By day, chasing the scum of the universe. Come midnight, you're the wedding fairy.'

Kai Owen gets another opportunity here to shine as Rhys, having been barely seen since making his most prominent appearances to date in 'Meat' and 'Adam' earlier in the run. He too shows a fine talent for playing humorous dialogue and action, as witnessed to great effect in the sequence where he picks up a chainsaw in a stable and prepares to attack the Nostrovite – in the form of his mother, Brenda, a part clearly relished by the perfectly-cast guest star Nerys Hughes of *The Liver Birds* fame – only to find that the motor cuts out on him. His mortified reaction here is priceless.

The scene in the stable – an appropriate setting for the narrowly-averted 'virgin birth' – is significant for another reason, too, as it effectively brings closure to the unstated competition between Rhys and Jack for Gwen's affections, as alluded to in the flashback to 'Kiss Kiss, Bang Bang' at the start of the episode and, more humorously, in the scene where Jack bursts in and calls a halt to the registrar's first attempt at the marriage ceremony, naturally right at the 'speak now or forever hold your peace' part, somewhat in the manner of Dustin Hoffman's character gatecrashing the wedding and whisking away the bride at the end of the 1967 Mike Nichols movie *The Graduate*. Jack appeared to accept back at the end of 'Meat' that he could never have a conventional romantic relationship with Gwen, and here, after blowing the Nostrovite away with his 'bigger gun', he symbolically places Gwen's hand in Rhys's and says 'The hero always gets the girl.' This is not to say that he and Gwen don't still have strong feelings for each other, or indeed an intense attraction, as is quite apparent when they dance together at the reception – interrupted only when Ianto cuts in, amusingly not to dance with Gwen, as she initially assumes, but with Jack – but the wedding really draws a line under this ongoing plot strand, at least for the time being.

One does actually have to feel a little sorry for Ianto here. It is clear that he regards his relationship with Jack as a serious and committed one – when, in 'A Day in the Death', Owen implies that it is just about the sex, he replies 'It's not like that' – but it is by no means certain that Jack feels the same way. In a comment he makes while dancing with Gwen, Jack even seems to equate having sex with Ianto with eating a pizza, suggesting that he sees it as essentially recreational. Even after Ianto cuts in – a significant move for him, as it brings the relationship fully into the open before the rest of the team for the first time – it is obvious that Jack only has eyes and thoughts for Gwen.

A poignant coda to this comes in the final scene of the episode, before the 'Next Time' trailer, as Jack returns to the Hub and looks wistfully through some yellowing old black-and-white portrait photographs of himself, including finally one of him in a morning suit seated beside a woman in a wedding dress – presumably his bride from some long-ago relationship that can only have ended with the woman growing old and dying while Jack remained young and immortal. The viewer is put in mind here not only of Jack's relationship with Estelle Cole from 'Small Worlds' but also of how, in *Doctor Who*, the Doctor's longevity has condemned him always to lose his human friends and lovers, leaving him bereft and alone, a sadness foregrounded in episodes such as 'School Reunion' and 'The Girl in the Fireplace'. Small wonder that Jack felt that he had to let Gwen go to Rhys, regardless of the hurt this clearly caused him.

These scenes are very well played by John Barrowman, who is on excellent form throughout the episode, showing no signs of the fatigue he would subsequently tell interviewers that he was feeling by this late stage of production on Series Two. He even gets a chance to portray, briefly, an evil version of Jack, as the Nostrovite temporarily adopts his form and moves in on Gwen, initially as if to kiss her – prompting Gwen to admit that if she hadn't met Jack, she would have already been married to Rhys by now – but actually with the intention of ripping her open and retrieving its baby from her belly. This is just one of a number of instances where the Torchwood team's rather clichéd insistence on splitting up leads to uncertainty, both for them and for the viewer, as to whose appearance the Nostrovite is currently mimicking – a confusion that brings some amusing consequences, such as when Jack, mistaking the real Brenda for the Nostrovite copy, holds a gun on her and shouts 'Get back, you ugly bitch!', earning himself a punch from Rhys when her true identity becomes apparent as Gwen recognises Brenda's 'bloody awful perfume'. The fact that the Nostrovite is never actually seen to switch identities in shot just adds to the fun of trying to spot which of the characters it is masquerading as – and no doubt it also helped to save some money from the show's visual effects budget, as there is very little CGI in evidence in this episode.

A word of praise should go here to actress Collette Brown – previously seen as a regular in *Casualty*, *Ultraviolet*, *Holby City* and *Doctors*, to name but a few of her credits – who, in the role of Carrie, the form taken by the Nostrovite for much of the action at the wedding, gives a suitably sinister-but-sexy performance as a literal *femme fatale*. The horrific yet darkly amusing scene where she starts devouring Mervyn, the wedding DJ, while performing oral sex on him is one of the most astonishing to have been presented by *Torchwood* to date, and surely unique in the history of genre TV shows.

The make-up effects used for the Nostrovite when its alien form starts to break through its various human disguises are relatively simple but highly effective, the long talons, red eyes, dark veins on the face and double row of sharp, blackened teeth giving it something of a vampire-like appearance. This recalls Owen's own undead status, one of the few references to which in this episode comes when the Nostrovite, still in Jack's form, refuses to kill him – even though Owen says 'Come on then, do me a favour' – presumably because, as Owen later puts it, 'It thought I'd gone off'. Psychologically, the Torchwood medic seems almost back to his old self by this point, and even invites Toshiko to dance with him at the reception, albeit with the distinctly bad-taste question, 'Are you ready to see that dead man dance, Tosh?'

The life-cycle of the Nostrovite – in which the threatened 'father' implants eggs in a human host by way of a bite, then the 'mother' forcibly extracts the baby the following day when it is ready to be 'born' – is well worked out by Phil Ford and gives the episode a solid science fiction basis, albeit that, like that of the Mayfly creature in 'Reset', it is essentially just another variation on the familiar *Alien* theme. It is admittedly hard to credit that all the wedding guests would so readily accept that Gwen is suddenly showing all the signs of a full-term pregnancy – particularly given that some of her friends actually spent the previous evening with her at her hen do – but this is really just another of those issues that is best glossed over in an episode so heavily geared toward humour. The friends' rationalisation that they failed to spot the bump due to 'camouflage dressing' by Gwen and the amount of alcohol they had consumed deals with it neatly enough. Having said that, the disappearance of Mervyn will surely be more difficult to explain, or at least require some exceptionally good cover-up work by Torchwood, notwithstanding the fact that all the guests are retconned by Jack at the end – although, on the other hand, his death and the other traumatic events they have witnessed haven't actually stopped them from going ahead with the wedding, or enjoying themselves at the reception!

That *Torchwood* can present ultra-dark episodes like 'Dead Man Walking' and 'A Day in the Death' alongside light and humorous ones like 'Something Borrowed', and do both equally well, is testament to the strength and flexibility of the show's format. Its wide variety of stories is surely one of the main reasons why it has been such a big hit with the general viewing public, and bodes very well for its long-term future.

2.10 – FROM OUT OF THE RAIN

Writer: Peter J Hammond
Director: Jonathan Fox Bassett

DEBUT TRANSMISSION DETAILS
BBC Three
Date: 12 March 2008. Scheduled time: 9.50 pm. Actual time: 9.50 pm.
BBC Two
Date: 19 March 2008. Scheduled time: 9.00 pm. Actual time: 8.59 pm.
Duration: 45' 31"

Pre-watershed version
BBC Two
Date: 20 March 2008. Scheduled time: 7.00 pm.
Duration: 45' 23"

ADDITIONAL CREDITED CAST
Julian Bleach (Ghostmaker), Camilla Power (Pearl), Craig Gallivan[99] (Jonathan[100]), Gerard Carey (Greg)[101], Steven Marzella[102] (Dave Penn), Hazel Wyn Williams (Faith Penn), Lowri Sian Jones (Nettie[103]), Eileen Essell (Christina), Anwen Carlisle (Restaurant Owner), Yasmin Wilde (Senior Nurse), Caroline Sheen (A&E Nurse), Alastair Sill[104] (Young Dad), Catherine Olding[105] (Young Mum)

PLOT: The reopening of the Electro Cinema with a screening of vintage black-and-white film coincides with a peak of rift activity and allows two supernatural circus performers, the Ghostmaker and Pearl, members of a group known as the Night Travellers who were in the Joshua Joy travelling show in the 1920s, to escape from the film and take on physical form. They attack a number of Cardiff residents, the Ghostmaker stealing their last breaths and Pearl absorbing all the water from their bodies, leaving them in a cataleptic state. They intend to abduct their victims to become an eternal audience for their travelling show, and also aim to liberate the others of their kind from the film. Jack realises that the Night Travellers can be

---

99 Role mistakenly credited to 'Stephen Marzella' in *Radio Times*.

100 Surname given as 'Penn' in the episode.

101 Not credited in *Radio Times*, and does not appear in the episode. This appears to be a credit mistakenly carried over from 'Meat', in which the character does feature.

102 Credited for incorrect role and first name spelt differently in *Radio Times*.

103 Surname given in dialogue as 'Williams'.

104 Not credited in *Radio Times*.

105 Not credited in *Radio Times*.

destroyed by taking their pictures again and exposing the film to sunlight. He puts this plan into action, and it works – but not in time to prevent the Ghostmaker, in an act of revenge, releasing all the victims' last breaths from the flask in which they have been stored. Ianto manages to catch to the flask in time to save just one breath, which Jack then uses to revive the victim from whom it was taken: a young boy, who has been lying close to death in hospital.

QUOTE, UNQUOTE
- Ianto: 'That film was beautiful. All those acts performing for us. Part of history, trapped on film forever.'
  Jack: 'Their days were numbered. Cinema may have saved their images, but if finished off the travelling shows; killed them.'

- Pearl: 'Make her cry … I want to drink her tears.'

- Christina: 'Your eyes are older than your face.'
  Jack: 'Is that a bad thing?'
  Christina: 'Yes. It means you don't belong. It means you're from … nowhere.'

DOCTOR WHO REFERENCES
- None.

ALIEN TECH
- None.

CONTINUITY POINTS
- Toshiko says that the Electro Cinema has a history of rift activity but has been quiet for years. The Cinema is also referred to by its proprietor as the 'Electro Museum', and is said to be in Hope Street (a fictional address).

- Jack says that the Night Travellers performed only in the dead of night. 'It was just a tale that was around at that time. A ghost story. They came from out of the rain – that's how people described them.' He adds that they 'left a trail of damage and sorrow wherever they performed'. Jack himself was part of a different show, a small company working the UK, in which he was billed as 'The Man Who Couldn't Die'. He tells Ianto that he was 'sent to investigate rumours of the Night Travellers', but will not say who sent him, noting simply 'Long story'. (Could his time in the travelling show be when he had a relationship with twin acrobats, as mentioned in 'They Keep Killing Suzie'?)

PRODUCTION NOTES
- Made with 'Fragments' as part of Block 5 of production.

- The scenes of the travelling show were shot overnight on 13 September 2007 in Cardiff's Bute Park, previously used for the Hooverville sequences in the *Doctor Who* story 'Daleks in Manhattan'/'Evolution of the Daleks'. Those of the empty open-air swimming pool visited by the Ghostmaker and Pearl were done the following day at the disused Ynysangharad Park lido in Pontypridd. The Electro exterior scenes and some of the interiors were recorded from 7 to 10 October at the Paget Rooms in Penarth, previously featured in the same writer's Series One episode 'Small Worlds'; the use of heavy simulated rain on the evening of 10 October resulted in the cast members getting soaked in cold water. The exteriors of Jonathan's flat were shot just around the corner, in Station Road. The cinema interiors were done elsewhere, at the Phoenix Cinema in Pentre, Mid-Glamorgan. The hospital scenes were taped at the District Miners' Hospital in Caerphilly, previously used as a location on 'Reset'. The Windsor Café, where the Ghostmaker and Pearl attack the owner, is a genuine establishment in Windsor Road, Penarth. Further location recording took place on 17 October in Romilly Crescent, Cardiff, for the scenes of the exterior area where Jonathan is seen running down a flight of steps and past a graffiti-covered wall with a can of film five minutes into the episode, and where the Ghostmaker is captured on film and destroyed at the end.

- As usual on the show, water from a decommissioned fire engine was used to make the roads wet and create the simulated rain during location recording.

- As on 'Small Worlds', writer Peter J Hammond was given *carte blanche* by the production team to come up with his own ideas for this episode. He drew inspiration from one of his earlier *Sapphire & Steel* stories, sometimes referred to as 'The Man Without a Face', in which images of people from old black and white photographs come to life. (This same story had previously been a source of inspiration for aspects of a number of *Doctor Who* stories, most notably 'The Idiot's Lantern'.) Hammond's script originally called for the Ghostmaker to steal people's shadows as well as their last breaths, but this was changed as it was considered too time-consuming and difficult to realise effectively.

- The version of this episode shown on the BBC HD channel inadvertently omitted all the opening credit captions, including the title.

- For the first and only time during Series Two, the original BBC Three transmission of this episode did not have the channel's bright pink logo – otherwise known as digital onscreen graphic (DOG) – superimposed in the top left corner of the picture. This departure from the norm was warmly welcomed by many fans but is believed to have been inadvertent on the channel's part.

OOPS!

- Watching the old film projected in the Hub, Jack says of two clowns, who are later revealed to be Night Travellers, 'I knew those two. They argued day and night.' Shots of

Jack's own act are also interspersed with those of the Night Travellers. Later in the same scene, however, he says that he never worked with the Night Travellers and never knew anyone who did.

PRESS REACTION

- 'It's been hard to track a consistent thread through *Torchwood*, but this week's ghost story, "From Out of the Rain", was the kind of haunting tale that *The X Files* used to do so well. Featuring old school funfair characters who stepped out of black and white film to steal the last breath of life from their victims, there was a visual poetry at play that caught the spirit of Fellini. If John Barrowman had just cranked the camp button down a notch, it would have been perfect.' Keith Watson, *Metro*, 20 March 2008.

- 'It's less *Doctor Who*, more *Tales of the Unexpected* or *Sapphire & Steel* (one of writer Peter J Hammond's old scripting gigs) ... as this chunk of *Torchwood* pitches a solid old-fashioned ghost story ... If you stop and think about the plot, you'll find there are gaps in the logic of it all that you could drive Torchwood's flashy 4x4 through, but documentary realism this ain't, and more importantly you can't fault the creepy atmosphere.' Ceri Thomas, *London Lite*, 19 March 2008.

- 'Twenty minutes in, my girlfriend piped up, "Why do they keep repeating things?" My answer: "Cos this is what TV drama was like 30 years ago, when audiences were 'less sophisticated'." P J Hammond, creator of surreal '70s spookfest *Sapphire & Steel*, is the man responsible for "From Out of the Rain", and it feels like a script he's had in his drawer for 30 years. Problem is, once the episode has set out its stall, it totally fails to develop. It's glacially slow, with an awful lot of people standing around reiterating information in case the audience was too slow-witted to get it the first time, and endless shots of Cardiff roundabouts.' Ian Berriman, *SFX* Issue 170, June 2008.

FAN COMMENT

- 'If *Torchwood* wants to be a supernatural series, I wish they'd just go ahead and admit it. Even *Star Trek*, which did fairly stretch the definition of sci-fi on occasion, managed to devote at least two lines of technobabble to any given crisis in order for it to stay within the realms of science fiction. My issue with *Torchwood* doing the supernatural is that when it's being its sci-fi self the rest of the time, it's unremittingly sci-fi. You have rifts in time, aliens, temporal schisms ... These do give you the latitude to encompass supernatural happenings under the general umbrella of science fiction, but there's not even a vague attempt to do that ... Perhaps *Torchwood* is still suffering somewhat from a lack of firm direction. You can see this in the way that [different episodes] seems to address the same things in different manners. In "Meat", Jack wants to save aliens, in "Reset" he's happy to kill them. Character interactions are handled differently from episode to episode. Is it any wonder that fans are left a little confused and with no clear idea of where things are going? Yes, it's a million times better than the first series, but it's still somewhat chaotic. However, if you look at "From Out of the Rain", and divorce yourself from the expectations you might hold it to because of *Torchwood*'s "official" science fiction leanings (although, I suppose now would be a good time to mention that the BBC simply classifies *Torchwood* as "drama"), you actually have a very good episode. It's different. It gives us some quiet character scenes. It gives a genuine sense of being creepy in some places. The solution isn't violence, but cleverness.' 'Jewels', www.b-jewelled.co.uk, undated.

- 'It was immediately clear that this episode was written by the same writer as "Small Worlds". Jack hearing strange whispering noises in the Hub, check. Big mystic portentous things happening that make no sense, check. A few striking images, but no emotional involvement, check. Bad things happening to a cardboard suburban family with small children, check. Jack playing Grab-a-Granny again, check. And indeed, P J Hammond was the writer of both episodes. And unfortunately so, because, to be brutally frank, I think that this and "Small Worlds" are contenders for the worst *Torchwood* episodes ever. Why? Because as a writer, he seems to have no interest at all in the Torchwood characters or their personalities or relationships or anything that makes the show engaging, entertaining or watchable. This could almost have been an episode of anything: the Torchwood team were there only to move around like sock puppets, spouting plot points and advancing the mystic and portentous storyline. The only one [Hammond] seems at all interested in is Jack, and only because his immortality seemingly makes him a good vehicle for mystic portentousness, despite the fact that it's nothing like anything the Jack we know would ever say. I really like *Torchwood* … and … the characters and their interaction are why I enjoy it so much. Sure, the team are flawed and inconsistent and impulsive and immature, but that's why they feel like real people, and that's why I care about them. But here there was nothing. A few spots of atmosphere, but virtually no relevance to anything that has gone before in the series or (I'm guessing here) anything that will come after … Loads of scenes featuring just Jack and Ianto should be a great opportunity, yet all they ever did was engage in endless plot exposition. What a sad waste.' Red Scharlach, LiveJournal blog, 13 March 2008.

- 'While the idea is glorious and timeless (in that Hammond is playing with the idea of souls stolen by the art and mechanics of photography, drawing on Ficino's idea of *Spiritus de Vita*, or breath of life) the end result has more in common with film stock discarded on the cutting room floor than with a finished, successful, completed film. Er … episode. Why? Well, no-one we care about, even a little, is in jeopardy. And despite the glorious sense of the weird and otherworldly – mainly created by the "mermaid" character, who I thought was fabulous – at no time did I get a visceral sense that anything was really at stake. Not even when those who *came from out of the rain* targeted children. Oh, team Torchwood rushed around Cardiff, ran upstairs and downstairs at the Electro – in scenes vaguely reminiscent of the Keystone Cops – but somehow all that rushing failed to impart urgency. Also lacking was much of a sense of teamwork or continuity in terms of characterisation … Furthermore I found it unfathomable that Jack would need to turn to Ianto for local knowledge, when it's been implied that Jack has been in and around Cardiff since before the end of the last century … And I would have expected him to be undercover with the carnival in some way that didn't involve or imply *blowing his own head off night after night as the man who can't die*. In the '20s … they'd have cried foul. Accused him of Satanism. There would have been public outcry. And, even leaving all that aside, if Jack was trying to keep a low profile on the slow road through history, he'd surely catch a bullet between his teeth or be the other end of a knife thrower's act. I can't see him dying nightly to amuse a select audience.' 'Boji', LiveJournal blog, 13 March 2008.

- 'Even by the end of the episode, the Ghostmaker's motive is never really established. Seemingly his quest is to stay alive, then it's about being remembered, then it's about stealing a person's last breath, then it's about having an audience, then it's about watching the ghosts, and then about taking over the city. Pearl … seems to crave/need water – in a city that is mostly bordered by water, you'd think she would come by it easily enough. It even crossed my mind that she'd require fresh water … until she mentions wanting to drink tears. The whole idea of dehydration seems to just be a mechanism to give a special nod to the make-up team – the point of sucking the moisture out of people never really materialises. Jack's presence in the film footage is improperly explained, at different times leading the viewer to believe he both travelled with and never met the Night Travellers. The audience are left shaking their heads in confusion, desperately trying to make sense out of all these riddles.' Ceres D'Aleo, Torchwood Guide website, undated.

ANALYSIS: Writer Peter J Hammond is held in high esteem by many genre TV fans in the UK for the outstanding work he did on iconic 1970s series such as *Ace of Wands* and his own creation *Sapphire & Steel*, but his Series One contribution 'Small Worlds' led some to question just how well-suited his approach was to *Torchwood*. On the evidence of 'From Out of the Rain', those doubts were well-founded.

Hammond's trademark style is far more science fantasy than science fiction. His fertile imagination produces stories replete with creepy imagery and spooky incident, but the explanations provided – if any – tend to be couched in abstract, metaphysical terms. This sits awkwardly with the rational, scientific ethos of the *Doctor Who/Torchwood* universe. 'Small Worlds' just about got away with it by virtue of the fact that its evil fairies were ultimately just as much of an enigma to Torchwood as to the viewer – the only way Jack could describe them was as 'something from the dawn of time … part of our world, yet we know nothing about them … with a touch of myth, a touch of the spirit world, a touch of reality, all jumbled together'. In 'From Out of the Rain', however, Jack not only seems unfazed by the fantastical, *Sapphire & Steel*-inspired notion that images of people captured on a piece of celluloid could somehow escape from it and take on corporeal form, but actually manages to come up with a way of destroying them – by filming them again, and then exposing the footage to sunlight – even though this is totally barmy and he can have no reason to suppose that it will actually work. It is as if, for this episode only, Jack has started to think in a completely different way, abandoning his normal scientific worldview and proposing a solution that really defies reason. And, what's more, the other members of the team don't challenge him on this, but actually go along with it – and, lo and behold, it works! This is not a case where an apparently supernatural occurrence can be attributed to the operation of an alien artefact with properties not fully comprehensible in current scientific terms – as, for instance, with the Dogon eye in 'Random Shoes' or the resurrection glove in 'Dead Man Walking' – but is tantamount to the use of magic, with Jack acting as a sort of wizard.[106]

Then there is the business about the Ghostmaker putting people into a cataleptic state by capturing their last breath in a flask, which seems to equate the victims' breath with what might be described in pseudo-scientific terms as their life force – a phrase that Jack does actually use at one point – or in religious terms as their soul. Thus when all the breaths are collected together in the flask they do not simply become a homogenous mixture of exhaled air, as would be the case in reality, but somehow stay separate and discrete, so that there remains the possibility of them being returned to those from whom they were taken – as happens at the end with the young boy in the hospital, who immediately revives. This would be unproblematic if breath was used as a metaphor for life force throughout, and would actually accord rather well with concepts established in earlier episodes such as 'They Keep Killing Suzie', where Suzie leeches Gwen's life force from her and eventually reduces her to a state of unconsciousness. At times, though, it does seem to refer literally to the victims' breath, and this comes across as just another piece of pure fantasy. The notion of Pearl being able somehow to drain the water from people's bodies – implied, if not shown, to be distinct from the Ghostmaker's stealing of their breath – is rather more plausible. No clue is given as to the nature or origin of the mysterious Night Travellers – which is fine in itself, although it precludes them being given any real characterisation – so it is perfectly possible to imagine that they might be creatures possessing such powers. Even so, there is a lack of coherence in the way that all these ideas are put together. Presumably what Hammond was aiming for with the Ghostmaker's stealing of breath and Pearl's absorption of water was to show that the Night Travellers pose a variety of different but equally macabre threats. (After air and water, maybe heat and substance would have been what two of the others sought to extract from their victims' bodies, invoking the four classical elements of air, water, fire and earth from Greek mythology.) But, at the same time, there is already the threat of people being abducted by the Night Travellers to become an eternal audience for their show, and at one point we see that a number of the victims have already been gathered together to stand silent and motionless in what appears to be an empty storeroom at a deserted lido. This all seems very muddled.

Another problem with Hammond's script is that he doesn't seem to have a very good grasp of the Torchwood team's characters. Even leaving aside Jack's aforementioned plunge into the realms of fantasy, the regulars' dialogue is for the most part very generic and fails to capture their familiar personalities. The idea of Ianto harbouring a love of vintage cinema, stemming from his father having taken him to the Electro as a boy, is admittedly a very fitting one, tying in well with his established professional interest in historical record-keeping for Torchwood, but

---

106 A similar idea of characters being liberated from a film and coming to life was featured in the episode 'Chick Flick' in Season Two of the witchcraft-themed US series *Charmed*, where it was indeed explained in purely magical terms.

his sudden transformation into an overtly emotional person with a great empathy for children is very odd, albeit that Gareth David-Lloyd gives another fine performance here. The idea that Jack might once have used his immortality as the basis of a carnival act is suitably dark for *Torchwood*, but also rather jarring, not only because it inappropriately trivialises his multiple deaths, but also because it seems to overlook the trauma he suffers each time he comes back to life – a sensation he describes in 'Kiss Kiss, Bang Bang' as 'like being hauled over broken glass'. Poor Toshiko, meanwhile, barely gets a look in this time, being confined to the Hub for the whole episode and given very little dialogue. At one point, Jack even walks off in the middle of a conversation with her!

Worst of all, though, and astonishingly given Hammond's reputation and wealth of experience, the script simply doesn't pass muster as a piece of drama. The Torchwood team initially have no real reason to connect the attacks on the apparently comatose victims with the mystery of the self-playing film at the Electro, other than that they occurred quite close by, and yet they obviously do, as no sooner have they agreed on the urgency of finding out who is responsible for the attacks than they all go back to the Hub to watch some old black and white movies! Then there is the dreadful scene where a nurse at the hospital overhears Jack use the phrase 'from out of the rain', is able by virtue of a jaw-dropping coincidence to connect this with a psychiatric patient she once had – 'She was a strange one,' she reflects, as if this was unusual for a psychiatric patient – and then, presumably breaking every medical confidentiality rule in the book, proceeds to tell Jack and Ianto all about the woman. When the two men go to visit the patient, who was indeed witness to an earlier visit by the Night Travellers (although surely not in 1901, as the following scene seems to suggest, as that would make her over 110 years old), it turns out that she does not seem mentally challenged at all, just unusually perceptive – a terrible cliché. The attempt to manufacture a happy ending when Jack and Ianto manage to save the young boy's life, which even moves Ianto to tears of joy, falls completely flat when one realises that all of the boy's immediate family have been killed, not to mention numerous other Cardiff residents. (Intriguingly, this is almost a reversal of the situation at the end of 'Small Worlds', where Jack effectively sacrifices the life of one child in order to save everyone else – except that in 'From Out of the Rain' he has even less of a choice and just saves the only life he can.) To cap it all, the episode is packed with incredibly repetitive exposition, which Jack in particular seems to spout at every conceivable opportunity. It has been said by some reviewers that this reflects the typical narrative style of telefantasy shows of the 1960s and 1970s, implying that Hammond's approach to scriptwriting in this genre has failed to keep pace with the times, but that is really an unwarranted slur on those classic productions of earlier eras, which very rarely showed so little confidence in their viewers' ability to follow a plot.

On the plus side, there is no denying the potency of Hammond's inspired imagery; and his decision to place the Night Travellers in the context of a travelling show was very astute, given how many people find carnival acts inherently scary and the way this has been exploited on screen before in, for instance, the 1983 movie adaptation of Ray Bradbury's *Something Wicked This Way Comes*, the US TV series *Carnivàle* (HBO, 2003-2005) and indeed the 1988/89 *Doctor Who* story 'The Greatest Show in the Galaxy'. In addition, this episode has some of the best production values yet seen in *Torchwood*. Director Jonathan Fox Bassett, making his debut contribution on this block, does a great job, demonstrating an excellent feel for the show's trademark urban, rain-soaked visual style and bringing the creepy atmosphere of Hammond's story very effectively to the screen. The scenes of the Joshua Joy travelling show are superbly shot, having an appropriately luminous, filmic quality to them – something one comes to appreciate even more on seeing in *Torchwood Declassified* how ingeniously it was achieved with relatively limited resources – and the Ghostmaker and Pearl are suitably eerie figures. The former in particular benefits from some wonderful make-up and costume design and is brilliantly portrayed by Julian Bleach, later to take on the iconic mantle of Davros in *Doctor Who*. The episode's effects work is also top notch, the emergence of the Night Travellers from the old film footage being particularly well-realised. The chosen locations are excellent, too, the sequences shot at the disused lido being especially memorable. (As crime novelist Raymond Chandler famously put it, nothing ever looks emptier than an empty swimming pool.) There is, though, one truly bizarre element in the production: the young man Jonathan's flat seems to be part of, or perhaps behind, a row of ordinary terraced houses, but turns out to be some sort of disused warehouse, with a bath placed incongruously in the middle of one floor!

In the final analysis, despite some imaginative ideas, fantastic imagery and first-rate production standards, 'From Out of the Rain' simply doesn't work as a *Torchwood* story, and sadly has to be counted the weakest episode of either series to date.

2.11 – ADRIFT

Writer: Chris Chibnall
Director: Mark Everest

DEBUT TRANSMISSION DETAILS
BBC Three
Date: 19 March 2008. Scheduled time: 10.00 pm. Actual time: 10.00 pm.
BBC Two
Date: 21 March 2008. Scheduled time: 9.00 pm. Actual time: 9.00 pm.
Duration: 48' 34"

Pre-watershed version
BBC Two
Date: 25 March 2008. Scheduled time: 7.00 pm.
Duration: 48' 07"

ADDITIONAL CREDITED CAST
Tom Price (PC Andy), Ruth Jones (Nikki[107]), Robert Pugh (Jonah[108]), Lorna Gayle (Helen), Oliver Ferriman (Young Jonah[109])

PLOT: Gwen is persuaded by her former colleague PC Andy to look into the strange disappearance seven months earlier of a 15-year-old boy named Jonah Bevan, which turns out to be one of an unusually large number of unsolved missing persons cases in Cardiff. She discovers with Toshiko's help that the disappearances have all coincided with negative rift activity spikes – so the rift does not just deposit people in the city, it also takes people away. Jack seems to know more about this than he is letting on and instructs Gwen to drop the investigation. Disregarding this, she eventually learns that some of the missing people are being held in a secret, run-down care facility established by Jack on Flat Holm island in the Bristol Channel. They were all taken by the rift and subsequently returned, but in highly damaged states. Jonah is there, but has aged some 40 years since he disappeared and has been left physically and emotionally scarred by his ordeal. Despite Jack's continued misgivings, Gwen insists on bringing Jonah's mother Nikki to the island to be reunited with her son. However, the full extent of Jonah's madness then becomes clear: he screams for 20 hours each day, and is getting worse all the time. Nikki is left distraught.

---

107 Surname given in dialogue as 'Bevan'.

108 Credited as 'Old Man' in *Radio Times*, to avoid revealing in advance the fact that Jonah ages during the course of the story. Surname given in dialogue as 'Bevan'.

109 Credited as simply 'Jonah' in *Radio Times*.

QUOTE, UNQUOTE

- Andy: 'Look, sorry, is this beneath you now?'
  Gwen: 'No.'
  Andy: 'Then what's with the attitude? You've got a face like a slapped arse.'

- Jonah: 'I was walking home. There was a light. I woke up and the land was on fire, and the flames were miles on end. A man pulled me from the flames, took me to a building and tried to work on the burns. I thought I was gonna die. I don't remember when the ground started shaking. And then I realised, it wasn't a building at all, it was a rescue craft. The last off a burning planet. We watched a solar system burn. It was so beautiful.'

- Gwen: 'They say you can visit, whenever you like, when he's in a good phase.'
  Nikki: 'Promise me you won't do this to anyone else. Before, I had the memory. Whenever I thought of him, I'd see him laughing with his mates, playing football, scoffing his breakfast. But now I just hear that … that terrible noise.'
  Gwen: 'I thought you wanted to know what happened to him.'
  Nikki: 'I did. I was wrong. It was better when I didn't know. Before you, I had hope.'

DOCTOR WHO REFERENCES

- None.

ALIEN TECH

- None.

CONTINUITY POINTS

- Gwen and Andy may have been lovers for a time around 2005. Andy says that he did not attend Gwen's recent wedding because he did not want to sit there and see her pledge her life to Rhys: 'I'm not like a bloody tap. I can't just switch it off.' Gwen replies: 'But this was like, what, three years ago. Look, I didn't know, I didn't realise you still had feelings.'

- While previous episodes such as 'Out of Time' and 'Kiss Kiss, Bang Bang' have shown that it is possible to enter the time rift intentionally during a period of rift activity, 'Adrift' is the first to reveal that the rift actually takes people (and presumably objects) away, this showing up as a negative spike of rift activity on the Hub's systems. It later returns some of them, though by no means all, as there are only 17 returnees in Jack's facility but far more missing persons cases recorded.

- Jack tells Gwen that when he took over Torchwood (revealed in 'Fragments' to be at the start of 2000), there were two people like Jonah, ravaged from falling through the rift, left neglected in the vault at the Hub. He set up the secret facility on Flat Holm because he wanted them looked after, telling the staff that they were 'experiments that had gone wrong'. The number has increased over the past year, 'like the rift is trying to correct its mistakes'. They are 'sick in ways you can't imagine'.

PRODUCTION NOTES

- Made as a single-episode Block 7 of production, 'double banked' with Block 5 ('From Out of the Rain' and 'Fragments'), hence the limited availability of some of the regular cast members to feature in the action and the involvement of Sophie Fante as producer alongside Richard Stokes.

- The Cardiff Bay Barrage is the scene of Jonah's original disappearance, as subsequently investigated by Captain Jack – a sequence that appears to have been recorded much earlier than the rest of the episode, on 4 July 2007. Nikki's house, seen by Jonah from the Barrage, is on Llwyn Passat in Penarth Marina. The scenes of the missing persons meeting organised by Nikki were shot at the Church of All Saints on Victoria Square, Penarth, on 22 September. Two days later, the café sequences with Gwen and Andy were recorded in Fortes Café in Barry Island. The argument between Gwen and Rhys was shot in Bute Park. Flat Holm island, where the time-displaced refugees are looked after by Captain Jack's team, is a real location in the Bristol Channel, the exterior scenes of which were recorded at the end of September. There is a derelict cholera isolation hospital on the island, but the interior scenes of the Torchwood facility were actually shot elsewhere, at MoD Caerwent in Caldicott, previously used as a location on 'Sleeper'. The marina jetty at the Port of Cardiff was the venue for the scene of Gwen taking the boat out to Flat Holm, leaving Andy behind.

- The music heard in the café the first time that Gwen and Andy meet there is 'Serious' by Richard Hawley from his 2007 album *Lady's Bridge* and the second time is 'Hard to Beat' by Hard-Fi, a 2005 single from their album *Stars of CCTV*. The music playing in the background in the scene where Gwen brings Rhys toast in bed is 'Other Side of the World' by K T Tunstall from her 2005 album *Eye to the Telescope*.

- The script for this episode underwent less rewriting than any other *Torchwood* script to date; the final version was essentially just a second draft. Gwen was originally to have adopted Rhys's surname, Williams, but this idea was dropped as Eve Myles felt that the strongly independent professional woman would want to continue using her maiden name. Ianto was originally to have given Gwen the Flat Holm coordinates on a Post-It note rather than a GPS device. A minor change made in editing of the finished episode was the excision of a short scene hinting at a romance developing between Nikki and Andy; this is one of the deleted scenes included on the Series Two DVD box set.

- The 'Next Time …' trailer at the end of this episode features a Captain Jack voiceover: 'Some people believe that in the moments before your death, your life flashes before your eyes'. It was recorded especially for this purpose and is not heard in 'Fragments'.

OOPS!

- In the scene where Gwen sends Andy to get cups of tea for them as a ruse so that she can bribe the boat owner to take her to Flat Holm alone, there is a shot where it is obvious that the two polystyrene cups that Andy is holding are actually empty.

PRESS REACTION

- 'It's a largely lovely episode, if predictable; a quiet, grief-ridden character piece that also scores by including Andy, Gwen's policeman mate, and some more superb Rhys/Gwen scenes that aren't afraid to show the ugliness as well as the wonder of relationships. (We dropped our collective sandwiches when Rhys shouts "Sometimes I fucking hate you!" at Gwen. Kai Owen and Eve Myles do excellent work here.) But it's also an episode that's almost ruined by an astonishingly anachronistic scene where Gwen walks into a half-naked tryst between Ianto and Jack, playing "naked hide and seek".' Jes Bickham, *DeathRay* Issue 12, April 2008.

- 'Chris Chibnall's poignant script neatly brings out the conflicting components within Gwen's character, aided by a great performance from Eve Myles. In light of recent high-profile disappearances, the subject matter is very contempory and boosts the impact of the story, and forces us to consider what we'd do in Gwen's circumstances. Is it best to reveal the truth and remove the hope from the parents of the missing, or conceal the truth and allow them to go on searching in vain? Captain Jack's shady but benevolent dealings with the off-shore facility build intrigue and ultimately demonstrate that it's not only space whales that he can show compassion towards, with his realism clashing with Gwen's idealism. The welcome return of PC Andy offers a nice external perspective on the world of Torchwood and the fiery domestic barneys between Gwen and Rhys are always great fun. Crucially, the episode's ability to heighten emotions is maximised by the haunting performance of Robert Pugh as the lonely, tortured Jonah.' Ben Rawson-Jones, Digital Spy website, 21 March 2008.

FAN COMMENT

- 'Jack was an arse in this. Why he couldn't just have been honest in the first place is beyond me. It would have saved them all a heap of hassle if he'd just been straight to them all about it from the get-go and then Gwen would have found out about it last year. Of course that would mean that there was no plot. Also there wouldn't have been so much Andy. Gwen really does treat him shamefully, almost as shamefully as she treats Rhys at times. Isn't it wonderful that two episodes after their marriage they're already having issues and arguments and she's sleeping on the couch. Their honeymoon period was awful short. (Then again, who knows how much time passes between episodes? It could be that it's been bloody months since the wedding.)' 'aryas zehral', LiveJournal blog, 19 March 2008.

- 'Frankly, Gwen got a well-earned smackdown this week, and I don't feel all that sorry for her. I don't dislike her, and I know she's supposed to be the anti-Jack, but she needed the lesson in trusting his judgment, not to mention treating her old friends with a bit more respect if she plans to keep them. And how marvelous were Rhys and Andy? This has definitely been Rhys's series, and I think Chibnall let Andy say all the things about Gwen that have been frustrating the fans, even those of us who like her.' 'manekikonekp', LiveJournal blog, 19 March 2008.

- 'I think this episode is much more important than it appears at first blush. For almost two full seasons ... Gwen has caused a string of miscues with results ranging from embarrassing to fatal. At first, the team was willing to cut the newbie some slack, but over the course of Series Two it appears that [they have become] increasingly intolerant to her mistakes – particularly since in all but one episode, somebody has either died or been gravely injured.

  o If Gwen had handed Owen the screwdriver in "Day One", 12 men would not have been turned to ash.
  o If Gwen had obeyed Jack in "They Keep Killing Suzie", she would not have ended up nearly dead and Suzie would not have murdered her father.
  o If Gwen had not disobeyed Jack in "End of Days" and led a mutiny to open the rift, Jack would not have been "killed" by Abbadon.
  o If Gwen had listened to Jack in "Kiss Kiss, Bang Bang", she would not have been nearly killed by the lip gloss.
  o If Gwen hadn't tried beyond trying to "save" Beth [in "Sleeper"], she wouldn't have been held hostage at sword(?)point.
  o If Gwen had listened to Jack in "Meat", Ianto and Rhys would not have been put in the direct danger they faced.
  o If Gwen had listened to Jack in "Something Borrowed", her husband's friend would not have been gruesomely murdered.

That's a hell of a track record for a person who was *supposed* to be a cop!' 'antelope writes', LiveJournal blog, 22 March 2008.

ANALYSIS: After the welcome extra screen time given to Rhys in Series Two, particularly in 'Meat', 'Adam' and 'Something Borrowed', now it is the turn of an even lower-profile semi-regular character to get a bigger share of the limelight as down-to-earth PC Andy Davidson plays his most important part yet in a *Torchwood* episode. This is a pleasing development, as *Torchwood* is always at its most effective when it juxtaposes the ordinary with the extraordinary, the everyday with the exceptional, the familiar with the alien. Previously the vital connection with normality has been provided mainly by Rhys, but Andy fulfils the same function equally well, if not more so now that Rhys is getting increasingly drawn into the murky world of Torchwood – as is demonstrated in this episode as he initially berates Gwen for failing to keep her home life separate from her work life but ultimately sits and listens sympathetically as she pours out her Torchwood troubles to him, he having apparently accepted that any talk about the possibility of them starting a family will have to be put on hold indefinitely (although it was possibly a little insensitive of him to have raised this so soon after the events of 'Something Borrowed' in any case). It helps considerably that Tom Price, in the role of Andy, is a thoroughly likeable and engaging performer with a great lightness of touch, and someone that the viewer is very happy to see more of. The hints given here of some past romantic entanglement between Andy and Gwen, and of a consequent lingering resentment between him and Rhys, give extra depth to his character in a very economical way, and his naïve hope that he might be considered for a job with Torchwood – something for which Gwen knows he is simply too much of an innocent to be suited – is endearing.

It is through Andy's eyes, too, that the viewer sees just how much Gwen has changed since she joined Torchwood. 'Do you know what's happened to you, Gwen?' he says. 'You've got hard.' He is right, too, as having started out at the beginning of Series One as very much an audience identification figure whose role it was to bring a caring, human dimension to Torchwood, she has inevitably become increasingly assimilated into the team, to the point where she is now just as fully a part of it as Toshiko, Owen and Ianto and largely shares their more pragmatic, more cynical worldview. 'One of them now, aren't you?' says Andy. 'Too busy to bother with one missing child. What is it, not major enough for you? Not spooky enough?'

This is really the crux of the story in 'Adrift' as, having been manipulated by Andy into taking an interest in the mystery of Jonah Bevan's disappearance, Gwen tries to go back to her old way of thinking and indeed her old way of being, using tried-and-trusted police investigation techniques to collate all the information on Cardiff's unsolved missing persons cases and, with Toshiko's help, cross-reference it with the negative rift spike data in what is essentially a solid piece of conventional detective work. And the outcome is not at all what she wants, as although it results in Jonah's mother Nikki finally learning what has become of her son, she bitterly regrets it, as she has now lost all that she had left to her: her happy memories, blotted out by the sound of Jonah's scream, and her hope. It seems, in a way, even worse for her than if it had turned out that Jonah was dead, as at least that would have afforded some closure. This raises the question that many fans have pondered: why does Gwen not simply retcon Nikki to return her to her earlier state of relatively blissful ignorance? Given Gwen's previous scepticism about the use of retcon, though, it seems likely that she just couldn't bring herself to do this, perhaps still believing deep down that it is better for Nikki to live with the truth, however painful that might be, than to go on without knowing. This would be very much in keeping with her characteristic self-righteous streak, which is again very much in evidence in the earlier part of the episode as she presses determinedly ahead with her investigation despite having been instructed by Jack to desist. And, who's to say, maybe she is right to do so? It is certainly arguable that, in the long run, Nikki is indeed better off knowing her son's fate; and maybe once she has got over the initial shock she will even want to go and see him again. As is generally the case in real life, there are no straightforward rights or wrongs here.

It is tempting to suggest that this episode would actually have fitted rather better into the overall pattern of Series Two had it been slotted in much earlier in the running order. The main reason for this is that it seems rather strange that Gwen should become quite as suspicious of Jack as she does, given the deep bond of trust they normally share, whereas had these events occurred only shortly after his return from his mysterious absence, when the whole team was still getting used to having him back again, it would perhaps have been more understandable. It also seems surprising that Ianto should effectively betray Jack by going behind his back to slip Gwen the Flat Holm coordinates, given the way the relationship between the two men has developed over the course of this series. It is telling, though, that Jack has chosen to keep the Flat Holm facility secret from Gwen – and from Toshiko too, although there are hints that Owen may know about it – presumably in order to avoid her reacting in precisely the way that she does react when she eventually finds out. This indicates an awareness on his part that his bond with Gwen, as strong as it is, will not be sufficient to ensure that she accepts his judgment if it goes against what she strongly believes to be right. The fact that, once she has gained access to the facility, he still doesn't tell her the full extent of Jonah's insanity (assuming he actually knows the details of all the victims' conditions) but allows her to carry on and witness it for herself suggests that he wants her in the process to learn a lesson; but whether or not he is morally justified in doing this – particularly given the impact it also has on Nikki – is open to question. It is strongly implied, too, that one of Jack's reasons for wanting to keep the victims a secret is simply to prevent their families, and thus the public more widely, from finding out about what Torchwood does, and about the rift – a motivation that was bound to cut little ice with Gwen. Would Gwen react any differently if a similar situation were to arise in future? The jury is still out on that one.

The focus of the action being so much on Gwen, Eve Myles has a more demanding role here than in any other Series Two episode, and she rises to the challenge admirably, delivering another stellar performance. Kai Owen also gets some more good scenes, particularly the one where Gwen and Rhys argue in the park over Gwen's preoccupation with her work. Myles, Price and Owen aside, the major acting honours this time really go to two guest stars, Ruth Jones – previously best known for her comedy work, including as co-writer and star of BBC Three's *Gavin and Stacey* – who gives a sensitive and affecting performance as Nikki, and Robert Pugh – another highly-regarded Welsh actor – as the tragic figure of the old Jonah, whose tortured, incessant scream is truly disturbing and unforgettable.

In many ways, though, the star of this episode is actually Chris Chibnall's script, which is just brilliant. Russell T Davies has likened it to a *Play for Today* entry, and one can easily see why he might say that. It is an intense and moving piece that, although it accords perfectly with the *Torchwood* ethos, is really quite unlike any episode previously featured in the show. There is very little humour included to leaven the essential darkness of the story – the main exception being a delicious little scene where Gwen inadvertently walks in on a semi-naked Jack and Ianto getting to grips with each other in the Hub's hothouse, leading Jack to quip, 'Well, there's room for one more. We could have used you an hour ago for naked hide-and-seek' – and the drama arises purely out of human emotions and interactions rather than the usual overt science fiction elements such as monsters and alien technology. In fact, this has the lightest special effects content of any *Torchwood* episode to date, and features no CGI whatsoever. The only really jarring line in the whole thing comes when Gwen, in an explanatory voiceover, says that Jonah's psychosis is due to him having 'looked into the heart of a dark star', which seems an unnecessary attempt to shoehorn in a science fiction idea when it would have been far preferable had the precise cause of his condition been left unspecified. There are one or two other incidental details in the script that could be quibbled over – surely, for instance, Jack could have found some more money in Torchwood's coffers to refurbish the Flat Holm facility so that the rift victims didn't have to live in such squalid conditions? – but all in all this is an outstanding piece of work.

The direction by *Torchwood* newcomer Mark Everest is also superb – in fact, some of the very best of Series Two. The location sequences of Gwen taking the boat to the island and then exploring the island itself are beautifully shot, and the powerful character material, such as the heartbreaking scene where Nikki finally comes face to face with her long-lost son, unnaturally aged by some 40 years since she last saw him and both physically and emotionally damaged by his experiences, is equally well handled. Hopefully this is not the last time that Everest will be engaged to work at Upper Boat.

While it would be unbearably depressing if every *Torchwood* was as bleak as this, one of the great things about the show's format is that it can accommodate a wide variety of different types and styles of story, and this approach again bears fruit here, as 'Adrift' is a truly remarkable episode.

2.12 – FRAGMENTS

Writer: Chris Chibnall
Director: Jonathan Fox Bassett

DEBUT TRANSMISSION DETAILS
BBC Three
Date: 21 March 2008. Scheduled time: 10.30 pm. Actual time: 10.29 pm.
BBC Two
Date: 28 March 2008. Scheduled time: 9.00 pm. Actual time: 9.02 pm.
Duration: 49' 06"

Pre-watershed version
BBC Two
Date: 3 April 2008. Scheduled time: 7.00 pm.
Duration: 48' 26"

ADDITIONAL CREDITED CAST[110]
Amy Manson (Alice Guppy), Heather Craney (Emily Holroyd), Paul Kasey (Blowfish/Weevil), Skye Bennett (Little Girl), Julian Lewis Jones (Alex), Simon Shackleton (Bob), Gareth Jones (Security Guard[111]), Claire Clifford (Milton), Noriko Aida (Toshiko's Mother), Andrea Lowe (Katie[112]), Richard Lloyd-King (Doctor[113]), Catherine Morris (Nurse), Selva Rasalingam (Psychiatrist)

PLOT: While Gwen oversleeps, Jack, Owen, Toshiko and Ianto investigate what appear to be alien life signs at a disused warehouse. This turns out to be a trap: four bombs detonate just as they reach them, and they are trapped in the rubble of the wrecked building. While they lie there, each of them recalls the circumstances that led to them joining Torchwood Three. Having been driven to the scene by Rhys, Gwen eventually manages to rescue her colleagues. They leave the warehouse to discover that the SUV has been stolen. Jack then receives a hologram message from Captain John Hart, confirming that he has found Jack's long-lost brother, Gray, and threatening to tear his world apart.

---

110 James Marsters features as Captain John Hart and Lachlan Nieboer as Gray in the closing scene of the episode, the characters appearing in the form of holograms, but neither is credited. The actress playing the unseen woman who speaks to Toshiko over an intercom system when she is locked in her cell at the UNIT prison is also uncredited, and her identity is unknown at the time of writing.

111 First name given in dialogue as 'George'.

112 Surname given in dialogue as 'Russell'.

113 Name given in dialogue as 'Jim Garrett'.

QUOTE, UNQUOTE

- Toshiko: 'Who are you?'
  Jack: 'Nobody. I don't exist. And for a man with my charisma, that's quite an achievement.'
  Toshiko: 'Are you a lawyer?'
  Jack: 'Do I look like a lawyer?'

- Jack: 'Look, any conversation between us, no matter what the subject, is over, finished, done, forever. I'm getting back behind the wheel of that car. If you're still standing in the road, I'm gonna drive through you.'
  Ianto: 'So, you're not gonna help me catch this pterodactyl, then?'

- Jack: 'Owen, why did you become a doctor?'
  Owen: 'I thought if I could save one life, mine would be worthwhile. But when you've saved one, there's another and another, clawing at you, demanding to be saved, and even if you do succeed, you can never save enough.'
  Jack: 'Maybe here you can.'

- Captain John: 'Okay, here's what's gonna happen. Everything you love, everything you treasure, will die. I'm gonna tear your world apart, Captain Jack Harkness, piece by piece, starting now. Maybe now you'll wanna spend some time with me.'

DOCTOR WHO REFERENCES

- Jack, obviously still feeling bitter about having been abandoned by the ninth Doctor on the Game Station at the end of 'The Parting of the Ways', has been careless with his talk in Victorian-era Cardiff, possibly while under the influence of alcohol. Alice Guppy reads out transcripts of some of his 'conversations with strangers in various drinking dens' since he first came to Torchwood Cardiff's attention: 'The Doctor, he'll be able to fix me'; 'When the Doctor turns up, it'll all be put right'; 'You wait till I see the Doctor. First I'm going to kiss him, then I'm going to kill him.' Emily Holroyd says: 'The Torchwood Institute was created to combat the threat posed by the Doctor and other phantasmagoria.' This accords with what was established in 'Tooth and Claw'. Jack replies: 'The Doctor's not a threat. He's the one who will save you from your phantasma-hoojits.' He tells the two women that he does not know where the Doctor is: 'He left me behind. I came here to find him. He refuels from that rift you have. Hoping if I stayed here long enough, we'd find each other.' This also accords with what has been established in *Doctor Who*, in episodes such as 'Boom Town' and 'Utopia'.

- The Tarot girl, previously seen in 'Dead Man Walking', tells Jack: 'He's coming, the one you're looking for. But the century will turn twice before you find each other again.' This is a reference to Jack's quest to be reunited with the Doctor. 'You mean I have to wait a hundred years to find him?' he asks the girl.

- A Torchwood report about Jack, seen being typed on a computer screen (date unknown), reads: 'Torchwood field agent Captain Jack Harkness was once again found to be operating covertly and out of Torchwood jurisdiction to set in place enquiries to find the target known as "The Doctor".'

- Ianto again refers to having witnessed the Battle of Canary Wharf, as featured in 'Doomsday'.

ALIEN TECH

- Torchwood Cardiff of the Victorian era possess an anachronistic device, possibly of alien origin, that generates an electric current; Emily Holroyd uses this to shock Jack via a pair of electrodes attached to his chest. 'You ladies are ahead of yourselves,' comments Jack.

- The sonic modulator that Toshiko constructs from stolen Ministry of Defence plans may possibly be of alien design – it is similar in appearance to the Doctor's sonic screwdriver, albeit somewhat bulkier. As Jack explains, the plans contained mistakes and had been filed away; but Toshiko instinctively corrected the mistakes in the process of putting the device together.

- Ianto tells Jack that he found the pterodactyl using a 'rift activity locator' that he appropriated from Torchwood London. This is not seen on screen.

CONTINUITY POINTS

- Jack's flashback to the Victorian era begins with the caption '1,392 deaths earlier'. It is possible that a considerable number of these deaths came during the year when he was chained up on board the *Valiant* by the Master, as indicated in the *Doctor Who* episode 'Last of the Time Lords'. Emily Holroyd says that Torchwood Cardiff have been monitoring Jack and that he has been 'killed' 14 times in the previous six months.

- Emily Holroyd tells Jack: 'Your liberty is at our discretion. Work for us, and you assist the Empire. Sever that tie, you become a threat.' Alice Guppy adds: 'And you've seen how we deal with threats.' Jack reluctantly agrees to work for Torchwood Cardiff on an 'uncontracted' – i.e. freelance – basis, needing a source of income and something to occupy his time during the hundred years or so that he knows he will have to wait before he is reunited with the Doctor.

- Jack appears to have prior knowledge of the Blowfish race. He says that stealing 'is like an addiction with your species'. He adds, 'This planet's over a century away from official first contact with alien life. You're upsetting the schedule.'

- Alice Guppy says 'The rift only goes one way', confirming that, in the Victorian era, Torchwood are unaware that things can sometimes pass into the rift as well as out of it.

- The lower levels of the Victorian-era Hub are underwater, and a Torchwood submarine is seen to be docked there. This of course pre-dates the modernisation of Cardiff Bay and the construction of the Roald Dahl Plass.

- Toshiko's flashback is prefaced by the caption '5 years earlier'. She is working at that time – around spring 2004 – at the (fictional) Lodmoor Research Facility, a division of the Ministry of Defence.

- It is possible that Toshiko never sees her mother again after the events related in her flashback. Her mother sustains a cut to the forehead when her kidnappers subject them both to the effects of the sonic modulator that Toshiko has constructed for them, and this is how Toshiko will later remember her looking in a vision conjured up by Bilis Manger in 'End of Days'. Jack explains that he has retconned her mother to cause her to forget the kidnapping, but that in future Toshiko can have only limited communication with her by sending postcards.

- Jack tells Toshiko that he is owed a few favours by UNIT. (Could he possibly have helped UNIT covertly during the 1970s by taking steps to prevent Torchwood from finding out that the Doctor – their number one target – was acting as its scientific adviser at that time?)

- Ianto's flashback begins with the caption '21 months earlier'. This must be around the summer of 2007, just after the Battle of Canary Wharf. Ianto has not previously met Jack but obviously knows about him, presumably from having seen information about him held at Torchwood One. He even seems to know how to make coffee just to Jack's liking – or perhaps his coffee is exceptionally good by anyone's standards – and is not fazed by Jack's mention of having '51st Century pheromones' as a consequence of which he never wears aftershave.

- Jack tells Ianto, in the 2007 flashback, 'We're nothing to do with Torchwood London. I severed all links.' This severing of links presumably occurred some time after Jack took control of Torchwood Three at the beginning of 2000, at which point he would have begun to remake the organisation in the Doctor's honour, as stated in the Doctor Who episode 'The Sound of Drums'. Ianto says of Torchwood London, 'Yet when it burned, two members of your team scavenged the ruins.' 'We don't want the equipment getting into the wrong hands,' explains Jack. It is unspecified which two members of Jack's team were responsible for the scavenging, but the most likely candidates would seem to be Suzie and Toshiko. Ianto claims, dishonestly, that his girlfriend Lisa Hallett is 'deceased'.

- The only thing Jack has in the Torchwood SUV to aid in catching the pterodactyl is a large, tranquilliser-filled hypodermic. He wryly comments that he does not keep dinosaur nets in the vehicle, to which Ianto replies, 'Torchwood London would have.'

- Jack says: 'Dinosaurs? Had 'em for breakfast. Had to. Only source of pre-killed food protein after the asteroid crashed.' This suggests that, when he was a Time Agent or subsequently a conman, he was on Earth around 65 million years ago, at the time when the dinosaurs became extinct. (*Doctor Who* fans, unlike Jack, will know that what hit the Earth was not in fact an asteroid but a space freighter, as seen in the 1982 story 'Earthshock'.)

- Owen's flashback is preceded by the caption '4 years earlier', dating the start of it to around spring 2005. The hospital where Owen is seen working, and where his fiancée Katie is also a junior doctor, is almost certainly Cardiff Hospital; he was based there in 2001, as established in 'Greeks Bearing Gifts', and the fact that Jack is on hand when Katie dies also suggests that it is in Cardiff. The cemetery where Katie is buried is probably not local to the hospital, as when Jack meets Owen there some time later he tells him, 'I need someone like [you] to work with me in Cardiff'. Katie is not Welsh (or, at least, does not have a Welsh accent) so it is possible that she has been taken to her original home town for burial, particularly if her parents or other family members still live there.

- Jack says of the alien parasite that kills Katie, '[It] incubates in the brain, disrupting the shape and functions. When it's attacked or threatened, it emits a toxic gas that's fatal to humans; it clears pretty quickly'.

PRODUCTION NOTES

- Made with 'From Out of the Rain' as part of Block 5 of production.

- This episode had the working titles 'Prequel' and 'Blast from the Past'. It was originally mooted for the sixth slot in the series rather than the twelfth.

- The location used for the building where Jack, Ianto, Owen and Toshiko get caught in the explosions was a disused warehouse at MoD Caerwent in Caldicott, previously the site of some of the recording for 'Sleeper' and 'Adrift'. The scene of Jack and Ianto talking outside the entrance to Torchwood's fake tourist information office on Mermaid Quay was shot on 19 September 2008. Later the same day, the crew moved on to the Cardiff Royal Infirmary in Newport Road, where the hospital sequences involving Owen were shot. The scene of the first meeting between Ianto and Jack, as the former helps the latter to restrain a Weevil, was recorded late in the evening on 25 September in the same area of Bute Park previously used as a location for 'From Out of the Rain'. John Barrowman's stunt double stood in for him for part of the fight. The crew then went on to record a short scene with the SUV in Maindy Road, Cardiff, incurring the wrath of one local resident who emerged from her house in dressing gown and slippers to complain about the commotion. The scenes of Toshiko in the MoD offices were shot on BBC Wales premises. The subsequent sequences of her taking the stolen plans to the building where her mother is being held hostage, and of her then being arrested by

UNIT troops, were taped on the evening of 28 September at a building behind Cardiff Central railway station. The cemetery used for the scene where Owen encounters Jack for the second time was Glyntaff Cemetery in Pontypridd.

- Jack's initial meeting with Toshiko was originally to have been rather lighter in tone; at one point, he was to have said to her: 'We have equipment that'll make your hair curl. That's a metaphor. We don't just have curling tongs.'

- The 1999 segment of Jack's flashback shows a TV screen displaying an archive clip of a genuine news report, presented by Natasha Kaplinsky, from the Millennium Eve celebrations of that year.

OOPS!
- It is clear from the 1899 segment of 'Flashback' that Torchwood have long known about the Blowfish creatures, but in 'Kiss Kiss, Bang Bang' Toshiko says 'Species type not on record'.

PRESS REACTION
- 'What a geekgasm. The rescue is filler between the flashbacks, but who needs plot when two-series-old questions are being answered? Each flashback provides an intriguing glimpse at what makes the characters tick. Owen's is the standout (the reasons for his relationship issues are now clear) while Jack's is so packed with revelations about Torchwood's history that repeated watching is advisable.' Richard Edwards, *SFX* Issue 170, June 2008.

- 'There were a lot of threads from the season pulled into the one cohesive story – the Torchwood of old, the innocent looking girl with the gift of foresight, a Blowfish without a sports car and more importantly how Jack came to work for the Institute. The flashbacks to Jack's past were incredibly similar to those from *Angel*, charting the tortured past of Angelus and his reluctant quest for atonement and redemption. Back alley fights, knowledge of the paranormal and an unwanted task of defending the helpless are only a few of the correlations between the two characters.' Alan Stanley Blair, SyFy Portal website, 24 March 2008.

FAN COMMENT
- '[Jack] is complicated the way real people are complicated, only on a much grander scale. He is horribly, horribly *damaged*, and has been hurt in ways few of us could ever fathom. Watching his father die and brother vanish in a war? Watching his best friend die in war at 16? Realising that his action to make a cheap buck was going to result in the deaths of all of London? Ouch. Loving somebody enough to go on what he had to know was a suicide mission, watching everybody around him fall to the ground, and dying alone in another man's war? Having that same person (sort of) abandon him for dead, tell him

he shouldn't exist and he couldn't bear to be in his presence, and then out-and-out *use* him to do a series of increasingly nasty jobs simply because there isn't anybody else alive who can? Double ouch. Especially when followed by a year in chains being tortured beyond imagining. Having the people whom he loved and trusted like family sacrifice him to a demon, sentencing him to yet more unimaginable torment … It's amazing the man is still sane, or even something passing close to sane. "Fragments" is a character exploration of one Jack Harkness, as seen by other people around him. It's pretty safe to say that Jack is Torchwood, post-Canary Wharf, and Torchwood is Jack. The two could not exist without one another. It is a reflection of the man who runs it and all of his imperfections – from what he does right down to the people he hires. It's hard to see, especially in Series One, which is told largely through Gwen's eyes, but Jack is a man of such staggering compassion, empathy, and soul that the mind boggles at what he has done.' 'antelope_writes', LiveJournal blog, 23 March 2008.

- 'Seems like Jack has been getting drunk and muttering in his cups about his favourite Time Lord in every grog shop in town. This would explain why he no longer drinks in public. Curiously, [Torchwood] don't torture him for everything he knows, but stop at the few scraps that he tells them, which they have probably already got from any Doctor-witness. Instead they offer to hire him as a freelance alien catcher, only it turns out that "catcher" means "hit man" even though someone else actually pulls the trigger. That's quite a fall, from Doctor's companion to alien assassin, and Jack feels every inch of it. Barrowman conveys Jack's pain, anger, repugnance, and frustration very well. But he's told that Torchwood will consider him an enemy if he leaves, and the Doctor won't show up again until the 21st Century, so he's left with few other choices, especially since he would have to change his ID completely every few years if he didn't work for them. After a century on the job, he's made it from freelancer to field operative, surely one of the slowest career paths on record, and inherits Torchwood Three in 1999 after his last boss goes nuts and kills everyone else. By my count this means that the only Torchwood Three boss we've seen who doesn't wind up crazy (and I include Jack) is the one from "To the Last Man", who retired early shortly after we met him. No, people, it's not that Jack's a bad leader, it's that he's got a very bad job.' 'crabby_lioness', LiveJournal blog, 6 April 2008.

ANALYSIS: The 'origins story' idea has probably been most fully exploited in comic book superhero sagas and their movie adaptations, but it is a staple of genre TV as well, having featured in shows as diverse as *Friends* – 'The One with the Flashback' – and Joss Whedon's *Firefly* – 'Out of Gas' – the latter of which would almost certainly have been seen by many of the key figures involved in *Torchwood*'s production, given how influential Whedon's work has been on them. Chris Chibnall's 'Fragments' is *Torchwood*'s own take on this popular subgenre, and although it would no doubt be the least accessible episode of all for anyone coming fresh to the show, it is a real treat for regular viewers.

The explosion at the warehouse is obviously just a plot device to provide a reason for the flashback sequences that make up the greater part of the episode, but although it serves that purpose admirably, it is not as well thought-out as it might have been: the fact that the countdowns on the four bombs reach zero just as Jack, Owen, Toshiko and Ianto find them is too much of a coincidence; and it is not really credible, given that the four team members are standing more or less on top of the bombs when they go off, that Jack is the only one to sustain 'fatal' injuries, while the others come through more or less unscathed, bar a dislocated shoulder in Ianto's case and some bruised ribs and a broken arm in Toshiko's. Having said that, the scenes of Gwen and Rhys carrying out their impromptu rescue operation are well shot and full of tense moments – Gwen's struggle to free Owen from the rubble beneath a precariously hanging broken window full of jagged glass, which threatens to fall at any moment and slice through either one or both of them, is particularly nerve-wracking – so perhaps it is a little churlish to grumble about this. It was certainly a wise decision to omit Gwen from the flashbacks, given that the viewer already knows from 'Everything Changes' how she came to join Torchwood – although apparently consideration was given at one point to presenting a brief montage of clips from that episode to cover her back-story.

Jack's flashback is the first to be presented and, fittingly, spans the longest period of time, a hundred years or so, from the end of the 19th Century, when he has his first encounter with Torchwood Cardiff, to New Year's Eve 1999, when he is left to take charge of the organisation and recruit a new team in the wake of a tragedy that leaves all his former colleagues dead. The Victorian-era scenes are the most entertaining of the whole episode, as the viewer is introduced to the team's original leader Emily Holroyd and her partner – sexual as well as professional, it seems – Alice Guppy. Everything about these two characters is great – their conception, their names, their dialogue, their costumes, their portrayal by Heather Craney and Amy Manson respectively – and they are really just crying out to be given their own spin-off, or at the very least be featured in another flashback episode or two. After all, if the BBC's medical drama *Casualty* can spawn the one-off special *Casualty 1906* (BBC One, 2006) and the mini-series *Casualty 1907* (BBC One, 2008), why shouldn't there be a *Torchwood 1899*? A show featuring Jack protecting the British Empire against alien threats in an uneasy alliance with a pair of feisty-cum-psychotic Victorian lesbians reporting directly to the Queen is surely something that a lot of people would pay good money to see.

Jack himself looks particularly dashing in these Victorian scenes, sporting sideburns, a more rakish hairstyle than usual and a fetching cape in place of his familiar greatcoat. As a bonus, the viewer gets to see another of the Blowfish creatures introduced in 'Kiss Kiss, Bang Bang', amusingly attracting Torchwood's attention in exactly the same way as before, by stealing and joyriding – in this case in a horse and carriage rather than a shiny red sports car! Then comes the icing on the cake, in the form of Jack's first meeting with the Tarot girl from 'Dead Man Walking', looking exactly the same as she would over a hundred years later and still having a Tarot card bearing his likeness.

This is an inspired piece of writing by Chibnall and gets the flashbacks off to a really cracking start. It is not the end of Jack's story, either, as time then moves forward via an excellent montage sequence to the point where 1999 becomes 2000 and, while the rest of the world is indulging in millennium celebrations, Jack enters the Hub to find a scene of absolute carnage. The previous leader, Alex, has murdered the rest of the team – 'mercy killings', he says – after looking into a mysterious locket and seeing the future. 'It was the kindest thing I could do,' he adds. 'So that none of us sees the storm. I'm sorry I can't do the same for you. The 21st Century, Jack. Everything's gonna change. And we're not ready.' So saying – in a neat reversal of Jack's usual opening voiceover lines, for the first time giving them real meaning – he shoots himself in the head, spattering Jack with blood. This is an incredibly grim sequence that leaves the viewer wondering just what sort of a 'storm' Alex can have foreseen that has caused him to take such drastic action, and whether or not this will be followed up in some future storyline.

Jack features in the other three flashbacks as well, providing a common thread running through them as he assembles his familiar team around him. Even Suzie Costello gets a mention, although sadly she does not actually reappear on this occasion. It's Toshiko's turn to be featured next. Her flashback is, if possible, even darker than Jack's, as she is blackmailed into stealing secrets from her Ministry of Defence employers, cruelly treated by her mother's kidnappers and then locked up by UNIT in a grim prison facility, where she is denied her basic human rights – surely an intentional allusion to the situation at the US government's Guantanamo Bay detention camp, previously evoked in 'Sleeper'. Some fans have expressed surprise at this unsympathetic depiction of UNIT, which certainly makes for a startling contrast with its rather cosy image of the 1970s; but the *Doctor Who* novels ranges have long hinted at a darker side to the organisation, making mention of a prison facility known as the Glasshouse, and there would inevitably have been changes of approach over the years to reflect harsher global circumstances. Great credit is due here to Naoko Mori, who gives a fantastic performance throughout, skilfully conveying Toshiko's desperation as she uses all her resourcefulness and intelligence to steal the plans for and construct the sonic device, and showing the full extent of her despair in the cramped, featureless confines of her cell at the prison – a really harrowing sequence.

This flashback concludes with an excellent scene where, having appeared like some mythical figure silhouetted in the doorway of her cell, Jack sits with Toshiko at a solitary table in the middle of one of cavernous concrete areas that seem to characterise the main part of the prison and offers her the chance to come and work for him – although, given that her only alternative is to remain locked up by UNIT indefinitely, it is not as if she really has a great deal of choice. This possibly throws a slightly different light on the conversation in 'To the Last Man' where Tommy says of her job at Torchwood 'But you weren't conscripted; it's your choice, right?' and she replies 'Yeah, I suppose it is'. The fact remains though that, notwithstanding the mitigating circumstances of her mother's kidnapping and the shockingly draconian nature of her punishment, Toshiko has committed a criminal act of espionage in stealing official secrets and passing them to a hostile power, so Jack is essentially saving her from the consequences of her own actions and giving her a chance to redeem herself. And although Jack initially tells her that her only contact with her now-retconned mother can be through sending postcards, the viewer knows that she will later see other members of her family again – at the beginning of 'Captain Jack Harkness', she is on her way to attend her grandfather's eightieth birthday celebration.

Next comes Ianto's flashback. Chibnall has said that he intended this to have the feel of a romantic comedy, and that's just how it comes across. *Torchwood* is possibly the first show ever to take exactly the sort of stories that might be found in its fan fiction and actually present them on screen, and this is a prime example. Ianto's persistent attempts to persuade Jack to take him on as an employee of Torchwood Three, culminating in their joint efforts to catch what will later become the Hub's resident pterodactyl, are sweet, funny and sexy, and will certainly have delighted all the shippers. What is really clever about the way Chibnall has written this, though, is that there is at the same time a much darker, unspoken subtext, as the viewer, unlike Jack, knows that the *real* reason why Ianto is so desperate to become a member of the team is that he wants to smuggle his part-Cyberman girlfriend Lisa into the Hub's basement and try to find a way of restoring her to normality, as seen in 'Cyberwoman'. Just how much of Ianto's flirting with Jack is genuine at the outset, and how much simply calculated to further his hidden agenda? It is an intriguing question, and one that will doubtless be hotly debated by fans for years to come.

Last but by no means least, Chibnall turns the spotlight on Owen's back-story. It comes as no surprise to see that the Torchwood medic started out working as a doctor at Cardiff Hospital (although the hospital is not specifically named here), as this was established as far back as in 'Greeks Bearing Gifts', but what does come as a revelation is to find him in a happy, loving relationship with a woman called Katie, to whom he is engaged to be married. This would not be *Torchwood*, though, if there were not a much darker aspect to the story, and it turns out that Katie is suffering from what is at first diagnosed as early-onset Alzheimer's disease and then as a brain tumour but eventually turns out to be an alien brain parasite. The scenes where Katie is losing her memory, unable to recall how to make a cup of tea or the words 'tea' and 'milk', and even at one point forgetting Owen's name, are truly heart-rending, and there are some more fantastic performances here from Burn Gorman and, as Katie, Andrea Lowe. As in Toshiko's case, Jack appears on the scene as a kind of saviour figure, unable to do anything to prevent Katie from being killed but offering Owen a new sense of purpose, to save countless lives as part of the Torchwood team.

There was obviously a risk, in presenting four brief vignettes plus a framing story all within a single 50-minute episode, that each of the individual elements could end up seeming too slight and insubstantial, rendering the whole thing deeply unsatisfying. In the event, though, Chibnall has managed in 'Fragments' to achieve quite the opposite: each of the four flashbacks is so well conceived, richly detailed and dramatically involving that it feels almost like a separate episode in its own right, and there is also a great variety of setting and tone between them, so that the overall impression is of an episode that packs an enormous amount into its running time and is verging on the epic in scope. Also admirable is the way that the flashbacks give fresh insights into the psyche of the four featured regulars that fit perfectly with their established characters and help the viewer to understand just how they came to be in the place they were, mentally speaking, when first seen at the start of Series One – a great bit of retrospective continuity-building by Chibnall. The back-stories have some interesting parallels, too, in that Toshiko, Ianto and Owen all come to join Torchwood through trying to protect someone they love – Toshiko's mother, Lisa and Katie respectively – but whom they subsequently lose.

Having had to cope with realising so many different and contrasting scenarios within the space of a single episode must also have been quite a challenge for director Jonathan Fox Bassett, but he has risen to that challenge admirably, demonstrating great versatility, bringing the best out of all the cast and delivering a near-faultless production.

Yet another twist comes right at the end as Jack receives a hologram message from Captain John Hart – making a welcome return after his well-received debut in 'Kiss Kiss, Bang Bang' – who not only admits that he set the explosives in the warehouse but also has an even bigger surprise for Jack: 'Say hi to the family' he sneers, as beside him appears the hologram of a young man – apparently Jack's long-lost brother, Gray. Concluding with Captain John threatening to destroy everything that Jack holds dear, this makes for an excellent cliff-hanger, setting things up very nicely for the series finale.

2.13 – EXIT WOUNDS

Writer: Chris Chibnall
Director: Ashley Way

DEBUT TRANSMISSION DETAILS
BBC Two
Date: 4 April 2008. Scheduled time: 9.00 pm. Actual time: 8.59 pm.
Not shown on BBC Three as part of original run.
Duration: 48' 22"

Pre-watershed version
BBC Two
Date: 15 April 2008. Scheduled time: 7.00 pm.
Duration: not known.

ADDITIONAL CREDITED CAST
James Marsters (Captain John Hart), Tom Price[114] (PC Andy), Paul Kasey (Weevil), Golda Rosheuvel (Dr Angela Connolly), Lachlan Nieboer (Gray), Syreeta Kumar (Nira Docherty), Cornelius Macarthy (Charles Gaskell), Amy Manson[115] (Alice Guppy), Paul Marc Davis (Cowled Leader)[116]

PLOT: Rhys drives the Torchwood team back to central Cardiff in his car. John takes Jack captive at the Hub and uses the rift manipulator to set off a series of 15 devastating explosions around the city, having already instigated a spate of attacks by Weevils and other alien creatures on strategic targets. He then takes Jack back in time to 27 AD, where he reveals that he has been acting under duress – attached to his arm is an explosive device that can be triggered by remote signal if he fails to follow instructions. They are joined by Gray, who reveals that he is the one who has been giving the instructions. He hates Jack because he holds him responsible for the fact that he got abducted and repeatedly tortured by the alien creatures that attacked the Boeshane Peninsula when they were children. Gray orders John to bury Jack alive, so that he will suffer the torment of an endless cycle of death and resurrection. John, however, is able to slip Jack a ring that emits a distinctive signal. This signal is detected by Torchwood Cardiff in 1901, and they dig Jack up. At his request, they then freeze him in the Hub's morgue, where he remains for the next 107 years or so. He revives just in time to rejoin his team in the present day, where they are still struggling to cope with the chaos caused by Gray in the city. Jack renders Gray unconscious with

---

114 Not credited in *Radio Times*.
115 Not credited in *Radio Times*.
116 Credited in *Radio Times* but not on screen.

chloroform, but not before he has shot Toshiko in the stomach. Toshiko dies shortly afterwards and is unable to prevent Owen from also being killed when the chamber he is in at the Turnmill Nuclear Power Plant, where he has been trying to stop a meltdown, is flooded with lethal radiation. Jack places Gray in cryogenic suspension in the Hub, but allows John to go free.

QUOTE, UNQUOTE
- Andy: 'Whoa, Rhys, what are you doing here? This is a crime scene, and a confidential crime scene at that. If it gets out what happened here there'll be a city-wide panic.'
Gwen: 'Rhys isn't gonna go blabbing.'
Rhys: 'I'm keeping more secrets than you'd ever believe.'
Andy: 'Yeah, like what?'
Rhys: 'Like a Time Agency based in Cardiff.'
Gwen: 'Oh, it's not based in Cardiff.'
Andy: 'Brilliant secret. I ask, you tell. Well done.'

- Jack: 'Where's Gray? What have you done with my brother?'
John: 'You don't realise. Actions, ramifications. Ripples in a pond. It's beyond my control.'

- Jack: 'I've forgiven you. I give you absolution. Now do the same for me.'
Gray: 'I prayed for death! Those creatures, the things they did to us, because of you, the favourite son, the one who lived, who'll always live. The only strength I have is my hatred for you.'
Jack: 'I didn't know. I didn't realise until it was too late.'
Gray: 'I begrudge you everything. I wanna rip it all from you, to leave you screaming in the dark. I will never absolve you. All of it, it's your fault.'

- Toshiko: 'Owen, just stay calm.'
Owen: 'Oh, why should I do that? Where's the fun in that? I'm gonna rage my way to oblivion.'
Toshiko: 'Please stop.'
Owen: 'Why? Give me one good bloody reason why I should, one good reason why I shouldn't keep screaming.'
Toshiko: 'Because you're breaking my heart.'

DOCTOR WHO REFERENCES
- Owen tackles a Hoix – a type of alien introduced in the Doctor Who episode 'Love & Monsters', where it was not named in dialogue but identified in the closing credits. He says, 'The only profile we have is that it lives to eat; it doesn't matter what. Caught one in Barry last year in a kebab shop. It went through seven döner sticks in 20 minutes.'

- Toshiko recalls that in Owen's second week at Torchwood, when he was hungover and unreachable, she had to cover for him by pretending to be a medic sent to examine a 'space pig'. This is a reference to her debut appearance in the *Doctor Who* episode 'Aliens of London'. It is not explained why someone from Torchwood Three rather than Torchwood One was involved in that incident, given that it occurred in London.

ALIEN TECH

- John is seen to consult a hand-held scanner device similar to those often used by Toshiko and other members of the Torchwood team. Possibly he has appropriated this from the Hub after breaking in.

- John has a wrist-strap-mounted explosive device, no doubt of alien origin, molecularly bonded to the skin of his arm so that he cannot remove it. He describes it as a 'ninth generation detonator'. It also has a surveillance circuit to monitor his every word and action. He takes Jack to 27 AD because he thinks that will be sufficiently far back in time to be out of range of the trigger signal. However, Gray follows them there.

- John gives Jack a ring that, as he later tells Toshiko, puts out 'an etheric particle signal NME transmitting at 200 betacycles'. He adds that the transmitter was 'guaranteed for five millennia through three ecological permalayers'.

- Gray uses a vortex manipulator – presumably John's – to travel between time periods. He also uses the same device to emit a signal that causes the Weevils to come out and run wild on the streets and to operate the locking mechanisms on the cell doors in the Hub's vault. John later adapts a hand-held scanner-type device, different in design from the ones seen previously, to send a recall signal; it is unclear where he obtains this device from, as he is locked in one of the cells at the time.

- Torchwood in Victorian-era Cardiff have a portable device, presumably alien in origin, capable of detecting and tracking the signal emitted by John's ring.

CONTINUITY POINTS

- John says that the explosive devices he planted in the warehouse in 'Fragments' 'were just prototypes' to test out the theory of their operation.

- Gwen notes that the Central Server Building in Cardiff 'houses servers for the military, police, NHS, even looks after the service systems for the nuclear station at Turnmill.'

- Jack tells Gray: 'I looked for you. I searched for you for years. You were my first thought every day.'

- Owen refers to himself at one point as 'King of the Weevils', recalling how the creatures cowered away and deferred to him in 'Dead Man Walking'.

- Although not shown on screen, Jack must presumably be naked when Alice Guppy and Charles Gaskell dig him up in 1901, as his clothes must have rotted away to nothing over the two thousand years he has been in the ground. In the next scene in the Hub, however, he is seen wearing his usual 1940s-style attire, including the familiar greatcoat. The most likely explanation for this would seem to be that he first started regularly wearing clothes in that style shortly after his initial encounter with Torchwood in 1899, and had several sets made up to the same design – possibly for symbolic reasons, because it was the style of clothes he was wearing when he first met the Doctor? – at least one of which he kept in storage in the Hub as a spare, which he was then able to put on after being taken back there in 1901. This might also account for the fact that the design of the coat differs slightly from that of a genuine Second World War RAF greatcoat. An alternative explanation is that his clothes did not in fact rot away, as they were made of exceptionally durable or even self-repairing material, far in advance of anything known in the 21st Century. This seems less likely, however, as it is uncertain how Jack would have got access to such material (unless he salvaged it along with other flotsam and jetsam that came through the rift) and doubtful that he would have thought it worthwhile to have clothes made from it.

- Gray has gained dominance over John by placing an explosive device on his arm, immovably bonded to the skin, and threatening to detonate this by way of a remote signal if he steps out of line. He must have achieved this at some point after John's departure into the rift at the end of 'Kiss Kiss, Bang Bang' – when John first tells Jack that he has found Gray – but the precise circumstances are left unspecified. John says of Gray's relationship with Jack: 'They were separated as children. Gray was abducted. When I found him, he was chained to the ruins of a city in the Bedlam Outlands, surrounded by corpses. He was the only one left. The creatures had long since gone. I don't know how long he'd been there. He thought I was the rescuing hero, so it took me too long to realise, he'd learned terrible things, watching those creatures. He let me trust him.' Gray releases the explosive device from John's arm toward the end of the episode and lets him go free.

- As it seems very unlikely that two nuclear power stations would be built in close proximity to each other just outside Cardiff, Turnmill is presumably a new name for the Blaid Drwg facility. The latter was originally planned for construction to a catastrophically faulty design on the site of Cardiff Castle by former mayor Margaret Blaine – who was actually a disguised Slitheen – as detailed in the *Doctor Who* episode 'Boom Town'. Following Blaine's demise, however, it was eventually built in a different location, away from the city centre, to corrected plans, as mentioned in the *Torchwood* novel *Another Life*.

- Gray calls his brother 'Jack', suggesting that this may in fact be his real name, in which case it would be simply a coincidence that the Captain Harkness from whom he acquired his false identity in 1941 also happened to be a Jack. It may even be the case that he chose to adopt Harkness's identity, rather than that of any other deceased serviceman, precisely because he had the same first name. Alternatively, Gray may call him Jack simply because John has told him that that is the name his brother now prefers to use, although this seems less likely given the hatred he feels toward him.

- The radiation from the meltdown of the Turnmill Nuclear Power Plant is channelled into the containment chamber within which Owen is trapped. This presumably means that the facility is rendered safe, but permanently inaccessible.

- Judging from what Jack says in 'They Keep Killing Suzie' about what happens to deceased Torchwood officers, it seems likely that Toshiko's body will be placed in cryogenic storage in the Hub after the events of this episode and that all her possessions will be kept in storage. It seems unlikely that Owen's body will be recovered from the Turnmill facility, if indeed any of it still remains intact after it is exposed to the decomposing effects of the released radiation.

PRODUCTION NOTES

- Made with 'Something Borrowed' as part of Block 6 of production. The scenes at the beginning, following directly on from the conclusion of 'Fragments', are an insert from Block 5, directed by Jonathan Fox Bassett and shot on location at MoD Caerwent in Caldicott.

- This episode was rumoured to have the working title/descriptor 'Spaceship Under Bay'. However, since this has nothing to do with the plot, it seems that either the rumours were unfounded or that this was the working title of an earlier, abandoned idea.

- Some of the police station interiors, including the sequences with the Weevils in the cell, were taped in a real police station in Clifton Street, Splott on 25 October 2007. The same location had also been featured in the Series One episodes 'Small Worlds' and 'End of Days'. The scenes of Toshiko and Ianto venturing out of the Central Server Building to find the streets infested with Weevils were shot just across the river from the Millennium Stadium on 12 November. The Central Server Building itself was actually Stadium House in Cardiff, the tallest building in Wales. The sequence of the two Captains at Cardiff Castle was also done on the night of 12/13 November. Further shots of the Weevils on the loose were recorded on 14 November on Cargo Road in the Cardiff Docks area. The location used for the sequence where Jack meets Gray in 27 AD and is buried alive by John was Ogmore Farm near Bridgend, where recording took place on 15 and 16 November. However, the setting where the Victorian-era Torchwood Cardiff find Jack and dig him up again was actually an area of Bute Park. 15 November was also the date when the scene of Ianto and Toshiko witnessing the bombs going off around Cardiff was shot, on the roof of British Gas's Helmont House premises in Churchill Way, previously featured in 'Kiss Kiss, Bang Bang'.

Location work for Series Two concluded on 19 November, when a scene was recorded of Owen witnessing the explosions from the roof of the Tower Building of Cardiff University's School of Psychology, previously featured as the scene of his conversation with the suicidal Maggie in 'A Day in the Death'.

- The episode opens with some clips from 'Fragments' by way of a recap.

- Apart from before the opening titles, an identifying place and time caption is briefly superimposed over the picture each time the setting of the action changes.

- The decision to bring Captain John back for a return appearance was taken only after the production team saw how good James Marsters was in the role during production of 'Kiss Kiss, Bang Bang'. In the earliest drafts of the script, it was Captain John rather than Gray who was the main villain, and he and Captain Jack were at one point supposed to indulge in a dramatic swordfight. The tone was originally to have been much like that of 'Kiss Kiss, Bang Bang', but this changed during the course of redrafting, particularly with the development of the Gray storyline, casting Captain John in a more sympathetic light. Because of time pressures and work on other episodes of the series, Chris Chibnall was late completing the script, and it was only half-written when the tone meeting for the episode took place, which meant that much subsequent discussion was required.

- The guns with which Captain John shoots Captain Jack are Heckler and Koch MP-5K sub-machine guns, fitted with 9mm blank cartridges for recording. Jack's weapon of choice is a vintage .38 Webley revolver, while the other Torchwood team members use SIG P228 semi-automatic pistols with 'Torchwood' engraved on the side.

- The episode features a number of flashback clips of the Boeshane Peninsula sequences from 'Adam'.

- The part of Gray was Lachlan Nieboer's first professional acting job. He was one of a number of actors considered for the role, and director Ashley Way was impressed by his audition tape and by the fact that he resembled John Barrowman sufficiently to be convincing as his brother.

- The song that Captain John plays to Captain Jack, saying 'It's our song', is the 1978 single 'I Lost My Heart to a Starship Trooper' by Sarah Brightman and Hot Gossip. This replaced the scripted 'Ain't No Pleasing You' by Cockney novelty act Chas 'n' Dave.

- The shot of Captain John saying 'It's just sex, sex, sex with you people' is a different take from the one used in the series preview sequence at the end of 'Kiss Kiss, Bang Bang'.

- Actress Heather Craney was invited to reprise her 'Fragments' role as Emily Holroyd in the brief 1901 scenes, alongside Amy Manson as Alice Guppy, and was disappointed to have to decline as she was already committed to appearing in a play at the Soho Theatre in London's West End. The new character Charles Gaskell, played by Cornelius Macarthy, was created as a substitute.

- Neither Burn Gorman nor Naoko Mori had expressed a wish to leave *Torchwood* at this point; it was the production team's decision to write out their characters. This was partly in order to ensure that the show did not become too cosy, by demonstrating to the viewing audience that the dangers the Torchwood team face are genuinely life-threatening for them. In an interview published on 4 April 2008 on the Digital Spy website, Naoko Mori commented: 'I found out [that Toshiko was going to be killed off] probably a good two months before, in September of last year. When I was told, I was obviously shocked and sad, but to be honest, it made sense to me. The show needed a big season finale. It also made sense because Tosh has been through so much. She's come a full circle and had her journey ... I remember when there was talk of Tosh and Owen exiting, and the first thing I asked was "How is it going to be done?" The great thing about Russell [T Davies] and Chris [Chibnall] is that they keep you informed and have a real two-way conversation. One of the things that I wanted to ensure was that it made sense, and that the connection between Owen and Tosh had the right balance. All through the series I didn't want it to come across as her being this stalker girl with a crush on Owen. I wanted it to be deeper than that, because as a colleague and as a human being she cared for him. I wanted their last conversation to be delicately and well put ... I hope we got the balance right. Sometimes when these deaths occur, one of the dangers is that it's just done for shock value. I wanted it to be shocking, but not just for the sake of that. Hopefully it comes across that way. It wasn't in vain and there was a purpose.'

- The final scene to be recorded for Series Two was of Toshiko's tearful last conversation with Owen. This was done in one take at around 1.00 am on 23 November 2007 – *Doctor Who*'s forty-fourth anniversary.

OOPS!
- When Jack revives after being shot with machine guns by John, his shirt is soaked in blood but there seems to be little bullet-hole damage to it. (Is it possible that his clothes are self-repairing? – see discussion under 'Continuity Points'.) His shoes have also changed design.

- The details given about the operation of the Turnmill Nuclear Power Plant and its threatened meltdown are not scientifically accurate.

PRESS REACTION
- 'Okay, it was pretty certain Owen's days were numbered, but Tosh as well? I'm still in shock. This is a brave, brutal end to a series that's spectacularly reinvented itself after an inconsistent

start. Although an entire city's gone to hell, Chibnall's script keeps the storytelling small-scale, focusing on the characters trying to put it back together. It's hard-hitting stuff, with Jack buried for 2,000 years by his pissed off sibling, and two interweaving death scenes delivered with gut-wrenching power. If there's a criticism, it's that the episode wallows in grief for the final five minutes, but that's excusable – it's respite after all the tension.' Ian Berriman, *SFX* Issue 170, June 2008.

- 'As with Nikki in "Adrift", Jack seeks a resolution to the loss of a close family member, and only when it happens, realises that he would have been better off unreconciled – the price of knowing is too great. The series ends with a kind of closure, as the wounded players, Tosh and Owen, achieve a kind of peace with one another, and closes with the impact of their loss on their remaining fellows. If the theme of the series has been loss, separation and bereavement and how we learn to continue after it, its final message is that these losses will keep occurring, and there is no final hiding place from them other than death itself. That option, of course, is denied Jack Harkness, who we know far better after these 13 episodes. As with its parent series, *Torchwood* centres on a man whose relationship with time and mortality separates him from everyone else. Also like *Doctor Who*, *Torchwood* fills in its mysteries gradually, making them all the more exciting. It's been very rewarding to catch glimpses of Torchwood and its staff over the decades past, and just as rewarding to see the supporting players in the present filled out. Learning more about Rhys and Andy, their jobs, families, and feelings, is just as important to making *Torchwood* compelling, as learning how many times Jack has threaded through the 20th Century or where the Weevils come from.' Dave Owen, *Doctor Who Magazine* Issue 395, 28 May 2008.

- '[James] Marsters once again makes his art look effortless, delivering sexually-charged wisecracks along with chilling commands with fantastic flair and presence. Indeed, his cryptic comments regarding the real reasons for his actions during the first half of "Exit Wounds" [take on] added gravitas after a second viewing ... And it's not just Marsters who lights up the screen with emotion. Another round of wonderful acting is once again displayed from all involved, whether it's from Burn Gorman as Owen facing death for a second time, or Naoko Mori, who genuinely moved her co-stars to tears during the [recording] of Tosh's wonderfully understated death scene. We really hope that both of these fine actors go on to receive some huge (and well-deserved) mainstream success in the future ... Writer Chris Chibnall is once again on fine form, delivering a fantastic episode filled with action, drama, plot twists and little snippets of character background ... The terrorist overtones makes the episode all the more effective when Cardiff begins to explode, and the added threat of a nuclear meltdown would have come across as over-egging the pudding had a lesser writer tackled the story. Here, the plot point serves a purpose rather than just ramping up the level of danger.' Uncredited reviewer, Joo-See.com website, 6 April 2008.

- 'A few stupendous sequences, a couple of fine intimate moments, and some genuine nail-biting tension … But overall this finale to *Torchwood* Series Two is a little disappointing really. It's not badly directed or poorly acted or clumsily written – in fact just the opposite. It's just that, as a whole, it doesn't quite seem to come together, and it looks a little flat. This may be because the effects budget had been blown earlier in the season, meaning that all we get here are a few explosions and some previously used flashback footage to Jack's past. But the disappointment is also partly due to the anticlimax of James Marsters' return as Captain John. He starts off well enough in great villainous mode – if a little too much like Spike – but his role in the plot eventually seems to peter out. Shame.' Brigid Cherry, Total Sci Fi website, 4 April 2008.

FAN COMMENT

- 'Gray has got to be the worst Big Bad in the history of science fiction television … Nothing can possibly prepare you for the sulky Matt Le Blanc-alike who conspires to blow up Cardiff because he's incapable of holding onto somebody's hand. What next? A villain who hunts down Torchwood when they park their SUV in front of his garage? In the season finale??!!! While I'm fairly certain that the events Gray lived through were suitably horrific (they did make him catatonic after all), his revenge is so over the top (bombs, bombs and then some more bombs) he merely comes across as a second-tier, nuttier-than-squirrel-shit threat-of-the-week, rather than a tortured and misdirected soul that warrants our attention and/or respect. We don't even get a glimpse of the nightmare that drove him insane (this is a post-watershed show, is it not?), which wouldn't be quite so bad if the images conjured up by Gray weren't so prosaic and delivered in an unconvincing whine … Insanity is all very well, but Gray's motives are both petulant and brazenly disproportionate to the original crime (which isn't even a crime). What's even worse is that the episode presents you with what appears to be the worst motive ever ("You won't spend any time with me!") only to replace it with an even lamer one ("You didn't hold my hand!"). But the golden rule you should always adhere to when it comes to super-villains is that you either have to understand where they're coming from … or they must exude some sodding charisma. You just want to slap Gray. When he's saved from a pile of rotting corpses by Captain Spike, how does he repay him? He welds a fucking bomb onto his arm.' Neil Perryman, Behind the Sofa website, 12 April 2008.

- 'The emotional centerpiece of the episode, of course, was the fates of Toshiko Sato and Owen Harper. Both characters had experienced tremendous growth throughout the season, and had Owen not been in an undead state they likely would have consummated their relationship by now. As it stood, that relationship never really got off the ground. The writers did a really great job of setting up a final scene between the two without even having them in the same room. Via the comm system, they were able to share intimate moments together before Owen succumbed to the nuclear coolant venting. Now, one could argue that as Owen is already dead he could possibly survive this, but I don't think his body would survive the decomposition. We already know it won't heal. Perhaps [the production team decided to write the character out] simply because it was proving increasingly difficult to write [for him] as he'd been re-established post-death, or maybe their intention was to eliminate him after this year regardless. Certainly, the fact that he could never heal from even the smallest of scrapes made his continued presence in the field problematic. The fact that he took zero damage in last week's explosion is nigh on impossible [to believe]. I loved how selfless Tosh was in concealing her own injuries while talking with Owen so that he would not worry about her well-being or have to focus on anything potentially negative in his own dying. He instead could pass thinking she was good and his death was a noble sacrifice to save the city of Cardiff. That last part was true at least.' Jason Hughes, TV Squad website, 20 April 2008.

- 'The episode is a continuous race against and interaction with time. Time is at the foundation of the relationship between Jack and John: they're both ex-Time Agents, their love affair was influenced by time perceived versus time effectively elapsed, there's time travel after John asks for comfort. What happens to Gray takes place in our future, which is Jack's past, and then wreaks havoc and consequences upon our present, which is where Jack lives. Jack himself can't cross his own timeline, so he choses to willingly sacrifice himself. Just like Tommy, who willingly tells [1918] Torchwood to lock him in the vaults. Just like Owen, who asked to be drawered so that Death would be stopped from roaming the planet. Time is important while [the team members] are locked in the vaults, in the oh-so-pleasant company of stunned Weevils, who could wake up at any moment and attack them. Time is of the essence as Toshiko and Owen try containing the nuclear meltdown, which is where it gets real and close-to-home for all of us. We know that aliens aren't real. We know that time travelling can't effectually happen. We know that a dead person stays dead. Yet, we also know radioactive particles interacting with the environment cause damage. Long term damage, even, as they interfere with DNA and cause mutations and affect us in ways that aren't positive. Whenever there is nuclear involved, it is meant to make us uncomfortable and respond emotionally to whatever is going on. Time is, in the end, what kills Toshiko and Owen, as they battle for the greater good. Toshiko doesn't stitch herself up or ask for help. She simply shoots up alien-enhanced painkillers and keeps directing Owen, and then talking to him so he won't be alone when the nuclear meltdown finally kills him. Time seems to stretch on endlessly after she tells him that he's breaking her heart and they say goodbye. I couldn't have loved it more if they'd been in the same room, holding onto each other. It is also extremely fitting that Jack was there with Tosh. He's saved her, and simultaneaously sentenced her to an early death, because this is Torchwood, they all die young.' 'utopia83', LiveJournal blog, 5 April 2008.

- 'What I most loved? *Penance.* I was floored. Because in any other story we'd be thinking and saying, "What happened to Gray wasn't Jack's fault", and I was thinking that, weren't you? But Jack saw right through all that as a smokescreen: it didn't matter whether it was his fault or not, that wasn't the point, the point was taking responsibility, and he took it without hesitation. Two thousand years of penance. An act of expiation all the more remarkable in its spiritual extremity. And yes, we've seen Jack paying for his various sins over and over. The sin of almost killing mankind in "The Empty Child". The sin of being a conman. The sin of his friend's torture and death, the sin of letting go of Gray's hand, and so on. The redemption theme. And Jack has paid the price over and over: dying for the Doctor in "The Parting of the Ways", dying for mankind in "End of Days", and so on. Just as the Doctor in *Doctor Who* Series One had his own redemption story: he killed his own race (and symbolically his past) in order to destroy the Daleks, and then offered his race, himself, Jack, mankind and the future as sacrifice in "The Parting of the Ways". I love redemption themes. This totally took me by surprise: that Jack's triumph came not by fighting Grey but capitulating to him, forgiving him, loving him, and essentially putting another "mercy killing" to Torchwood's credit. As heroic figures go, Jack's is not so much the obvious contemporary superhero or action hero – he's a medieval martyr. It has nothing to do with justice or even atonement, because the wrongdoing was not his own – but in a mystical sense, there was a spiritual price to pay. So: who'd've thought Jack could outdo his messiah resurrection act from last season? But he did. Wow.' 'fajrdrako', LiveJournal blog, 6 April 2008.

- 'Owen and Tosh were my two favourite characters in *Torchwood* and the moment I found out they were going to die I was heartbroken. Watching the episode and their last scenes was so upsetting. I started crying the moment Tosh was shot and I didn't stop until the credits rolled. I watched the last 15 minutes through tears and I couldn't help but sob. Tosh's "Because you're breaking my heart" was the saddest line of all two series. There was such a connection between the two and the fact that they spent their last few minutes talking to each other … I can't help but believe that Owen knew that she too was dying – no-one is in that much pain from a broken arm. The fact they died together … Burn [Gorman] and Naoko [Mori] did an amazing job and they deserve recognition for their fantastic acting. I hope to see them in a lot more stuff over the years. I think the line that really got me for Owen was when he went "Oh God" just before the screen went to white. For two tinny words, it was so powerful and immensely upsetting. It just summed up his feelings and what was about to happen to him. The final scene where their stuff was being packed away and Ianto was signing them out just made me cry even more. I think it was Ianto closing their files that really hit me – they're dead. It was so very final and the image of the folder fading away … They really gave two amazing characters a fabulous (and heartbreaking) ending.' 'miss_boleyn17', LiveJournal blog, 5 April 2008.

ANALYSIS: Series Two of *Torchwood* closes with an episode that draws together a number of strands from earlier storylines – Captain John's love/hate relationship with Captain Jack, the mysterious long-ago disappearance of Gray, the death and resurrection of Owen, the appearance of Weevils *en masse*, the Victorian-era Torchwood Cardiff, the increased involvement of Rhys and Andy, the developing relationship between Owen and Toshiko – and brings things to a highly dramatic conclusion, ending with a terrible tragedy that leaves the regular team, and the show itself, irrevocably changed.

It was an excellent idea on the production team's part to bring James Marsters back for a further guest appearance as Captain John, and the development of his character is very well handled here. While he could never be described as a sympathetic figure, having proved himself in 'Kiss Kiss, Bang Bang' to be a ruthless killer, the fact that on this occasion his destructive actions turn out to have been perpetrated under extreme duress – and not, as it initially seems, for the petty reason that he sees himself as having been snubbed and belittled by Jack – does lead the viewer to feel a little more favourably disposed toward him, as does the fact that he tries to make amends by helping the Torchwood team once he is free to do so. The pre-titles scene in the Hub where he tells Jack that he loves him and then turns around and shoots him with a pair of machine guns is memorably shocking. It is clear, though, that he really does regret having to mistreat his former partner in this way – as his subsequent pained comments when he has got Jack chained up by the wall further attest. 'Whatever your plan is, we're gonna stop you,' says Jack. 'Oh, okay,' replies John. 'Go on then, stop me. I hope you can. Really.'

The true culprit, Gray, arguably has even less justification for wanting to harm Jack, quite apart from the fact that they are brothers. Even though Jack clearly blames himself for the fact that they got separated as children – as seen in 'Adam' – and that Gray was subsequently captured and horrifically tortured by the creatures that attacked the Boeshane Peninsula, this is obviously a classic case of survivor guilt, and no objective observer would ever hold him at fault for what happened. Gray, though, is far from being an objective observer, and one can only conclude that he has been driven insane by his traumatic experiences. Although he shows no outward signs of madness, it is fair to say that no sane person would ever contemplate the terrible retribution that he metes out to Jack, having John take him back in time to 27 AD and bury him under the ground on which Cardiff will one day be built, to remain there – as far as Gray is concerned – indefinitely, suffering a never-ending cycle of dying and being brought back to life again. In the event, by virtue of John having managed to slip him a signal-emitting ring, Jack is rescued by his Victorian-era Torchwood associates after 'only' the best part of two thousand years, but the fact that he has avoided being driven insane himself in the process must surely indicate that it is not only his physical injuries that are automatically healed each time he revives, as witnessed on numerous prior occasions, but also any mental injuries, so that his mind effectively gets reset to its former state. (The constant bodily restoration would also presumably explain why his hair and nails have not grown while he has been buried and why he has suffered no apparent weight loss despite having not eaten or drunk for almost two millennia.) Even so, this must still be a truly horrendous ordeal for him to have to endure – recalling that in 'Kiss Kiss, Bang Bang' he likened the sensation of coming back to life to being 'hauled over broken glass' – and the fact that when he eventually sees Gray again in 2009 he simply tells him that he forgives him speaks volumes about his strength of character and depth of compassion. It is tempting to suggest that he is inspired here by the example set by the Doctor who, in very similar fashion, forgave the Master for the terrible crimes he had committed in 'Last of the Time Lords' – an event that Jack was present to witness – but, then again, he had already demonstrated his own extraordinary capacity for forgiveness after his Torchwood Three colleagues all turned on him and betrayed him in 'End of Days'.

It has been suggested by some commentators that the Gray storyline is disappointingly anticlimactic, particularly for a series finale, in that the threat derives simply from a deranged personal vendetta against Jack rather than something grander like an alien invasion attempt or even, as in 'End of Days', the unleashing of a demonic beast. Some fans have also been harshly critical of Lachlan Nieboer's portrayal of Gray, having found it to be weak and unconvincing to the extent that it undermined the effectiveness of the drama. This is not *Doctor Who*, however, and stories involving dark, twisted, intensely personal conflicts suit *Torchwood* far better than less emotionally-intense plots concerning alien invasions or villainous master plans; and while it is undeniably true that Nieboer – making his professional acting debut here – lacks the presence and charisma of a John Barrowman or a James Marsters, it is arguable that this is entirely appropriate to the role of Gray, in light of the evident weakness of his character, and that a more assured performance would have failed to provide the necessary contrast to Jack's strength of personality and moral conviction. Nieboer certainly looks the part, as he has sufficient physical similarities to Barrowman to pass as his brother; and, to his credit, he makes a very good job of emulating Barrowman's American accent.

Jack's rescue in 1901 affords a welcome opportunity for a return appearance by Alice Guppy, again appealingly played by Amy Manson, as previously seen in the 1899 segment of 'Fragments'. Sadly, on this occasion, she is without her leader, Emily Holroyd, due to actress Heather Craney's unavailability, but in her place we are introduced to another previously-unseen Torchwood Cardiff member, Charles Gaskell, a small role of which actor Cornelius Macarthy makes the most. Once again the viewer is left thinking how wonderful it would be to see more of the exploits of this Victorian-era Torchwood Three.

Also making a second appearance in this episode is the St Helen's Hospital doctor played by Golda Rosheuvel who in 'Dead Man Walking' treated Martha after she was aged by her brush with the resurrection glove. She is named here for the first time as Angela Connolly and becomes involved in the action after she encounters a ravenous Hoix – a nice incidental crossover of a minor monster from *Doctor Who*. Owen is given the task of neutralising the creature, which he does by distracting it with a tasty packet of cigarettes supplied by the doctor and then injecting it with an all-species sedative, commenting 'You really are quite stupid, aren't you'. This is one of a number of nicely humorous sequences in the episode. Another stand-out amongst these is one where Ianto and Toshiko are threatened by a group of three scythe-wielding black-cowled figures vaguely recalling the traditional image of the Grim Reaper – another nod to 'Dead Man Walking', perhaps? – and deal with them simply by shooting them down, Ianto casually remarking 'There we are then' and Toshiko adding 'Sorted' – a neat variation on the famous *Raiders of the Lost Ark* joke where Indiana Jones calmly waits until an assailant finishes an impressive display of sword-twirling and then nonchalantly shoots him dead. As in 'Kiss Kiss, Bang Bang', Captain John also gets some amusing lines of dialogue, particularly in the early part of the episode; when Jack protests at being chained up, for instance, he replies, 'Oh, what, suddenly you're anti-bondage?' His 'Eye Candy' nickname for Ianto also gets another airing.

As the episode continues, though, it gets progressively darker in tone, leading up to the shattering conclusion where Owen and Toshiko are both killed – the former for the second and presumably final time. These tear-jerking closing sequences, in which the two friends and colleagues share their most intimate and heartfelt conversation despite being in physically separate locations, are superbly written by Chris Chibnall – making what could well be his last contribution to *Torchwood*, given his subsequent departure to the production team of the in-preparation ITV1 show *Law and Order: London* – and brilliantly acted by Burn Gorman and, possibly even more so, Naoko Mori. Indeed, this is probably Mori's best-ever performance in the show, making the viewer regret even more that it is to be her swansong. The aftermath of the deaths, as Jack and Gwen pack away their departed colleagues' possessions and Ianto logs them out of the Hub's computers for the final time, is also incredibly poignant, as is Toshiko's pre-recorded video message, left for her colleagues to find in the event of her death, in which she expresses her love for Owen and the others and ends 'I hope I did good.' By this point, many viewers would no doubt have been in floods of tears.

Thus ends another outstanding episode, boasting some typically assured direction from Ashley Way, the high production values now customary to the show, and fine performances not only from Gorman and Mori but also from all the other regulars too – Eve Myles is again afforded some excellent material here, particularly in the scenes where Gwen valiantly rallies her former police colleagues despite her own self-doubts about her ability to cope, and only the generally-underused Gareth David-Lloyd is left without a great deal to do. And although the overall tone of the episode is decidedly downbeat – inevitably so, given that if features the horrifying deaths of two well-liked regular characters – it does at least end on a relatively hopeful note, as the three remaining team members come together in their grief and look to the future:

Jack: 'Now we carry on.
Gwen: 'I don't think I can, not after this.'
Jack: 'You can. We all can. The end is where we start from.'

SERIES OVERVIEW

Prior to transmission, much was said and written within fandom and the genre TV press about how Series Two of *Torchwood* might, or indeed ought, to differ from Series One. In the event, the changes were quite subtle, but nevertheless significant. The same line-up of regular characters was retained, but some of the rough edges were knocked off them, and their interrelationships were made more harmonious. The same preoccupation with death and darkness ran through the stories, but there was more of a sense of fun and humour too. The same sexually liberal ethos infused the drama, but there was less swearing, no sex scenes and no nudity – even Kai Owen's backside remained fully covered throughout this run.

These changes were warmly welcomed by most telefantasy fans – not surprisingly, perhaps, as they took the show a bit further away from the domain of mainstream adult drama and a bit closer to the world of standard telefantasy; a world in which the heroes are always likeable, invariably friendly to one another and never swear or have illicit sex, and in which the villains are similarly clearly defined as thoroughly nasty and irredeemably evil. This is no doubt an over-generalisation, but the tendency toward simple moral absolutes is arguably one of the defining features of standard telefantasy that sets it apart from conventional adult drama; and it is, by and large, something that most genre TV fans want to see maintained. Series One of *Torchwood* didn't really play by those rules, and thus, while it was a huge hit with the general viewing public, it alienated many within what might have been predicted to be its most committed audience. Time and again, fan reviews and internet forum postings – albeit from a particularly vociferous minority – lambasted the show because some of its regulars were not altogether likeable, or acted on occasion in morally dubious ways, or had emotionally messy infidelities, or used realistically coarse language, as if these were self-evidently bad things rather than – as would be readily accepted in the generality of post-watershed drama – typical, uncontroversial, even expected elements of good, truthful characterisation. In Series Two, however, *Torchwood's* subtle shift in tone gave it a little less in common with shows such as *Dexter*, *Damages*, *Spooks* and *Skins* and a little more in common with ones like *Stargate SG-1*, *Heroes*, *Primeval* and indeed its own parent show, *Doctor Who*.

The difference is a fine one, but can perhaps be encapsulated as follows: while it is easy to imagine that a character in a mainstream adult drama such as *The Sopranos* might ask something like 'When was the last time you screwed all night? When was the last time you came so hard and so long that you forgot where you are?' – something that Owen says to Gwen in Series One of *Torchwood*, in the episode 'Countrycide' – it is inconceivable that anyone in a standard telefantasy show like *Smallville* might deliver such a line of dialogue – and similarly unthinkable that Owen might say such a thing to Gwen in Series Two of *Torchwood*. This has little to do with the target age range for telefantasy shows – popular examples such as *Charmed*, *Battlestar Galactica* and *Ghost Whisperer* all typically get 12 or 15 ratings for their DVD releases and are not specifically tailored to a family audience. Nor is it always due to restrictions imposed by broadcasters – *Stargate SG-1* was, after all, made for the US Showtime network for its first five seasons, where it was seen alongside far more sexually-explicit and expletive-laden fare such as *Queer as Folk* and *Red Shoe Diaries*. Rather, it is dictated primarily by the conventions of the genre. One is reminded here of Russell T Davies's comments prior to transmission about wanting to give the Torchwood team more of the sense of unity of the various crews of the *Enterprise* in the *Star Trek* franchise.

Of course, there is nothing inherently wrong with standard telefantasy shows – all the above-mentioned examples are excellent, and *Doctor Who* is really beyond compare – but what made *Torchwood* so incredibly distinctive in Series One was that it *didn't* adopt the standard telefantasy approach. Instead, it took the science fiction and fantasy elements characteristic of the genre and coupled them with the aesthetic and mode of expression of a mainstream adult drama; and in that respect it was arguably unique. This is not to suggest that the show completely lost its distinctiveness or was effectively neutered in Series Two – it still contained a fair sprinkling of expletives the like of which one would never hear in, say, *Primeval*, and enough violence and bloodshed to keep it clearly delineated from *Doctor Who*, earning it the same 15 rating as Series One on its DVD release – but it did unquestionably lose some of its rawness, some of its edginess, some of its downright outrageousness. Although many fans were initially surprised by the decision to screen pre-watershed repeats of Series Two, in retrospect it makes perfect sense that the BBC should have wanted to broaden the show's audience reach in this way, given that the shift in tone meant that in most cases the amount of editing required to bring the episodes within pre-watershed parameters was fairly minimal.

Another notable consequence of the retooling of the format was that Series Two proved markedly less controversial than Series One. The fact that telefantasy fans overwhelmingly approved of the changes meant that the show was now far less discussed, debated and generally argued over than it had been before. Whereas Series One had attracted reams of impassioned comment, both pro and con, on TV-related websites and blogs and in genre magazines such as *TV Zone*, *SFX* and *DeathRay*, Series Two saw this fall to a fraction of its previous level. So, paradoxically, while Series Two was more popular than Series One, it was also less talked about. This was even reflected in more mainstream press coverage: there were no pithy Charlie Brooker critiques of the show in the *Guardian*'s TV pages *this* year, as there had been in 2006.

Also lacking in Series Two was some of the sheer spontaneity evident in Series One. The fact that the production team had been given relatively little preparation time for that debut run meant that they had been left having, in effect, to make things up as they went along – certainly there was no preconceived story arc for it – and this in turn meant that developments such as the affair between Gwen and Owen and the resurrection of Suzie emerged organically as the episodes were written, and the viewer could never tell what was going to happen, or what type of story was going to be presented, next. This was unusual and refreshing, and helped to create a real sense of dangerous unpredictability. On Series Two, by contrast, the production team had much longer to formulate ideas and plans, and this was reflected in a sense of events unfolding more in accordance with an orderly, predetermined pattern. At times, in fact, it seemed that things had been almost over-thought. Thus, for instance, while the obvious, immediate-reaction thing to have done when presented with the opportunity of a three-episode guest appearance by Freema Agyeman would have been to make this a trilogy of stories focused on her character, the production team actually chose to do something quite different: so keen were they, it seems, to fit into this series the storyline they had long been planning about Owen dying and being brought back to life, that they actually made this the central aspect of two of the three episodes, bizarrely relegating Agyeman to a background role. The wisdom of this decision seems even more questionable in light of the fact that Owen was to be killed off permanently at the end of the series, the impact of which would inevitably overshadow that of his first death.

However, what Series Two lacked by comparison with Series One in terms of rawness, controversy and spontaneity, it easily made up for, and arguably more than made up for, in terms of increased consistency, confidence and overall quality. With the sole exception of the very disappointing 'From Out of the Rain', which just didn't suit the *Torchwood* format or even work as a story in its own right, all the episodes this time around succeeded in every important respect, being imaginatively conceived, tautly plotted, skilfully scripted, convincingly acted, superbly directed and excellently produced. All five regulars were given some strong material to work with over the course of the 13 episodes, the only notable omission in this regard being the regrettable lack of any storyline allowing Ianto to take centre stage (although 'From Out of the Rain' came close to doing so); a wonderful new recurring villain was introduced in the form of Captain John Hart, played with great presence and charisma by guest star James Marsters; Freema Agyeman's Martha made her much-anticipated transition from *Doctor Who* and turned out to work equally well as a character in the spin-off, particularly in the one episode, 'Reset', where she *was* allowed to shine; and even the deservedly popular semi-regulars Rhys and PC Andy were given a bigger slice of the action this time around. *Torchwood*'s key recurrent themes of death and loss – another factor marking it out as unique within the telefantasy genre – were again very much to the fore and gave rise to some of the darkest storylines yet seen in the show, culminating in the shocking deaths of Toshiko and (for the second and presumably final time) Owen in the climactic 'Exit Wounds', proving that, Captain Jack aside, no-one in this show is guaranteed to make it through to the final credits.

It is also worth reflecting here that *Torchwood* remains the only TV drama, certainly in the UK and probably anywhere in the world, to have made a bisexual (strictly, omnisexual) character its central figure and hero, and as such it holds an important place in the nation's TV culture, and arguably even in the nation's culture more generally. It is easy to forget that just a few years ago, the sight of two people of the same sex doing so much as kissing in a programme shown before the 9.00 pm watershed would have been enough to generate outraged tabloid editorials and mounds of complaining correspondence to the relevant broadcaster, industry watchdogs and even the government. While it would obviously be wrong to give *Torchwood*, or indeed Captain Jack's original home show *Doctor Who*, sole credit for changing these public attitudes, never before has a high-profile, popular-appeal drama such as this brought stories involving gay and bisexual characters so successfully into the mainstream, and in a completely matter-of-fact way that has drawn remarkably little adverse comment let alone controversy. Significantly, Russell T Davies was adamant that one thing that would *not* be cut from the Series Two episodes for their pre-watershed repeats was scenes of same-sex kissing; and even independent regulator Ofcom has stated that it now views such scenes no differently than those of opposite-sex kissing. This was an issue addressed by journalist Sarah Lyall in a perceptive article about Davies published in June 2008 on the websites of the *New York Times* and its global edition, the *International Herald Tribune*, which read in part:

'[Davies] … pushes the envelope the whole time, not in terms of taste and decency but in terms of ideas and emotional intelligence, the size of feeling and epic stroke of narrative breadth,' said Jane Tranter, the BBC's Head of Fiction. She said that no-one at the BBC had ever had a problem with Captain Jack or with any of Mr Davies's plotlines. 'How ridiculous would it be that you would travel through time and space and only ever find heterosexual men?' Ms Tranter said.

…

'I thought, "It's time you introduce bisexuals properly into mainstream television,"' [Davies] said, laughing. He tends to see the joke in most things and talks about television with a words-spilling-over-each-other enthusiasm. What better way to introduce a charming bisexual character, he asked, than to make him 'an outer space buccaneer?' 'The most boring drama would be' – here he put on a whiny, fractious voice – '"Oh, I'm bisexual, oh my bleeding heart" night-time drama. Tedious, dull. But if you say it's a bisexual space pirate swaggering in with guns and attitude and cheek and humour into prime-time family viewing: that was enormously attractive to me.'

Torchwood has unquestionably made its mark on the broadcasting landscape, not only in the UK but also, increasingly, in the USA and in the many other countries where it has been screened.[117] In the final assessment, there is no arguing with the official viewing statistics.[118] With an average audience reach of almost five million viewers per episode, plus about half a million more watching via the BBC's iPlayer and other download services, and Appreciation Index figures consistently in the upper eighties, Series Two of *Torchwood* proved to be an even bigger hit than the groundbreaking Series One. With the show due to be promoted to BBC One for the 'special event' Series Three in 2009, following its move from BBC Three to BBC Two for Series Two, it looks set to win a still bigger audience in future, and all the signs are that it will continue to go from strength to strength with each successive run, hopefully for years to come.

---

117 In a 2008-published *Buffy the Vampire Slayer* comic book, *Season Eight* Issue 12 (Dark Horse), a storyline sanctioned by Buffy's creator Joss Whedon surprised many fans by having her sleep with another woman – the first indication of any bisexual tendencies on her part in that show's official canon. Is it possible that *Torchwood*, which has always owed a big debt of inspiration to the Buffyverse, is now effectively returning the favour …?

118 See Appendix D for full details.

APPENDIX A – TIE-IN MERCHANDISE

From the latter months of 2007, officially-licensed *Torchwood* merchandise, previously very thin on the ground, started to become more plentiful.[119]

DVDs

Following three double-disc DVD sets containing four or five episodes apiece plus extras, a complete DVD box set of Series One was issued in the UK on 19 November. This contained all the material that was on the individual sets, along with a selection of amusing outtakes and a commentary by members of the cast and crew on each of the 13 episodes, making for a very impressive overall package. Later announced to go on sale on 30 June 2008 was a Blu-ray version of the Series One set plus a standard DVD box set of Series Two, with no individual releases preceding it on this occasion.[120] The Series Two set would have far fewer extras than the previous one, however, and there would be no episode commentaries this time around. A Region 1 version of the Series One box set came out in both the US and Canada on 22 January 2008, and a Region 4 version in Australasia on 11 February.

MAGAZINE

Long-established genre publisher Titan Magazines was granted a licence to produce *Torchwood: The Official Magazine*, the launch of which was announced by the company as follows:

> Following the success of *Torchwood*, the BBC's award-winning sci-fi drama, Titan Magazines presents *Torchwood: The Official Magazine* – the essential guide to the adrenalin-fuelled exploits of Captain Jack Harkness and his team.
>
> *Torchwood: The Official Magazine* includes the latest news from the *Torchwood* set in Cardiff, exclusive cast and crew interviews, behind-the-scenes features on the show's special effects, regular columns from *Torchwood*'s lead writer Chris Chibnall and producer Richard Stokes, plus 10 pages of original *Torchwood* comic strip fiction!
>
> The launch issue includes interviews with *Torchwood* lead John Barrowman and guest star James Marsters (Spike, *Buffy the Vampire Slayer*), plus exclusive photography and concept artwork of the Hub.
>
> Explore *Torchwood* from a different angle, only with *Torchwood: The Official Magazine*!

The first issue, dated February 2008, went on sale on 24 January. Subsequent issues then followed on a four-weekly basis, with Issue 4 in April being a 100-page special.

In an interview posted on 1 February on the UK SF Book News website, Titan Magazines' senior comics editor Steve White gave an insight into how the *Torchwood* comic strip was

---

119 See Appendix B for more detailed information about the novels, audios and comic strip stories released during the period covered by this book.

120 Plans for an HD-DVD version of the Series One set were abandoned after the effective demise of that format.

produced: 'We have to stay within fairly tight guidelines, and because we're running behind the TV series, there has been the occasional stumble over an idea or storyline already under way in the show. In these sorts of situations, you tend to have [to] move in a sort of circular history. You can do whatever you want – tear holes in the space/time continuum, destroy planets, leave cast members for dead – so long as by the end, it's all back to normal …

'One of the biggest challenges was finding the right creators [for the strip] that everyone's happy with! Editorially that's been the driving force behind the strip – at least during the initial stages. Everyone has had differing views on approach and style and it took a fair while to actually reach a consensus. But after a bit of struggle, we got there and things can now seriously get under way.

'Not that's it's been a constant struggle or such like, but every stage of the process has been hard work. Still, [penciller] Shannon [Gallant] did get a pretty smooth ride through the approvals process [on the first strip story] and did a miraculous job turning the pages around in under two weeks – which were then approved pretty much as was. You have no idea the sense of relief on that one!

'The stories we have planned for the first year of the magazine will feature one overall story arc, although we will have standalone strips that will reflect what's going on in the main storyline. Simon Furman has been responsible for developing the story arc and will write several issues, but we're hoping for star turns on the individual strips. We also have a number of artists in the pipeline including D'Israeli, Paul Grist and Steve Yeowell. But this is early days and we're still pulling together a final line-up.'

CDs

Abridged talking-book versions of the first three *Torchwood* novels, *Another Life* by Peter Anghelides, *Slow Decay* by Andy Lane and *Border Princes* by Dan Abnett, had been released as three-disc CD sets by BBC Audiobooks back on 2 April 2007, read by John Barrowman, Burn Gorman and Eve Myles respectively.[121] The next two *Torchwood* audio releases, however, were original stories exclusive to that medium. *Everyone Says Hello*, written by Dan Abnett and read by Burn Gorman, and *Hidden*, written by Steve Savile and read by Naoko Mori, were both issued by BBC Audiobooks as double-disc CD sets on 4 February 2008. A third audio-only story, *In the Shadows*, was originally planned to appear at the same time, but this had to be put back to 11 September as its author, Joseph Lidster, was delayed completing the text due to work on his TV episode 'A Day in the Death'. Lidster's Radio 4 *Torchwood* drama was also scheduled for a CD release on 11 September.

BOOKS

For younger readers, the tenth entry in the *Doctor Who Files* series from the BBC Children's Books imprint of Penguin Character Books was *Captain Jack* by Justin Richards, published on

---

121 John Barrowman later recalled in interviews that it had required two days of intensive work for him to complete his audiobook reading and that he had done it 'cold', as due to lack of time he had not had an opportunity to read the book in advance. He mused that if any further audiobooks were produced, a good idea might be to have each of the show's regular cast members reading his or her own character's dialogue, with the linking material provided by a narrator, such as his friend Sir Ian McKellen.

30 August 2007. This contained lots of facts and photos and a short piece of original fiction, although understandably the focus was entirely on the character's *Doctor Who* appearances rather than his *Torchwood* role.

Although not strictly a *Torchwood* book, of interest to many fans was John Barrowman's autobiography *Anything Goes*, co-written with his sister Carole E Barrowman, which was published in hardback by Michael O'Mara books on 24 January 2008. An abridged talking-book version read by the actor himself followed from BBC Audiobooks on 4 February.

The next three *Torchwood* hardback novels from BBC Books were published on 6 March 2008, mid-way through the on-air run of Series Two. These were *Trace Memory* by David Llewellyn, *Something in the Water* by Trevor Baxendale and *The Twilight Streets* by Gary Russell. The first three novels meanwhile had a debut paperback publication, exclusive to the Book Club mail-order company. Scheduled for release on 2 October 2008 were three further novels, *Skypoint* by Phil Ford, *Pack Animals* by Peter Anghelides and *Almost Perfect* by James Goss, and a hardback guide book called *The Torchwood Archives* by Gary Russell.

Titan Books meanwhile got in on the act with *Torchwood – The Official Yearbook 2009*, scheduled for publication on 22 August 2008.

MISCELLANEOUS

With an eye on seasonal sales, Danilo released the *Official Torchwood Calendar 2008* on 1 November 2007, presenting various publicity images from the show. This sold sufficiently well for a 2009 equivalent to be scheduled for 15 September 2008. November 2007 also saw Cartamundi issue a pack of 55 photo-illustrated *Torchwood* playing cards, which were generally reckoned by fans to be of superior quality to the same company's three previously-produced sets of *Doctor Who* cards.

The ScifiCollector company, based at the Stamp Centre in the Strand in central London, added a number of *Torchwood* items to its successful range of attractively-designed stamp sheets and commemorative stamp covers, some of which it made available signed by either John Barrowman or Eve Myles.

Two new 36 x 24-inch *Torchwood* posters were issued by 1art1 on 19 February 2008, presenting standard Series Two publicity images of Captain Jack and the five Torchwood team regulars respectively. In a similar vein, Mysterious World made available high quality mounted 10 x 8-inch photo prints of a selection of standard *Torchwood* publicity shots.

G E Fabbri, who had scored a big hit with their *Doctor Who – Battles in Time* trading card series and associated magazine, followed this up with a set of 200 *Torchwood* trading cards, released on 16 April 2008. These came in packs containing nine or sometimes ten cards each, and consisted of 160 common cards (eight in every pack), 25 rare (one in every pack), ten super rare (one in every six packs) and five ultra rare (one in every 24 packs). Reflecting the fact that these were aimed very much at the collectors' market, the packs cost £2.99 each – virtually twice the £1.50 price of the *Battles in Time* ones. They were supplied to shops and dealers in boxes of 32 packs each. Unlike with *Battles in Time*, there was no accompanying magazine.

Although not strictly qualifying as merchandise, because they were given away rather than sold, several postcards featuring Series Two publicity images were produced by the BBC for promotional purposes.

Alongside all the official items, numerous unofficial ones continued to appear, often on the eBay auction website. These included standard fare such as mugs, T-shirts, key-rings and the like, and a fairly basic video game.

COMING SOON ...

News of an important new range of forthcoming *Torchwood* merchandise broke on 12 December 2007 with a much-anticipated announcement by ScifiCollector that it – or, more precisely, the associated company GetRetro, of which it was the retail arm – had been granted a licence to produce five-inch-tall *Torchwood* action figures, to be launched as early as possible the following year. A formal press release to this effect was put out by GetRetro on 16 January 2008. As the company refined its plans over the next few months, a first wave of four figures – Jack, Gwen, a Weevil and a Cyberwoman – was scheduled for release around August or September 2008, with a second wave of five – Owen, Toshiko, Ianto, Captain John and a Blowfish – to come later that year. Impressive prototypes of some of the figures – each of which would be mounted on a detachable plinth but in other respects would be compatible with those in the equivalent *Doctor Who* range produced by Character Options[122] – were previewed at toy fairs and at the 26 April *Torchwood* convention The Rift, although attendees were asked not to take photographs of them as at that time they were still going through the BBC Worldwide approvals process.

On 11 April 2008, an indication of a plethora of further official products to come was given in a report by Samantha Loveday on the Licensing.biz website, which read in part:

> BBC Worldwide has signed up Underground Toys as the licensee for *Torchwood* in the UK and North America.
>
> The deal will see Underground Toys take on the international distribution of existing *Torchwood* product and the manufacturing of new lines including mugs, key chains, voice key chains, plastic prop replica items, playing cards and resin busts for the UK and US markets.
>
> In the US, action figures and Minimates are also included in the deal. Product will begin rolling out in both territories this summer.
>
> ...
>
> 'We're thrilled to embark on this project with Underground Toys,' said Anna Hewitt, head of international licensing at BBC Worldwide. 'The partnership follows the success of the *Doctor Who* range, which Underground Toys distributes in North America, and we're looking to tap into the amazing TV success [of *Torchwood*] on both sides of the pond to attract toy sales across a range of premium product.'

The first mugs and key chains were subsequently scheduled for release at the end of August. It seemed that exciting – and expensive! – times lay ahead for collectors of *Torchwood* merchandise!

---

122 In 2007, Character Options had itself considered producing a range of *Torchwood* action figures, but this idea had not been progressed.

APPENDIX B – ORIGINAL NOVELS, AUDIOS AND COMIC STRIPS

NOVELS[123]

4: SOMETHING IN THE WATER
Publication date: 6 March 2008
Author: Trevor Baxendale
Commissioning Editor: Albert DePetrillo
Series Editor: Steve Tribe
Production Controller: Phil Spencer
Cover Design: Lee Binding

PLOT: The lone survivor of the lost planet Strepto arrived on Earth in the Middle Ages via the time rift in Cardiff and has since been scheming to breed a new generation of her race. Thriving in stagnant lakes and bogs, the creatures have given rise to the myth of the water hag. Taking on the guise of a woman named Saskia Harden, the progenitor disseminates her spores into the population of South Wales, starting at a local medical centre. The spores spread like a contagious infection, causing an epidemic of severe flu-like symptoms. In men, they grow into a grotesque homunculus, which eventually breaks free – ripping the victim's throat apart in the process – and develops into a new water hag. Torchwood become involved when the creatures cause a spate of rift activity sparks. Toshiko manages to find a cure for the epidemic, but the creatures that have already been born converge on the Hub, intent on using the rift to take control of the Earth. Jack manages to kill the progenitor, and the other creatures, which were all linked to her, die as well.

DOCTOR WHO REFERENCES
- The planet Strepto is said to have vanished, tying in with the disappearing planets theme of Series Four of *Doctor Who*.

ALIEN TECH
- None.

CONTINUITY POINTS
- In the 1970s, Jack had an affair with a man named Professor Len Morgan, and also saved his life at one point. Morgan features briefly in the novel but is killed by the principal water hag, known to him as Sally Blackteeth.

---

123 For information on the first three *Torchwood* novels, see *Inside the Hub: The Unofficial and Unauthorised Guide to Torchwood Series One* (Telos Publishing, 2007).

NOTES

- There is a reference to the 'recent time shift with 1918', and Rhys does not yet know what Gwen's job entails. This places the novel between the TV episodes 'To the Last Man' and 'Meat'.

REVIEW: *Something in the Water* is written in a highly descriptive style, with some very memorable imagery of the water hags and of the truly disgusting flu-like infection spreading through the population, starting with the sympathetically-drawn character of local GP Bob Strong. On the downside, the plot doesn't hang together too well – for instance, it is unclear why the principal water hag has waited until 2008 to launch her colonisation attempt in earnest if she has been on Earth since the Middle Ages, and uncertain exactly how the creatures intend to use the rift to achieve their purposes – and the ending is somewhat anticlimactic, with Jack ultimately defeating the menace simply by ripping off the principal water hag's head while she is in a state of transformation. The Torchwood team members are well depicted, but – particularly in Owen's case – more in line with how their characters were in Series One than in Series Two. Overall, a bit disappointing.

5: TRACE MEMORY

Publication date: 6 March 2008
Author: David Llewellyn
Commissioning Editor: Albert DePetrillo
Series Editor: Steve Tribe
Production Controller: Phil Spencer
Cover Design: Lee Binding

PLOT: A Vondraxian Orb – an ancient alien artefact that acts as a tachyon radiation storage cell – is found buried in the Arctic ice in 1953 and transported to Cardiff by ship to be placed in the charge of Torchwood Three. On the ship's arrival, however, the Orb reacts with energy from the rift and explodes. A young dock worker, Michael Bellini, is exposed to the tachyon radiation. This causes him to make a series of jumps through time: to his home street during the Blitz in 1941; to Cardiff around 2001, where he is admitted to hospital and seen by Dr Owen Harper; to Torchwood Three in 2008, where he is found in the basement area of the Hub where the broken Orb is held in storage; to Torchwood One in February 2006, where Ianto Jones has just started work; to Osaka, Japan, where he meets a five-year-old Toshiko Sato; to Cardiff around 2004, where he encounters PC Gwen Cooper and her new partner PC Andy Davidson; and finally to Cardiff in 1967, where he appears in a car being driven by Captain Jack Harkness. On each occasion, he is pursued by the Vondrax – emaciated creatures dressed incongruously in suits and bowler hats – who wish to retrieve the tachyon radiation from him. In 1967, he and Jack are captured by a group of spies from KVI, a Soviet equivalent of Torchwood, and taken to their secret base in the abandoned

Hamilton's Sugar warehouse on the docks. Chaos ensues when the Vondrax arrive, and Michael and Jack jump from the roof of the building into the Bay. Michael dies in the water, and the Vondrax finally leave Earth.

DOCTOR WHO REFERENCES

- Reference is made to alien-related incidents at the Albion Hospital in 1941 – as seen in 'The Empty Child'/'The Doctor Dances' – and at Maiden's Point in 1943 – as seen in 'The Curse of Fenric'.

ALIEN TECH

- The Orb is one of a number of such devices created by the Vondrax to store tachyon radiation, on which they feed. This radiation is generated each time a new parallel universe is created by a choice being made. It was plentiful at the time of the Big Bang, because there were so many possible choices then, but has become less so ever since, hence the Vondrax's need to store it.

CONTINUITY POINTS

- During the Cold War era, Torchwood were concerned to prevent information about aliens falling into Soviet hands. Torchwood agents in 1953 included two men named Cromwell and Valentine. Cromwell remained loyal to the organisation, and came out of retirement in February 2006 to advise Torchwood One on the case of Michael Bellini, in which he had been involved over the years. He was killed by the Vondrax. Valentine, on the other hand, defected to the USSR sometime before 1967 and worked with their Committee for Extraterrestrial Research, known as KVI for short – a 1920s Soviet rebranding of a department set up under the Tsar sometime after the Tunguska explosion of 1908.

NOTES

- This book had the working title *Horaizan*, which was changed at quite a late stage on its route to publication – the heading of the BBC Books press release for this batch of novels still erroneously listed it as the title.

REVIEW: Always fascinating to *Torchwood* fans are stories in which new insights are given into the lives of the regular characters or new titbits of information revealed about the history of Torchwood itself. *Trace Memory* does both those things, and puts the reader somewhat in mind of the TV story 'Fragments'. Here we get to learn about the life of Toshiko as a young girl in Osaka; about Owen's early career as a doctor; about the start of Ianto's second week of work at Torchwood Tower, by which point he has already become friendly with a young fellow-employee named Lisa; about Gwen's first meeting with her police colleague PC Andy Davidson; and, most significantly of all, about Jack's work as a Torchwood agent in 1967, when the USSR is jealously eyeing the Institute's secrets. The narrative is very cleverly constructed, and author David Llewellyn's prose style is excellent, really drawing the reader in and maintaining interest in Michael Bellini's tragic story right to the very end. Possibly the strongest *Torchwood* novel to date.

6: THE TWILIGHT STREETS

Publication date: 6 March 2008
Author: Gary Russell
Commissioning Editor: Albert DePetrillo
Series Editor: Steve Tribe
Production Controller: Phil Spencer
Cover Design: Lee Binding

PLOT: The Tretarri area of Cardiff has long been the subject of reported hauntings and other strange phenomena, and for some reason Jack has never been able to go there: it makes him feel physically ill to approach. It eventually emerges that in 1876, the area was the scene of a battle for control over the rift between two fearsome but partly-buried beasts, Abaddon and Pwccm, the former supported by Bilis Manger and the latter by the physically identical Cafard Manger. Abaddon seemed to be defeated, but actually faked this in order to prepare and gain strength. Light and Dark energy creatures from the rift were held in balance by the opposing powers of Abaddon and Pwccm. When Jack killed Abaddon in 2008, he inadvertently upset this balance and allowed the Dark energy to gain prominence. In one possible future, of which the Torchwood team members see visions, Owen, Toshiko and Gwen get taken over by the Dark energy and turn against Jack, imprisoning and repeatedly killing him in order to use the energy generated each time he resurrects as a means to control the rift and establish a supposedly benign Torchwood Empire on Earth. Bilis has been preserving the Light energy since Abaddon's death and has made Tretarri inaccessible to Jack as a trap to lure him there at the right time. He now wants Torchwood to help restore the balance between Light and Dark and thus prevent the Dark gaining sway in the terrible future that has been foreseen. They drain the Dark energy via the huge satellite dish atop Stadium House into a wooden prison box supplied by Bilis, which is then to be buried in concrete. The Light energy is dispersed into the ground. Hence both Dark and Light are neutralised, and Bilis vanishes again.

DOCTOR WHO REFERENCES

- This novel features the character Idris Hopper from the *Doctor Who* episode 'Boom Town', the events of which are referred to. (It is believed that Hopper was at one point intended to be a regular character in *Torchwood* but was replaced by Ianto Jones after Gareth David-Lloyd was cast in the role.)

ALIEN TECH

- The current alien cryogenics equipment is said to have been installed in the Hub in 1906 after being discovered by 'Charlie Gaskill's team'. This confirms a suggestion in one entry on the official *Torchwood* website that the current system replaced an earlier one, which was already in place in the Victorian era – as stated by Toshiko in 'To the Last Man' – and was used to freeze Jack in the 1901 sequence of 'Exit Wounds', in which Charles Gaskell (note different spelling) was seen on screen.

CONTINUITY POINTS

- This story features Bilis Manger, as seen in the Series One TV episodes 'Captain Jack Harkness' and 'End of Days'.

- In 1941, the Hub could be entered via a lift concealed in a dockside warehouse.

NOTES

- This book has an additional credit at the front: 'Bilis Manger created by Catherine Tregenna and Russell T Davies and used with gratitude'. There is however no similar credit for the use of Davies's character Idris Hopper.

REVIEW: Like *Trace Memory*, *The Twilight Streets* tells a story spanning several different time periods and gives a fascinating glimpse into the Torchwood of an earlier era, specifically in this case August 1941, where we are introduced to another previously-unseen team in the Hub. There are some nicely evocative descriptions of the contrasting aspects of Cardiff, both in the past and in the present day, and even in a terrifying potential future that is ultimately averted. The reappearance of Bilis Manger is very welcome, and author Gary Russell has managed to strike a fine balance between revealing more about him and preserving his essential mystery. The main shortcoming of the book is that the plot involving the two rival beasts, Abaddon and Pwccm, and the alien Light and Dark energies with which they are associated, becomes pretty convoluted, and risks losing the reader at times. All in all, though, this is another enjoyable read, and maintains the run of worthwhile *Torchwood* novels.

AUDIO CDs

1: HIDDEN
Release date: 4 February 2008
Written by: Steven Savile
Read by: Naoko Mori
Produced by: Andrew Lawrence
Project editor: Gary Russell
Executive producer: Michael Stevens
Torchwood theme music composed by: Murray Gold
Cover design by: Paul Hocking

PLOT: Torchwood investigate a spate of killings that appear to be linked. Jack, who knew one of the victims, disappears, and the others deduce from records of his recent phone calls that he is involved in some way. The police make this connection too, and arrest Jack. A number of the dead were involved in an archaeological dig in the Brecon Beacons, where a ruined church has been discovered containing numerous Hermetic statues and other artefacts, including three canisters of parchments documenting the work of Thomas Vaughn, a 17th Century scientist devoted to the study of alchemy. Also tied in to the mystery is a fertility clinic in Caerphilly, where Ianto finds the staff murdered. It transpires that Vaughn had discovered the secret of immortality and, under the new identity Robert Craig, had been using the clinic to carry out research that enabled him to clone himself and produce a son, as he was infertile. The killings were carried out by a secret society dedicated to protecting Craig's work. In retribution for these crimes, Jack deliberately caused a car crash in which Craig died. Owen and Toshiko manage to steal Craig's body from the police mortuary and, as the man never officially existed, there is no longer any crime that can be pinned on Jack. Craig's cloned son lives on, under the protection of his secret society.

DOCTOR WHO REFERENCES
- None.

ALIEN TECH
- None.

CONTINUITY POINTS
- None.

NOTES
- A two-disc set. The back cover of the CD bears the notes 'This story takes place during the first series of *Torchwood*' and 'Contains adult themes and language'.

REVIEW: There are a lot of good ideas in this story, but it doesn't hold together too well and ultimately fails to satisfy. The fact that Jack is locked up in the police station away from the main action for most of the time doesn't help matters, and it seems out of character that he would cold-bloodedly kill someone as an act of retribution. There is a long build-up to the eventual revelation that Thomas Vaughn and Robert Craig were one and the same man, and the ending then comes as something of an anticlimax, with Vaughn's murderous secret society being allowed to get away with their crimes. On a more positive note, Steven Savile's writing style is pacey and engaging, and Naoko Mori does a very good job with the reading, managing some effective imitations of the accents of the other Torchwood regulars. It is a pity, though, that there are no sound effects or incidental music on this release, as these would have enlivened proceedings considerably.

2: EVERYONE SAYS HELLO

Release date: 4 February 2008
Written by: Dan Abnett
Read by: Burn Gorman
Produced by: Andrew Lawrence
Project editor: Gary Russell
Executive producer: Michael Stevens
Torchwood theme music composed by: Murray Gold
Cover design by: Paul Hocking

PLOT: All bar an unusually-resistant few amongst Cardiff's population are affected by a telepathic field that turns them into 'Heralds', compulsively greeting everyone they meet and relating information about themselves. Chaos ensues in the city. The Torchwood team are able to resist the influence with chrome wristband field-jamming devices, but it severely damages the Hub's systems when Toshiko scans for its source. Jack's wristband is damaged and he eventually succumbs to the influence. He is taken to a disused garage where other Heralds are gathered around a bright light emitted from a multi-limbed black metal sphere of alien origin. He discovers that the sphere is an exploratory craft that has come through the Rift and sent out the telepathic field in order to gather information about its new surroundings. The impact this has had on the Cardiff residents is an unintended side-effect. The alien within the craft died on landing, and the probe is now running on automatic. Jack still has sufficient presence of mind to be able to use a mobile phone to send the probe a nonsense signal concocted by Toshiko and Ianto in the Hub. Unable to communicate with the signal, the probe switches off, ending the crisis.

DOCTOR WHO REFERENCES
- None.

ALIEN TECH
- The alien probe, operating on automatic following the death of its occupant, is at the root of the crisis in this story. Once it is deactivated, Jack determines to take it into storage.

CONTINUITY POINTS
- Gwen encounters an old police colleague of hers, PC Tony Pratt.

NOTES
- A two-disc set. The back cover of the CD bears the notes 'This story takes place during the second series of *Torchwood*' and 'Contains adult themes and language'.

REVIEW: The idea of an alien probe accidentally causing chaos in Cardiff by compelling virtually everyone to greet each other incessantly provides an excellent basis for this story. Burn

Gorman is a superb narrator and successfully adopts a wide variety of different accents for the many incidental characters featured, although the one inflection he does seem to have a little more trouble with is Captain Jack's American twang. The only real problem with this release is that the plot is rather too simple to sustain the approximately two-and-a-half-hour running time. The action tends to be very drawn out and repetitive, particularly on the first disc, and the denouement is ultimately relatively simple. The lack of sound effects and incidental music is again regrettable.

COMIC STRIPS

1: THE LEGACY OF TORCHWOOD ONE!

Published: 24 January 2008, in Issue 1 of *Torchwood: The Official Magazine*
Script: Simon Furman
Art: S L Gallant
Colours: Hi-Fi Design
Lettering: Richard Starkings/Comicraft

PLOT: In Cardiff, Ianto encounters Rupert Howarth, former head of Torchwood One's Biochemical Research Division. Howarth was believed dead, but he claims that he faked this and went into hiding after incurring the wrath of pharmaceutical companies with a breakthrough that would wipe out all viral disease. This turns out to be a lie: he had actually been working to create a hybrid human-alien DNA strand for use by special anti-terrorist forces, drawing on alien tissue that provoked a primal fear response. Most of the down-and-outs on whom he experimented died; one survived and became a creature known as Chimera, which can tap into people's fears in order to attack them. Chimera has now followed him to Cardiff. With Owen's help, Howarth completes a series of computer analyses he started at Torchwood One in order to find a combination of drugs that will neutralise Chimera. He injects the drugs into the creature, which dies, but is killed himself in the process.

DOCTOR WHO REFERENCES
- In a Chimera-induced vision, Ianto is a attacked by something that strongly resembles a Cyberman – presumably a lingering fear from the time when he was caught up in the Battle of Canary Wharf.

ALIEN TECH
- None – the story involves alien DNA, not alien technology.

CONTINUITY POINTS
- Rupert Howarth was Ianto's mentor when he first joined Torchwood One.

REVIEW: The first-ever *Torchwood* comic strip story has a solid if rather simple plot and succeeds quite well in capturing the ethos of the TV show. The likenesses of the five Torchwood Three team members are well captured, but for some reason Rupert Howarth is drawn to resemble very strongly the well-known British comedian, actor and musician Bill Bailey.

2: JETSAM

Published: 20 March 2008, in Issue 3 of *Torchwood: The Official Magazine*
Script/Art: Brian Williamson
Colours: Kris Carter
Lettering: Jimmy Betancourt/Comicraft

PLOT: A ship carrying a cargo of crates containing alien artefacts dumps them at sea as it approaches Cardiff. The crates wash up on shore and Torchwood mount a recovery operation, but one of a pair of large war machines is missing. These machines are used by an alien race for duelling. The missing machine is now operated by Drew Blayney, leader of the local Brimstone Skulls biker gang, who has got inside and been taken over by its systems. Investigating the other machine, Toshiko suffers the same fate. She is beset by images from Japanese myths, drawn from her subconscious. By getting her to recall the Zen parable of the Samurai and the tea master, Owen enables her to overcome the machine's influence. By threatening to cause both machines to self-destruct, Toshiko then forces Blayney to surrender. Emerging from his machine, Blayney advances on Jack, Gwen and Toshiko with a knife, but the machine shoots him with a deadly beam for breaking the surrender protocol. Jack then instructs both machines to shut down.

DOCTOR WHO REFERENCES
- One of the Welsh biker gangs is named Blaid Drwg – which translates as Bad Wolf in English.

ALIEN TECH
- Apart from the two alien war machines, which somewhat resemble huge motorbikes, the artefacts that wash up on the shore include something that looks like a giant Rubik's Cube, inside which a number of locals become temporarily trapped, and a small device that allows the user to see through people's clothes and even their skin to their skeletons beneath. The Torchwood SUV carries both an EMP (electromagnetic pulse) gun, which can be used to disable some alien tech, and a Klydian pulse gun.

NOTES
- It is not specified in the story where the crated alien artefacts come from in the first place or where they are being transported to. One possibility is that they have been salvaged from the wreckage of Torchwood London and are being taken to Torchwood Cardiff for storage,

but this is just speculation.

- Due to production difficulties, no comic strip had been included in Issue 2 of *Torchwood: The Official Magazine*.

REVIEW: An excellent story by Brian Williamson, this is a definite step up from 'The Legacy of Torchwood One!', having both a less generic premise and a more compelling plot. The artwork is strong, too, although the likenesses of the Torchwood team members are very obviously based on photo references of the cast.

3: RIFT WAR!

Published: 17 April 2008 (**Part One**), 15 May 2008 (**Part Two**) and 19 June 2008 (**Part Three: Funhouse!**), in Issues 4, 5 and 6 of *Torchwood: The Official Magazine*
Script: Simon Furman
Art: Paul Grist (Parts One and Two), S L Gallant (Part Three)
Colours: Kris Carter (Parts One and Two), Hi-Fi Design (Part Three)
Lettering: Jimmy Betancourt/Comicraft (Parts One and Two), Richard Starkings/Comicraft (Part Three)

PLOT: (Part One) Creatures of a species previously unknown to Torchwood appear in Cardiff via a spate of rift storms and begin to kill indiscriminately. Jack and his team go to deal with them but quickly realise that this has been just a distraction designed to lure them away from the Hub. Interrogating one of the creatures, Jack learns that they regard this as a war; they believe that Torchwood have been attacking them with the use of the rift manipulator. Toshiko is the first to get back to the Hub. When the others arrive, they find that both she and, incredibly, the whole area of the Hub incorporating the water tower fountain and the rift manipulator have vanished, taken by the creatures. (Part Two) Toshiko is able to use the rift manipulator to suspend herself and the stolen part of the Hub, plus its resident pterodactyl, in a temporal void. There she meets a man called Vox, who explains that the creatures that attacked Cardiff are the Harrowkind, storm troopers of the Sanctified. Vox has a pocket rift manipulator of his own, and by using this, Toshiko is able to restore the Hub, and herself, to the correct location. Vox accompanies her. He tells Jack and the others that he is an enemy of the Sanctified and the Harrowkind, who are a rapacious empire powered by energy from the rift. (Part Three.) Gwen and Owen are sent by Jack to investigate rift activity at Cardiff Castle and get caught up in a kaleidoscopic disturbance surrounded by figures from different historical periods. From the readings on the Hub's computers, Toshiko determines that these are illusions. When Gwen tries to shoot a medieval knight who is threatening Owen, the illusion shatters and they both find themselves stood beside a giant baby. This time it is no illusion: Vox identifies the baby as one of a race called the Zanzi, who were subjugated by the Sanctified many centuries earlier. The Zanzi raise their young in rift bubbles, using psychic projections to entertain and stimulate them, and this is exactly what has appeared at the Castle. Gwen and Rhys agree to look after the baby for its six week development period, and a perception filter is put around the Castle to render the giant child invisible to passers-by. The child eventually reverts to its true form – a kind of purple octopus – and returns home through the rift, thanking Gwen and Rhys for the care they have given it. Vox tells Jack that with the rift becoming ever more erratic in his galaxy, this latest incident having been just one manifestation of the instability, further attacks by the Sanctified are inevitable. He offers to help seal the rift forever.

DOCTOR WHO REFERENCES
* One of the things that Jack gives the Zanti baby to keep it amused is a book of Venusian lullabies. These have been mentioned before in *Doctor Who*, most notably in the classic era stories 'The Curse of Peladon' and 'The Monster of Peladon'.

ALIEN TECH
* Vox has a pocket rift manipulator. It burns out when it restores the Hub to its correct location in space and time.

* Jack supplies numerous pieces of alien technology to help Gwen and Rhys keep the Zanti baby entertained. These include some Malcadian Dream Tellers, which apparently conjure up dream-like story images.

CONTINUITY POINTS
* Vox states: 'Your "rift" has many openings in my part of the galaxy, and the Sanctified have grown strong and dangerous by weaving its energy to their own ends.'

NOTES
* This sets a precedent by launching the first multi-part comic strip story. It is still ongoing and has yet to reach its conclusion as this book goes to press.

REVIEW: The first two parts of this story have a strong, action-packed plot and set things up nicely for what promises to be a good long-running arc. On the downside, although Paul Grist has many fans, his artwork here is distinctly unimpressive, his attempted likenesses of the regular team members being particular poor. In the third part, the situation is basically reversed. S L Gallant's artwork here, as on *The Legacy of Torchwood One!*, is pleasing on the eye and features faithful likenesses, but Simon Furman's script takes a truly bizarre turn, with a plot that puts one in mind of a 1970s *Doctor Who Annual* story and is really totally unsuited to *Torchwood*. It remains to be seen how things will pan out in future issues, but hopefully the subsequent instalments will be more akin to the first two than the third!

APPENDIX C – TORCHWOOD DECLASSIFIED

As in the show's first year, each new *Torchwood* episode was accompanied by its own *Torchwood Declassified* mini-documentary, focusing on some of the key behind-the-scenes aspects. The standard debut time slot for this – in England and Wales at least[124] – was 7.50 pm on Thursdays on BBC Two, immediately after the edited, pre-watershed repeat of the episode to which it related – which had the rather curious result that viewers were occasionally shown clips of 'adult-viewing' sequences that had been cut from the version of the episode just transmitted. There were however four exceptions: the sixth, tenth, eleventh and twelfth in the run first went out immediately after the debut BBC Two transmission and were then repeated immediately after the pre-watershed version of the episode to which they related. ('Immediately' here means as the very next programme; there were generally one or two trailers shown in between the *Torchwood* and *Torchwood Declassified* episodes.)

Although shorter, and thus necessarily less detailed, than the similar *Doctor Who Confidential* documentaries, these *Torchwood Declassified* programmes continued to give an excellent insight into many aspects of the production of *Torchwood*. Unlike in the first series, they followed *Doctor Who Confidential*'s precedent by featuring commercial rock and pop tracks as incidental music, sometimes – as with the use of Pink Floyd's 'The Great Gig in the Sky' in the eighth episode, 'Finger on the Pulse' – to very impressive effect. (The tracks used most prominently are listed in the episode summaries below. All these tracks were omitted from the versions of the episodes included on the Series Two DVD box set and replaced with library music.)

SERIES CREDITS

PRODUCTION TEAM[125]

Runner: Stuart Laws, Rob Wootton
Edit Assistant: Rhian Arwel
Researcher: Nathan Landeg (all except 2.02), Jamie Lynch (all except 2.10)
Assistant Producer: Catherine Chappell[126] (2.01, 2.02, 2.03, 2.05, 2.06, 2.10, 2.13), Geoff Evans (2.01, 2.02, 2.03, 2.04, 2.05, 2.06, 2.08), Donovan Keogh (2.01, 2.02, 2.03, 2.07, 2.08, 2.09, 2.10, 2.11, 2.12, 2.13)
Production Team Assistant: Amanda Buckley
Production Accountant: Elaine Stephenson
Production Co-ordinator: Clare Rutteman

---

124 Viewers in Scotland and Northern Ireland generally had to wait until a later date to see the episodes, as different schedules were adopted in their regions.

125 Where an episode number (or more than one) appears in brackets after a person's name in the listing, this means that they were credited only on the episode (or episodes) indicated. Otherwise, the person concerned was credited on all 13 episodes. Some production roles were credited only on certain episodes.

126 Credited as 'Cat Chappell' on 2.03, 2.06, 2.10 and 2.13.

Production Manager: Kirsty Reid
Production Executive: Paul Williams
Camera: James Daniels (2.08)
Graphics: Louise Hillam, Aled Jones
Editor: James Brailsford (2.01, 2.03, 2.09, 2.11), Marius Grose (2.01, 2.02, 2.05, 2.06, 2.07, 2.09, 2.11, 2.12, 2.13), Fiona Pandelus (2.02, 2.04), Rob Franz (2.02, 2.03, 2.04, 2.05, 2.06, 2.07, 2.08), Mike Crawford (2.05, 2.08, 2.10), Rahim Mastafa (2.06)
Dubbing: Mark Ferda, Owen Thomas (2.04)
Edit Producer: Nathan Landeg (2.02), Cat Chappell (2.04, 2.07, 2.08, 2.09, 2.11, 2.12), Donovan Keogh (2.04, 2.05, 2.06), Jamie Lynch (2.10)

Executive Producers for *Torchwood*: Russell T Davies, Julie Gardner
Executive Producer: Mark Cossey

Senior Producer: Mark Proctor
Series Producer: Gillane Seaborne

A BBC Wales production

EPISODE GUIDE

The durations quoted below are for the debut transmissions. These were generally a couple of seconds shorter than the complete episodes on the BBC's master tapes, as each episode tended to be cut into very slightly by the preceding and/or following continuity caption and announcement. (Note also that the versions of the second and tenth episodes included on the Series Two DVD box set are shorter than the transmission versions.) The transmission times quoted are the scheduled times for England and Wales as advertised in advance in *Radio Times*; the actual times sometimes varied from these, but never by more than a few minutes.

2.01 – HOME AND HART

DEBUT TRANSMISSION DETAILS
BBC Two
Date: 23 January 2008. Scheduled time: 7.50 pm.
Duration: 13' 04"

INTERVIEWEES (IN ORDER OF APPEARANCE)
James Marsters, Chris Chibnall, Richard Stokes, John Barrowman, Russell T Davies, Ashley Way, Tom Lucy, Curtis Rivers (Captain Jack's Stunt Double), Eve Myles, Burn Gorman, Naoko Mori, Gareth David-Lloyd.

> SUMMARY: The character of Captain John Hart, and James Marsters' portrayal of him; the staging of the 'gun-slinging' fight scene between Captain Jack and Captain John in the bar; the recording of the rooftop confrontation between the two Captains, culminating in the stunt fall and subsequent resurrection of Captain Jack (the latter scene having been cut from the transmitted episode); and a preview of the later episodes of Series Two.

2.02 – SLEEPLESS IN CARDIFF

DEBUT TRANSMISSION DETAILS
BBC Two
Date: 24 January 2008. Scheduled time: 7.50 pm.
Duration: 12' 19"

INTERVIEWEES (IN ORDER OF APPEARANCE)
John Barrowman, Eve Myles, Russell T Davies, Colin Teague, Richard Stokes, James Moran, Danny Hargreaves, Nikki Amuka-Bird

SUMMARY: The scale of production and action-packed nature of 'Sleeper'; the planning and execution of, and press reaction to, the city centre explosion; and the character of Beth, her interaction with Gwen and her death.

2.03 – STEP BACK IN TIME

DEBUT TRANSMISSION DETAILS
BBC Two
Date: 31 January 2008. Scheduled time: 7.50 pm.
Duration: 8' 26"

INTERVIEWEES (IN ORDER OF APPEARANCE)
Naoko Mori, Russell T Davies, Anthony Lewis, Chris Chibnall, Andy Goddard, Helen Raynor, John Barrowman

SUMMARY: The love story between Tommy and Tosh; Tosh's doomed romantic relationships and emotional growth; and the staging of the chaotic final scene in the hospital. Features the track 'Monster Hospital' by Metric, from their 2006 album *Live it Out*.

2.04 – SAVE THE WHALE

DEBUT TRANSMISSION DETAILS
BBC Two
Date: 7 January 2008. Scheduled time: 7.50 pm.
Duration: 9' 30"

INTERVIEWEES (IN ORDER OF APPEARANCE)
Catherine Tregenna, Russell T Davies, Richard Stokes, Colin Teague, Eve Myles, Kai Owen, Barney Curnow

SUMMARY: The conception, design and realisation of the 'space whale' creature; the recording of the hangar scenes, with a 50-foot crane; the integration of real-life and CGI shots; the character development of Rhys; and the staging of the scene of Rhys getting shot in the shoulder.

2.05 – PAST IMPERFECT

DEBUT TRANSMISSION DETAILS
BBC Two

Date: 14 February 2008. Scheduled time: 7.50 pm.

Duration: 9' 58"

INTERVIEWEES (IN ORDER OF APPEARANCE)
John Barrowman, Russell T Davies, Bryan Dick, Catherine Tregenna, Andy Goddard, Ray Holman, Richard Stokes, Demetri Goritsas, Gareth David-Lloyd.

> SUMMARY: The character of Adam; the revelation of Jack's origins and family; the conception and realisation of the Boeshane Peninsula and its inhabitants; the alleyway sequences with Ianto; and Adam's death scene.

2.06 – ANIMAL PHARM

DEBUT TRANSMISSION DETAILS
BBC Two

Date: 20 February 2008. Scheduled time: 9.50 pm.

REPEAT TRANSMISSION DETAILS
BBC Two

Date: 21 February 2008. Scheduled time: 7.50 pm.

Duration: 12' 30"

INTERVIEWEES (IN ORDER OF APPEARANCE)
Russell T Davies, John Barrowman, Freema Agyeman, Ashley Way, Gareth David-Lloyd, Burn Gorman, Richard Stokes, Alan Dale, Mike Crowley (Special Effects Supervisor).

> SUMMARY: The *Torchwood* debut of Martha Jones, now a more mature character than in *Doctor Who* and working for UNIT; the reactions of the other team members to her arrival; the realisation of the alien Mayfly; Alan Dale's role as Copley; and the killing of Owen. Features the singles 'I Told You I Was Trouble' by Amy Winehouse, from her 2006 album *Back to Black*, and 'The First of the Gang to Die' by Morrissey, from his 2004 album *You Are the Quarry*.

2.07 – DEATH DEFYING

DEBUT TRANSMISSION DETAILS
BBC Two
Date: 28 February 2008. Scheduled time: 7.50 pm.
Duration: 11' 07"

INTERVIEWEES (IN ORDER OF APPEARANCE)
Andy Goddard, Matt Jones, John Barrowman, Richard Stokes, Freema Agyeman, Burn Gorman, Russell T Davies, Ruari Mears (Movement Artist), Mike Crowley (Special Effects Supervisor)

> SUMMARY: The return of Owen as a 'living corpse'; the closeness of his relationship with Jack; the resurrection glove, the realisation of its movement and its ultimate destruction by gunshot; and the appearance of the Weevils *en masse*.

2.08 – DEAD EYES OPEN

DEBUT TRANSMISSION DETAILS
BBC Two
Date: 6 March 2008. Scheduled time: 7.50 pm.
Duration: 13' 11"

INTERVIEWEES (IN ORDER OF APPEARANCE)
Joseph Lidster, Burn Gorman, Andy Goddard, Richard Stokes, Ray Holman, James Leigh (Underwater Camera Operator), Richard Briers.

> SUMMARY: Owen's adjustment to his life after death; the decisions made in the depiction of his zombie state; his leap into Cardiff Bay; the shooting of the underwater scenes; and Richard Briers' role as Parker. Features the track 'The Great Gig in the Sky' by Pink Floyd from their 1973 album *The Dark Side of the Moon*.

2.09 – SOMETHING NEW

DEBUT TRANSMISSION DETAILS
BBC Two
Date: 13 March 2008. Time: 7.50 pm
Duration: 12' 31"

INTERVIEWEES (IN ORDER OF APPEARANCE)
Ashley Way, Phil Ford, Kai Owen, Eve Myles, Russell T Davies, Richard Stokes, Mike Crowley

(Special Effects Supervisor), Nerys Hughes, Chris Chibnall, Peter J Hammond

SUMMARY: The excitement of making a 'Torchwood wedding' episode; the shooting of the stunt scene where the Nostrovite leaps through a window; the comedy of the episode; Gwen's relationships; Rhys the hero; the nature of the Nostrovites; Nerys Hughes' role; the realisation of the stable scene where the Nostrovite explodes; and a preview of the next week's episode. Features the song 'Chapel of Love' by the Dixie Cups.

2.10 – IN LIVING COLOUR

DEBUT TRANSMISSION DETAILS
BBC Two
Date: 19 March 2008. Time: 9.50 pm

REPEAT TRANSMISSION DETAILS
BBC Two
Date: 20 March 2008. Scheduled time: 7.50 pm.
Duration: 13' 00"

INTERVIEWEES (IN ORDER OF APPEARANCE)
Russell T Davies, Bev Gerard (Standby Art Director), Richard Stokes, Camilla Power, Chris Chibnall, Peter J Hammond, Ray Holman, Marie Doris, Jonathan Fox Bassett, Ben Foster

SUMMARY: The clever and economical design of the travelling show set erected in Bute Park; the casting of the circus acts; the light balloons used to illuminate the Bute Park location; the fantastical nature of the story and its villains; the Ghostmaker's costume and make-up design; the character and look of Pearl; the challenges of recording the bus-stop scene with heavy simulated rain; the episode's incidental music; the 'horror moment' where Pearl rises from the bath water. Features the tracks 'Biscuit' and 'Mysterons' by Portishead from their 1999 debut album Dummy.

2.11 – QUID PRO QUO

DEBUT TRANSMISSION DETAILS
BBC Two
Date: 21 March 2008. Time: 9.50 pm

REPEAT TRANSMISSION DETAILS
BBC Two

Date: 25 March 2008. Scheduled time: 7.50 pm.
Duration: 9' 44"

INTERVIEWEES (IN ORDER OF APPEARANCE)
Eve Myles, Chris Chibnall, Ruth Jones, Mark Everest, Russell T Davies, Tom Price, Richard Stokes

SUMMARY: The emotional subject matter of the story of the missing boy; the character development of Gwen; the semi-regular role of PC Andy Davidson, and his relationship with Gwen; and Bob Pugh's performance and make-up as the old Jonah.

2.12 – CLEAN SLATE

DEBUT TRANSMISSION DETAILS
BBC Two
Date: 28 March 2008. Time: 9.45 pm.

REPEAT TRANSMISSION DETAILS
BBC Two
Date: 3 April 2008. Scheduled time: 7.50 pm.
Duration: 10' 24"

INTERVIEWEES (IN ORDER OF APPEARANCE)
Chris Chibnall, Russell T Davies, John Barrowman, Richard Stokes, Naoko Mori, Jonathan Fox Bassett, Burn Gorman, Gareth David-Lloyd

SUMMARY: The ideas behind the telling of the regular characters' back-stories.

2.13 – AVULSION

DEBUT TRANSMISSION DETAILS
BBC Two
Date: 4 April 2008. Time: 9.50 pm.

REPEAT TRANSMISSION DETAILS
BBC Two
Date: 15 April 2008. Scheduled time: 7.50 pm.
Duration: 10' 58"

INTERVIEWEES (IN ORDER OF APPEARANCE)

James Marsters, John Barrowman, Chris Chibnall, Richard Stokes, Ashley Way, Lachlan Nieboer, Eve Myles, Burn Gorman, Naoko Mori

SUMMARY: Captain John's character and its development; Jack's unhappy reunion with Gray; the roots of Gray's anger; the decision to kill off Owen and Toshiko; and the characters' death scenes. Features the 2003 single 'Time is Running Out' by Muse.

APPENDIX D: RATINGS AND RANKINGS

An important measure of the success of any TV show is its performance in the official ratings compiled by the Broadcasters' Audience Research Board (BARB). Series One of *Torchwood* had done spectacularly well in this regard, its opening double bill of episodes setting a new viewing-figure record for a non-sport programme on a digital channel. But how would Series Two fare, now that the show had been promoted from BBC Three to BBC Two? Would it get overshadowed by higher-profile BBC Two offerings and overpowered by stronger competition from the other terrestrial channels? Or would it continue to outshine the opposition and maintain *Torchwood*'s excellent track-record?

Any fears that the show's production team or fans might have had were quickly allayed when four of the first five episodes topped the BBC Two chart for their week of transmission, with the other ('Meat') taking second place – a tremendous achievement. In line with the well-recognised phenomenon whereby the opening instalment of any new series benefits both from novelty value and from stronger-than-usual advance publicity, 'Kiss Kiss, Bang Bang' won a particularly impressive 4.22 million viewers on first screening; a 16% share of the total TV audience at that time. These would remain the best figures for any single transmission of a Series Two episode. The late-evening BBC Three repeats also performed well, regularly drawing over 300,000 viewers.

The succession of top two BBC Two chart positions was broken only when, to the bemusement of many fans, the schedulers reversed things so that, from 'Reset' onwards, the episodes made their debut on BBC Three and were then repeated on BBC Two. Even so, *Torchwood* remained in the BBC Two weekly top ten throughout Series Two – its lowest position was a still-very-creditable sixth for 'Dead Man Walking' – and the change did at least have the positive effect of boosting the BBC Three screenings into a regular place in *that* channel's weekly top ten as well. Further scheduling manoeuvres complicated matters toward the end of the run: the show was moved from Wednesdays to Fridays after 'Adrift', one consequence of which was that 'Adrift' and 'Fragments' both premiered in the same week; and the series finale, 'Exit Wounds', then had its debut transmission back on BBC Two. Indeed, like 'Adam' a few weeks earlier, 'Exit Wounds' was curiously omitted from the BBC Three run altogether. Despite all these potentially confusing changes, the ratings for the closing episodes remained consistently good, suggesting a high degree of audience loyalty; and 'Exit Wounds' saw the series end on a high note by regaining the top spot in the BBC Two weekly chart. Overall, the show had performed significantly better than *Heroes*, which had averaged 2.9 million viewers per episode in the same Wednesday evening BBC Two slot at the end of 2007, and on a par with the most popular of BBC Two's other dramas, amply fulfilling the channel's hopes for it.

As always, the ratings tell only part of the story; also significant are the Appreciation Index (AI) figures, compiled by the BBC itself, which give a percentage measure of the extent to which viewers have enjoyed what they have seen. In this respect, too, *Torchwood* continued to do exceptionally well. The average AI figure for a drama programme broadcast by the BBC or ITV is 77, but even the lowest figure recorded for a Series Two episode, 84 for the BBC Two transmission of 'From Out of the Rain', was well above this, and the highest, 90 for 'Exit

Wounds', was absolutely outstanding. The average for the series as a whole was 86 for the BBC Two screenings and 87 for those BBC Three screenings for which figures are available; an excellent result – and, what's more, a notable improvement on the already-strong Series One figures of 81 and 84 respectively. The slightly higher figures for BBC Three are not unexpected: programmes with smaller ratings tend to get higher AI figures, as their audiences generally have a higher proportion of viewers who have specifically sought them out and are predisposed to like them (as opposed to casual viewers who have tuned in more on a whim). That there is not a bigger difference between the BBC Two and BBC Three figures in *Torchwood's* case is arguably, again, a testament to the audience loyalty inspired by the show.

The table below presents, for each episode's initial BBC Two and BBC Three transmissions (the changes in the order of which are reflected in the order of the entries): the estimated total number of viewers aged four and over (corrected and adjusted to include those who recorded the episode to watch within the week following transmission) in millions (RATING); percentage share of total TV audience at that time (SHARE); position in that week's chart of programmes on the channel of transmission (C); position in that week's chart of programmes on all digital channels (not applicable – N/A – in the case of the BBC Two transmissions) (MC); and the Appreciation Index as a percentage (AI). The entries marked n/a are not available, generally because the number of viewers for the transmission in question was below the threshold for the data to be recorded. As mentioned above, 'Adam' and 'Exit Wounds' were not shown on BBC Three as part of the initial run.

EPISODE	CHANNEL	RATING	SHARE	C	MC	AI*
'Kiss Kiss, Bang Bang'	BBC Two	4.22 m	16%	1st	N/A	84
	BBC Three	0.35m	5%	n/a	n/a	n/a
'Sleeper'	BBC Two	3.78 m	15%	1st	N/A	85
	BBC Three	0.31 m	4%	n/a	n/a	n/a
'To the Last Man'	BBC Two	3.51 m	14%	1st	N/A	85
	BBC Three	0.31 m	3%	n/a	n/a	n/a
'Meat'	BBC Two	3.28 m	12%	2nd	N/A	85
	BBC Three	0.37 m	4%	n/a	n/a	n/a
'Adam'	BBC Two	3.79 m	15%	1st	N/A	85
	BBC Three	N/A	N/A	N/A	N/A	N/A
'Reset'	BBC Three	0.85 m	5%	5th	11th	87
	BBC Two	3.22 m	12%	5th	N/A	87
'Dead Man Walking'	BBC Three	1.01 m	6%	2nd	6th	87
	BBC Two	3.31 m	13%	6th	N/A	86
'A Day in the Death'	BBC Three	1.18 m	6%	2nd	3rd	88
	BBC Two	3.08 m	12%	3rd	N/A	85
'Something Borrowed'	BBC Three	0.98 m	5%	2nd	4th	87
	BBC Two	2.76 m	11%	3rd	N/A	86

'From Out of the Rain'	BBC Three	0.95 m	5%	9th	15th	87
	BBC Two	2.90 m	12%	3rd	N/A	84
'Adrift'	BBC Three	0.97 m	5%	5th	12th	87
	BBC Two	2.52 m	n/a	5th	N/A	86
'Fragments'	BBC Three	0.72 m	5%	7th	27th	88
	BBC Two	2.98 m	12%	2nd	N/A	88
'Exit Wounds'	BBC Two	3.13 m	13%	1st	N/A	90
	BBC Three	N/A	N/A	N/A	N/A	N/A

Source for viewing figures: BARB
Source for AI figures: BBC

As *Torchwood* was no longer a BBC Three show, it no longer benefited from that channel's standard practice of giving episodes multiple repeats within the week of their debut transmission. A major innovation for Series Two, however, was the introduction of the edited pre-watershed repeats on BBC Two. These attracted significant numbers of additional viewers in their own right, despite the fact that they were sometimes bumped from the schedule in Scotland and Northern Ireland in favour of other, regional programming. A good indication of the total TV audience for each episode can therefore be obtained by adding together the figures for all three of its transmissions – the initial unedited BBC Two and (where applicable) BBC Three airings and the edited BBC Two repeat.[127] The combined totals thus arrived at, and the averages for the series as a whole, are set out in the table below.

EPISODE	BBC TWO	BBC THREE	BBC TWO REPEAT	TOTAL
'Kiss Kiss, Bang Bang'	4.22 m	0.35 m	1.19 m	5.76 m
'Sleeper'	3.78 m	0.31 m	0.91 m	5.00 m
'To the Last Man'	3.51 m	0.31 m	1.15 m	4.97 m
'Meat'	3.28 m	0.37 m	1.09 m	4.74 m
'Adam'	3.79 m	N/A	0.99 m	4.78 m
'Reset'	3.22 m	0.85 m	0.96 m	5.03 m

---

127 General research into TV ratings has shown that the great majority of viewers who tune in for repeats are additional, i.e. they have not already seen the programme on one or more of its earlier transmissions. Some sources suggest that the figure is as high as 90 percent. It may however be a little lower in the case of Series Two of *Torchwood*, as no doubt a proportion of those adult viewers who watched one or other of the unedited transmissions each week will subsequently have seen the edited pre-watershed version as well, alongside younger members of their families. The totals given in the table may thus slightly overstate the actual numbers of unique viewers.

'Dead Man Walking'	3.31 m	1.01 m	0.94 m	5.26 m
'A Day in the Death'	3.08 m	1.18 m	0.86 m	5.12 m
'Something Borrowed'	2.76 m	0.98 m	1.02 m	4.76 m
'From Out of the Rain'	2.90 m	0.95 m	0.97 m	4.82 m
'Adrift'	2.52 m	0.97 m	1.00 m	4.49 m
'Fragments'	2.98 m	0.72 m	0.87 m	4.57 m
'Exit Wounds'	3.13 m	N/A	1.00 m[128]	4.13 m
Average	**3.27 m**	**0.62 m**	**1.00 m**	**4.88 m**

Source for viewing figures: BARB

While these figures would suggest only a marginal increase on the average combined total of 4.62 million viewers per episode recorded by Series One, an additional factor to be borne in mind this time is that it was now no longer necessary for people to tune in to (or record) the scheduled TV transmissions in order to see the show. Some estimates suggest that up to half a million additional viewers accessed each episode via the BBC's new iPlayer service, and tens of thousands of others by using 'on demand' cable TV services or by downloading to their iPod or iPhone from the Apple iTunes Store. All in all, there can be no doubt that Series Two was a resounding ratings success.

AI figures are available for only the first six of the pre-watershed BBC Two repeats, but these averaged a very healthy 85, exactly the same as for the original BBC Two screenings of the same episodes, indicating that they had been equally well-received.

The full ratings statistics produced by BARB for the main BBC Two transmissions (which go into too fine a level of detail to be reproduced in their entirety here) reveal three other points of particular interest. First, the episodes consistently had above-average scores for drama programmes under a range of viewer-response headings, including 'Made a special effort to watch', 'High quality programme', 'Feels original and different', 'Liked the storyline', 'Liked the characters' and 'Would recommend'. The main exception was 'Learned something new', under which heading the episodes tended to score just below average. Secondly, the average split of viewers by sex was 54% women to 46% men, and the biggest proportion of the audience – approaching a quarter – was in the 35 to 44 age band. This supports the evidence of the equivalent figures from Series One – and from *Doctor Who* – that the clichéd image of the typical fan of TV science-fiction in the UK as an adolescent male is well wide of the mark. Thirdly, although the proportion of the audience in the 4 to 15 age band was unsurprisingly lower for the main BBC Two transmissions than for the pre-watershed repeats, it was not quite as low as might perhaps have been expected: an average of 7.5 percent for the former against

128 Estimated figure – actual data not available for this transmission.

an average of 15.6 percent for the latter. This indicates that significant numbers of children were watching even the unedited versions of the episodes – although presumably most of them would have been nearer the top end of the age band than the bottom. On the other hand, the 15.6 percent average for the pre-watershed versions was still lower than the typical figure of approaching 20 percent for episodes of *Doctor Who*, suggesting that, even with the edits, the spin-off was still seen as being less family-friendly than the parent show.

An indication of the relative merits of the episodes from the perspective of fans – or, at least, of *Doctor Who* fans, who may not always be *Torchwood* fans – can be gleaned from the online episode polls conducted on the hugely popular *Doctor Who* Forum at www.doctorwhoforum. com (formerly hosted by the Outpost Gallifrey website). An average of 1,426 voters participated in these polls – ranging from an exceptional high of 2,199 for 'Kiss Kiss, Bang Bang' to a low of 1,168 for 'Adrift' – in which each episode was given a mark of between one and five, with five being the highest. The percentages in the table below have been calculated by adding together the total number of marks received by each episode (as of 6 May 2008) and dividing by the maximum that could have been achieved if everyone who voted had given the episode a five.

EPISODE	FAN RATING
'Kiss Kiss, Bang Bang'	75.16%
'Sleeper'	76.18%
'To the Last Man'	80.16%
'Meat'	73.85%
'Adam'	82.79%
'Reset'	86.43%
'Dead Man Walking'	78.16%
'A Day in the Death'	77.93%
'Something Borrowed'	77.52%
'From Out of the Rain'	68.38%
'Adrift'	82.53%
'Fragments'	86.91%
'Exit Wounds'	84.57%

Based on these figures, the fans' order of preference, working downwards from favourite to least favourite, would thus seem to have been:

1. 'Fragments'
2. 'Reset'
3. 'Exit Wounds'
4. 'Adam'
5. 'Adrift'
6. 'To the Last Man'
7. 'Dead Man Walking'
8. 'A Day in the Death'
9. 'Something Borrowed'
10. 'Sleeper'
11. 'Kiss Kiss, Bang Bang'
12. 'Meat'
13. 'From Out of the Rain'

Lastly, set out below, for what it's worth, is this author's own ranking of the Series Two episodes, again working downwards from favourite to least favourite – although I should add that my views on this tend to change quite frequently, and I have found it particularly difficult to separate some of the episodes in this highly-consistent run.

1. 'Dead Man Walking'
2. 'Fragments'
3. 'Adrift'
4. 'Exit Wounds'
5. 'Kiss Kiss, Bang Bang'
6. 'Meat'
7. 'Reset'
8. 'Something Borrowed'
9. 'Adam'
10. 'Sleeper'
11. 'To the Last Man'
12. 'A Day in the Death'
13. 'From Out of the Rain'

APPENDIX E – WEBWATCH[129]

Torchwood's already-impressive internet presence grew even stronger during 2007 and the early months of 2008.

THE OFFICIAL BBC WEBSITE

Although the Torchwood Institute System Interface, one of the two official websites originally set up for the show by bbc.co.uk, was closed down prior to the start of Series Two, the other, at www.bbc.co.uk/torchwood, was retained and given a major overhaul. Responsibility for this was assigned to the freelance Carbon Studio agency in Cardiff[130], who commented in a 9 April 2008 posting on their company blog:

> We were very honoured to be asked to redesign the website for worldwide hit TV series *Torchwood*. Preparation for this included a private tour around the set and a chance to meet some of the cast, which was very cool! The brief required that we create all the content from scratch. The end result? We created an above-ground Cardiff cityscape for the homepage, then head down below ground for further content.

This further content included regular news updates, brief character and cast profiles of the five regulars, an assortment of computer wallpaper images and – added on a weekly basis as Series Two progressed – a selection of video clips relating to each new episode, comprising trailers, highlights compilations and, most impressive of all, four or five short 'making of' video diaries and interviews with members of the cast and crew. The *Torchwood Declassified* mini-documentaries were not included this year, however, and as before the website was not readily accessible outside the UK.

THE ALTERNATE REALITY GAME

The most innovative feature of the redesigned official website was the interactive *Torchwood* alternate reality game (ARG). Believed to be the first ever created for a TV show in the UK, this was written by Phil Ford, who had also been responsible for the Series Two episode 'Something Borrowed', and took the form of a series of 11 missions for players to complete in order to prove their suitability for recruitment to Torchwood. Carbon Studio said on their blog:

> 'A genetics professor has gone missing! It's probably nothing, but he had just claimed that he was being hunted by aliens. It's an ideal opportunity to test out the potential candidates. If you think you've got what it takes, give it your best shot!'

---

129 Please note that neither Telos Publishing Ltd nor the author has any connection with, or can take any responsibility for the content of, any of the websites mentioned in this Appendix. The use of appropriate anti-virus and firewall software is always recommended for anyone accessing the internet.

130 The same agency had also been responsible for designing bbc.co.uk's official website for *The Sarah Jane Adventures*.

We were very excited to create the design for the *Torchwood* ARG, a series of games that encouraged users to move from the TV show to their computers to continue the adventure on-line. We were responsible for the design and illustration of the computer interface, the icons and all the games. Another very cool project to work on!

The first mission went live on the website a few hours after the BBC Two transmission of 'Kiss Kiss, Bang Bang' on the evening of 16 January 2008, and this precedent was then followed for subsequent episodes up to and including 'Adrift'. Each mission had to be completed before the next started. Those players who filled in an online registration form were given their own account recording their progress and received regular e-mails from Ianto Jones reminding them every time a new mission was due to start. Each mission consisted of a puzzle or challenge introduced by a video message from Ianto and supported by a variety of background files, briefing documents, electronic tools, information relating to the episode just televised (which would sometimes be alluded to in the mission), a 'story so far' video recap from Ianto and a video message from Toshiko giving heavy hints on how to proceed. After the successful completion of each mission, a further video message from Ianto conveyed congratulations and wrapped things up.

The basic plot of the game, as it eventually unfolded, was as follows. Genetics professor Conrad Fischer phones the pirate radio show *Dark Talk*, presented by Abigail Crowe, and claims he is being hunted by aliens. The next day, he disappears, having last been seen at the New Eden research foundation with girlfriend Natalie Blake, whom he met through a dating website. Blake is then found dead in her burned-out car. Torchwood learn that she was actually a private eye hired by New Eden to root out a whistleblower. Fischer's son Michael uncovers notes of a phone call between the professor and the whistleblower, who had evidence that New Eden were in possession of inert alien DNA. Fischer is in hiding. He leaves a webcam message on his blog, telling Torchwood that he has put details of what he knows on his laptop; but the message ends with him being shot by Blake, who faked her own death – it was actually her twin sister Naomi who was in the car. Blake takes the laptop to the Cardiff Century Hotel where, in an unrelated development, she is murdered by the assassin employed by the PHARM, who have been using her as a guinea pig for their Reset drug. She was not in control of her actions when she killed Naomi and Fischer; Dr John Winters, head of New Eden, had injected her with the alien DNA. The whistleblower, research chemist Roger Griffiths, attempts to contact Torchwood via *Dark Talk*, but he too is killed. Torchwood learn from Fischer's laptop that cosmetic surgery patients at the Venus Clinic, run by Winters' wife Laura, are being injected with the alien DNA in preparation for an invasion attempt at the molecular level; it will cause them to metamorphose, but only when triggered by an ultrasonic signal, due to be transmitted on 21 March from the *Dark Talk* studio.[131] Ianto and Gwen go to shut this down. Abigail Crowe turns out to be one of the alien virulents and is shot by Gwen. Torchwood then neutralise the other alien hosts and remove the alien cells from the Venus Clinic patients.

---

131 This must be 21 March 2009, as there are indications in the game that the events take place around the same time as those of the TV episodes 'Adam' and 'Reset' – see the *Torchwood* timeline in Chapter Eleven.

A number of tie-in websites were set up for players to access as part of the game. These were: *Dark Talk* at www.darktalk.co.uk, Blake Enquiries at www.blakeenquiries.co.uk, Cardiff Century Hotel at www.centurycardiff.co.uk, Conrad Fischer's blog at www.conradfischer.co.uk, New Eden at www.newedenbiotech.co.uk, Singles SOS at www.singlessos.co.uk, Standard Mail at www.standardmail.co.uk and Venus Clinic at www.venusclinic.co.uk. Some of Conrad Fischer's snapshots were put on the flickr photo hosting website at www.flickr.com/photos/conradfischer, and Abigail Crow was given a MySpace profile page at www.myspace.com/darktalk. Most of the tie-in websites had several pages of content, and some presented further video clips as well. The *Dark Talk* one presented a weekly podcast by Crowe, and the BBC set up a phoneline – 0845 610 1503 – allowing callers to leave messages about their own sightings of strange goings-on in Cardiff; the best of these were added to the podcast each week.

Gareth David-Lloyd and Naoko Mori recorded their video messages for the game in a number of separate sessions on different areas of the Hub set, reading their dialogue from cue cards. David-Lloyd had to be recalled later on to record a short additional piece when it became apparent that, due to the rescheduling of episodes toward the end of Series Two, players would have only two days rather than the usual week in which to complete the penultimate mission. He and Eve Myles also recorded a scene together on the *Dark Talk* studio set – the main set specially built for the game – for the conclusion of the final mission where the alien plot is foiled. This was Myles's only contribution to the game. Amongst the other actors appearing in the video clips were Renu Brindle as Natalie Blake and, featured most prominently, Siwan Morris as Abigail Crowe – who was even made the subject of a fictional interview, written by Phil Ford, in the second issue of *Torchwood: The Official Magazine*.

On 4 April, a final video message from Ianto appeared on the game area of the official website, telling potential Torchwood recruits that things were bad and that they were now needed more than ever – a reference to the tragic events of the just-transmitted 'Exit Wounds'. Then, on 16 April, all 11 missions were reinstated on the website for visitors to play at their leisure, although there was no longer any facility for players to set up accounts and track their progress, and no further e-mails were sent to those who had already registered. The various tie-in websites remained live, as these were essential to the completion of some of the missions, but Abigail Crowe's MySpace page was taken down.

OTHER OFFICIAL WEBSITES

There are other official *Torchwood* websites set up by merchandise licensees such as trading card company G E Fabbri – see www.torchwoodcards.com – and overseas broadcasters such as Channel Ten in Australia – see http://ten.com.au/ten/tv_torchwood.html – and BBC America – see www.bbcamerica.com/content/262/index.jsp. A particularly notable feature of the latter is its series of Captain's Blog entries, supposedly written by Captain Jack during the course of the televised episodes, the content of which was supplied by the show's production team.

FAN WEBSITES

All of the other *Torchwood* websites are unofficial, fan-created ones. Amongst the most impressive of these is Torchwood.TV at www.torchwoodtv.blogspot.com, which is one of the best places on the internet to pick up *Torchwood* news and also features a short section of user comment on each episode, a tag board and even a chat room. Another excellent example is the Torchwood Guide at www.torchwoodguide.co.uk, which, as the name suggests, presents an episode guide to the show, along with a number of pages of related information, although these seem not to be updated as frequently now as they once were.

A must-visit is The Torchwood Institute at www.community.livejournal.com/torch_wood, a LiveJournal community that forms a repository of stimulating *Torchwood* discussion and debate, and is probably the best jumping-off point for the large amount of other *Torchwood*-related material on LiveJournal – click on the 'User Info' or 'Other T_Wood Communities' links on the front page to find a list of all the relevant communities, which number over 100 at the time of writing – twice as many as existed at the end of Series One. A fair few of these communities are devoted to fan fiction, much of which is well worth a read, although – as is generally the case with such things – the writers often seem preoccupied with telling stories in which the regular team members indulge in all manner of sexual activity with outsiders, each other and even occasionally themselves, placing these very much in the 'not for the easily shocked' category.

Those wishing to know more about the places where the show's location recording has taken place should check out Torchwood Locations at www.torchwoodlocations.com and the *Torchwood* section of The Locations Guide at www.doctorwholocations.net.

A site specifically devoted to fan discussion of *Torchwood* and all related matters is The Torchwood Forum at www.torchwoodforum.co.uk. This even has its own Facebook group at www. facebook.com/group.php?gid=5349051506. Another similar forum is the beguilingly named Torchwood's Secret, which can be found at http://s6.invisionfree.com/TWEverythingChanges. The *Torchwood* area of the Doctor Who Forum at www.doctorwhoforum.com is also highly recommended for anyone wishing to debate aspects of the show with fellow fans.

A number of other fan-created *Doctor Who* websites have *Torchwood* content that is well worth checking out. These include The Doctor Who News Page – the best source of *Doctor Who*-related news, bar none, at www.gallifreyone.com/news.php – A Brief History of Time (Travel) – which provides a useful basic guide at www.shannonsullivan.com/drwho/torchwood.html – and, good for reviews (albeit with a generally rather cynical and negative slant), Kasterborous – see www.kasterborous.com – and Behind the Sofa – see www.behindthesofa.org.uk.

ACTOR WEBSITES

All of the show's regular cast members except Naoko Mori have active websites devoted to them, which naturally offer a considerable amount of *Torchwood* content. John Barrowman has his own official site at www.johnbarrowman.com, and is the subject of a number of unofficial, fan-created ones, probably the best of which are at http://john-barrowman.net/ and http://john-barrowman.org/. Gareth David-Lloyd also has an official site, at www.garethdavid-lloyd.co.uk, and an unofficial one, at www.garethdavidlloyd.com. The leading Eve Myles and Burn Gorman sites are both fan-created ones; these are at http://evemyles.net/ and www.burn-gorman.com respectively. Myles does however have her own official MySpace page at http://www.myspace.com/evemylesofficial. Series Two guest star Freema Agyeman also has an excellent unofficial site, which can be found at http://freemaagyeman.com/.

GENERAL

Two other sites well worth visiting for their *Torchwood* content, both of them American, are AfterElton.com – see www.afterelton.com/TV/Torchwood – and The Recapist – see www.recapist.com/tv-shows/torchwood – both of which present highly amusing recaps – essentially running commentaries in print – on all the transmitted episodes, and in the former case some good interview material as well.

ABOUT THE AUTHOR

Stephen James Walker became hooked on *Doctor Who* as a young boy, right from its debut season in 1963/64, and has been a fan ever since. He first got involved in the series' fandom in the early 1970s, when he became a member of the original Doctor Who Fan Club (DWFC). He joined the Doctor Who Appreciation Society (DWAS) immediately on its formation in May 1976, and was an attendee and steward at the first ever *Doctor Who* convention in August 1977. He soon began to contribute articles to fanzines, and in the 1980s was editor of the seminal reference work *Doctor Who – An Adventure in Space and Time* and its sister publication *The Data-File Project*. He also became a frequent writer for the official *Doctor Who Magazine*. Between 1987 and 1993 he was co-editor and publisher, with David J Howe and Mark Stammers, of the leading *Doctor Who* fanzine *The Frame*. Since that time, he has gone on to write, co-write and edit numerous *Doctor Who* articles and books – including *Doctor Who: The Sixties*, *Doctor Who: The Seventies*, *Doctor Who: The Eighties*, *The Doctor Who Yearbook 1996*, *The Handbook* (originally published in seven separate volumes) and *The Television Companion* – and he is now widely acknowledged as one of the foremost chroniclers of the series' history. He was the initiator and, for the first two volumes, co-editor of Virgin Publishing's *Decalog* books – the first ever *Doctor Who* short story anthology range. More recently, he has edited the three-volume *Talkback* series of *Doctor Who* interview books and written *Inside the Hub: The Unofficial and Unauthorised Guide to Torchwood Series One* and *Third Dimension: The Unofficial and Unauthorised Guide to Doctor Who 2007*. He has a BSc (Hons) degree in Applied Physics from University College London, and his many other interests include cult TV, film noir, vintage crime fiction, Laurel and Hardy and an eclectic mix of soul, jazz, R&B and other popular music. Between July 1983 and March 2005 he acted as an adviser to successive Governments, latterly at senior assistant director level, responsible for policy on a range of issues relating mainly to individual employment rights. Most of his working time is now taken up by his writing projects and by his role as co-owner and director of Telos Publishing Ltd. He lives in Kent with his wife and family.

Other Telos Titles Available

TIME HUNTER
A range of high-quality, original paperback and limited edition hardback novellas featuring the adventures in time of Honoré Lechasseur. Part mystery, part detective story, part dark fantasy, part science fiction ... these books are guaranteed to enthral fans of good fiction everywhere, and are in the spirit of our acclaimed range of *Doctor Who* Novellas.

THE WINNING SIDE by LANCE PARKIN
Emily is dead! Killed by an unknown assailant. Honoré and Emily find themselves caught up in a plot reaching from the future to their past, and with their very existence, not to mention the future of the entire world, at stake, can they unravel the mystery before it is too late?
An adventure in time and space.
£7.99 (+ £1.50 UK p&p) Standard p/b
ISBN: 1-903889-35-9

THE TUNNEL AT THE END OF THE LIGHT by STEFAN PETRUCHA
In the heart of post-war London, a bomb is discovered lodged at a disused station between Green Park and Hyde Park Corner. The bomb detonates, and as the dust clears, it becomes apparent that *something* has been awakened. Strange half-human creatures attack the workers at the site, hungrily searching for anything containing sugar ...
Meanwhile, Honoré and Emily are contacted by eccentric poet Randolph Crest, who believes himself to be the target of these subterranean creatures. The ensuing investigation brings Honoré and Emily up against a terrifying force from deep beneath the earth, and one which even with their combined powers, they may have trouble stopping.
An adventure in time and space.
£7.99 (+ £1.50 UK p&p) Standard p/b
ISBN: 1-903889-37-5
£25.00 (+ £1.50 UK p&p) Deluxe signed and numbered h/b ISBN: 1-903889-38-3

THE CLOCKWORK WOMAN by CLAIRE BOTT
Honoré and Emily find themselves imprisoned in the 19th Century by a celebrated inventor ... but help comes from an unexpected source – a humanoid automaton created to give pleasure to its owner. As the trio escape to London, they are unprepared for what awaits them, and at every turn it seems impossible to avert what fate may have in store for the Clockwork Woman.
An adventure in time and space.
£7.99 (+ £1.50 UK p&p) Standard p/b

ISBN: 1-903889-39-1
£25.00 (+ £1.50 UK p&p) Deluxe signed and numbered h/b ISBN: 1-903889-40-5

KITSUNE by JOHN PAUL CATTON
In the year 2020, Honoré and Emily find themselves thrown into a mystery, as an ice spirit – *Yuki-Onna* – wreaks havoc during the Kyoto Festival, and a haunted funhouse proves to contain more than just paper lanterns and wax dummies. But what does all this have to do with the elegant owner of the Hide and Chic fashion chain ... and the legendary Chinese fox-spirits, the Kitsune?
An adventure in time and space.
£7.99 (+ £1.50 UK p&p) Standard p/b
ISBN: 1-903889-41-3
£25.00 (+ £1.50 UK p&p) Deluxe signed and numbered h/b ISBN: 1-903889-42-1

THE SEVERED MAN by GEORGE MANN
What links a clutch of sinister murders in Victorian London, an angel appearing in a Staffordshire village in the 1920s and a small boy running loose around the capital in 1950? When Honoré and Emily encounter a man who appears to have been cut out of time, they think they have the answer. But soon enough they discover that the mystery is only just beginning and that nightmares can turn into reality.
An adventure in time and space.
£7.99 (+ £1.50 UK p&p) Standard p/b
ISBN: 1-903889-43-X
£25.00 (+ £1.50 UK p&p) Deluxe signed and numbered h/b ISBN: 1-903889-44-8

ECHOES by IAIN MCLAUGHLIN & CLAIRE BARTLETT
Echoes of the past ... echoes of the future. Honoré Lechasseur can see the threads that bind the two together, however when he and Emily Blandish find themselves outside the imposing tower-block headquarters of Dragon Industry, both can sense something is wrong. There are ghosts in the building, and images and echoes of all times pervade the structure. But what is behind this massive contradiction in time, and can Honoré and Emily figure it out before they become trapped themselves ... ?
An adventure in time and space.
£7.99 (+ £1.50 UK p&p) Standard p/b
ISBN: 1-903889-45-6
£25.00 (+ £1.50 UK p&p) Deluxe signed and numbered h/b ISBN: 1-903889-46-4

PECULIAR LIVES by PHILIP PURSER-HALLARD
Once a celebrated author of 'scientific romances', Erik Clevedon is an old man now. But his fiction conceals a dangerous truth, as Honoré Lechasseur and Emily Blandish discover after a chance encounter with a strangely gifted young pickpocket. Born between the Wars, the superhuman children known as 'the Peculiar' are reaching adulthood – and they believe that humanity is making a poor job of looking after the world they plan to inherit …
An adventure in time and space.
£7.99 (+ £1.50 UK p&p) Standard p/b
ISBN: 1-903889-47-2
£25.00 (+ £1.50 UK p&p) Deluxe signed and numbered h/b ISBN: 1-903889-48-0

DEUS LE VOLT by JON DE BURGH MILLER
'Deus Le Volt!'…'God Wills It!' The cry of the first Crusade in 1098, despatched by Pope Urban to free Jerusalem from the Turks. Honoré and Emily are plunged into the middle of the conflict on the trail of what appears to be a time travelling knight. As the siege of Antioch draws to a close, so death haunts the blood-soaked streets … and the Fendahl – a creature that feeds on life itself – is summoned. Honoré and Emily find themselves facing angels and demons in a battle to survive their latest adventure.
An adventure in time and space.
£7.99 (+ £1.50 UK p&p) Standard p/b
ISBN: 1-903889-49-9
£25.00 (+ £1.50 UK p&p) Deluxe signed and numbered h/b ISBN: 1-903889-97-9

THE ALBINO'S DANCER by DALE SMITH
'Goodbye, little Emily.'
April 1938, and a shadowy figure attends an impromptu burial in Shoreditch, London. His name is Honoré Lechasseur. After a chance encounter with the mysterious Catherine Howkins, he's had advance warning that his friend Emily Blandish was going to die. But is forewarned necessarily forearmed? And just how far is he willing to go to save Emily's life?
Because Honoré isn't the only person taking an interest in Emily Blandish – she's come to the attention of the Albino, one of the new breed of gangsters surfacing in post-rationing London. And the only life he cares about is his own.
An adventure in time and space.
£7.99 (+ £1.50 UK p&p) Standard p/b
ISBN: 1-84583-100-4
£25.00 (+ £1.50 UK p&p) Deluxe signed and numbered h/b ISBN: 1-84583-101-2

THE SIDEWAYS DOOR by R J CARTER & TROY RISER
Honoré and Emily find themselves in a parallel timestream where their alternate selves think nothing of changing history to improve the quality of life – especially their own. Honoré has been recently haunted by the death of his mother, an event which happened in his childhood, but now there seems to be a way to reverse that event … but at what cost?
When faced with two of the most dangerous people they have ever encountered, Honoré and Emily must make some decisions with far-reaching consequences.
An adventure in time and space.
£7.99 (+ £1.50 UK p&p) Standard p/b
ISBN: 1-84583-102-0
£25.00 (+ £1.50 UK p&p) Deluxe signed and numbered h/b ISBN: 1-84583-103-9

CHILD OF TIME by GEORGE MANN
When Honoré and Emily investigate the bones of a child in the ruins of a collapsed house, they are thrown into a thrilling adventure that takes them from London in 1951 to Venice in 1586 and then forward a thousand years, to the terrifying, devasted London of 2586, ruled over by the sinister Sodality. What is the terrible truth about Emily's forgotten past? What demonic power are the Sodality plotting to reawaken? And who is the mysterious Dr Smith?
All is revealed in the stunning conclusion to the acclaimed *Time Hunter* series.
An adventure in time and space.
£7.99 (+ £1.50 UK p&p) Standard p/b
ISBN: 978-1-84583-104-2
£25.00 (+ £1.50 UK p&p) Deluxe signed and numbered h/b ISBN: 978-1-84583-105-9

TIME HUNTER FILM

DAEMOS RISING by DAVID J HOWE,
DIRECTED BY KEITH BARNFATHER
Daemos Rising is a sequel to both the *Doctor Who* adventure *The Daemons* and to *Downtime*, an earlier drama featuring the Yeti. It is also a prequel of sorts to Telos Publishing's *Time Hunter* series. It stars Miles Richardson as ex-UNIT operative Douglas Cavendish, and Beverley Cressman as Brigadier Lethbridge-Stewart's daughter Kate. Trapped in an isolated cottage, Cavendish thinks he is seeing ghosts. The only person who might understand and help is Kate Lethbridge-Stewart … but when she arrives, she realises that Cavendish is key in a plot to summon the Daemons back to the Earth. With time running out,

Kate discovers that sometimes even the familiar can turn out to be your worst nightmare. Also starring Andrew Wisher, and featuring Ian Richardson as the Narrator.

An adventure in time and space.

£14.00 (+ £2.50 UK p&p) PAL format R4 DVD

Order direct from Reeltime Pictures, PO Box 23435, London SE26 5WU

HORROR/FANTASY

URBAN GOTHIC: LACUNA AND OTHER TRIPS
edited by DAVID J HOWE
Tales of horror from and inspired by the *Urban Gothic* televison series. Contributors: Graham Masterton, Christopher Fowler, Simon Clark, Steve Lockley & Paul Lewis, Paul Finch and Debbie Bennett.
£8.00 (+ £1.50 UK p&p) Standard p/b
ISBN: 1-903889-00-6

CAPE WRATH by PAUL FINCH
Death and horror on a deserted Scottish island as an ancient Viking warrior chief returns to life.
£8.00 (+ £1.50 UK p&p) Standard p/b
ISBN: 1-903889-60-X

KING OF ALL THE DEAD by STEVE LOCKLEY & PAUL LEWIS
The king of all the dead will have what is his.
£8.00 (+ £1.50 UK p&p) Standard p/b
ISBN: 1-903889-61-8

ASPECTS OF A PSYCHOPATH by ALASTAIR LANGSTON
The twisted diary of a serial killer.
£8.00 (+ £1.50 UK p&p) Standard p/b
ISBN: 1-903889-63-4

GUARDIAN ANGEL by STEPHANIE BEDWELL-GRIME
Devilish fun as Guardian Angel Porsche Winter loses a soul to the devil ...
£9.99 (+ £2.50 UK p&p) Standard p/b
ISBN: 1-903889-62-6

FALLEN ANGEL by STEPHANIE BEDWELL-GRIME
Porsche Winter battles She-Devils on Earth ...
£9.99 (+ £2.50 UK p&p) Standard p/b
ISBN: 1-903889-69-3

THE HUMAN ABSTRACT by GEORGE MANN
A future tale of private detectives, AIs, Nanobots, love and death.
£7.99 (+ £1.50 UK p&p) Standard p/b
ISBN: 1-903889-65-0

BREATHE by CHRISTOPHER FOWLER
The Office meets *Night of the Living Dead.*
£7.99 (+ £1.50 UK p&p) Standard p/b
ISBN: 1-903889-67-7
£25.00 (+ £1.50 UK p&p) Deluxe signed and numbered h/b ISBN: 1-903889-68-5

HOUDINI'S LAST ILLUSION by STEVE SAVILE
Can the master illusionist Harry Houdini outwit the dead shades of his past?
£7.99 (+ £1.50 UK p&p) Standard p/b
ISBN: 1-903889-66-9

ALICE'S JOURNEY BEYOND THE MOON by R J CARTER
A sequel to the classic Lewis Carroll tales.
£6.99 (+ £1.50 UK p&p) Standard p/b
ISBN: 1-903889-76-6
£30.00 (+ £1.50 UK p&p) Deluxe signed and numbered h/b ISBN: 1-903889-77-4

APPROACHING OMEGA by ERIC BROWN
A colonisation mission to Earth runs into problems.
£7.99 (+ £1.50 UK p&p) Standard p/b
ISBN: 1-903889-98-7
£30.00 (+ £1.50 UK p&p) Deluxe signed and numbered h/b ISBN: 1-903889-99-5

VALLEY OF LIGHTS by STEPHEN GALLAGHER
A cop comes up against a body-hopping murderer.
£9.99 (+ £2.50 UK p&p) Standard p/b
ISBN: 1-903889-74-X
£30.00 (+ £2.50 UK p&p) Deluxe signed and numbered h/b ISBN: 1-903889-75-8

PARISH DAMNED by LEE THOMAS
Vampires attack an American fishing town.
£7.99 (+ £1.50 UK p&p) Standard p/b
ISBN: 1-84583-040-7

MORE THAN LIFE ITSELF by JOE NASSISE
What would you do to save the life of someone you love?
£7.99 (+ £1.50 UK p&p) Standard p/b
ISBN: 1-84583-042-3

PRETTY YOUNG THINGS by DOMINIC MCDONAGH
A nest of lesbian rave bunny vampires is at large in Manchester. When Chelsey's ex-boyfriend is taken as food, Chelsey has to get out fast.
£7.99 (+ £1.50 UK p&p) Standard p/b
ISBN: 1-84583-045-8

A MANHATTAN GHOST STORY by T M WRIGHT
Do you see ghosts? A classic tale of love and the supernatural.
£9.99 (+ £2.50 UK p&p) Standard p/b
ISBN: 1-84583-048-2

SHROUDED BY DARKNESS: TALES OF TERROR edited by ALISON L R DAVIES
An anthology of tales guaranteed to bring a chill to the spine. This collection has been published to raise money for DebRA, a national charity working on behalf of people with the genetic skin blistering condition, Epidermolysis Bullosa (EB). Featuring stories by: Debbie Bennett, Poppy Z Brite, Simon Clark, Storm Constantine, Peter Crowther, Alison L R Davies, Paul Finch, Christopher Fowler, Neil Gaiman, Gary Greenwood, David J Howe, Dawn Knox, Tim Lebbon, Charles de Lint, Steven Lockley & Paul Lewis, James Lovegrove, Graham Masterton, Richard Christian Matheson, Justina Robson, Mark Samuels, Darren Shan and Michael Marshall Smith. With a frontispiece by Clive Barker and a foreword by Stephen Jones. Deluxe hardback cover by Simon Marsden.
£12.99 (+ £2.50 UK p&p) Standard p/b
ISBN: 1-84583-046-6
£50.00 (+ £2.50 UK p&p) Deluxe signed and numbered h/b ISBN: 978-1-84583-047-2

BLACK TIDE by DEL STONE JR
A college professor and his students find themselves trapped by an encroaching horde of zombies following a waste spillage.
£7.99 (+ £1.50 UK p&p) Standard p/b
ISBN: 978-1-84583-043-4

FORCE MAJEURE by DANIEL O'MAHONY
An incredible fantasy novel. Kay finds herself trapped in a strange city in the Andes … a place where dreams can become reality, and where dragons may reside.
£7.99 (+ £1.50 UK p&p) Standard p/b
ISBN: 978-1-84583-050-2

TV/FILM GUIDES

DOCTOR WHO

THE TELEVISION COMPANION: THE UNOFFICIAL AND UNAUTHORISED GUIDE TO DOCTOR WHO by DAVID J HOWE & STEPHEN JAMES WALKER
Complete episode guide (1963 – 1996) to the popular TV show.
£14.99 (+ £4.75 UK p&p) Standard p/b
ISBN: 1-903889-51-0

THE HANDBOOK: THE UNOFFICIAL AND UNAUTHORISED GUIDE TO THE PRODUCTION OF DOCTOR WHO by DAVID J HOWE, STEPHEN JAMES WALKER and MARK STAMMERS
Complete guide to the making of *Doctor Who* (1963 – 1996).
£14.99 (+ £4.75 UK p&p) Standard p/b
ISBN: 1-903889-59-6
£30.00 (+ £4.75 UK p&p) Deluxe signed and numbered h/b ISBN: 1-903889-96-0

BACK TO THE VORTEX: THE UNOFFICIAL AND UNAUTHORISED GUIDE TO DOCTOR WHO 2005 by J SHAUN LYON
Complete guide to the 2005 series of *Doctor Who* starring Christopher Eccleston as the Doctor
£12.99 (+ £2.50 UK p&p) Standard p/b
ISBN: 1-903889-78-2
£30.00 (+ £2.50 UK p&p) Deluxe signed and numbered h/b ISBN: 1-903889-79-0

SECOND FLIGHT: THE UNOFFICIAL AND UNAUTHORISED GUIDE TO DOCTOR WHO 2006 by J SHAUN LYON
Complete guide to the 2006 series of *Doctor Who*, starring David Tennant as the Doctor
£12.99 (+ £2.50 UK p&p) Standard p/b
ISBN: 1-84583-008-3
£30.00 (+ £2.50 UK p&p) Deluxe signed and numbered h/b ISBN: 1-84583-009-1

THIRD DIMENSION: THE UNOFFICIAL AND UNAUTHORISED GUIDE TO DOCTOR WHO 2007 by STEPHEN JAMES WALKER
Complete guide to the 2007 series of *Doctor Who*, starring David Tennant as the Doctor
£12.99 (+ £2.50 UK p&p) Standard p/b
ISBN: 978-1-84583-016-8
£30.00 (+ £2.50 UK p&p) Deluxe signed and numbered h/b ISBN: 978-1-84583-017-5

MONSTERS INSIDE: THE UNOFFICIAL AND UNAUTHORISED GUIDE TO DOCTOR WHO 2008 by STEPHEN JAMES WALKER
Complete guide to the 2008 series of *Doctor Who*, starring David Tennant as the Doctor. PUBLISHED DECEMBER 2008
£12.99 (+ £2.50 UK p&p) Standard p/b
ISBN: 978-1-84583-027-4
£30.00 (+ £2.50 UK p&p) Deluxe signed and numbered h/b ISBN: 978-1-84583-028-1

WHOGRAPHS: THEMED AUTOGRAPH BOOK
80 page autograph book with an SF theme
£4.50 (+ £1.50 UK p&p) Standard p/b
ISBN: 1-84583-110-1

TALKBACK: THE UNOFFICIAL AND UNAUTHORISED DOCTOR WHO INTERVIEW BOOK: VOLUME 1: THE SIXTIES edited by STEPHEN JAMES WALKER
Interviews with cast and behind the scenes crew who worked on *Doctor Who* in the sixties
£12.99 (+ £2.50 UK p&p) Standard p/b
ISBN: 1-84583-006-7
£30.00 (+ £2.50 UK p&p) Deluxe signed and numbered h/b ISBN: 1-84583-007-5

TALKBACK: THE UNOFFICIAL AND UNAUTHORISED DOCTOR WHO INTERVIEW BOOK: VOLUME 2: THE SEVENTIES edited by STEPHEN JAMES WALKER
Interviews with cast and behind the scenes crew who worked on *Doctor Who* in the seventies
£12.99 (+ £2.50 UK p&p) Standard p/b
ISBN: 1-84583-010-5
£30.00 (+ £2.50 UK p&p) Deluxe signed and numbered h/b ISBN: 1-84583-011-3

TALKBACK: THE UNOFFICIAL AND UNAUTHORISED DOCTOR WHO INTERVIEW BOOK: VOLUME 3: THE EIGHTIES edited by STEPHEN JAMES WALKER
Interviews with cast and behind the scenes crew who worked on *Doctor Who* in the eighties
£12.99 (+ £2.50 UK p&p) Standard p/b
ISBN: 978-1-84583-014-4
£30.00 (+ £2.50 UK p&p) Deluxe signed and numbered h/b ISBN: 978-1-84583-015-1

HOWE'S TRANSCENDENTAL TOYBOX: SECOND EDITION by DAVID J HOWE & ARNOLD T BLUMBERG
Complete guide to *Doctor Who* Merchandise 1963–2002.
£25.00 (+ £4.75 UK p&p) Standard p/b
ISBN: 1-903889-56-1

HOWE'S TRANSCENDENTAL TOYBOX: UPDATE No 1: 2003 by DAVID J HOWE & ARNOLD T BLUMBERG
Complete guide to *Doctor Who* Merchandise released in 2003.
£7.99 (+ £1.50 UK p&p) Standard p/b
ISBN: 1-903889-57-X

HOWE'S TRANSCENDENTAL TOYBOX: UPDATE No 2: 2004-2005 by DAVID J HOWE & ARNOLD T BLUMBERG
Complete guide to *Doctor Who* Merchandise released in 2004 and 2005. Now in full colour.
£12.99 (+ £1.50 UK p&p) Standard p/b
ISBN: 1-84583-012-1

THE TARGET BOOK by DAVID J HOWE with TIM NEAL
A fully illustrated, large format, full colour history of the Target *Doctor Who* books.
£19.99 (+ £4.75 UK p&p) Large Format p/b
ISBN: 978-1-84583-021-2

TORCHWOOD

INSIDE THE HUB: THE UNOFFICIAL AND UNAUTHORISED GUIDE TO TORCHWOOD SERIES ONE by STEPHEN JAMES WALKER
Complete guide to the 2006 series of *Torchwood*, starring John Barrowman as Captain Jack Harkness
£12.99 (+ £2.50 UK p&p) Standard p/b
ISBN: 978-1-84583-013-7

SOMETHING IN THE DARKNESS: THE UNOFFICIAL AND UNAUTHORISED GUIDE TO TORCHWOOD SERIES TWO by STEPHEN JAMES WALKER
Complete guide to the 2008 series of *Torchwood*, starring John Barrowman as Captain Jack Harkness
£12.99 (+ £2.50 UK p&p) Standard p/b
ISBN: 978-1-84583-024-3
£25.00 (+ £2.50 UK p&p) Deluxe signed and numbered h/b ISBN: 978-1-84583-025-0

BLAKE'S 7

LIBERATION: THE UNOFFICIAL AND
UNAUTHORISED GUIDE TO BLAKE'S 7 by
ALAN STEVENS & FIONA MOORE
Complete episode guide to the popular TV show.
Featuring a foreword by David Maloney
£9.99 (+ £2.50 UK p&p) Standard p/b
ISBN: 1-903889-54-5

SURVIVORS

THE END OF THE WORLD?: THE UNOFFICIAL
AND UNAUTHORISED GUIDE TO SURVIVORS
by ANDY PRIESTNER & RICH CROSS
Complete guide to Terry Nation's *Survivors*
£12.99 (+ £2.50 UK p&p) Standard p/b
ISBN: 1-84583-001-6

CHARMED

TRIQUETRA: THE UNOFFICIAL AND
UNAUTHORISED GUIDE TO CHARMED by
KEITH TOPPING
Complete guide to the first seven series of *Charmed*
£12.99 (+ £2.50 UK p&p) Standard p/b
ISBN: 1-84583-002-4

24

A DAY IN THE LIFE: THE UNOFFICIAL AND
UNAUTHORISED GUIDE TO 24 by KEITH
TOPPING
Complete episode guide to the first season of the
popular TV show.
£9.99 (+ £2.50 p&p) Standard p/b
ISBN: 1-903889-53-7

TILL DEATH US DO PART

A FAMILY AT WAR: THE UNOFFICIAL AND
UNAUTHORISED GUIDE TO TILL DEATH US
DO PART by MARK WARD
Complete guide to the popular TV show. PUBLISHED
SEPTEMBER 2008
£12.99 (+ £2.50 p&p) Standard p/b
ISBN: 978-1-84583-031-1

FILMS

A VAULT OF HORROR by KEITH TOPPING
A guide to 80 classic (and not so classic) British
Horror Films.
£12.99 (+ £4.75 UK p&p) Standard p/b
ISBN: 1-903889-58-8

BEAUTIFUL MONSTERS: THE UNOFFICIAL
AND UNAUTHORISED GUIDE TO THE ALIEN
AND PREDATOR FILMS by DAVID McINTEE
A guide to the Alien and Predator Films.
£9.99 (+ £2.50 UK p&p) Standard p/b
ISBN: 1-903889-94-4

ZOMBIEMANIA: 80 MOVIES TO DIE FOR
by DR ARNOLD T BLUMBERG & ANDREW
HERSHBERGER
A guide to 80 classic zombie films, along with an
extensive filmography of over 500 additional titles
£12.99 (+ £4.75 UK p&p) Standard p/b
ISBN: 1-84583-003-2

SILVER SCREAM: VOLUME 1: 40 CLASSIC
HORROR MOVIES by STEVEN WARREN HILL
A guide to 40 classic horror films from 1920 to 1941.
PUBLISHED OCTOBER 2008.
£12.99 (+ £2.50 UK p&p) Standard p/b
ISBN: 978-1-84583-026-7

SILVER SCREAM: VOLUME 2: 40 CLASSIC
HORROR MOVIES by STEVEN WARREN HILL
A guide to 40 classic horror films from 1941 to 1951.
PUBLISHED OCTOBER 2008.
£12.99 (+ £2.50 UK p&p) Standard p/b
ISBN: 978-1-84583-029-8

TABOO BREAKERS: 18 INDEPENDENT FILMS
THAT COURTED CONTROVERSY AND
CREATED A LEGEND by CALUM WADDELL
A guide to 18 films which pushed boundries and
broke taboos. PUBLISHED SEPTEMBER 2008.
£12.99 (+ £2.50 UK p&p) Standard p/b
ISBN: 978-1-84583-030-4

IT LIVES AGAIN! HORROR MOVIES IN THE
NEW MILLENNIUM by AXELLE CAROLYN
A guide to modern horror films. Large format, full
colour throughout. PUBLISHED OCTOBER 2008.
£14.99 (+ £4.75 UK p&p) h/b
ISBN: 978-1-84583-020-5

CRIME

THE LONG, BIG KISS GOODBYE by SCOTT MONTGOMERY
Hardboiled thrills as Jack Sharp gets involved with a dame called Kitty.
£7.99 (+ £1.50 UK p&p) Standard p/b
ISBN: 978-1-84583-109-7

MIKE RIPLEY

Titles in Mike Ripley's acclaimed 'Angel' series of comic crime novels.

JUST ANOTHER ANGEL by MIKE RIPLEY
£9.99 (+ £1.50 UK p&p) Standard p/b
ISBN: 1-84583-106-3
ANGEL TOUCH by MIKE RIPLEY
£9.99 (+ £1.50 UK p&p) Standard p/b
ISBN: 1-84583-107-1
ANGEL HUNT by MIKE RIPLEY
£9.99 (+ £1.50 UK p&p) Standard p/b
ISBN: 1-84583-108-X
ANGEL ON THE INSIDE by MIKE RIPLEY
£12.99 (+ £1.50 UK p&p) Standard p/b
ISBN: 978-1-84583-043-4

HANK JANSON

Classic pulp crime thrillers from the 1940s and 1950s.

TORMENT by HANK JANSON
£5.00 (+ £1.50 UK p&p) Standard p/b
ISBN: 1-903889-80-4
WOMEN HATE TILL DEATH by HANK JANSON
£5.00 (+ £1.50 UK p&p) Standard p/b
ISBN: 1-903889-81-2
SOME LOOK BETTER DEAD by HANK JANSON
£5.00 (+ £1.50 UK p&p) Standard p/b
ISBN: 1-903889-82-0
SKIRTS BRING ME SORROW by HANK JANSON
£5.00 (+ £1.50 UK p&p) Standard p/b
ISBN: 1-903889-83-9
WHEN DAMES GET TOUGH by HANK JANSON
£5.00 (+ £1.50 UK p&p) Standard p/b
ISBN: 1-903889-85-5
ACCUSED by HANK JANSON
£5.00 (+ £1.50 UK p&p) Standard p/b
ISBN: 1-903889-86-3

KILLER by HANK JANSON
£5.00 (+ £1.50 UK p&p) Standard p/b
ISBN: 1-903889-87-1
FRAILS CAN BE SO TOUGH by HANK JANSON
£5.00 (+ £1.50 UK p&p) Standard p/b
ISBN: 1-903889-88-X
BROADS DON'T SCARE EASY by HANK JANSON
£5.00 (+ £1.50 UK p&p) Standard p/b
ISBN: 1-903889-89-8
KILL HER IF YOU CAN by HANK JANSON
£5.00 (+ £1.50 UK p&p) Standard p/b
ISBN: 1-903889-90-1
LILIES FOR MY LOVELY by HANK JANSON
£5.00 (+ £1.50 UK p&p) Standard p/b
ISBN: 1-903889-91-X
BLONDE ON THE SPOT by HANK JANSON
£5.00 (+ £1.50 UK p&p) Standard p/b
ISBN: 1-903889-92-8

Non-fiction

THE TRIALS OF HANK JANSON by STEVE HOLLAND
£5.00 (+ £2.50 UK p&p) Standard p/b
ISBN: 1-903889-84-7

The prices shown are correct at time of going to press. However, the publishers reserve the right to increase prices from those previously advertised without prior notice.

TELOS PUBLISHING
c/o Beech House, Chapel Lane, Moulton, Cheshire, CW9 8PQ, England
Email: orders@telos.co.uk
Web: www.telos.co.uk

To order copies of any Telos books, please visit our website where there are full details of all titles and facilities for worldwide credit card online ordering, as well as occasional special offers, or send a cheque or postal order (UK only) for the appropriate amount (including postage and packing – note that four or more titles are post free in the UK), together with details of the book(s) you require, plus your name and address to the above address. Overseas readers please send two international reply coupons for details of prices and postage rates.